Praise for

KAREN YOUNG

"The suspense is almost unbearable."
—*Romantic Times BOOKclub* on *Never Tell*

"Karen Young is a writer who delivers
intense, gripping and dark suspense…
bound to keep you hooked."
—*Romantic Times BOOKclub*

"Young skilfully mixes romance with
edge-of-your-seat suspense."
—*Library Journal*

"Karen Young is a spellbinding storyteller."
—*Romantic Times BOOKclub*

D0766817

Also by **Karen Young**

NEVER TELL
PRIVATE LIVES

KAREN YOUNG

BELLE
POINTE

MIRA

DID YOU PURCHASE THIS BOOK WITHOUT A COVER?
If you did, you should be aware it is **stolen property** as it was
reported *unsold and destroyed* by a retailer. Neither the author nor
the publisher has received any payment for this book.

All the characters in this book have no existence outside the
imagination of the author, and have no relation whatsoever to anyone
bearing the same name or names. They are not even distantly inspired
by any individual known or unknown to the author, and all the
incidents are pure invention.

All Rights Reserved including the right of reproduction in whole or
in part in any form. This edition is published by arrangement with
Harlequin Enterprises II B.V./S.à.r.l. The text of this publication or
any part thereof may not be reproduced or transmitted in any form
or by any means, electronic or mechanical, including photocopying,
recording, storage in an information retrieval system, or otherwise,
without the written permission of the publisher.

This book is sold subject to the condition that it shall not, by way of
trade or otherwise, be lent, resold, hired out or otherwise circulated
without the prior consent of the publisher in any form of binding or
cover other than that in which it is published and without a similar
condition including this condition being imposed on the subsequent
purchaser.

MIRA is a registered trademark of Harlequin Enterprises Limited,
used under licence.

Published in Great Britain 2007.
MIRA Books, Eton House, 18-24 Paradise Road,
Richmond, Surrey, TW9 1SR

© Karen Stone 2006

ISBN: 978 0 7783 0191 2

63-1107

Harlequin Mills & Boon policy is to use papers that are
natural, renewable and recyclable products and made from
wood grown in sustainable forests. The logging and
manufacturing processes conform to the legal environmental
regulations of the country of origin.

Printed and bound in Spain
by Litografia Rosés S.A., Barcelona

Acknowledgements

As in all my books, I'm indebted to so many people who helped make this one happen. I took a leap of faith when I chose to build the story around a professional baseball superstar. Most of what I know about baseball I learned at school. Therefore, I relied on guidance from Doug Simmons, my son-in-law, for the technicalities of the game and the effect of injuries. For guidance on the workings of a cotton plantation, I relied on Peggy Peal, my grandson's other grandmother, whose family has lived on and worked a cotton plantation in the Mississippi Delta ever since God invented dirt. For insight into the social culture of the Delta, I owe thanks to Gloria Dunbar. For the business stuff, Bob Wood, my lawyer son-in-law, proved, as always, a fabulous asset. Finally, to my editor, Valerie Gray, for insightful critique.

Thanks to you all.

For my grandson, Josh.
Baseball, football, basketball –
the family's very own super athlete!

One

As it always happened at these events, the room was filled to capacity. Scanning the crowd, Anne Whitaker estimated the number at better than three hundred, well surpassing the goal of the nonprofit sponsor. Amazed that all it took for folks to plunk down five hundred dollars a plate was the appearance of the star pitcher of the St. Louis Jacks—who just happened to be her husband. Buck's name was a strong draw, so he was constantly in demand. Not only was he a gifted speaker and utterly relaxed in front of an audience, but he was genuinely funny. And, perhaps most appealing of all, he came across as modestly unimpressed with his superstar status.

Anne smiled politely and murmured in response to a comment from the baseball commissioner's wife seated on her left. With the din of voices and the music of a live band, it was impossible to have any real conversation. As distracted as she was, she wouldn't have been able to talk anyway. She was ten weeks pregnant and feeling distinctly ill. It wasn't the classic nausea that came with pregnancy, but something different and it filled her with panic. During the cocktail hour, she'd made no less than four visits to the powder room fearing the worst, but so far nothing. More than anything, she wanted to go home. But a glance at her watch told her it would be a while yet before that was possible.

When she glanced up to find Gene Winston, Buck's agent, watching her narrowly, she managed what she hoped was a natural smile. No surprise that Gene had picked up on her distraction. Even if he knew the reason she was distracted, he would be unmoved. Buck's public image was all he cared about. He never needed to remind her of her role at these events. She knew it and played it well.

Buck, finally sensing something, let his napkin fall to the floor. Leaning close on a pretext of retrieving it, he murmured in her ear, "You feeling okay, sugar?"

"I'm just a little…queasy," she told him, hoping against hope that what she feared wasn't happening.

"We'll be out of here soon." He squeezed her hand and turned his attention back to the commissioner.

She longed to lean against him just for the comfort it would bring but—again—not possible here and now. Even if she weren't okay, there was nothing to be done about it. The sponsor's spokesman would soon be up introducing Buck.

She shifted to allow a waiter to refill her water glass and caught the concerned look on Marcie Frederick's face. Marcie, wife of Monk Frederick, one of the Jacks' managers, had already commented on the odd fact that Anne was refusing wine lately. Although Marcie was a friend, she didn't know about the pregnancy. No one knew.

Not even Buck.

Which was the cause of much of Anne's agitation. She was

going to have to tell him and soon. Probably tonight. But after the initial surprise, she told herself he was bound to be pleased. He knew she'd dreamed of having a baby for years. Time would tell if he'd be happy enough to forgive her for the way she'd gone about getting pregnant.

A waiter removed her untouched dessert, while another appeared at the table with after-dinner coffee. Anne put a hand over her cup to refuse just as sharp pain struck in her lower abdomen. She gave a small, involuntary gasp but, in the noisy ballroom, nobody noticed except Marcie. For a stunned moment, Anne didn't move, and then another searing pain struck.

Rising shakily to her feet, she murmured a distracted apology to the table at large. Buck looked a little surprised at her untimely exit. It had been barely fifteen minutes since she'd last left. But she was too intent on getting to the now all-too-familiar powder room to explain.

Flashing a strained smile to a waiter who courteously opened the exit door, she slipped out and dashed down the hall. Thankfully, the powder room was empty. Her heart thumping with dread, she entered the first stall.

Please, don't let it be blood.

But it was. Not much, but it was there. She closed her eyes and fought an urge to scream a denial. But no time now to panic. It wasn't so much that it signaled disaster, she told herself, but she would have to leave. She had strict instructions from her doctor if there was ever any sign of spotting.

Go to bed immediately. Feet up. Total bed rest.

She would have to ask someone to deliver a note to Buck so that they could leave. As for Buck's speech, he would just have to make some kind of explanation. Their baby's life was at stake.

A few moments later, she stood at the ballroom door and saw, to her intense relief, that Buck was not on the podium yet. But it would not be long until he was introduced. She stopped a passing server and thrust a note into the startled man's hand. "Will you give this note to Buck Whitaker, please?"

Slipping back out of sight, she watched as Buck was handed the note which he read without any show of emotion. He was good at that. He had plenty of practice keeping his cool under extreme pressure. No one who played major league baseball panicked easily.

Meanwhile, waiting for him, it was all she could do not to panic. With her insides in a knot and dread in her heart, she took a deep breath. The cramping was irregular, but every nerve in her body screamed at her to run to the escalator and leave. Which would definitely cause a stir. As it was, she was not going to be voted most popular when, because of her, the guest speaker had to bow out early, but there it was.

Their baby's life was at stake!

Another peep through the crack in the door and she saw Buck finally making his way toward the exit. The instant he reached her, she opened her mouth to tell him, but he shushed her with a look. Taking her arm, he guided her toward an alcove across a sea of hotel carpeting. Even then, before he said anything, he checked to see that they were well out of earshot of anybody. Facing her finally, he asked bluntly, "What's wrong?"

She struggled to keep a tremor from her voice. "Buck, we have to leave."

"What are you talking about? We can't leave. I'm on in five minutes."

"I know, I know, but we have to go. Now." She closed her eyes. "I'm sorry, I didn't want to tell you this way, but I'm bleeding."

His mouth dropped open. "Bleeding? What—"

"I'm pregnant, Buck."

With a smile that didn't quite reach his eyes, he said, "Are you kidding me?"

She couldn't keep the terror from her voice. "No! No, I mean it, Buck. I'm pregnant and I'm cramping and there's spotting."

He made a restless movement, turning away before looking at her again. "How could you be pregnant?"

She shook her head, impatient with the question. "Can we just not talk about it, at least not right now? Right now I need to go home and go to bed."

He rubbed at the side of his neck, still struggling to take in what she was saying. "I thought the Pills— I mean, they're supposed to be just about foolproof, aren't they?"

"Didn't you hear me, Buck? I'm bleeding!" Her voice rose frantically. "Something is going wrong. Bleeding is a warning that can't be ignored."

"Ah…I guess you've sort of caught me off guard here." He glanced back at the closed doors of the ballroom where three hundred plus guests waited. "Does…uh, this…uh, bleeding necessarily mean that something serious is happening?"

"I'm not sure, but I'm not willing to take that chance. Are you?" She'd had ten weeks to adjust to her pregnancy and he'd had less than ten minutes. Maybe he was entitled to a shocked reaction, but she didn't have time to deal with his feelings. "I'm telling you we have to go home, Buck, now," she repeated firmly.

"We can't, Anne. Think about what you're saying. I'm the freaking guest of honor. I can't just up and leave. These people have paid a lot of money."

"Money? Money? I don't care about money! This baby is what I care about." She pressed her fingers to her mouth, trying to calm herself. "Don't you care at all, Buck?"

"I'm still trying to take it in that you're pregnant. But one thing I do care about is that I have an obligation to three hundred people waiting in that room."

What about their baby? Didn't he feel an obligation there? She felt her heart sink. To her mind, the threat to their baby overruled everything else, but he was worried about disappointing a bunch of people who, if he'd just go in there and explain, would probably understand what was at stake. But from the look on his face, that wasn't going to happen. His agent would be aghast and Jacks management wouldn't be too happy either.

"Be reasonable, Anne," he pleaded, looking at his watch. "It's too late to walk out."

"And I'm sorry, but the baby—" Words caught in her throat as she sighed. "I just don't want to risk losing this baby, Buck."

"Jesus." He stood for a minute, thinking. Anne saw there was nothing on his face to reveal the gravity of their conversation. He had to be stunned to learn he was going to be a father, but he was so conditioned to keeping his feelings under wraps that she couldn't tell one way or another. "Can you hold on for thirty or forty minutes? I'll be done with the speech and as for the party afterward at the commissioner's house, I'll make some excuse for us to skip it."

"Oh, Buck…" Her voice caught and she fought back

tears. She didn't have his expertise at hiding her emotions. "I know it's awkward," she said, pleading with him, "but I'm sure they'll understand when you tell them it's an emergency."

"But is it really? You said yourself you're not sure." He frowned, struck with another thought. "You don't need to go to the hospital, do you? It's not that serious, is it?"

"I don't know whether it's serious or not, Buck," she said, with bitter disappointment. "I just know my doctor told me if there was any spotting I was to go to bed immediately."

"And you will." He started back, taking her hand. "It'll be okay to delay it an hour or so, won't it? I'll cut the talk short."

She leaned into his shoulder and gave a dispirited sigh. "I guess another thirty or forty minutes won't make much difference."

"You'll be sitting down the whole time," he said, throwing a reassuring arm around her shoulders. He was already guiding her across the floor toward the doors. Before entering, he dropped a quick kiss on the top of her head. "C'mon, beautiful, let's knock 'em dead."

It was the longest forty minutes of her life. While waiting for Buck to make his excuses after the speech, she'd gone again to the powder room and found fresh spotting. Although it was still minimal, she was scared. Desperate to leave, she caught his eye across the ballroom and something in her face must have told him she was nearing the end of her rope. With a last quiet word to Gene Winston, he started toward her. She had to admire his skill in avoiding the many attempts to hail him in passing. Finally, he reached her and, with a flash of his famous smile, slipped his arm around her waist and whisked her away.

"You okay?" Buck said, as they pulled away from the hotel.

"I'm not sure. I just need to get home."

"You can recline that seat," he told her.

At least she was now in a prone position, she thought. Buck was quiet, winding his way toward the interstate ramp. Once on a straight stretch, he opened up the Porsche with a roar. He liked speed and tended to exceed the legal limit, especially when he was upset. "How could you be pregnant? Did you forget to take the Pill?"

"No, it was nothing like that."

Hearing something in her voice, he glanced at her. "Then what?"

She thought about asking him to wait until they got home, but maybe it was best to get it behind them now. "It isn't an accident that I'm pregnant, Buck," she said quietly. "I quit taking the Pill."

In the muted glow of the dash, she saw his features darken in a fierce frown. "You quit? Just like that?"

"Not just like that." Her hand rested protectively on her abdomen. "I didn't do it on a whim. I thought about it a long time."

"I wish you'd thought to consult me." Not quite openly sarcastic, but close.

"I'm not proud of the way I went about it, Buck ,and for what it's worth, I apologize. We've gone round and round about this forever and you always come up with a thousand reasons to put off having a child. I knew what your answer would be if I told you." With both her hands cradling her abdomen, she longed to make him understand. "I'm thirty-four years old, Buck. The longer we wait, the harder it'll be for me to conceive."

"I thought we agreed to put off having kids."

"For how many years? Another four or five? Eight? Ten?" She swallowed disappointment. She'd so longed for a joyous reaction from Buck, but she now had to let that wish go. "It was your idea to wait, Buck, not mine."

"So you just decided to ignore my wishes and go ahead with your idea."

She turned away. They were in open country now and she was looking at total darkness. "I guess that's one way to put it," she said quietly.

"I don't see any other way to put it," he said, shifting restlessly in his seat. "This is something we should have decided together, Anne. Having a baby isn't like going to the pound and picking out a puppy. A baby changes everything in a couple's life."

"And would it be such a bad thing to change our life, Buck?"

He gave her a quick look. "Does that mean you think something is missing?" When she took too long to answer, he added, "I guess you do. And you think having a baby will make it all better? Don't you think that's a bit naive?"

"Maybe to you, but not to me," she said, bracing as he downshifted and shot past a huge semitrailer truck. If she'd been uncertain about his state of mind, she now had no doubt that he was angry. "You should slow down, Buck," she cautioned.

He did...barely. "I didn't realize you were so miserable," he said after a moment.

She thought about that, trying to fix on her feelings before deciding to get pregnant without telling him. Slightly bored? Somewhat unfulfilled? She'd had an interesting and successful career as a television journalist when she first met Buck at a Special Olympics event. She'd asked for that assignment when her research had revealed that Buck Whitaker was from Tallulah, Mississippi. During the civil rights struggle, her father, a journalist, had spent a summer in Tallulah with a PBS crew from Boston filming a documentary. Anne had grown up listening to him tell about his experience, which had so influenced him that he'd later written a book about it. She'd been thrilled at a chance to meet someone from Tallulah.

She studied Buck's profile now, sternly set. So unlike that day at the Special Olympics when he'd smiled constantly at the kids. He had been so kind, so natural and at ease with them. She'd thought then what a great father he'd make. And within six months of that meeting, they'd been married.

Deep in her thoughts now, she was blind to the view out her window. She supposed other people might look at her situation and say she had it all. She was married to a pro baseball superstar who was generous and loving. He never forgot her birthday or their anniversary. He was outgoing and sociable on the surface—few people knew Buck was actually an extremely private man—so they had a busy life. Off season, they traveled extensively to interesting and exotic places. As a result of his incredible contract as the Jacks' star pitcher, they had a fabulous home in St. Louis, condominiums in Vail and Palm Beach. But sometimes—more and more frequently of late—Anne had begun to wonder if she weren't one of Buck's possessions, too. Arm candy to his sports hero image. To her way of thinking, the prospect of a baby promised to give some measure of reality to their bizarre lifestyle. Children had a way of grounding a marriage.

In an attempt to make him understand, she said, "We live in a fishbowl, Buck, you posing for fans, me playing the adoring wife and smiling when I don't always feel like smiling. And yes, I admit it. I haven't found all that so fulfilling." She paused, searching for words. "To me, a constant round of fun and games has become sort of…I don't know…empty, I guess. Maybe I've outgrown it."

"I didn't hear all these complaints when I signed that last multimillion-dollar contract. And I didn't see any misery when I bought you that sweet little Mercedes for your birthday. I also didn't notice any pain on your face when we paid cash for the condo in Vail." His foot was heavy on the accelerator again.

"I've never denied enjoying the things your job makes possible for us," she said quietly. "But they're only things, Buck. They don't take the place of a baby. At least, not for me. I want us to be a real family."

"What's a real family? I can tell you from experience that mine is a dysfunctional, screwed-up bunch. You and I don't need a baby to feel like a family."

"I know you don't have a good relationship with the Whitakers, but that doesn't mean you won't make a good father. You'd have a chance to change the things your parents did that were wrong."

He gave a bitter laugh. "I couldn't live long enough to do that."

"Just think about it, Buck. Already you've endowed a program for inner city kids and almost every year you participate in Special Olympics. You make time to talk to high school athletes about avoiding drugs and getting a diploma. You do any number of things that show you've got a good heart. You sell yourself short when you say you wouldn't make a good father."

As an adopted only child, Anne's childhood had been lonely. In spite of having very loving adoptive parents, she'd longed for brothers and sisters. When she married Buck, she'd dreamed of having her own babies, her own family. Buck's heritage as the son of a "gentleman planter" in the Mississippi Delta was intriguing, so different from her rather ordinary roots in New England. Belle Pointe, his family home, fascinated her. Why couldn't he see all the reasons they should start their own family?

"How far along are you?" he asked abruptly.

"Ten weeks." But maybe not for long. While they'd been on the road, the cramping had worsened. Maybe she should call her doctor. Maybe going straight to bed wouldn't be good enough. She might very well wind up in the hospital tonight. With a glance at the speedometer, she saw the needle pushing eighty and, feeling anxious to get home, she said nothing.

"To tell the truth, I'm having trouble with this, Anne," Buck told her. He sat hunched over the steering wheel, a sure sign of his agitation. "I've got a lot on my mind that we haven't had a chance to discuss. The Jacks are playing hardball in the negotiations on my new contract. It's a disadvantage that I'm thirty-seven years old. They claim they're uncertain whether my arm will hold out. Plus, they're harping on the bad publicity that came after Casey's death. I couldn't help it that he was at my house when his heart gave out, but they don't see it that way. The press hinted at steroid abuse and no matter how I deny it, I think the Jacks suspect I had something to do with it. So a baby right now is a complication I didn't expect. I guess you could say it's…well, it's just bad timing. Frankly, I feel blindsided."

He saw their baby as a complication? "When would have been a good time, Buck? I've apologized for the way I went about getting pregnant, but I'm not sorry for conceiving the baby. It's done."

"I would never have expected you to do something like this, Anne."

"Well, I did it." She crossed her arms stubbornly. "And I'm sorry it's bad timing for you. You'll simply have to get over it. It's not like I can just reverse a pregnancy. There's only one way to do that and I know you don't want me to have an abortion. Do you?"

The words were tossed off impulsively, but when Buck didn't instantly deny it, she looked at him in shock. He had a right to be upset, she gave him that, but surely he wasn't contemplating aborting their baby. Appalled, she stared at his stony profile. "I'm waiting to hear you answer that, Buck."

"Hell, Anne, it's just that—" He broke off abruptly. "Hold on!" he shouted over the screech of brakes.

Anne's startled gaze caught sight of a deer square in the Porsche's headlights. Later, she'd recall the flash of its white tail as Buck instinctively swerved to avoid the animal. But with the maneuver, the Porsche fishtailed off the pavement onto the gravelly shoulder of the road. As it careened wildly, Anne realized they were going to crash. She had the odd sensation that the whole thing was happening in a kind of distorted slow motion. Her mind took it all in, the blur of trees as the car hurtled at breakneck speed, the sudden specter of a green highway sign and Buck's desperate wrench on the wheel to miss it, then the drag as pavement gave way to a grassy bank. With the car now moving sideways at a dizzying speed, she realized it was going to tumble down into a deep ravine. Her last thought before the sickening impact was of her baby.

Please, God...

When Anne was wheeled out of the recovery room it wasn't Buck who appeared instantly at her side. It was Marcie Frederick. Anne had no strength—or heart—to greet her. She still reeled from the news delivered by her doctor in recovery as she regained consciousness.

Miscarriage. Her baby, gone forever.

"So, how're they treating you, sweetie?"

Anne felt a tear leak out of the corner of her eye. "I can't say I recommend this place."

"I know, darlin'." Marcie lifted her hand and squeezed it. "I'm so sorry."

"I d-don't think I can b-bear it, Marcie," she whispered brokenly. "I wanted this baby more than anything in this world."

"Of course, you did." Marcie dug in her purse for a tissue and gently blotted at Anne's tears. "I feel silly for not guessing you were pregnant. After three pregnancies myself, I should have recognized the signs."

"Nobody knew. I wanted to wait until all chance of m-miscarriage was over." She felt another overwhelming urge to cry. "I'm sorry. I just can't—"

"It's okay, you just go right ahead and cry, honey. You've had more than enough trauma tonight to make anyone cry. That was a bad crash. I'm just thankful you both survived."

Her mind was fuzzy, but she had no trouble recalling the accident. Buck, angry and speeding. The deer appearing out of nowhere. The horror as the car tumbled down into that steep gully. Anne closed her eyes. "Is Buck okay?"

"He's banged up, but okay," Marcie said as an orderly appeared. She didn't volunteer details and Anne didn't ask. Nobody spoke as they rode in the elevator to the third floor. Anne had been told that most patients recovered quickly from a miscarriage, but she'd taken a bump on her head in the crash and a few scrapes and bruises, so she would probably be staying in hospital for a day or two.

"Here we are," the orderly said, maneuvering the gurney out of the elevator. "Third floor. We'll just get you tucked in all nice and cozy, then the nurse will get a reading of your vitals and you can take a nice long rest."

When he was gone, Marcie looked at her watch. "I expect Monk to show up any minute now. He's with Buck on another floor and I made him promise to call us as soon as he can get away." When there was no response from Anne, she asked, "Do you recall much of what actually happened in the accident?"

"I had my seat belt on, but my head hit the side window and I think I was out for a minute or two."

"Time and details have a way of becoming distorted in a situation like that," Marcie remarked.

"I remember enough." Anne's gaze was focused on the view from the window. "People were on the scene right away and the EMTs had me out and on a stretcher pretty quickly, I think." She paused, remembering. "All I was aware of is blood…so much blood…"

"And Buck?"

"He was unconscious. I remember that. He didn't have his seat belt on."

Marcie clucked with disapproval. "That guy! What was he thinking? The high muckety-mucks at the Jacks aren't going to be happy to hear that." She picked up Anne's chart and studied it with a professional air. She was a nurse, but hadn't worked since having her first child. "They didn't give me much information while I was waiting for you in the O.R."

"Will I live?" Anne asked. Not that she cared at the moment. She didn't care about anything.

"Yes, darlin'. And you'll have more babies, too. Don't you fret." Marcie slipped the chart back into a holder on the wall. "I just wanted to make sure nothing was removed to keep that from happening. You and Buck can still have a houseful of young'uns."

"I don't think that's in Buck's life plan," Anne said, turning her face to the window.

"Aww, no man thinks he wants a baby until he gets a look at that precious little face."

"Buck is different, Marcie. He really doesn't want any children."

"Well, you could fool me. He's so good with kids. They hover around him like bees to a honey pot wherever he shows up."

"Those are other people's children," Anne said bitterly.

She saw the look on Marcie's face and regretted saying anything. Fortunately, they were interrupted when a nurse appeared to get Anne settled. She was told how to use the remote which operated the television set, how to lower or raise the bed, how to turn a light on and off and how to summon help, should she need it. Since anybody could have figured it all out without help, Anne tuned the woman out long before the monologue was over.

"While you were in surgery your daddy called," Marcie said when the nurse left. "He and your new stepmother were frantic. They were as surprised as the rest of us to hear about your pregnancy. Even though they know you're okay, they'll want to hear it from you. I told them you'd probably need to sleep off the anesthetic before making any calls."

"That's good. Thank you." She didn't want to talk to anyone. She turned her head to look outside. The view framed in the wide window was spectacular. Although it was long after midnight, high-rises were fully lit and traffic still flowed on the streets. "It's so late, Marcie. You shouldn't be here."

"Shoot, girl, if I wasn't here with you, I wouldn't have anything to do."

Anne managed a weak smile. "Tell that to somebody who doesn't know you have three kids under six."

"And they're with their nanny, so don't go worrying about them. You just worry about getting yourself on your feet again. The sooner you're up and healthy, the sooner you can try again."

Anne didn't have to reply to that. Marcie's cell phone buzzed. "It's Monk," she said, looking at the caller ID. She stepped outside the room, but Anne could hear bits and pieces of the call, but she had little interest. She was again gazing out the window when Marcie came back into the room.

"Well, looks like the two of you are in the same boat," Marcie said with a determinedly cheerful smile. "Buck's basically okay, but his knee took a bad hit. Also, he's got a nasty concussion, which is the reason he hasn't been up here checking on you."

"Frankly, I don't want to see him, Marcie. It's because of his recklessness that I've lost my baby."

"You can't be sure about that." Marcie moved closer and took one of Anne's cold hands in both of hers. "Didn't you say you were spotting at the hotel before you even got into the car?"

"Yes. And I wanted to leave, but he wouldn't."

"Oh, hon…" Marcie sighed and squeezed Anne's hands. "Before I had my first child, I had a miscarriage, too. It happens. I was an emotional wreck, too. I cried for weeks. Even now, today, I think about that baby and wonder what he would look like, what personality he'd have. So I can understand your heart is breaking. But this is a time when you need Buck and he needs you. He's suffered a loss, too. You know how these jocks are. Even when they're dying inside they don't whine, they don't cry, they don't get emotional. I understand you want to crawl in a hole and pull your grief in with you, but right now, you and Buck need each other."

"Maybe that's the way it is with you and Monk, Marcie, but Buck isn't going to grieve over losing this baby," she said sadly. "I actually think he's going to be relieved."

Marcie stared at her in amazement. "You can't believe that."

Anne tucked her hands beneath the blanket and wearily turned her face to the window again. "I'm not good company right now, Marcie. Please…just—" She swallowed, blinking back tears. "Will you please go out to the nurses' station and tell them I don't want any calls and I don't want to see anybody?"

Marcie studied her in silence for a long moment. "Yes, of course. If that's what you want. Your doctor has been pretty effective in keeping quiet that you're here, so if your stay is short, you'll probably be gone before the media figures out a way to bug you with a visit."

Out in the hall, the hospital intercom paged a doctor by some anonymous number. Anne looked wistfully out the window. "Don't you wish they could figure out a way we could be anonymous in this business, Marcie?"

"Most of the time, we wives are anonymous. It's the players who can't even go to the bathroom without somebody rubbernecking." She bent and picked up a jacket from the small settee. "Look, I'm not wishing Buck any grief, but maybe it's not all bad that this accident forces him to hang around the house awhile. The two of you can use the time to work through your problems."

"There's only one thing wrong with that plan, Marcie," Anne said quietly. "Since I'm no longer pregnant, Buck considers our problem solved. You're a good friend and I'm grateful you're here tonight. Thank you for that."

"Well, what are friends for, darlin'?" Then, with a resigned sigh, Marcie crossed her arms. "Okay, I can tell the nurses that you don't want any other visitors, but you have to see Buck." She held up a hand when Anne opened her mouth to argue and repeated, "You have to see Buck…for this reason. If I go out there with your no visitors message, the whole hospital would soon be abuzz with the juicy news that the wife of the St. Louis Jacks star pitcher, who was in the accident with him and has just suffered a miscarriage, has barred him from her room. How long do you think it would take that to reach talk radio and the six-o'clock news? They'll have a field day with it, Anne. And it won't stop here in St. Louis. Doggone it, they'll follow you to the ends of the earth. You know I'm right."

"I hate living in a fishbowl, Marcie," Anne cried. "I hate it!"

"It's not for wimps," Marcie agreed. As the wife of one of the team managers, she knew firsthand how hard it was to have a private life. For every move a player made, he had to keep in mind that there was someone watching.

Anne sighed deeply. "I guess I have to see him."

"You do." Marcie leaned over and kissed her cheek. "One look at that guy's pretty face and, trust me, you'll feel a lot better."

On Sunday mornings, Franklin Marsh enjoyed making breakfast for his wife. He was frying bacon for breakfast when he heard the phone ring. They'd both been anxious since learning of Anne's accident sometime after midnight. Thinking it was early for calls, he quickly removed the skillet from the hot burner, turned off the stove and by the time he reached the bedroom, Beatrice was already talking. He knew instantly by the look on her face that it was Anne.

"Yes, he's just starting breakfast, Anne. Oh, it's so good to hear your voice. We've been so worried. How are you?" With a hand on her heart, Beatrice sank down on the edge of the bed to listen. They'd both been holding their breaths waiting to hear from his daughter.

"It was such a close call, Anne, but thank God you're okay." She paused, nodding slowly. "Yes, he's right here." Reluctantly, she handed the phone to Franklin. "She wants to speak to you."

Franklin took the phone and sat down on the side of the bed beside Beatrice. "Hey, Annie-girl. You gave us a good scare last night, love."

"I know, Dad, but I'm all right. Is this too early? Did I wake anybody?"

"Oh, no, we've been up awhile, both of us. Are you sure you're okay? Marcie told us about…everything."

"Uh-huh. I'm just…" He heard a catch in her voice. "…just so sad."

"Of course you are. We're both as disappointed as we can be. I know how much you wanted a baby. Buck must be hurting, too. How's he doing?"

"He's okay. I don't know if you've heard the details of the accident yet. It's already all over the news here."

"And by the time I get to work, it'll be the talk of the town here," he predicted. "Tallulah's favorite son doesn't do anything that's not reported up one side and down the other."

"I wanted you to know some details since the media will distort it somehow." She drew a shaky breath. "Buck was speeding, which won't be a surprise to anybody. He swerved to avoid a deer that just appeared out of nowhere. It's kind of murky, but I remember the car went careening down a steep embankment. I had my seat belt buckled, but Buck didn't. He has a concussion and his knee is injured. I haven't seen him yet so I don't know how bad it is."

"Uh-oh, that could mean big trouble for the Jacks if he's out any length of time."

"I guess." He heard her take another unsteady breath and after a moment, she added in a different tone, "He should have thought of that before being so reckless."

Franklin met Beatrice's concerned gaze. "Are you sure you're okay, Anne?"

"I will be, Dad. Don't worry. I…I just haven't been able to…to…" Her voice caught on a sob. "Actually, that's why I'm calling. I was wondering if you would like some company."

Surprised, Franklin again looked at Beatrice, who was watching him with anxious eyes, her fingers pressed to her lips. "If by company, you mean you and Buck, nothing could be nicer."

"Not Buck, just me, Dad. I…I'd like to come for a visit, if that's okay."

"Well, sure, Annie-girl. But with Buck's injury—"

"Buck has all of the St. Louis fan base and the whole Jacks organization rallying around him," she said grimly. "He doesn't need me. So I'd like to come for a visit if it won't inconvenience you. I'm not sure how long I'll be staying."

"Come away. You're welcome to stay as long as you like, you know that." He stood up, now alarmed by her tone. "You sound…" He hesitated, worried about pushing her and maybe changing her mind about coming. Bea would kill him. "Are you sure it's the right thing to do—leaving Buck by himself at such a…well, such a delicate time? He's suffered a loss, too, you know."

"We'll talk about that when I get there. I just needed to let you know before making any flight reservations. I'll probably be discharged tomorrow morning. Once I get home, it'll take me a while to pack. I don't know which flight or my arrival time, but you needn't worry about meeting me at the airport. I'll rent a car and—"

"You'll do nothing of the kind," he told her. "I'll pick you up no matter what time it is, day or night." He glanced at Beatrice, who was nodding eagerly, pointing to herself. "We'll both be at the airport. Just let us know when."

"I appreciate this, Dad," Anne said in a husky tone. "I know it's short notice, but—"

He heard the catch in her voice. "Anne, a miscarriage can be emotionally devastating. You and Buck—"

"I need some time away from Buck, Dad. Don't ask me to explain just now." And before he had a chance to say more, she hung up.

"What's the matter?" Beatrice asked urgently. "Tell me."

Still holding the phone in his hand and looking troubled,

Franklin shook his head. "I'm not sure, sweetheart. She wouldn't say anything except she needed some time away from Buck."

"And she's coming here?" With a stunned look, Beatrice put both hands to her cheeks.

"That's why she called. She was apologetic as it's short notice, but she's made up her mind." He frowned. "She's in an emotional state, Bea. I wonder—"

"I knew we should have left last night! The minute her friend called, we should have gotten a flight. We'd be there for her right now, Franklin. She's all alone."

"Hindsight," Franklin said.

Beatrice stood at the window, looking out. "I know this is an awful thing to say and I grieve for her loss, but I'm thankful for an opportunity to have her visit. I had only a few hours with her on our wedding day before Buck whisked her back to St. Louis."

"He sure doesn't spend any time in his hometown if he can avoid it," Franklin said, rising to go to her. "And even though the circumstances aren't ideal, it's—as you say—an opportunity for you to get to know her."

With her hands clasped and pressed against her heart, Beatrice looked ready to cry. "I want that so much."

"I know, my darling." He went to her thinking to comfort her with a hug. Only when he tipped up her chin to kiss her did he see the tears.

Two

It was midmorning that same day before Buck made it to Anne's room. She was awakened by a light kiss on her forehead. She opened her eyes to find him leaning close, fumbling for her hand. She evaded his touch by clutching the blanket.

"Hi," he said.

She felt oddly detached, studying his face. One cheek was bruised and he had a black eye. Above it was a sizeable bandage covering what she assumed was the blow that caused his concussion. Day-old stubble darkened his jaws, giving him a rakish look that the nurses probably found sexy. "Hello, Buck."

"Finding a way to visit my wife around here is harder than trying to finagle a pass to get out of jail," he said with a smile. "Good thing I know some people."

He was going to play it with humor, she thought. Okay. Whatever. "Should you be walking around? Monk seemed concerned about your knee."

"Like they say, I feel like I've been rode hard and put up wet." His smile was a little off-center, aimed at charming her. "But I'm okay. How're you doing?"

"I'm fine." She turned to look out the window. "How's the Porsche?"

"Totaled," he said wryly. Then a pause. "Anne, I—"

"The staff at the hospital's buzzing over you being here." She watched a couple of birds—blue jays, she decided—quarreling in flight. "More than one person has told me we're both lucky to be alive."

"Yeah. It was a close call...and stupid on my part. I was speeding and I didn't have my seat belt on. Thank God you did."

"The Jacks will no doubt think of some way to exonerate you."

"But will you?"

"I don't know, Buck."

He put out a hand and caught her chin. "Anne, please look at me." Reluctantly, she raised her eyes to his. "I'm sorry. I know those words won't begin to be enough for you, but I am so sorry. I wouldn't have this happen for the world."

"You wouldn't?" Her eyes locked with his. "Really? Even to rid yourself of a baby you didn't want?"

He was shaking his head. "I know that's how it sounded and I wish I had those few minutes in the hotel to live over again. I wish I'd left when you asked me to. I wish I hadn't driven so fast." He made a distressed sound. "I...you... I guess I was just floored when I heard you were pregnant. I know that's no excuse—"

"You're right. It's no excuse." She turned away again. "So what's the point of talking? I've miscarried. The baby's gone. I accept that you're sorry. It's just—" She shrugged. "I guess it just seems...too little, too late."

"I need you to forgive me for this, Anne," he said. "I want us to go home and spend some time talking. I want us to—"

She made an impatient sound. "It's always what you want, isn't it, Buck? Well, right now I really don't care what you want. I don't think you even begin to suspect what has happened to us—to our marriage. I know you made it plain that you didn't want a baby, but I honestly thought that you'd come around once you knew we had created a child. I was wrong about that and you can rest easy that you won't have to cope with my silly wishes for a baby ever again."

She felt a wild urge to throw the covers aside. She wanted to go at him nose to nose to tell him exactly how completely beyond redemption he was to her now. Instead, she made an effort to draw a calming breath. "I want you to leave now, Buck, before we both say things we'll probably regret."

His face had gone pale at her attack. Shaken, he said, "I don't want to leave you like this."

"Too bad." She sighed then and gave him a sad look. "Are we strangers, Buck? After six years of marriage, do we actually know each other? Did you really not realize how important it was to me to have a child?"

"I don't think I did," he said slowly, looking like a man walking a path through a minefield. "I know that sounds selfish and egotistical, but we can work this out, Anne."

"I don't know if I want to work it out."

"You don't mean that." He paused, choosing his words cautiously. "I mean, you're upset and you have a right to be. When we get home and you've had a chance to rest and…you know, sort of recover, we'll talk."

She gave him a straight look. "Recover from losing my baby? Just like that?"

"Not 'just like that.' Of course not." Looking exhausted,

he rubbed a hand over his beard. "I was told you're going to be released tomorrow morning. Is that right?"

She was so emotionally spent that it was a moment before she answered. "I don't know. I'd leave now, but my doctor insists that I stay another day. Which is irrelevant as far as you're concerned. The Jacks aren't going to let you leave."

"I want to take you home." He shifted on his feet, squared his shoulders and got a stubborn look on his face. "I mean, I'm going to take you home. They—the Jacks—do want to keep me in here, but I'm leaving when you do, so don't go without me. As ticked off as you are, I wouldn't put it past you to check out early."

"What're you going to do to stop me? Camp out in the parking lot?" She sighed, too tired for sarcasm. "Besides, you can't drive with that knee. You're in pain. I know the signs whether you admit it or not." She could tell by the strain pulling at his mouth and the fact that he was sweating. "If you've really got a concussion, I don't think it's smart for you to be driving. If you don't worry about your own safety, then I care about mine. Marcie will come for me if I call her."

"I'll hire a limo and driver. We'll go home together. Then we'll talk."

"A limousine?" He blinked at the sudden fury on her face. "Do. Not. Hire. A limousine. I repeat, Buck, do not do it. I hate the publicity this has already stirred up. All I need is to get discharged and find a forty-foot limo with a driver waiting to take me away in style. I'm leaving to escape that kind of smothering publicity."

He frowned as if he hadn't heard her correctly. "What do you mean, you're leaving?"

She closed her eyes and looked away again, unwilling to

get into it with him now about her plans. "I'm tired, Buck. I don't have the energy to talk about this anymore. You can go home with me tomorrow morning…if you're able to leave. Otherwise, I will ask Marcie."

"Is that a promise?" he asked.

She turned to look at him. "I don't want more gossip, so that's the way it has to be."

"Then I'll be here," he said, speaking with a clamped jaw. "Come hell or high water, I'll be here."

She waved a hand weakly. "Whatever, Buck."

"I'm sorry, Anne." When the words came out huskily, he cleared his throat. "I swear to God I'll make it up to you."

She turned back to the window without speaking and after a minute, she heard him leave.

Buck was in mortal pain when he got back to his room. In order to get his doctors—and the Jacks on-staff sports medicine physician—to allow him a visit to his wife, he'd finally agreed to being pushed in a wheelchair by an orderly. Turned out, the guy was a Jacks fan and Buck bribed him with prime seat tickets to park him outside the door and wait. Somehow, in spite of his throbbing knee, he had managed to limp to Anne's bedside. He had been determined not to be in a wheelchair when they talked.

But he was glad to be wheeled back to his room. The effort had taken a toll and he was shaken by Anne's reaction. She might never forgive him for this. He didn't know how he'd manage to drive her home tomorrow, but he was determined to do it. No way was he going to let her check herself out of the hospital and him not be there. Judging from her mood today, he wasn't sure she wouldn't go to a hotel to keep from looking at him. With his knee throbbing now, he was on the point of buzzing for a nurse when a huge black man strolled into the room.

"Time for your meds, Mr. Whitaker."

Buck made an attempt to look less than half-dead. "Call me Buck. Mr. Whitaker is my big brother."

"And you can call me Eddie." He looked more like a wrestler than a nurse, but he moved with the grace of a dancer. He held out the tiny paper cup. "I brought you something that'll take you to paradise…temporarily. Considering how you look, it should be welcome." He watched Buck toss it back and offered water from a decanter on the bedside table to swallow it down.

"How long do these things last?" Buck asked, shuddering.

Eddie tossed the paper cup. "The concussion, the banged-up knee, the bruised ribs, the narcotics or your rotten mood?"

Buck rubbed a hand over his face wearily and grunted an obscenity.

"I guess you mean the dope," Eddie opined. "With that concussion, a couple hours. It wears off, you can call me and there's more where that came from."

"I don't want to sleep through checkout time tomorrow morning."

"Why, you got a ball game?"

Everybody's a comedian, Buck thought, staring at his knee, now elevated on some kind of foam wedge-thing and wrapped securely. It was worse than he'd thought at first. He'd seen athletes with similar injuries and he was worried that it could be a long time before he played ball again. "I can veg at home just as well as here," he told Eddie. "I don't want to sleep past six-thirty."

"No problem there," Eddie said cheerfully as he adjusted the wedge. "You know that old saying, doncha? A hospital is no place to get any rest. There'll be folks in and out of here starting around daybreak. Sleep through all that and you're closer to dead than alive."

With that bit of macabre humor, he stripped off his disposable gloves and tossed them into a receptacle near the door. "You take my advice, you'll do what your orthopedic man recommends with that knee. I can't see him liking it that you want to leave here while it's puffed up like that. You mistreat your knee now, you'll pay for it later." At the door, he added, "Whatever your reason for wanting to leave, you might ask yourself if it's worth your career. 'Cause if you don't treat it right, that knee can ground you for good." He flashed a grin as he pulled the door open. "Just my take on it, buddy."

Buck closed his eyes and prayed for the drug to kick in. He didn't need homespun advice from anybody to know what to do to be back on his feet the soonest. The concussion was nothing new. He'd had more than a few. In a day or so he wouldn't even have a headache. But the knee was serious. It could give him grief long enough to knock him out for the season. He worried whether or not he had the time. The Jacks had a major investment in him and would pull out all the stops to give him the treatment necessary to put him on his feet again. He wouldn't have a choice about it. But Anne was the wild card here. She wasn't thinking about his career. Hell, she wasn't even thinking about him as he'd just discovered.

Jesus, he'd really screwed up this time.

Ten minutes later, he had a nice buzz on from the narcotic Eddie had given him. He turned drowsily at a cursory tap on his door as the coach of the St. Louis Jacks let himself in the room. Buck instantly came alive.

Gus Schrader was a squat, red-faced man with attitude. While most of the team he coached was bulked-up athletes who towered over him, Schrader, at about five foot nine, took no guff from anybody. His word was law and Buck respected him more than any coach he'd ever had. Last year, with Buck as starting pitcher, Schrader had shepherded the Jacks into a wild card status and it was his mission in life to actually win the league championship this year and wind up in the Series. He would not be happy that his star pitcher was laid up with a bum knee, especially when he heard how it happened.

"How's it going, Buck?"

Buck struggled to clear a narcotic haze from his brain and stuck out his hand to greet Schrader. "I'm okay. Ears ringing a little from cracking my head on the windshield," he said, tossing a grin and hoping not to show how he dreaded whatever the next few minutes would bring. "Otherwise, nothing's broken."

Schrader looked at the knee. "Think you'll be able to walk on that anytime soon?"

"A couple weeks, give or take." Buck used the remote to raise the head of his bed.

"That so?" Arms crossed, Schrader eyed him skeptically. "What were you thinking, Coach?"

"I'm thinking your guestimate is a little too optimistic. Grissom's take on it is more realistic." He paused. "Plumb grim, if you want the truth."

Buck winced. Steve Grissom was head of the sports medicine team for the Jacks. "What did he say?"

"Said he examined it within an hour of you checking in.

No estimate of how long, but he thinks you'll need extensive physical therapy before you can pitch. You put any pressure on that knee prematurely and get out on the mound… *blam—*" He snapped his fingers. "You think it's in bad shape now. Wait'll you see the damage then. No, we don't want to be risking that."

"I'm with you there, Coach."

"So Grissom's arranging a program," Schrader said, as if Buck hadn't already agreed. Not that it mattered. Nothing Buck could say was going to change Schrader's mind if Steve had already passed judgment on the extent of damage to his knee. "It starts the day you leave the hospital."

"That'll be tomorrow."

"Tomorrow?" Schrader's eyebrows rose.

"I need to get out of here, Gus," he said, shifting to sit up straight. He had to pause to quiet a shaft of pain from his rib cage before he could speak again. "I know the knee will still give me some grief, but I need to be at home right now. I've got some personal issues I need to deal with. I'll cooperate with the physical therapy. Whatever Steve suggests I'll go along with a hundred percent."

"Damn right you will." He gave Buck a keen look. "What kind of personal issues? I know Anne's in a room on another floor. Word is the accident brought on a miscarriage." Schrader didn't consider anything private if it interfered with an athlete's performance.

"She's having a bad time, Gus. I need to be with her right now."

"Well, I'll leave it to you whether you go home tomorrow, but if you damage that knee beyond repair, you'll be writing your own ticket to nowhere. You know that, don't you?"

"I hear you."

"Bad publicity's following you like stink follows a skunk, Buck. I don't like it."

"Tell me," Buck muttered.

"What the hell were you thinking driving that automobile at top speed with your wife beside you and your seat belt off?"

"It was stupid. I was speeding. I admit it. Then that deer just materialized out of nowhere. I acted on pure instinct to avoid it."

He cut Buck off with a disgusted snort. "Excuses. I don't hear a reason for anything I mentioned." His bushy eyebrows beetled with the force of his frown. "I don't know what's goin' on with you and your wife, but after this caper, I'm surprised the woman isn't ready to walk away from you. I'm assuming that's part of the personal issues you mentioned, so I'm not ordering you to stay put here in the hospital. Been my experience that a man handling marital problems is almost as useless as tits on a boar hog. You get out on the mound, you need your head clear. You see where I'm coming from, Buck?"

"Yeah."

"Then I'll leave you to think it over…that is, if that stuff they've given you for pain hasn't turned your brain to mush." He turned on his heel without waiting for a reply and stalked to the door. Then, just before pulling it open, he turned back. "I'm heading up to see Anne right now. I've always considered you a lucky man having a woman like that for a wife. You screw that up, you're more than a fool."

Which pretty much summed up what Buck thought of himself. When Schrader was gone, he closed his eyes with a tired sigh and welcomed the oblivion of the narcotic.

Anne waited until the sound of the Fredericks' SUV faded away before sitting up and tossing aside the soft throw that Marcie had thoughtfully tucked about her. The bedroom she shared with Buck was beautiful, a tasteful blend of buttery yellows with touches here and there of red and brown. The art on the walls was original, carefully chosen. The furniture was top-of-the-line. And why not? When they'd built the house, money had been no object and she'd taken a lot of pleasure in decorating it. Unfortunately, it would not echo with the sound of tiny feet, nor would she rock her baby in the chair she'd bought a month ago and secretly stowed away from Buck in the attic.

Her baby. Before she was engulfed in anguish, she went to the sumptuous walk-in closet and took down a piece of luggage. At the chest of drawers built in on her side, she began removing what she'd need for the foreseeable future—bras, panties, socks, T-shirts, pajamas. After packing them, she went back to the closet and chose a few pairs of pants and jeans, some tops, blouses, a running suit. It was too chilly right now for shorts.

Coming out of the closet she lifted her head to see Buck propped in the doorway on his crutches. He looked at the half-packed suitcase and then back at her with a ferocious frown. "What are you doing? You're supposed to be in bed."

"I'm leaving. And you're supposed to be off that knee." She dropped the clothes on the bed and began folding them.

"C'mon, Anne. This is no way to deal with our situation."

"It's the way I choose," she told him. Her hands were shaking, so she kept them moving, folding, placing this piece and that in the suitcase, reaching for the next one. "However you deal with it is up to you."

He was at the bed now, trying to get a look at her face. "I've said I'm sorry for the way I acted…about the baby and the accident. I mean it, I'm sorry. But it was…hell, I guess I was in a state of shock or something, Anne. For you to just quit taking the Pill…I never expected you to do something like that."

Moving back to the closet, she picked up a pair of running shoes and came out with the shoes in one hand and another smaller carryall in the other. "I never thought I'd do something like that either," she said, "but I did."

"And you think what you did is justified because you wanted a baby?"

She stopped in the act of stuffing the shoes in the bag and looked him squarely in the eye. "I'm going to tell you this one more time, Buck, and if you don't get it, then it's plain that the differences in the way we think are so major that we really won't be able to get beyond it."

She briefly closed her eyes to gather her thoughts before laying it on the line. "My ovaries are thirty-four years old, which means I'm already past peak childbearing years. I simply couldn't wait any longer for you to change your mind about having a family. I convinced myself that once you knew I was carrying our child, you'd be as thrilled as I was and your objections would just fade away. Okay, that was dumb. I was wrong about that. It was a serious betrayal of trust and I sincerely apologize." She gave him a weak smile. "Serious mistakes require serious thinking and I need to be away from you to do it."

With a bleak look, he watched her throw more stuff in the suitcase. "You blame me for the accident and bringing on the miscarriage, don't you?"

She paused with a makeup bag in her hand. "Yes, I guess so," she said slowly. "I wish you'd left when I begged you to."

"I'll make it up to you, Anne, I swear I will."

"Just…leave it, Buck. Don't go there right now. I need to be away from you for a while." She closed the suitcase and began zipping it up. "I need to decide whether there's anything left of our marriage worth saving."

Seeing he was about to argue, she stopped him by raising a hand. "Please, don't say any more. It's not only our differences about whether we should have a baby, Buck. We have differences about the way we live our lives. I'm uncomfortable living in a fishbowl, you know that. I've said it enough. But I accepted it for the joy of one day having your babies. That's something else that went with this miscarriage. I'm not so sure I'm willing to compromise about that anymore."

"Jesus, are you saying you're through? You want a divorce?"

"I'm not sure what I want right now. I am sure that I need some time to sort out my thoughts. So I'm going to stay with my dad and Beatrice."

Buck sat down hard on the side of the bed. "You can sort your thoughts out here," he said. "You don't have to be in another part of the country—especially not there."

"Like where, Buck? A hotel? How long do you think it would be before the media would be all over me if I were to check into a hotel? Or maybe the condominium in Vail? Same thing and you know it."

"Yeah, but Tallulah?" He looked incredulous.

"My dad will welcome me. And Beatrice, too, I hope. I've called and made arrangements. It's done, Buck."

"Just like that?"

"Yes, just like that."

He got up abruptly, forgetting his knee, then swore when it almost folded beneath him. Grabbing a single crutch, he glared at her. "This is bullshit, Anne! I'm up to my ass in trouble with the Jacks. I'm grounded with this damn knee for who knows how long and now my wife ups and leaves. Add that to the scandal of Casey dying at my house and the gossips will have a field day."

"Well, too bad, Buck. I'm dealing with some pretty difficult stuff myself, in case you haven't noticed. Your trouble with the Jacks is temporary—you're too valuable to be out and your knee will heal. The thing with Casey will eventually fade away, too." She straightened then and looked him squarely in the face. "But my baby is gone forever."

"I tell you, we can work this thing out here, Anne. You don't have to go to Tallulah."

"That would save you the embarrassment of explaining my disappearance, wouldn't it? And it's understandable for you to assume I'd fall in with what you want since before, when we've come to these bumps in the road, I've always been the one to compromise. Well, I'm not compromising this time, Buck. I need this time and I'm taking it."

"Do you realize what's at stake here? We could lose everything we've worked for all these years."

"Everything *you've* worked for."

"For God's sake, Anne, be reasonable."

"Reasonable." She looked at him, shaking her head. "You know what? I don't feel like being reasonable. I've had it with the struggle, the ego stuff, the loneliness when you travel and I'm home alone. I haven't been able to pursue a career because we've never been in one place long enough. I don't expect you to understand because I've been remiss in telling you, and that's my fault. I'm sorry, Buck, but my mind is made up."

With the suitcase now packed, she got ready to lift it off the bed, but he stopped her with a hand on it. "At least wait a few days. Christ, you just went through an ordeal losing the baby and the accident. You just got out of the hospital."

"Meaning you think I'm overreacting because my hormones are in an uproar." She smiled bitterly. "Wrong. My hormones probably are in an uproar, but I know exactly who I am and what I'm doing. And if you don't like the real me, then for sure our marriage is over."

She tugged the handle out of his grasp and walked to the door. Hampered by his crutches, it took him a moment to get going. "I'm driving myself to the airport," she told him as she reached the stairs. "I'll leave a message on your voice mail telling you where to send someone to pick up my car."

Three

As if to challenge Anne's decision about leaving Buck, the weather turned bad and she had to spend several hours in the airport waiting for her flight to depart. By the time she got off the plane in Memphis, she'd had too much time to think, but not enough to change her mind.

She caught the first glimpse of her father and Beatrice at Baggage Claim before they spotted her. Franklin Marsh was a tall man, lean and gangly. Anne's nose barely came to the third button on his shirt, an Oxford button-down that appeared almost a size too large. As was the tan corduroy jacket he wore. He looked exactly what he was—an academic and an author/journalist whose thoughts were often engaged elsewhere.

With tears clogging her throat, she let herself be folded into his embrace. "Don't ask," she whispered, guessing that she must look ready to splinter into a thousand pieces. He held her for a long moment, sensing that she needed it, just as he'd done countless times when she was a child.

"Thanks for coming to meet me, Dad," she managed to say with a little sniff.

He made a *tsk*-ing sound. "And wouldn't I go to the moon to meet my Annie-girl. How are you, love?"

"I'm okay." Swallowing a lump in her throat, she looked beyond her father and met the anxious blue eyes of her stepmother. "Beatrice. I've kept you away from your shop today, haven't I?"

"A welcome break," Beatrice said, holding out her arms. "Is there a hug for me, too?"

Her stepmother was about Anne's height, an attractive woman whose once-dark hair styled in a casual pageboy was rapidly turning gray. The long sweater she wore over a gauzy tiered skirt made her look exactly what she was—an aging child of the sixties. Anne stepped naturally into a warm embrace that made her throat go tight, and her doubts about her welcome disappeared.

"I'm so happy you're here," Beatrice said in her ear. Pulling back, she studied Anne's face intently.

Anne brought both hands to her cheeks. "Is my makeup a mess? I know I look like something the cat dragged in."

Beatrice shook her head, smiling. "Was I staring? If so, it's just to check that you're as lovely as I remembered on my wedding day."

Again, to her consternation, Anne felt herself on the verge of tears, but somehow managed a laugh. "I guess that means I don't look as bedraggled as I feel." They'd met only a year ago. And once Anne got over the shock of the idea of her father remarrying, she'd liked his new wife from the start. "And thanks for being so gracious about having me. You must think I've got some nerve just calling and saying I'm on my way without giving you any notice."

"You don't have to give notice to visit us, Anne…ever."

"That's nice of you to say, but it has to be an inconvenience."

"Inconvenience?" Franklin, watching them with a smile, spoke up. "What kind of nonsense is that? I wish you'd stay a month."

"Be careful what you wish for, Dad," she said dryly.

An hour later, as they exited Interstate 55, the gently rolling terrain of north Mississippi abruptly changed to the stark flatness of the Delta. Now in early April the land lay fallow, but in high summer the fields turned lush and green with cotton plants and in August the bolls swelled in the scorching Mississippi sun until they finally burst. Everything that had been green turned suddenly, dramatically, to snowy white. It still seemed so different to Anne, reared in New England where winters were long and gray and cold and summers all too brief.

As they neared the city limits of the town, she read a signing proclaiming Tallulah as the proud hometown of Buck Whitaker. It was a reminder that, to the folks in Tallulah, Buck was a bigger-than-life hero. At the same time, she was reminded that his celebrity would make it hard for her to keep a low profile while she was here.

Another mile and she noticed a profusion of political signs. To her surprise, the biggest and most prominent featured Buck's brother, Pearce. "I didn't know Pearce was involved in a political campaign."

"No?" Franklin frowned. "I would have thought he'd contact Buck for an endorsement. The state senate is turning out to be a horse race and Buck's name would definitely be an asset to Pearce."

"His opponent is giving him a run for his money," Beatrice said, "but in the end I don't see how anyone can beat a Whitaker."

Franklin chuckled. "My wife is supporting the opposition."

"And who are you supporting, Dad?"

"The *Spectator* remains neutral," he said piously. "So far."

Beatrice gave Anne a knowing smile. "I'll win him over yet."

"All it would take for Pearce to win, with or without an endorsement from the *Spectator*," Franklin said, as they approached a huge billboard picturing Buck in pitcher's stance, "is an endorsement from Buck."

"I forget how big Buck's name is in this town," Anne said, now looking at his face painted on the side of the high school gym.

"It's understandable when you consider the odds of a town this size producing a world-class athlete," Franklin replied.

"I guess they've forgotten how long it took before he was recognized as world-class," she remarked.

On her first visit to Belle Pointe just before their wedding, Buck had still been stuck in the minor leagues, frustrated and keenly ambitious, but it had not mattered to Anne whether he ever made it into the pro ranks. She was that much in love with him. What did matter was that he spent so little time with his family. His father had died before they ever met, but his mother and Pearce, his older brother, were in Tallulah. Although Buck harbored resentment and hurt over things that had happened after his father died, she wondered if he hadn't overreacted. People said things, did things, in the wake of a family trauma that could be worked out. To Anne, it seemed a shame to simply withdraw from his family when he had such an interesting heritage.

"There's the turn to Belle Pointe," Franklin said now, as they approached the ornate iron gate. "Won't be long before folks around here find out you're back for a visit. They'll wonder where Buck is. What's your plan to deal with that?"

"I don't have a plan," she said, gazing at the house where Buck was born. Stretching on all sides were endless cotton fields, but the house itself was surrounded by shade trees, mostly oak, sycamore and the unique and stately magnolia. Brightening the grounds nearer the house were hot-pink azaleas in full bloom.

"It is a fantastic sight, isn't it?" Beatrice said, following her gaze.

"Yes." She knew she would never forget her first look at Belle Pointe. It was high summer when Buck took her to meet his family. They'd driven past miles of lush cotton fields and suddenly there it was, an antebellum gem of classic Greek Revival design. She'd gazed enthralled, thinking the place looked like something out of *Gone with the Wind,* a white pearl in a green sea.

Franklin slowed the car. "When I see it, I sometimes get a feeling that the clock at Belle Pointe stopped somewhere in the nineteenth century. Same thing with a few other landowners around here as well. How they've managed to hold on to such a unique lifestyle is truly remarkable."

"Yes, remarkable," Anne murmured, studying a tall water tower painted like a cotton boll. "I thought the same thing myself when I first saw Belle Pointe."

"Of course, most of the original plantations were divided up as families came on hard times. Beatrice can tell you something about that."

"My daddy lost our land when it was sold for back taxes," she explained at Anne's puzzled look.

"Oh, no," Anne murmured.

"He was a very stubborn man," Beatrice said.

"I'll say." With Belle Pointe behind them now, Franklin picked up speed. Anne guessed there was a story there, but neither offered more details.

"On the other hand," Beatrice said, "the Whitakers have managed to hold on to Belle Point for five generations. They've even added to the original acreage. And with your mother-in-law managing things, that's not likely to change— at least not in this lifetime."

Anne welcomed any scrap of information about Victoria Whitaker. From the start, she'd been a bit in awe of Buck's mother. "Buck doesn't talk much about Belle Pointe…or his family, so while I'm here I'm going to try to get better acquainted."

"The *Spectator*'s archives are a good place to start," Beatrice said. "With your journalism background, you should feel right at home poking around down there, right, Franklin?"

He slowed as a farm vehicle pulled onto the road in front of him. "More than poking around in those dusty old shelves, I'd love to have you working right alongside me. I could use a good journalist."

She hadn't thought about going to work. She hadn't thought about anything much beyond getting away. At the sound of an airplane, she turned her gaze skyward and watched a crop-duster preparing to land at a small airfield. Another mile or two and they would be at Tallulah's town square, which was about all the downtown amounted to.

"Considering my own fascination for the Delta and its

culture," Franklin said, "it puzzles me how someone with Buck's heritage could stay away for years, even with the exciting career he chose."

"Maybe his career is exactly the reason," Beatrice said. "He's bound to be thinking about what he'll do when it's over, so I don't think it's unreasonable that he'll want to spend more time here. I know John Whitaker expected Buck would eventually wind up farming at Belle Pointe. When he was a boy, he had a real connection to the land, far more than his brother, Pearce."

She gave Beatrice a surprised look. "You knew Buck then?"

"I knew of him," she said, smiling. "Remember, Tallulah's a small town and I've been here all my life. Actually, I went to school with Victoria." When Franklin stopped at the only traffic light on the square, she waved at two elderly women crossing the street. "We were classmates, but we didn't socialize much and never at all after Victoria married John. My goodness, I remember the buzz when John surprised everyone and picked a local girl to marry."

"It sounds like a storybook romance," Anne said, fascinated at this glimpse of Buck's parents. She was dying to know more. From the start, she'd been curious about her mother-in-law, but in their rare visits she'd found Victoria to be a very private individual, almost severely so. And although Buck talked about Belle Pointe and his childhood, he rarely said much about his parents.

Franklin eased away from the light. "Like I said, folks always figured Buck would come back to his roots one day."

"Well, looks like folks were wrong," she said as Franklin negotiated the square.

"Speaking of John Whitaker," Franklin said, as if picking

up a thread of conversation, "I met him when I came down in 1971 with that PBS crew. He was a real Mississippi aristocrat. I recall us getting into a discussion of the literary influence of Faulkner and Hemingway and other great Southern writers."

"He gets into those discussions frequently if he can find any takers," Beatrice said, with a wink at Anne.

Franklin cleared his throat loudly. "Well, it was right up my alley, that discussion. I've always regretted not having a chance to know John a lot better. His death a few years later was a great loss to this town."

"Buck was in his senior year of college when it happened," Anne said. "He was devastated. It was so sudden."

"Yes, indeed." Franklin slowed for another stop sign. "At the time, your mother and I were still in Boston, of course." He glanced over and smiled at Beatrice. "I never dreamed then that I'd wind up here."

"That makes two of us," Anne said dryly.

"Surprised you, didn't I?" he said, chuckling.

"On a scale of one to ten?" she asked. "Only about ten and a half."

"If we want to talk of surprises, how about the one where my daughter wound up married to John Whitaker's son?" Shaking his head, he added, "Now there was a whirlwind courtship if ever there was one."

"He warned me that I didn't know Buck well enough," Anne said to Beatrice.

Franklin braked as a pickup backed out of a parking space in front of the Piggly Wiggly. "Well, isn't that what fathers do?"

Anne, fighting a smile, put a finger to her temple. "I believe you said something like, 'Marry in haste, repent at leisure.'"

Beatrice made a face. "Not very original, was it?"

"Fathers don't have to be original," Franklin said sagely.

"And apparently they have one set of rules for offspring and another for themselves," Anne said, still teasing him. "What if I'd said the same thing when you suddenly retired and moved here, then while I was still trying to catch my breath over that, you announced you were marrying again?"

Franklin reached for his wife's hand, brought it up and kissed it. "I'd have done the same thing you did," he said, still smiling. "I'd have ignored you."

Watching them, Anne realized how right her father's decision had been to marry Beatrice. They seemed so much in love. And yet, shock had been her first reaction when, shortly after the death of her mother, Franklin suddenly retired from his job at a major newspaper in New England and moved to Mississippi to edit the town's small weekly *Tallulah Spectator.* Anne had worried he was having a midlife crisis. Buck, with a shrug, said she should be relieved that Franklin's crisis prompted only a job change rather than falling for some big-breasted gold digger. But even Buck was taken by surprise when Franklin called a year later and said he intended to marry a Tallulah woman. Fortunately, on meeting Beatrice, Anne had been instantly reassured.

"Were you serious when you said you needed a journalist at the *Spectator?*" she asked Franklin as they cleared the town square.

"As a heart attack," he quickly replied.

"I'm rusty," she warned him. "I've worked only sporadically since marrying Buck. I don't know if I can meet the *Spectator*'s high standards."

Franklin met her eyes in the rearview mirror. "You must be joking. Your career was on the upswing when you were able to pursue it. Even if you weren't my daughter, I'd consider a journalist with your talent and credentials an asset to the *Spectator.*"

Anne flushed at the warmth of her father's approval and, again, found herself on the verge of tears. Oddly, at the same time, underneath her emotional reaction was a sense of the rightness of what she was doing…and a stir of anticipation at the prospect of working again. She'd been too long without any true purpose in her life other than fulfilling her role as wife of the Jacks' star pitcher. She realized that her stepmother was watching her with a gentle smile on her face.

"Don't look now, Franklin," Beatrice said, "but I think you've just hired a reporter."

The Marshes' house was a classic Victorian built at the turn of the century. Franklin had bought it upon arriving in Tallulah and, although it was in good shape, he'd set about restoring many of its original features with as much attention to detail as he put in his books and articles. Anne had seen it only once—when she came for the wedding. She wondered about its history now. Who'd built it? Who'd had children and raised them here? Who had lived and loved and died here?

"I love your house," Anne told them as she climbed out of the car.

"So do I." Beatrice stood gazing at it fondly.

Franklin looked up after retrieving her luggage from the trunk of the car. "Ask her if she has any special reason for loving it."

"It once belonged to my family," Beatrice said, linking her arm with Anne's to walk with her to the front door. "Four generations of Joneses, for what it's worth," she added.

"Oh, that's wonderful!" Anne cried, genuinely thrilled. "I was just thinking about the people who'd lived here, imagining births and deaths and marriages. Now I can find out from my very own stepmother." She gave Beatrice a little hug. "How neat is that?"

"Bea is full of Tallulah history," Franklin said, pulling up the rear with Anne's luggage. "And she's probably dying to share it with you. But I have first dibs. For this reason, I can't see Buck letting you stay away all that long. With his injury and enforced downtime and the season just opening, he'll be in a very unsettled frame of mind. He'll want his wife nearby."

What Buck wanted did not concern her at the moment, but Anne didn't comment. She knew people often regretted saying things to others while in the throes of a personal crisis. Somehow, it didn't seem fair to Buck when he wasn't around to defend himself.

Beatrice seemed to sense her struggle to come up with a vague reply. "We'll both have lots of time for talking," she said, sweeping her over the threshold. Once inside, she turned and spoke softly. "Welcome to our home, Anne."

The woman was really a sweetheart, Anne thought. No wonder Franklin had fallen head over heels for her.

"And now," Beatrice said brightly, "what we need is tea. Franklin, if you'll take Anne's luggage to her room, I'll brew some of that nice Darjeeling." She turned to Anne. "I think I recall from your last visit that you're partial to Darjeeling."

"I am and thank you. I'd love it." As her father disappeared up the stairs, Anne followed Beatrice to the kitchen and found it stamped with her stepmother's warm personality. The walls were painted a buttery cream and the cabinets were a soft off-white. In the middle of the room was a polished oak pedestal table with four chairs set for tea. It was difficult to decide which was older, the table and chairs or the delicate china.

"You've made lots of changes in the house since Dad bought it," she said, admiring the room. "It was nice before, but now it's wonderful."

"We make a nice team," Beatrice said, her gaze following Anne's. "I'm not quite such a stickler for detail as your father, but I think I do have an eye for style. Franklin had furnished the house with antiques, but they were arranged without much style." She touched Anne's shoulder, gently urging her to sit. "Here, let me pour the tea. There's sugar and lemon…and if you like it, cream."

"No, it's fine just like this." Holding the cup with both hands, she closed her eyes and inhaled the bracing aroma before sipping cautiously. When she looked up, she found Beatrice watching her with a faint smile.

"There's just something about tea, don't you think?"

Anne nodded. "Yes, I do. It's so…comforting." She set her cup down with hands that weren't quite steady. "I don't know why I keep tearing up like this," she said, her voice rising with emotion. "Ordinarily, I never cry. Just do me a favor and ignore it, please."

"I would hardly call your present circumstances ordinary," Beatrice said gently. "You're dealing with two emotional crises, trouble in your marriage and a miscarriage. You're entitled to tear up. In fact, you're entitled to cry your heart out. In your shoes I know I would."

Anne studied the tea swirling in her cup. "I'm still having trouble believing all that's happened. If you'd asked me last week where I'd be and what I would be thinking, it wouldn't be here and I wouldn't be contemplating a divorce."

"Is it that serious, Anne? I know absolutely nothing about your personal life and I won't presume to make any judgments. I will only say that you've gone through an emotional upheaval with your miscarriage. Are you sure you want to end your marriage as well?"

"I'm not sure at all," Anne said with a sigh as her cell phone rang. Although there was nothing intrusive about her stepmother's remarks, Anne wasn't ready to confide in anyone that Buck hadn't wanted their baby and now that she'd miscarried, was probably relieved that their lifestyle was unchanged. It made him seem insensitive and selfish. She found she didn't want Beatrice—or her father—thinking of Buck that way.

Checking the caller ID, she saw that it was Buck calling. Feeling Beatrice watching, she let it ring and ring without answering, then turned it off. "It's Buck. I don't want to talk to him."

"Oh, Anne…"

"He'll keep trying. He's as tenacious as a bulldog." She crammed the phone in a deep pocket of her purse. "I told him I needed time to think, time away from him. So when I don't answer my cell, he'll try calling your number. I'm not taking his calls, Beatrice. I'd appreciate it if you would simply tell him that."

"If you're sure…"

Seeking to change the subject, Anne said, "I'm looking forward to a tour of your shop. I never got a chance to drop in when we came for your wedding, but a lot of people had nice things to say about it at the reception."

It took a moment, but Beatrice rallied. "I love my shop," she said, offering Anne cookies on a small platter. "I was critical of Frank furnishing this house in a hodgepodge way, but when you visit my shop, you'll see what real hodgepodge means."

Anne managed a smile. She was still a little shaky after refusing to talk to Buck. "Is that how you describe it?"

"It's not only how folks around here see it because I have such a wide array of things, but I named it Bea's Hodge-Podge."

"What does a wide array include?"

"Well, let's see…" Nibbling at a cookie, Beatrice brushed at a few crumbs on the table. "I'm partial to local artists, so there's a good selection of handcrafted pottery and quite a bit of jewelry—all signed pieces. A couple of local artisans make hand-dipped candles and soap for me. Oh, and linens. I have some really lovely linens, napkins, tablecloths, pillowcases."

"I thought your place was a bookstore."

"Oh, did I forget to mention books?" Beatrice poured herself more tea. "Yes, in fact, fully half my space is devoted to books." She touched her lips with a napkin. "See what I mean by a hodgepodge?"

"I can't wait to see it."

"Well, fortunately for you, it's too late today." Beatrice stood and began collecting their empty cups. "Because you must be tired. I know air travel just wipes me out. And after all you've been through, you'll want to rest for a while before we have dinner, which will be something light. Does that sound about right?"

"It sounds just perfect. Thank you." If it meant going out, she would have skipped eating altogether. As it was, she didn't know if she could manage to swallow food.

Beatrice looked up as Franklin appeared. "Did you put Anne's luggage in her room?"

"I did." He helped himself to cookies. "Yummy. Just what I need to hold me over until dinner."

Beatrice gave him a playful tap on his wrist. "Just what you don't need, you mean." She looked at Anne. "Do you have as wicked a sweet tooth as this guy? In spite of the fact that he never gains an ounce, I can't keep sweets in the house because as soon as they appear, he gobbles them up."

"It's not natural to go without a cookie now and then," Franklin said. "Isn't that right, Annie girl?"

"You and Buck should get together," Anne said. "He can't pass up anything loaded with sugar."

"Well, then," Franklin said, munching happily, "since it looks like I'm outnumbered here, the sooner he shows up, the better."

Anne turned, heading for the stairs. If her dad was counting on Buck to show up to balance the numbers, he was in for a disappointment. Buck might be determined to talk to her on the phone, but the last place he wanted to be was in Tallulah.

Four

Buck peered through the keyhole on the door and recognized Monk Frederick, then swore when he saw Steve Grissom standing beside him. Although he counted Monk as one of his best friends, he knew he didn't come in friendship if he was with Grissom. Instead, he'd be wearing his Jacks management hat. Dropping his head with a tired groan, Buck debated whether or not to ignore them until they went away. But even if they left, they'd try again tomorrow and the day after that. Sooner or later, he'd have to let them in and hear them out.

"Can I get y'all a beer?" he asked after ushering them into the den.

"Nothing for me." Grissom was known to be a teetotaler.

"Same here, Buck," Monk said with a nod at the crutches Buck was using. "Take a load off. You don't need to be walking around on that knee."

"It's okay." But he shuffled over to a recliner and after placing his crutches where he could grab them in a hurry, he carefully sat down. "I take it this isn't a social call," he said.

In Grissom's line of work, crabby and ailing athletes were a given, so he spoke in a tone meant to soothe. "Just checking on how you're doing, Buck. With a concussion, you can't be too careful. In fact, after I look at that knee and have a chance to judge the extent of your injury, I'm thinking of recommending a trainer around the clock for you." He hardly paused at Buck's muffled oath. "That way, there would be less chance of you doing further damage if you should fall or…" he paused, cleared his throat, "I mean, with Anne having left, it's risky to be alone with that kind of injury."

Buck shot Monk an accusing look. "How is it that folks know I'm alone?"

Monk's big shoulders rose in a shrug. "Not from me and not from Marcie, so be cool. You ought to know that you're too big a celebrity to have any privacy, Buck. Anybody could have seen Anne at the airport—without you. Words gets around."

"Shit." He turned his head and gazed out the window.

"So—" Grissom was on his feet now. "You don't object to me taking a look, do you?"

As much as Buck longed to, refusing was not an option. He was an owned asset of the Jacks and Grissom was here to inspect their property, after which he would report back to Gus Schrader about whether or not a multimillion-dollar investment was going south. Buck did his best not to wince as Grissom poked and probed and prodded. Then, as he pressed a certain spot, Buck nearly came up out of the chair.

"Holy shit, Steve!"

"That's where I'd inject steroid ordinarily," Grissom muttered, unmoved by Buck's agony. Frowning in thought, he rose and stood with his arms crossed. "Steroid would be only a short-term solution, of course, but in the long run…no, I don't think so."

"Short term sounds good to me," Buck said, shaken at the thought of an extended leave of absence. "I'll worry about long-term stuff later."

Grissom gave a stiff smile. "Fortunately, Buck, that decision isn't up to you."

Buck had been miserable before the two men showed up at his front door, but he was ten times worse after they were gone. He was shaken by Steve's stubborn refusal to do a quick fix. In spite of everything Buck could think of to argue otherwise, he'd hung tough. Steve's official report would land on Schrader's desk within the hour. With the season starting soon, sitting out could mean the death of his career.

He accepted that Jacks' management worried over their investment and were concerned for his rehabilitation, but he discounted everything else they said now that he knew they were recommending an extended leave of absence to get him on his feet again. It sounded like a kiss-off. No doubt about it, unless he made a startling recovery, his career was in jeopardy.

He reached for the handle on the side of the recliner and pulled up to a sitting position. Just that small movement triggered searing pain that went hot and deep. With his teeth set, he groped for his crutches and painfully managed to get on his feet. For a second, the room spun, reminding him that he'd also suffered a concussion.

Propped on his crutches with his vision blurred and his knee throbbing, he made his way cautiously out of the den and across the vast foyer, splendid in Italian marble, heading for the kitchen. By the time he reached the butler's pantry, he was sweating and feeling a little sick. He'd been injured many times, but mostly stayed away from painkillers. But this time, between the knee and the concussion, he'd been desperate for relief and it was telling on him now.

At the pantry he stood thinking. He wasn't washed up yet, by God. A few weeks favoring his knee and he'd pick up where he left off…provided they didn't put him out to pasture as Steve Grissom might recommend and as the powers that be might sanction. Grissom was not known for his creativity as regards rehab, so any plan he devised would be traditional, slow to achieve results and in the end, possibly not particularly successful.

Head hanging low, Buck faced facts. He hadn't survived in the cutthroat world of professional baseball by just sitting back and accepting what a couple of so-called experts said. If he'd done that, he would have quit before he was twenty-five years old. Nearly ten years in the minors had taught him a thing or two about survival. Hell, being raised by his cold-hearted mother had taught him a thing or two about survival. Balanced on the crutches, he opened the door to the pantry.

Using one of his crutches, he snagged the leg of a stool and, moving cautiously, climbed a couple of rungs until he could reach the topmost shelf where he stored liquor, purchased by the case. Fumbling behind a case of Dewar's, he found a small box containing a vial of a clear substance and a syringe. Stepping down from the stool, he stood for a moment with his head pressed back against a shelf loaded with bottles of champagne. He took several long, deep breaths until the pain subsided to a bearable level.

A few minutes later—still sweating like a pig—he made

his way out of the pantry, through the kitchen and the huge foyer to the den and finally to his recliner. This time, he simply dropped his crutches to the floor without caring whether he would be able to reach them if needed and sank into the chair. He was whipped.

A long, long three minutes passed. Then, with shaking hands, he fumbled at the seal on the box. No way he'd be able to inject his knee until he could hold the syringe steady, he thought. But he had the vial out now and he'd watched the procedure enough in the hands of other athletes to know what to do and how to do it. By the time he had the syringe filled with the powerful steroid, he was calm.

Fortunately, he wasn't wearing jeans, but pajama bottoms, which had been a gift from Anne at Christmas. Since he always slept buck naked, when he'd opened the box on Christmas morning and saw what was inside, they'd both laughed at the absurdity.

"Wear them just once…for me," she'd teased that day. "I have a reason."

"Such as?" Suspicious, but he'd played along.

"Since you always have so much fun taking mine off," she said, smiling and kissing him at the same time, "I thought I'd try the same thing."

What would Anne think if she saw him now?

He quickly banished his wife from his thoughts and ripped the side seam of the pajamas all the way up to the knee. Steve's exam and the trek to the kitchen and back hadn't done good things for the injury. Gingerly feeling it up, Buck found the spot he thought would be about right and took a calming breath. Holding it, he pushed the needle into the spot and blinked rapidly at the pain. Slowly and carefully, he injected the drug.

For a minute, he was caught in a blankness of thought and time. Anne's face floated before him. She looked so sad. Was she still crying for the baby, he wondered, or was it because of what he'd just done? What had he done, he asked himself as tears welled in his eyes. With sudden and profound shame, he flung the needle across the room and bowed his head in his hands.

In spite of the many opportunities he'd had over the years, he had never used chemicals to enhance his performance on the mound or for any other reason. It was cheating, pure and simple. How had he reached such a low that he turned his back on every honorable standard he'd prided himself on from the time he first held a baseball in his hand while his father smiled at him proudly? The game was sacred to him. The ethics of play were sacred. What did it say about him that staying in the game was so vital to him that he'd not hesitated before shooting up if it meant he'd play again?

A sudden deep, agonizing need for Anne welled up in him. Jesus, she would be horrified over what he'd just done. Using the fingers of both hands, he wiped his cheeks and let his gaze move to a photo of the two of them when they'd been married only a few months. Anne was leaning into Buck who was Mr. Cool in sunglasses, a crooked smile and shirtless, while she laughed and raked at strands of her dark hair whipping in the wind. No sunglasses, so you could see her eyes, those incredible, beautiful turquoise-blue eyes. God, he missed her. He hadn't realized how empty the house was without her. Or how long the nights could be. Or how desperate he was to hear her voice. A dozen calls and she still refused to talk to him. He was flat-out scared that he'd hurt her so much she might never forgive him.

It came to him then that he needed to get his life in order. Still reclined in his chair, he considered what that entailed. First of all, he needed to win his wife back, but he could hardly do that if she was in another state and wouldn't even talk to him. Next, he needed to get back in shape enough to play baseball. In time, the concussion would take care of itself, but the knee was a problem. The chemical he'd just injected was only a temporary fix. A lengthy physical therapy plan was vital. He sat up in the chair. But who said that it had to be done here? There were physical therapists all over the planet, even in Mississippi.

Hell, he could kill two birds with one stone. The Jacks wanted him nearby so they could keep an eye on his progress. But what could they do if he left? He wasn't going to be able to play and Schrader wouldn't want him visible to the fans walking like a cripple. If he arranged to have his physical therapy in Mississippi, he could be near Anne. He'd have to pay for it out of his own pocket, but it was an expense he'd gladly bear.

His adrenaline was flowing now. He was a man of action. Instead of sitting on his butt, he was going to do something. But first he had to get to Mississippi. With his knee messed up, he couldn't drive. And he didn't want to fly commercial. Too public. Too embarrassing. He'd have to charter a plane. Simple enough. For the first time since driving the Porsche off into that ditch, he felt he was in control again. He could handle Gus Schrader's reaction, no matter what it was. His biggest worry was what kind of reaction he'd get from Anne.

By the third day in Tallulah, Anne was sick of her own company. The baby was her first thought upon waking and her last at night, a sore and tender spot on her heart that felt as if it might never heal. She appreciated the fact that Beatrice and Franklin took her at her word that she wasn't ready to talk, but a part of her wanted to tell someone how she'd felt when all was well in her pregnancy. She'd been so joyful. If a boy, she'd imagined him a carbon copy of Buck, complete with that rakish smile and easy charm. Or a girl with those same gifts. Would she be a tomboy? Would Buck's son have his athletic gifts or would his talents be similar to hers? Or would their baby be nothing like either of them?

Lord, enough of that. To keep from dwelling on her troubles, she was headed to the *Spectator* to take her dad up on his job offer. She was genuinely eager to resume her career, but it was icing on the cake that she'd have access to the *Spectator* archives. According to Beatrice, who had proved to be a walking encyclopedia of Tallulah's history, the archives would be chock-full of references to Buck's family. The things Buck told her about his family had only whetted her appetite to learn more. It was a golden opportunity to fill in the blanks.

She had not spoken with Buck. She simply wasn't up to arguing with him. After she'd refused to take his calls, he'd stopped trying. Maybe after thinking it over, he was relieved that she was the one who dared to say their marriage was in trouble. Maybe he'd been looking for a way out and just hadn't found a way to tell her. God knows, there were scads of women who'd love to be with Buck Whitaker. And not a single one of them would complain about not having his baby.

Her stepmother had generously offered the use of her car and Anne was halfway to the newspaper office when she realized the gas light was on. She was torn between irritation and amusement at Beatrice. The woman was a crackerjack businesswoman with a creative bent but Anne noticed that, in practical matters, such as keeping gasoline in her car or stocking the pantry with groceries or picking up clothes at the cleaners, she was woefully forgetful. Franklin groused about it when it affected him directly, but Anne had seen right away that he was so besotted with Beatrice that it would take a lot more than a depleted pantry or a wardrobe mishap to make him truly angry with his wife. In the time that Anne had been their houseguest, she was completely convinced that her father was happier than he'd ever been. She suffered a pang of conscience every now and then, feeling a bit disloyal to her mother, but Beatrice really was a sweetheart.

At the service station, she swiped her card and prepared to pump gas into the tank of the small car. For just a second, she thought of her Mercedes and wondered if Buck was driving it in St. Louis. He shouldn't be driving at all, but she couldn't imagine him staying cooped up in the house even when ordered to stay put. Of course, he may have already replaced his wrecked Porsche with something equally fast and expensive. And for just a second, she wondered if he was missing her.

"Anne! Anne Whitaker? What the hell—"

With her hand on the nozzle, Anne turned to see who'd spoken. Coming around the hood of a large black Lexus on the opposite side of the pump station was Buck's older brother.

"Jesus, it really is you, Anne." While still a yard away from her, Pearce Whitaker opened his arms wide and smiled, showing a lot of teeth. He swept her up in a bear hug, his kiss just missing her lips when she turned at the last second. Then, holding her by the arms, he looked her over. "Talk about surprises, honey, I about drove into the pump when I saw who it was gassin' up Beatrice's bug. How the hell are you?"

"I'm fine, Pearce. And you?"

"Couldn't be better." He'd removed his sunglasses and was still studying her as if he wasn't sure she was real. Her own sunglasses were firmly in place in the hope that she'd go unrecognized once she left her father's house. And of all those who might have recognized her, she would have wished it anybody but Pearce. Or possibly his mother.

"Where's Buck?" He glanced at the passenger seat of the Volkswagen looking for his brother. "After the accident, I thought he'd be confined to quarters in St. Louis by the Jacks. You're looking great, but how's our fair-haired boy?"

"He's okay."

"He didn't sound okay when I called him Sunday. Grouchy as a bear with a burr up his—" He caught himself. "And he didn't say a damn thing about coming to Tallulah. So, how long y'all been here?"

"Just since Tuesday." Skirting the truth. If she could get by without telling him outright that Buck was not with her, she would avoid questions about why. Let Buck break the news.

"And you haven't called us at Belle Pointe?" He was shaking his head. "I know Buck would rather kiss a snake than have a conversation with Mama, but y'all can't hole up at your daddy's house and pretend she's not just five miles down the road. She'll have a fit like you never saw when she finds out. Hey!" His eyes lit with a new thought. "I assumed Buck would be playing, which is why I haven't called him to set up an appearance in my campaign, but now you're here it changes things. He's able to get around?"

"More or less." She looked at the gauges on the pump and willed the gas to flow faster. "How is your campaign going?"

"Couldn't be better," he repeated, reaching into the breast pocket of his jacket. He took a business card out of a small leather case and used the surface of the pump to scribble a number. "Here's my cell. Tell Buck to call me. Today. Within the hour. His name's gold around here. I've been lucky the way support is growing, but word gets around that Buck's gonna make an appearance, the voters will love it!" He grinned, handing her the card. "This is just great. Couldn't happen at a better time. The polls say I'm the front-runner, but it's early yet and you can never be too far out front. A couple of appearances with the great Buck Whitaker and it may even scare my opponent into pulling out!"

The pump clicked off automatically. "You'll need to talk directly to Buck about that," she told him, with a glance at her watch. "I'm sorry to run, but—".

"No problem. Got things to do, huh?"

"I'm heading for Dad's office."

He spread his hands wide with another grin. "Another major advantage for me, having connections at the *Spectator*. I'm hoping Franklin will do more than just an endorsement. I'd like a nice profile piece, from the standpoint of the Whitakers. You know, playing up the contributions made to the town—hell, the state!—by my ancestors, emphasis on me, of course." He gave her a playful wink. "Get folks thinking it's the natural thing, having a Whitaker in the Capitol."

Anne bent to screw the cap of the tank in place thinking

Pearce had found his calling as a politician. With his profound conceit he assumed not only the cooperation of her father in his campaign, but Buck's as well. Fortunately, it wasn't her place to disabuse him of this notion.

She closed the lid with a thump. "Good luck, Pearce."

"Wait a minute." He opened her car door for her with the courtesy that seemed innate in Southern men. "How about coming out to Belle Pointe tonight? No joke, Buck can't hole up at the Marshes' and avoid Mama. Y'all need to make an appearance, if nothing else."

"I'm sorry, but I really can't speak for Buck." She reached over and turned the key in the ignition. "And I'm afraid I really do have to run, Pearce. Tell Claire I said hello, will you?"

"Sure, sure." He stepped back as she put the car in gear. "And you tell Buck I'll be looking to hear from him today, okay?"

With a smile and a wave, she drove off. He would know the truth before the day was done, but he was right about one thing. Now she was here, out of courtesy she must pay Victoria a visit. And soon. But she didn't have to look forward to it.

"Hello, Tyrone?"

"Yeah. Who's this?"

Nursing a Coke in one hand and the phone in another, Buck leaned back in his recliner. "Somebody who knows you were the one who tied Ray Dixon's jockstrap in a knot fifteen years ago, then forced Coach Randall to use you to pinch hit for him while Dixon spent precious minutes trying to straighten it out."

A moment of stunned silence. "Buck? This Buck Whitaker?"

Buck grinned and felt something ease in his chest. "Yeah, you sonofagun, who else?"

"Buck! Man, how you doin'? I saw on TV where you like to've killed yourself and your wife in that expensive car. Y'all okay, man?"

"Yeah, we were both lucky. I'm stove up some, but with a little physical therapy, I'll be okay." He took a sip of Coke. "How you doin'?"

"Fine. Fine. But I gotta say if what they reported is anything like accurate, you got a knee injury that needs more than a little physical therapy. You gotta be careful underestimating the damage and what it takes to overcome it, you know what I mean?"

Buck held the Coke can against his forehead. Cold seemed to ease the ache. "That's why I'm calling, Ty. I hear you're one of the best physical therapists in the South."

Tyrone gave a snort and then chuckled low. "I don't know about that, but I'm enjoying regular employment here in Memphis."

"How would you like to spend the next, say six months working in a place outfitted with the best state-of-the-art equipment, be your own boss, right in your own hometown?"

"That would be Tallulah, right?"

"Right."

"I would say it would cost a nice chunk of change and where would it come from?"

"Here's what I was thinking, Ty. I've chartered a plane and I'll be flying in to Tallulah in a few days. I need a PT and you're the best. The setup will be wherever I'm staying in Tallulah, which is a little up in the air at the moment. But after you check me out, you'll have an idea what kind of equipment and all the other bells and whistles I'll need for therapy. Are you with me so far?"

"I guess…so far."

"We could meet, talk, work out the details. I'd leave it to you to set the schedule and start the torture."

"What time frame we talking here?"

"I need to start right away. And I'd like to hire you exclusively for as long as it takes, Ty. I realize this means you'd have to ask for a leave of absence from your employer. If you need me to make a call or even to see somebody personally, I'll do it."

When Ty remained silent, Buck said, "If a leave of absence puts your present job in jeopardy, I'd be willing to subsidize a private clinic here in Tallulah, Ty. That's how bad I need you. You have any heartburn about being in business in your hometown?"

"I've still got family there," Tyrone said. "I guess you know that."

"To tell the truth, I wasn't sure." After Buck had left Tallulah, he'd lost touch with Ty, who had been an athlete—a good one—but had never quite made it to the pros. From the time Buck was a boy, Oscar Pittman, Ty's daddy, had been employed by the Whitakers operating and repairing machinery at Belle Pointe. Buck and Ty had played together, gone to school together, been busted for smoking together. They'd done a few other things together that Buck didn't like to think about. Only by the grace of God and Ty's mother, Frances, they hadn't wound up as outlaws. The woman was a saint.

"I know it's a lot to ask, Ty, but I'd count it a personal favor if you'd consider my offer. I know you probably have a life in Memphis—"

"Like a wife and eight kids?"

"Holy—" Buck stopped himself. "Are you serious?"

Tyrone laughed. "Gotcha goin', didn't I? No kids, but I married Lily Thigpen, you remember her, don't you?"

"I do. Lucky you."

"She keeps reminding me. You say your lady's okay after the crash? I've seen her at the games and she's nearly as pretty as you are."

"Anne. I'll introduce you when you get here."

"Sounds good."

"So, you like the plan? You think you can wrap up things there in Memphis and be in Tallulah within, say a week or two?"

"For a chance to add to my credentials a patient whose name is as big as Buck Whitaker's? I think I can manage that."

For the first time in the conversation, Buck relaxed. "Then here's my cell phone and the number of the Jacks sports medicine director who can give you the technical details of my injury and will no doubt tell you the treatment regimen he recommends, which you can decide to follow or not. Name's Steve Grissom." He reeled off the numbers and waited as Ty wrote them down. "Give it a day before calling Grissom, okay?" he added.

"Why? I assume the Jacks are okay with this?"

"They don't know about it yet."

"Whoa now, Buck! How can you—"

"I'll handle it. And Ty…"

"Yeah?"

"I know what I'm asking is a lot, so I'm prepared to put my promises in writing. We'll have a contract, all right and tight and legal. You think it over and if you decide it's too risky or you just don't want to go there, I'll…well—"

"You'll think of another incentive," Ty said with a smile in his voice.

"Yeah, probably. But if you do this, I'll owe you and I won't forget it, Ty, I swear."

"I'll hold you to that, buddy."

Five

On her way to the *Spectator*, Anne impulsively decided to stop at Beatrice's shop. She'd probably be recognized, but now that Pearce had outed her at the gas station, she might as well satisfy her curiosity about her stepmother's place of business.

A bell tinkled over the door of the Hodge-Podge as she entered and somewhere in the back of the store Beatrice called out, "I'll be with you in a minute."

"It's just me," Anne said, wandering over to a display of pottery. She had always loved pottery and had once joined a class to learn the craft, but like other projects she'd undertaken, she'd had to quit when Buck's career forced yet another move. Somehow, she'd never re-enrolled.

"What a nice surprise," Beatrice said giving her an affectionate hug. "You've decided to come out of hiding."

"Might as well since my cover's blown," Anne told her. "I had to stop for gas and who else but Pearce pulled up at the same time. He assumes Buck is here with me and hasn't bothered to call his mother."

"Seems a reasonable assumption. Did you explain?"

Anne sighed. "No, I lied. More or less. I didn't admit Buck was still in St. Louis. I thanked him for his invitation to Belle Pointe and told him Buck would be in touch."

"Naughty girl." Beatrice clicked her tongue and wagged a finger at Anne.

"I know," Anne said with chagrin. "You can believe I'll soon have to come clean because he's counting on Buck's endorsement for his campaign. I bet he's trying to reach him right now, probably at your house, which is where he thinks Buck and I are staying." She stopped. "But enough of that. I'm here to see your shop. It's wonderful."

"Do you think so?" Beatrice said with a pleased look around. "I mean, is it wonderful? I try, of course. What you see is mostly the work of Mississippi artists, pottery, candles, soap and all local whenever possible. I—"

She stopped as the bell over the door tinkled. "Oh, shoot! Let me take care of this customer while you look around and—" She stopped again, recognizing the woman entering. "Oh, Victoria. Goodness, it's been a while. How are you?"

"I'm well, Beatrice." With a regal nod, Buck's mother headed toward them. "And you?"

"Good, I'm good."

Victoria's cool gaze shifted to Anne. "Hello, Anne. I thought I might find you here. Pearce called after running into you a while ago and no one answered the phone at the Marshes'. I was a bit surprised to hear you were in Tallulah."

"It was a spur-of-the-moment decision." Anne managed a smile, uncertain about greeting her mother-in-law with a hug. It would be like embracing a mannequin. When Victoria kept her distance, Anne relaxed. "And how are you?"

"Busy. Very busy. I imagine Buck has described the flurry

of activity at Belle Pointe this time of year. We're up at dawn and we don't stop until dark."

"It must be exhausting," Anne murmured. In fact, Victoria looked tired. Upon meeting her for the first time, Anne had been struck by the woman's vigor. She guessed her mother-in-law's age at about sixty, but she'd always looked fifteen years younger. Today, however, even with skillfully applied makeup, she looked her age.

"Well, of course, it is exhausting, but not so much so that I couldn't find time for a phone call, if not a visit, from Buck. His trips to Tallulah are rare enough that I would have decided to have a little celebration," she said. "Of course, I would have to know he was here."

Anne sighed. It was silly to think she could be in Tallulah and avoid explaining Buck's absence. "Buck is not here, Victoria," she admitted. "I came alone."

"Really?" Perfectly penciled eyebrows went up a notch. "Does that mean he was more seriously injured in the accident than he told me when I called?"

"I don't know what he told you."

"Well, knowing the media's habit of sensationalizing anything about him, I wanted to hear from him personally the extent of his injuries. When I finally got beyond his answer machine, he said the media exaggerated. He'd be up and playing before long."

Anne sighed. "He had a concussion, Victoria, and he'll need extensive physical therapy before he can pitch again. When I left, it wasn't clear just how long that would be."

"And you left…when?"

"We were both discharged from the hospital on Monday. I left Tuesday."

"I'm finding it somewhat puzzling that you chose a time when Buck is…handicapped to take a vacation."

"Buck would be the first to say he doesn't need me to hold his hand at any time, Victoria. You must know that he isn't the type to tolerate anybody hovering over him."

"Hmm…yes." Victoria paused, studying Anne as if sensing something more than what she was being told. "And have you recovered from your injuries? Buck danced around my questions about you, too."

"I'm just fine." If Buck hadn't shared the fact that she'd miscarried, Anne wasn't in the mood to tell her mother-in-law.

"So, how long do you intend to be here in Tallulah? Naturally, we'd like to have you over for dinner and soon."

"Thank you," Anne said. "In fact, I was just thinking today that I'd call and find a convenient time to visit. I've hardly done anything but putter around Beatrice's house. She and Dad have been very gracious in just giving me the run of the place."

"It's been our gain," Beatrice spoke up. "In just two days, Anne's got everything in the house spic and span. Next, I expect her to start doing yard work."

"That sounds as if you might be bored," Victoria said, still studying Anne's face keenly. "If so, there's plenty to do at Belle Pointe."

Anne smiled. "I'm afraid I don't know anything about farming cotton."

"And I wouldn't expect you to. I meant there were other diversions. You've never spent much time with us and Belle Pointe has an interesting history."

"I've always thought so. I'd love to know more."

"Well, now's a good time, wouldn't you say? I'll check with Pearce and Claire about their calendars and we'll fix it. Now, I should be on my way." With a nod, Victoria headed toward the door. Just short of her destination, she paused and turned back. "By the way, with Pearce's campaign in full swing, as he must have mentioned, it occurs to me you'd be an asset. I'll have Pearce call to see how best to use you." With a tinkle of the tiny bell, she was gone.

Anne met Beatrice's amused eyes. "Use me?"

Beatrice laughed. "I'm sure she didn't mean that the way it sounded."

Anne sighed. "That woman scares me to death and has from day one. I feel as if I'm back in the fourth grade and I've failed to turn in my homework."

"She has presence all right," Beatrice said. "But rest easy, you were very gracious and respectful. Which is as it should be." She watched Anne pick up a platter from one artist's display. "Maybe it would help to remember that Victoria hasn't always been the chatelaine of Belle Pointe. She wasn't born a Whitaker, you know. She married into the family."

"I know that, of course, but it's hard to imagine her as anything except the quintessential Southern matriarch."

"Which is exactly how she wishes to be perceived." Beatrice moved a beautifully glazed bowl to a different position. "However, in high school, she was Vickie Hinton."

"Vickie?" Anne gave Beatrice an astonished look. It was hard to visualize Victoria Whitaker as a schoolgirl, let alone being called Vickie.

"Yes, Vickie. Before she married John Whitaker, her father worked for the Whitakers. Benny Hinton was a master mechanic and since farming at Belle Pointe is highly mechanized, his job was important. Still, he was hired help. In fact, he died in an accident while on the job and Victoria's widowed mother moved somewhere up north, I believe."

"That is so amazing. It explains why Buck's memories of his maternal grandparents are pretty vague."

Beatrice studied her thoughtfully. "The Whitakers figure prominently in Tallulah history, which is the reason I've suggested you might want to drop in at the *Spectator* and poke around a bit in the archives." She paused, tweaking a quilt displayed on the wall. "If, as Victoria suggested, you're a bit bored, I'll bet that once you start digging, you won't be bored for long."

Anne wondered at Beatrice's prediction as she surveyed the newsroom at the *Spectator* a while later, finding it as calm and quiet as a doctor's office. The level of activity was nothing like the frenetic energy that characterized the newsrooms in a daily newspaper or a television station and, from her observation, unlikely to relieve anybody's boredom. On the other hand, one reason Franklin gave for leaving his job in Boston was his desire to work under less pressure. He'd certainly managed that.

His face brightened when he looked up and saw her. "Anne!" He rose from his computer and motioned her inside. "Bea called and told me you were headed this way."

"Don't let me interrupt whatever you're doing, Dad. I'll just look around and get acquainted until you're free to talk."

"You aren't interrupting anything and I mean that literally." He looked at the screen of his monitor with disgust. "I've spent the afternoon trying to write next week's editorial. So far, I've deleted almost everything I've written."

He waved at a chair. "Bea suggested you might want to look at the *Spectator* archives. Curious about the Whitakers, are you?"

"The Whitakers and other Tallulah history. The Mississippi Delta is a very unique place. Maybe I'll write a book."

Franklin looked delighted. "Good idea. And I think you'll find the Whitakers figuring pretty prominently in your research."

"I was kidding, Dad." Unwilling to interrupt him, she lingered at the door. "Actually, I was thinking that since there's a political campaign going on I might do something with that. I ran into Pearce as I was pumping gas and he gave me the idea himself. Of course, he suggested an article favorable to him, but I thought it would be interesting to put Pearce and his opponent in the same article, showing the contrasts in their platforms."

"Good idea. I'll schedule it for next week's edition."

She gave a small laugh. "Just like that? What if it doesn't meet your standards?"

"Then I'll act like an editor and demand revisions," he said.

"Gosh, you make it sound like I have a real job." But she was smiling. Just the idea of working again and her adrenaline was flowing. "By the way, who is Pearce's opponent?"

"Jack Breedlove, the current chief of police and a hometown boy who returned to Tallulah after a stretch in the army. He was discharged after an injury in the Gulf War. He's about the same age as Buck, so I bet he could give you a few insights into Jack's character." He gave her a sly look. "Of course, you'd have to call Buck to pursue that source for your research."

"Give it a rest, Dad," she told him. "I think I can research the article without Buck, who probably hasn't seen Jack Breedlove since they both graduated from high school."

Franklin, still smiling, shrugged. "Just a suggestion, Annie."

"Okay, now I'm really fired up." She gave two quick taps to the door frame and stepped back, ready to begin. "Just point me in the right direction and I'll get started." Without turning, she backed into a person hovering in the doorway. "Oh, excuse me! I didn't know there was someone there. Did I step on you?"

"No." The reply was terse, almost rude.

"You remember Paige, don't you, Anne?" Franklin asked.

"Of course." Somewhere beneath a mass of coal-black hair tipped with neon orange, Anne recognized the youthful and vaguely familiar face of Buck's teenage niece. She had missed seeing Paige at Franklin and Beatrice's wedding. The teenager had been away on a skiing trip to Colorado. "How are you, Paige?"

Appearing utterly bored, the girl turned, exposing an ear pierced with no fewer than six tiny silver rings. "I'm okay."

In light of her bizarre appearance, okay was not the word that came to mind, Anne thought. Paige's eyes were outlined in dark mascara, which matched the hideous purple on her lips and nails. Slim to near anorexic, she looked even more wraithlike in a long, straight black coat and boots, which appeared to be at least one size too large and more suitable for combat duty in a war zone than for the rigors of middle school.

"You've grown since I was here last," Anne said faintly, hoping her reaction wasn't revealed on her face.

"People grow." She looked beyond Franklin to the window that framed a view of the town square. "Is Uncle Buck with you? Is he going to recuperate from his accident here in Tallulah?"

"No, Buck stayed in St. Louis."

Paige frowned. "Shouldn't you be with him?"

"He has tons of people helping him," Anne said. "He won't miss me."

Paige turned then and studied Anne briefly. "They said you were in the accident, too. Were you hurt?"

"Not seriously."

"Paige," Franklin explained, "is spending some time here at the *Spectator* after school to earn extra credits toward her grade in English."

Paige rolled her eyes. "He makes it sound like I volunteered or something," she said to Anne. "It was do it or die. When my grades in honors English tanked, the Dragon spoke and the parents agreed, of course. I swear people in prison have more choices than I do."

"The Dragon," Anne repeated. "That would be your… teacher?"

"No, it would be my grandmother. My teacher is actually okay. Almost."

"Isn't honors English a class for students with exceptional talent?" Anne asked.

"I wouldn't know since I don't have exceptional talent," Paige replied dismissively. "Which I tried to tell everyone, but when have they ever listened to me? When has anybody ever listened to me? It's like I'm expected to turn into Maureen Dowd or Ann Coulter or somebody."

"Are you into politics?" Anne asked, trying not to smile at mention of the famous female pundits. It was remarkable that Paige even knew their names.

"God, no! One person in the family with politics on the brain is already one too many." She huffed out a disgusted sound. "That's all my dad ever wants to talk about and it's so, like, *boring.*"

"You know, it occurs to me that Paige's current project makes her the logical person to give you a tour of the archives," Franklin said. "She's organizing a shipment of records that came to me from the estate of a professor at Vanderbilt. Paige," he turned to the teenager, "would you show Anne around down there while I try and finish this editorial?"

"I guess so." Paige wasn't exactly gracious, but she didn't refuse. As Anne followed her down the hall, she wondered why Paige chose to dress as if auditioning for a role in a horror movie. What she'd read about kids who were into Goth was that they were, for the most part, troubled teens. Certainly, Paige's bizarre dress, grades that had tanked and open hostility to authority were danger signs. As much as she longed for motherhood, Anne wasn't blind to the challenges of raising kids.

"How is your mom, Paige?"

"Claire?" A shrug and an exaggerated look at her wristwatch. "Hmmm, probably on her way home from Memphis about now. She goes there at least three times a week. She's a shopaholic. But when I want something really, like, cool to wear, she flips out. Like my taste in clothes just sucks and her taste is perfect."

Claire was very attractive and dressed beautifully. Although Anne didn't know her sister-in-law well, Anne guessed that Paige's bizarre appearance probably drove her crazy. She wondered, too, what effect it had on voters that Pearce's teenage daughter seemed a bit out of the mainstream compared to other kids.

"Fashion tastes can be a generational thing," Anne suggested, seeking a reply that wouldn't set them at odds at the outset. "I remember trying to convince my mom to let me have a tattoo when I was about fifteen. I just couldn't understand why she refused to let me do it. It was going to be a butterfly…" With a smile, Anne lifted her hair and pointed. "…right here. Now I'm truly grateful that she put her foot down. Wouldn't it look ridiculous when I'm all dressed up for a formal event and there's an insect on my neck?"

"I think it would be way cool." Paige lifted her clingy little T-shirt beneath the heavy black coat and bared her tummy. Curling around her navel, which had a silver ring in it, was a snake.

"Oops." Anne covered her mouth to hide her dismay. "Guess your mom didn't put her foot down fast enough, huh?"

Paige gave another disgusted huff. "I don't know why Claire is so paranoid about my behavior considering what a real hellion she was at fourteen."

Anne wondered if Claire knew Paige referred to her by her first name. "How many tattoos does she have?"

"None. And if she had done it, my dad would have forced her to remove it. He doesn't want any of us to have an original thought or do anything without consulting him."

"Let me guess. He takes exception to…ah, the way you dress?"

"It drives him wild. But at least I have the guts to do stuff out in the open, which Claire could never get up the gumption to do."

"For example…" Anne held her breath, not having a clue what the girl would say next.

"Well, she objects to me smoking a few cigarettes," Paige continued, "while she goes through a pack a day."

Bad grades, smoking, tattoos, body piercing and what else, Anne wondered, feeling sympathy for "the parents." "Maybe she's trying to help you avoid making the mistakes she made."

"And maybe when she quits, I might listen. And how about Dad throwing away those smelly cigars? No way, Jose. Anything he does is fine." Paige threw open a door revealing steep stairs. "The archives and stuff are down here," she said, taking the stairs with surprising grace in her clunky boots. "Over there on those shelves is the stuff I'm working on that came from that old professor who croaked. Good luck trying to figure out the rest of what's in here."

Along with the archival material boxed and stacked to the ceiling, pictures of significant happenings in Tallulah lined the walls of the long and narrow room. The light was bad, air circulation poor and the dust thick enough to clog the sinuses. Anne didn't wonder that Paige was grumpy if she spent much time alone down here.

Studying the wall of pictures, she instantly recognized a photo of John Whitaker posing with a past governor. This was definitely the place to fill in the gaps about Buck's family before interviewing Pearce.

Paige looked around, wrinkling her nose. "Pretty bad, isn't it?"

"I would say that we have our work cut out for us," Anne said. "We'll just think of it as a treasure hunt."

"Huh?"

"Going by these photographs, there's probably oodles of stuff about your dad's family here…and since I married into it, I'm pretty curious, too."

Paige looked around as if viewing the place from a different perspective. "Can I ask you something?"

"Sure." Anne looked at her, expecting a question about the archives.

"What's it like being married to somebody like Uncle Buck? I mean, besides being famous and the Jacks star pitcher, he's like, really hot. Isn't it exciting just being his wife and getting to be with him every single day?"

Anne smiled. "Sounds like you see that as a wonderful life."

"Well, sure. At school, all the boys want to be like Uncle Buck. They want to know all about him. I get a lot of that because I'm his niece." She made a face. "I know it's not about me."

"But you do like baseball?"

"Sure, don't you?"

"I'll tell you a secret. Just because I'm married to a man who plays baseball doesn't mean that I have to love the game, too."

"But you go to the games. I see you on TV when they show special people in the stands, wives and all."

"I go because Buck's fans expect to see his wife at the games. And besides, I've learned to appreciate many aspects of baseball. But when I met Buck, it was a different story. I was a reporter and I knew next to nothing about sports. I wrote human interest pieces for the features section of the paper."

"Then how did you ever meet him?"

"I was assigned to cover a Special Olympics event and Buck was one of the athletes scheduled to appear. I was interested in meeting him, not because I cared anything about baseball, but because I knew he was from Tallulah, Mississippi."

Paige wrinkled her nose, puzzled. "Why did that matter? This place is, like, nowhere, the end of the universe."

"Oh, I think many people would argue with you there, my dad, for one. I grew up hearing him talk about the Mississippi Delta. The civil rights movement interested him, so when he came down with a PBS crew from Boston, what he saw made such an impact that he wrote a book about it."

"I know about the book. We had to read it in honors English."

"Did you like it?"

Paige nodded. "It was, like, way cool. All the stuff that happened back then seems like something out of a bad movie. So, what happened when you met Uncle Buck that day? Was it love at first sight?"

Anne's gaze shifted from the young girl's face to the gold band on her finger. Buck had bought her a large yellow diamond after signing his first million-dollar contract in St. Louis but it was in the wall safe back in St. Louis. Even in her disillusionment, she couldn't bring herself to take off her wedding band. "I don't know if it was love at first sight, but it was certainly something very powerful."

"Like a wild crush or something, huh?"

Smiling, she looked at Paige. "Have you ever had a wild crush?"

Paige shrugged. "Not really, but I can understand how it would happen, especially if the boy was like Uncle Buck. Which is impossible because there's nobody at school like Uncle Buck. He is *so* cool. I think you're just about the luckiest woman in the world to be married to him."

Anne's opportunity to interview Pearce came sooner than expected. When it was time for Paige to leave that day, it was her father, not Claire, who came to pick her up. When Anne asked if he had time to answer a few questions for an article in the *Spectator,* he was more than ready to make time.

"Before we get started," he said, making himself comfortable in front of her newly assigned desk, "tell me, where the hell is Buck? Nobody's home at the Marshes', he's not picking up his phone messages, nobody's seen him. Man, I need to talk to him."

Anne sighed. Apparently Victoria hadn't yet filled Pearce in. "He's not here. The Jacks are concerned about his injury. He's undergoing pretty intensive physical therapy in St. Louis."

"How long are we talking here?"

She shrugged. "Who knows? It was a serious injury. He could be out for the season."

He studied her thoughtfully. "And you're here…working for your daddy?" He let his eyes roam around the office. "What does Buck think about that?"

She crossed her legs and gave him a speaking look. "In this interview, I ask the questions, Pearce."

"O-kaaay…" He studied her, narrow-eyed, letting her know he guessed interesting things were going on in his brother's marriage, but he wouldn't press her…for now. "So, where do you want to start? The voters know my background, but it won't hurt to remind them that we Whitakers go back five generations here."

Anne wished for a tape recorder, but since she'd occupied the tiny office for less than half a day, she hadn't collected supplies, not even a notepad. At least there was a computer, albeit an aging one. She grabbed a few sheets of paper from the printer and prepared to take notes. "I have a standard list of questions that I use when interviewing," she told him, "but don't worry, I won't use everything we discuss. It just helps to know as much about an individual as possible."

"Well, sweetheart, you know about all anybody could know about me," he said, propping an ankle on his knee. "We're family, aren't we?"

"What I meant was this, Pearce. To decide how to shape the piece that eventually emerges, some of my questions that may strike you as personal, but most of that won't show up in print." She gave him a professional smile. "Okay?"

With the survival instincts of most good politicians, he took a while to consider the implications of that. "Hmm, I'm getting a little nervous." He didn't look nervous. Instead he looked relaxed and confident. Leaning back, he reached inside his jacket and brought out a cigar. "Do you mind if I light this?"

She glanced at the wall where a No Smoking sign was posted and clearly visible. "I'm new here at the *Spectator*," she reminded him, "but it appears there's a no smoking policy."

"I sure wouldn't want to get you in trouble with your boss," he said, winking at her as he tucked the cigar back in his pocket.

"Thank you," she replied dryly. With her pen poised, she asked, "What person do you most admire, living or dead?"

He laughed and shook his finger at her playfully. "Looking to trip me up, aren't you? If I say George Washington, I alienate half of the voters in the district. If I say Martin Luther King, I alienate the other half. Can't win for losing."

"I'm not looking to trip you up, Pearce. Knowing whom you admire gives me an idea of your value system."

"I'll match my value system with my opponent's any day," he said darkly, suddenly losing all trace of good humor.

"Your opponent," Anne said, her pen flying across the paper. "That would be Jack Breedlove."

He shifted in his chair, both feet now on the floor. "He's the chief of police…at the moment. Have you ever known an honest cop?"

"It sounds as if you're accusing Mr. Breedlove of something illegal. Would you care to be specific?"

He looked at her notepad and swore under his breath. "Erase that, sweetheart. It's off the record. I shouldn't have said it."

She made a mark on the paper. "Do you call every woman you talk to 'sweetheart'?"

He winked at her again. "No, only the pretty ones."

She made another note and without looking up asked, "What made you decide to run for the state senate?"

"Hey, wait a minute. I'm kidding. You put that in the article and every feminist in Mississippi will turn out against me."

She put her pen down and folded her hands on top of the desk. "Okay, if you act as if you're taking this interview seriously, I'll do the same."

"Agreed. So…let's start with why I think my opponent's qualifications to hold the office are pitiful."

She hid a smile. He was determined to control the interview and it suited her to let him think he was doing just that…for now. She could hardly wait to write up her notes and put in a call to his "pitiful" opponent.

The ring of his cell phone woke Buck from a half doze. Groggily, he stared at the caller ID. His mind cleared instantly upon seeing the area code for Mississippi. His wife…finally. "Anne?"

"No, Buck," Victoria Whitaker replied. "I'm sorry to disappoint you."

"Ma. Hey." He cleared his throat and settled back in the chair. "How are you?"

"I'm fine. How's that knee coming along?"

"I can't complain." Between his mother and Pearce, he'd received more phone calls from Mississippi in the last few days than he had in the past five years. "Everything okay there?"

"We're in the throes of spring planting, as you know. Up early, working late. It's demanding." Many women in her situation spent their days playing bridge or golf at the country club or shopping in Memphis, but not his mother. She was busy ramrodding the hired help at Belle Pointe.

"I hear you." And his mother wasn't one to call and chat either. Something was up.

"I was surprised to see Anne at Beatrice's shop this morning," she said. "It seems odd that she's here and you're there."

"Anne claims when I'm injured I'm like a bear with a sore paw, so she took off to visit Franklin and Beatrice." And he'd be joining her in a week. It was killing him to wait, but he was afraid of a setback if he put too much stress on his knee too soon.

"Yes, she mentioned that you didn't tolerate much coddling. What was it she said…hmm, something like you'd have the entire Jacks organization looking out for you. That you wouldn't need her."

Buck rubbed his eyes with a thumb and forefinger. His head ached. It wasn't the concussion. His mother always gave him a headache. "How's Pearce's campaign going?"

"That's one of the reasons I'm calling. Pearce is preoccupied with his campaign, which is a complication. It makes us shorthanded at Belle Pointe."

"Ma, you're not trying to tell me he ever gets his hands dirty at planting season or any other time, are you?" he asked.

"I can only tell you I miss every pair of hands, especially now that Will Wainwright gave notice."

"Will has quit?" Buck's mouth fell open.

"Retired." She gave an offended huff. "He gave me some excuse about wanting to see more of his grandchildren. It was terribly inconvenient."

"Holy sh— Um…holy schmolie," he breathed. Wainwright had been her right-hand man for fifteen years. "Now there's a pair of hands you'll definitely miss."

"I must agree with you there," she said. "However, I think I've resolved the problem, Buck. With Pearce caught up in this campaign and you idle for the season, the stars seem aligned."

"The stars seem aligned?" Now what, he wondered.

"Yes, indeed. We're in a bind at Belle Pointe and you always understood what was required to get the crops planted and maintained until it was time to start picking. You're well able to step right into Wainwright's shoes."

"Ma, if you're asking what I think you're asking, forget it. I've got my hands full with rehab. I—"

"Added to that," she went on, "it looks odd that you're in St. Louis and your wife's here. People talk. Do you really need more bad publicity, Buck? After that boy, Casey—"

"Ma, it's not a good time for me," he argued, keeping his travel plans to himself. If she knew he was heading for Tallulah, she'd probably meet him at the city limits on a tractor and hog-tie him to the nearest cotton field.

She sighed. "I expected just that reaction from you, Buck, but I also know that after you think about it, in the end you'll do your duty. You love Belle Pointe. Don't deny it. You won't be able to resist helping out. It's what your father would want you to do."

Somehow, he managed to keep his outrage in check. She had her nerve mentioning his father. Fifteen years ago when John Whitaker died, Buck had wanted nothing more than to step in and fill his father's shoes, but she'd had different plans then. "I appreciate the problem you're having, Ma, but I've got other priorities right now. You need to find a good manager to replace Will. As for somebody to step into Pearce's shoes, I can't think it would be too difficult since he never knew jack shit about growing cotton anyway."

"I don't appreciate your vulgarity, Buck," she said frostily. "And I might remind you of your responsibility as a Whitaker."

"What's different now from the day Dad died, tell me that. You reminded me then that Pearce was the primary heir to Belle Pointe, that when I finished my degree, I was to forget coming home to grow cotton."

"It worked out well, didn't it? You had excellent prospects for a career in professional baseball and you made it. I knew you could."

"After about ten miserable years in the minors, Ma!"

"And would you have tried as hard if your real goal was simply to return to Belle Pointe?" she replied. "I think not."

His laugh was short and mirthless. "You're telling me you practically disinherited me for my own good? And now, because Pearce is temporarily distracted, I should forget all that?" He stopped at a sudden thought. "What if he wins that senatorial seat as you predict and then decides he doesn't want to play at being a gentleman farmer anymore? What if he wants to live most of the year in the state capitol? What then, Ma?"

"Pearce knows where his duty lies. Which is exactly what I expect from you. To use a baseball metaphor, I expect you to step up to the plate, Buck. Do your duty."

He was shaking his head at the gall of her. "Again, no disrespect, Mother, but you'll have to find another pinch hitter."

It was almost a week after interviewing Pearce that Anne was able to secure an interview with Jack Breedlove and nothing about the man struck her as pitiful. Far from it, Breedlove was tall and lean with severe features that were not quite handsome, but powerfully male. She was used to world-class athletes with an excess of testosterone and this man, she thought, would fit right in with Buck and his teammates.

The slight limp was a souvenir of his tour of duty in the Gulf War, she thought, as he came around his desk to greet her, but she quickly forgot his handicap as he took her hand and smiled down at her from striking green eyes. "Anne Whitaker. I feel as if I know you considering how often I've seen you in the Jacks VIP box. Welcome to Tallulah."

"Thank you." A little flustered, she took the seat he offered. "I know you're busy, so I won't take up too much of your time. As I mentioned when I phoned you, I thought it would be interesting to contrast the platforms of the two leading senate candidates, especially since you're both from Tallulah."

He didn't return to his chair, but propped one hip casually on the side of his desk and crossed his feet at the ankles. "I'm up for that, of course, but first, how's Buck? Bad news, that accident. I've been following it in the media. Word is he's out for the season."

He probably knew as much as she. By refusing Buck's calls, she relied on Marcie for updates on his injuries. "He's undergoing pretty intensive physical therapy," she said. "And yes, he's out for the season."

"Rotten luck," he said. After a pause, he added, "We played baseball together in high school. He pitched. I played short-stop."

"The thinking man's position," she said, smiling.

"I don't know about that, but we made a good team." He gazed at his feet, remembering. "Those were good times. I was thrilled when he finally made it into the majors."

"Not as much as Buck, I bet," she said.

He turned his head to look at her. "And now here you are reporting on an obscure political race in Mississippi while he's recuperating in St. Louis. What's wrong with that picture?"

She pulled a tape recorder from her bag and set it on his desk. After checking to see that it was on, she asked, "Is that how you see the position as state senator in this district…obscure?"

He paused with a look of chagrin. "I apologize if I trespassed into personal territory."

"Apology accepted." She let her gaze wander to the window. Then, because she liked him, she said, "For what it's worth, Chief Breedlove, Buck belongs to his public, but I don't. So I'm just having a little break from all that while I'm here in Tallulah."

It was probably more than he wanted—or needed—to know, but it was the explanation she planned to give while in Tallulah. He wouldn't be the only person who would ask outright why she wasn't with Buck.

He straightened from his desk. "Call me Jack," he said.

She smiled. "Okay, Jack." While he went back to his chair, she checked to see the tape was still running, then opened the flap of her notepad and clicked her pen to start writing. She liked to have tape as backup, but she usually wrote from her notes. "First question: Why do you think you're the better man for the job than your opponent?"

"Are you kidding?" He grinned, enjoying himself. "How much time do you have? This could take a while."

Six

After interviewing Jack Breedlove, Anne shopped for groceries before heading home. She was forced to pull up behind a strange SUV parked in the Marshes' driveway. Frowning, she got out of Beatrice's car at the same time the driver door of the SUV opened. It was dusk, but had it been pitch-black, she would have recognized that profile.

Buck.

"Hey, babe." Tall, broad-shouldered, hips cocked, he braced on the door frame of the SUV with one hand and leaned on a crutch with the other. She stood in the open door of her car fighting back a rush of emotion. Paige's wrongheaded assumption that any woman was lucky enough to be married to him had left her feeling depressed because once upon a time, as Buck Whitaker's wife, she had felt like the luckiest woman in the world. So it was not joy she was feeling now, she told herself firmly. She was not happy to see him. Drawing in a long breath, she hitched the bag of groceries on one hip and walked toward him.

"What are you doing here, Buck?"

"At the moment trying to stay upright long enough to go inside if I get an invitation. Otherwise, I might just topple over on my face." He gave a boyish grin. "You wouldn't want that to happen, would you?"

She glanced at the huge SUV, then back at him in disbelief. "Have you driven all the way from St. Louis?"

"Only from the local airstrip. I chartered a plane to get here. The SUV's newly leased." He managed to shrug without losing his balance. "No matter how bad I wanted to see you I couldn't drive three hundred miles."

She glanced down at his knee, noting that he wasn't putting any weight on it. From the set of his mouth, she guessed he was in pain, but she knew from experience that, like many athletes, he made light of an injury that would put an ordinary person out of commission for days. "How did you get permission to leave?"

"I didn't exactly. I guess you could say I'm AWOL."

She frowned. "What?"

"Absent without leave. That's—"

She gave an impatient shake of her head. "I know what AWOL means. I'm just stunned that you've taken a chance on permanently damaging your knee." Her eyes narrowed. "Does Gus Schrader know you're here?"

"Physical therapy doesn't have to be in St. Louis." He shifted and she saw by the way he sucked in a breath that it hurt him. "Look, can we talk about this inside where I can sit down?"

There was little she was ready to talk to him about, but he probably wouldn't leave without making a scene until he explained why he'd come. He could be as stubborn as a mule when he had a plan.

Without a word, she brushed past him on the sidewalk,

climbed the steps and unlocked the door. Stepping back, she gave him ample space to shuffle past her and watched him make his way across the foyer to the sofa in Beatrice's formal living room. "I can't believe you did this, Buck. Gus Schrader must have had a stroke when you told him you were leaving."

"Almost, but he's too tough to have a stroke." He propped his crutch within easy reach and eased down on the couch, a dead giveaway that he was in pain.

"The air must have turned blue," she said dryly.

"I admit Gus and I have had friendlier conversations."

She sat gingerly on a chair, still holding the groceries. "Isn't there something in your contract that forbids you doing anything that might jeopardize your ability to play?"

"There's no jeopardy," he said stubbornly. "I'll do whatever Steve Grissom suggests, except it'll be here in Tallulah, not in St. Louis. It's taken care of."

"Here?" she repeated with astonishment. "In Tallulah?"

"Yeah, unless I can talk you into coming home with me. And we can talk about that after you tell me how you've been," he told her. "Are you okay? You wouldn't take my calls, so I've been keeping tabs on you through your dad and he says you are, but—" He broke off, seeing her surprise. "I asked him not to tell you. I figured you weren't in any mood to hear anything I said."

"You and Dad were talking behind my back?"

"I was pretty desperate to hear from you and Franklin was…understanding. I owe him. But I need to hear it from you that you're okay. I mean, Franklin says he thinks going back to work has been good for you and I think that's great, but—" He spread his hands, running out of words. "So…are you okay?"

"I'm fine, Buck."

"He tells me you've jumped into your job with both feet." His smile skewed sideways. "Already you've covered a meeting of the school board, a shoplifting at the Piggly Wiggly, a fender bender in front of the bank on the square and a domestic disturbance at the mobile home park."

She shrugged. "What can I say? Tallulah is just like the rest of the world, only in microcosm."

"Yeah." He was studying her intently. "So everything's fine?"

She bent over and set the groceries on the floor beside her. "Not really. I wanted that baby more than anything in the world, so it's taking some time to come to terms with losing it. With how I lost it."

"The accident," he guessed.

"Among other things, yes."

"Like the fact that I wouldn't take you home that night when you asked? My God, I wish I had that evening to live over, Anne."

She drew in a long breath. "Buck, if you're here thinking to talk me into going back to St. Louis, you've wasted a trip. I'm still not sure our marriage is worth saving."

"And I'm positive it is, Anne. I'm hoping to change your mind. Going up against Gus Schrader to get here was easy compared to the mountain I have to climb to win my wife back. I'm here for the duration."

"You hate it here! We've never visited more than a weekend at a time. Have you thought about being stuck here for weeks—months maybe—in a place you hate?"

"We need to talk about that. I mean, I need to try and explain why I never want to visit Belle Pointe, why you and I are poles apart on the subject of family."

"Dad and Beatrice will be here any minute, Buck. It's not a good time."

"Well, until they show up, please, Anne, let me get this out. I don't know when you'll give me another chance to talk to you." He made a face, shifting to stretch his leg out on the couch. "Muscle gets stiff if I sit too long," he explained, rubbing the muscle at the side of his knee. When it eased, he said, "Will you listen?"

She gave a resigned huff. "Go ahead."

"I guess the major turning point in my life was my dad's death." His gaze strayed to the grandfather clock, an antique from Beatrice's family. "I've never liked wallowing in the past. Seems to me obsessing about it never changes anything. So I've never told you why it was so devastating, other than the fact that my dad was dead and gone forever." He paused as the clock struck the hour. "It was an accident on the interstate. He was with Pete Wilcox, the Belle Pointe foreman. It was late and they were heading home after attending an auction of farm equipment. Pete was driving. We think he fell asleep at the wheel and the car ran head-on into a bridge abutment. They were both killed instantly."

"I know how it feels to lose a parent," Anne murmured.

He gave a wry laugh. "For me it turned out to be more than just the shock of losing Dad suddenly. It changed the career path that I'd been preparing for all my life." Without looking at Anne, he knew he had her full attention now.

"I was at Mississippi State and it was my senior year. I had a baseball scholarship, but even though I was being scouted by a couple of the teams in the minors, what were the chances of getting into the majors? Slim to none. So I didn't really plan to make baseball a career."

"I didn't know that," Anne said with a look of surprise. "You live and die for baseball now. I can't imagine you being interested in any other career."

"Well, as they say, shit happens. Two days after my dad died, I was in for another shock." While he spoke evenly, it was still such a bitter memory that he felt agitated just thinking about it. "I grew up with a real passion for the land, not just the Whitaker land at Belle Pointe, but for the whole Mississippi Delta. It's nothing we humans have done. Mother Nature took eons to create land so fertile and crops planted here grow like crazy. It's truly amazing."

"Now you sound like my father," Anne remarked.

"Yeah, well, like Franklin's obsession rubbed off on you, my dad's reverence for Belle Pointe—for the Delta—sure enough rubbed off on me. He respected and cherished the five generations of history rooted in Belle Pointe, but unfortunately my dad wasn't cut out to actually farm. In fact, if he hadn't been the only child of Southern aristocrats, he probably would have been a college professor. He would have had a lot in common with your dad."

"I was just thinking the same thing," she said.

"He was definitely an intellectual. He was a gentle, introverted man who was happy to leave the management of Belle Pointe to an overseer, at least, until he married my mother. I don't know this for sure, but I bet the ink wasn't dry on the marriage license before she was running things. I do know that from the time I was old enough to see it, she was in charge."

Anne was listening raptly, hearing things Buck had never confided before.

"I was due to graduate in a couple of months when Dad

died," Buck said. "My degree was in business and horticulture. As god-awful as it was to lose him, the timing could have been worse since I told myself I'd be able to step in and help my mother run Belle Pointe."

"Where was Pearce at this time?" Anne asked.

"Practicing law. He never had any interest in being a cotton farmer. All I heard when we were growing up was how boring it was. There's a lot of plain physical labor involved in growing cotton. You have to clear the fields, plow, plant, nurture and then defoliate the plants. Even mechanized, it's hard work. When the cotton matures, it has to be picked, then transferred from the fields to the gin for processing. There're times throughout the year when you're up early and work late. Even though there's a fine crew at Belle Pointe, not everybody is suited to it. But it's fulfilling…at least I found it fulfilling."

"But not Pearce," Anne guessed.

"No. From the start, he planned to do other things. That's why this foray into politics now doesn't surprise me."

"You've known about his run for the senate?"

"From day one. He's called me half a dozen times trying to get me over here to endorse him. I've put him off every time."

"I never knew he called."

He saw temper kindling in her eyes and rushed on. "It wasn't important enough to mention since I didn't want to get involved. But count on it, as soon as he realizes I'm here, he'll be all over my case."

"Why wouldn't you want to endorse him? He's your brother."

He bent his head, touching his bruised temple gently. "I

have some serious concerns about Pearce. In a position of power—and in the right circumstances—I'm not sure he wouldn't break the law. Or finagle a way around it. He can be really ruthless." He knew firsthand just how ruthless his brother could be, but he hoped Anne didn't ever have to know about it.

"You paint a pretty harsh picture," she said.

"Yeah, I know. And I've never said that to anyone else…" he paused, "that is, anyone who's living. I tried to talk to my dad once, but—" He shook his head. "Maybe it's best to just leave it at that." He was rubbing the muscle above his knee again. "Where was I?"

She spoke quietly. "You were going to step in and help your mother after John died."

"Yeah, that was always the plan. I'd do the actual farming and as Pearce interacted well with the gentry of the county and state, he'd eventually wind up in politics."

"Looks like half the plan is now set to go," Anne said. "What went wrong?"

"First, we made our plans without consulting my moth er," Buck said. Staring straight ahead and focused on the past, he saw it all as clearly as if it had happened yesterday.

With his father buried only two days, Victoria came into Buck's bedroom as he was packing to return to college. With only half of his final semester to go, he was tempted to just forget it since he couldn't see the value of a diploma. He'd already aced the courses for an undergraduate degree. And spring was a time of intensive work at Belle Pointe. With Pete Wilcox gone and his mother needing help, he planned to go back to Tallulah every weekend until graduation. But Victoria had a very different plan.

"Pearce will be assuming his role immediately as primary heir to Belle Pointe, Buck," she told him. "Arrangements are in place to begin planting Monday morning with Pearce supervising. I want you to continue to pursue a career in professional baseball."

Stunned, he dropped a double handful of toilet articles on the bed and stared at her. "Pearce is a lawyer, Ma. What are you talking about?"

"His law practice must take second place to his responsibilities at Belle Pointe now," she told him. "I'm aware that your father has given you a completely false notion of your role here. However, it is absolutely appropriate for Pearce to take John's place."

"Yeah, but not to actually get his hands dirty. Pearce hates dirt." *What false notion?* "You've found a replacement for Pete Wilcox already?"

"With Pearce stepping up to take his rightful place, that won't be necessary."

"Ma, this is crazy! He doesn't know shit from shinola about farming and he doesn't want to know. Have you talked to Pearce about this?"

"Don't be vulgar. And of course, I've talked to Pearce. He sees his duty."

Meaning, Buck guessed, that she'd talked to him and, bottom line, it was Victoria's way or else. "And he's okay with giving up his practice to farm cotton?"

"We've agreed that he doesn't have to give it up, but it has to be secondary, especially just now when we're in the throes of spring planting. I'm prepared to assist him, of course."

He looked at her in disbelief. She couldn't be serious. "You don't assist anybody now, Ma, you run things and Dad was good to go with that. But you always had Pete's help. Without a qualified manager, there's no way you can do this." He made a sudden decision and flipped the top of his suitcase closed. "Look, I can drop out of school. I'll graduate in a couple of months anyway. I won't get a diploma, but I don't need a piece of paper. My future is here at Belle Pointe and always has been. I have ideas about crop management. There are new seeds constantly being developed. They're resistant to disease, they're hardy. I was talking to Dad and he—"

"Buck." She spoke sharply, stopping him cold. "I've just told you what your future is. You will continue at the university until you have your degree. You are being courted by professional sports representatives—"

"In the minors, Ma, not majors."

"…and you have excellent prospects. You will continue to pursue a career in that arena. You will thank me later for urging this decision on you."

"No, Ma. Dad and I—"

"I have no interest in anything your father discussed with you!" she said with exasperation. "He was hopelessly sentimental and now he's gone. His will gives me full authority here, so this discussion is pointless. Pearce is his heir, not you. And I want him to immediately assume the role that he was born to."

He was shaking his head. "You can't be serious, Ma. You—"

"Stop addressing me by that ridiculous, childish name!" she snapped. "I am indeed serious and that's the end of it."

But he couldn't let it go. What she was suggesting was all wrong. He had to convince her. "Just hear me out, Mother. You may want Pearce to step up to the plate here, but he doesn't have any feel for the land. He doesn't like farming the way you do, the way I do. Since I was old enough to see the difference in your way and Dad's way, I've known that. I'm more in tune with the way you feel about Belle Pointe than Pearce will ever be. You have to admit that."

"I admit nothing," she said coolly. "On the contrary, while you've been in school, Pearce has progressed very satisfactorily in running Belle Pointe."

"I've been home every summer for three years and I haven't noticed Pearce having any interest in farming," Buck argued.

"He will do his duty," Victoria stated doggedly.

For a long moment, Buck simply stared at her. He knew there was no way in hell that Pearce would willingly choose farming at Belle Pointe over practicing law. Pearce liked hobnobbing with the state's movers and shakers. He liked wheeling and dealing. He liked using his birthright as a Whitaker of Belle Pointe as an asset, but he didn't like getting up at daylight to supervise the crews until dark. He didn't like to sweat or to get his hands dirty. So why was his mother pushing Buck out to hand Belle Pointe over to Pearce?

"What if my excellent prospects don't pan out, Mother?" he asked. "And if there's no place for me at Belle Pointe, where's my place in your plan?"

"You have an excellent education and you're intelligent," she said. "That is more than many young men start out with." She moved regally to the door. "Now, finish packing and Pearce will help you carry your things to the car."

Telling it to Anne now, Buck waited for the bitterness that always came when he thought of that conversation with his mother, but to his surprise it didn't hurt as much as it once did.

"How could she?" Anne whispered, shocked.

"The thing that galls me most to this day is that I begged her to change her mind," he said quietly. "She told me that my dreams for Belle Pointe weren't going to happen, that she was handing it over to Pearce who didn't give a damn about innovations in crop management or experimental projects like other planters to keep from depleting soil nutrients. Dad knew I had my heart set on trying new stuff, that I'd spent four years leaning to make a difference at Belle Pointe and she slammed the door in my face."

He read a mix of sympathy and bafflement in Anne's expression and gave a sheepish shrug. "I guess I sound like a big crybaby, don't I? Hell, she was right after all. My baseball career did take off—even though it took a few years. And now I have a very healthy portfolio, a house in St. Louis, condos in Vail and West Palm Beach, a couple of really fast cars, a beautiful wife—" He stopped with a wry grin. "I do still have a wife, don't I?"

She said nothing, simply shook her head.

"You're wondering why this has festered in my craw for so damn long."

"Wrong. I'm beginning to understand why baseball is so vital to you. And why you've been so reluctant about coming home."

"It's not my home anymore. She made that plain." He spoke with a tremor in his voice, but quickly cleared his throat. "You want to know something else that's really funny?"

"Please," she said with feeling.

"You'd think I was the last person she wanted working at Belle Pointe, but she called me at home a couple nights ago and asked just that. Seems Pearce is occupied with the demands of his campaign and since I'm not going to play ball this season, she thinks I should take up the slack."

Anne frowned. "Isn't there a manager?"

"Not anymore. Will Wainwright gave notice that he's retiring." He was unconsciously rubbing at the muscle above his knee again. "So I called Will and sure enough, he's had enough. He's sixty-nine years old and he told me the only way he can enjoy his grandkids is to retire." He studied his foot propped on the sofa, then spoke wryly. "I can only imagine a job with my mother as the boss."

"What did you tell your mother when she asked you to help out?"

"What do you think I told her? I refused flat-out." He gave a harsh laugh. "Not that she accepted it. She thinks she can bring me around. She makes everybody do what she wants eventually."

"I'm curious," Anne said, studying his stony profile. "Back when this happened, how did Pearce respond to your mother's edict? I can't see him just walking away from his practice to take up farming as she claimed he would."

"And you'd be right." He gave a scornful snort. "But Pearce is too shrewd to openly defy her. He gave it a couple of months, but mostly he was busy trying to find a replacement for Pete Wilcox. It was Pearce who found Will."

"Incredible," she murmured.

"He has a way, Pearce does," Buck said, nodding his head slowly. "I never knew how to get around my mother the way he did. And still does. I would have spent all day every day working my ass off at Belle Pointe, but not Pearce." With his eyes fixed at a point midway between them, Buck wrinkled his brow thinking about it. "Even today he needs his connection to Belle Pointe to build his law practice and to lay the foundation for his political aspirations, but he never gets his hands dirty. Actually, now that I think about it, he's slick enough to be a politician."

He swung his gaze back to Anne's. "I'm telling you all this to try and explain why I've got some pretty negative feelings about Belle Pointe and Tallulah…about family." He gave a self-conscious laugh. "Actually, now that you've heard it all, you may know way more about me than you wanted."

"No," Anne told him softly. "I'm just glad you finally decided to trust me enough to tell me."

"I've always trusted you, Anne."

She was shaking her head. "No, Buck, you haven't."

The kind of trust she was talking about scared him. Looking into her beautiful turquoise eyes, he wanted to take her into his arms. He wanted to kiss her anger and disappointment away. He wanted to promise her the moon and stars, but what she wanted was a baby. But would she want his baby now?

She stood up, but instead of picking up her groceries, she picked up his crutch. "Now that you're here, where are you planning to stay?"

He looked at her a long minute. "That's it? That's all you have to say?"

"You've given me a lot to think about, Buck. But I'm still struggling with the differences in the way we think about marriage and family and our future. I still need time away from you to work it out."

He swallowed disappointment. "I guess that means I won't be staying here."

"I'm occupying the guest bedroom," she told him. "There is no other."

After a long moment, he took his crutch from her and managed to get up from the couch. When he was on his feet, he reached out to tip up her chin and let his eyes rove over her face. "I've really done some damage, haven't I, Anne?"

"There's blame on both sides," she said quietly. "I just haven't been able to make peace with all of it yet."

He nodded and let his hand fall to his side. "I've had a lot of time to think since you left. I may not have this baby thing squared away yet and I don't have a good fix on a future after baseball, but I do know this, Anne: I love you and I don't want to lose you. I love baseball, too, and I won't deny I enjoy the limelight. But when you left, the shine was gone. It's no fun without you."

She took a step back. "It's late, Buck. I need to start dinner." She put up a hand before he could ask. "No, you aren't invited. But here's a thought. They're probably serving dinner at Belle Pointe about now."

He laughed softly, accepting defeat. "I'm hungry, but not that hungry, babe." He fixed the crutch firmly beneath his arm and started toward the door. "Now that you've refused to take me in, I may check out the family's hunting lodge. It's quiet, it's private and it's a long way from the big house at Belle Pointe."

She followed him, then waited as he used his crutch to push the door wide enough to get through. "Now that I know how far Victoria went to keep Pearce 'down on the farm,'" she said, "it makes me wonder if she's totally supportive of a career change that will distance him from Belle Pointe."

"From the way she talks," Buck said, "she assumes Pearce

feels the same visceral connection to Belle Pointe that she feels." He gave a snort. "It ain't so."

Anne looked thoughtful. "I wonder about Claire, too. To get a really complete picture, I'd like to get their take on all this before my article goes to press."

"What article?"

"Oh, didn't I say? I interviewed Pearce."

"The *Spectator* is endorsing him?"

"No, I'm doing a feature article on the candidates. I interviewed Jack Breedlove, too." Her lips curved in a small smile. "Neither is aware that they're both in the same article." She glanced up to find him watching her with an odd look on his face. "What?"

"You've missed your career, haven't you? You're getting a kick out of working at the *Spectator* even though it's small-town stuff."

"Yeah, I am. It's fun. More than that, it's fulfilling." This time her smile had a wicked tilt. "The fun may end when Pearce sees what I've written. Because I'm 'family,' he expects a puff piece."

Buck leaned against the doorjamb, enjoying a relaxed moment with her. "How about Jack? Are you trashing him, too?"

"I'm not trashing anybody," she told him. "I'm just not willing to ignore a few unsettling facts I've uncovered about Pearce. And as for his opponent, I'll just say that Pearce shouldn't underestimate Jack Breedlove. He's charismatic, he's smart, plus, unlike Pearce, he's a self-made man and a war hero."

Buck straightened up. "Whoa up there. If you admire Jack so much, maybe I should be worried."

"Don't be silly. By the way, why isn't he married?"

"He came close once." As if he couldn't resist touching

her, he stroked her cheek with the back of his fingers. "Claire almost eloped with him."

Her mouth fell open. "Claire Whitaker? Our Claire? Pearce's wife?"

"The same," he said with a shrug. "Her daddy's president of the bank. Word was that he nixed it. Jack's pedigree didn't measure up."

"And Pearce's did," Anne murmured. "Wow…"

"Jack's a good man. He was then and I'd bet my best glove he still is."

"He mentioned you played baseball together in high school."

"Yeah, we go way back." He glanced down at her, his gold eyes intent and oddly beseeching. "Are you sure about all this, Anne?"

"It's only in draft form so far, but—"

He made an impatient sound. "I'm not talking about your article. I'm talking about us. You and me. I'm here. We need to be together to work this out."

"To answer your question, I'm not sure about anything."

He stood looking at her for a long minute. "Well, you've got my cell phone if you need me," he said finally.

For some obscure reason, she felt her throat go tight. "Take care, Buck."

Seven

Beatrice walked into the kitchen and with one look at Anne's face knew she was upset. With her whole heart and soul, she wanted to ask what was wrong, but she dared not undo the delicate start they'd made in their relationship. It was absolutely wonderful to have Anne staying with her and Franklin, but she longed for the time when they were truly friends, close and loving friends who shared confidences. So Anne would have to be the one to make the first move.

"Something smells delicious in here," she said, shedding her jacket. "Tell me it isn't something fattening."

"Is fettuccine Alfredo fattening?"

"My God, yes." Beatrice crossed the kitchen as Anne turned off the gas. She dipped a finger for a quick taste and, closing her eyes, sighed with pleasure. "Please tell me you're never going to leave."

"I've made a pecan pie, too," Anne said, looking toward the door. "It's Dad's favorite. Where is he?"

"There's a city council meeting. He always likes to attend in the rare hope that something interesting will happen. He'll love it when he comes home to find you've made this lovely dinner."

"I like to cook when I'm upset."

Beatrice's smile gentled with concern. "Did something happen?"

Anne moved to the teapot and poured a cup for each of them. "Buck is here," she said quietly.

"Here?" Beatrice looked around as if he might be hiding in the pantry.

"He chartered a plane and now he's here in Tallulah." She handed a cup to Beatrice. "I drove up and there he was, parked in the driveway."

"Ah." Beatrice smiled with understanding and took a seat at the table while Anne went to the fridge for lemon. "I'm surprised he didn't get here sooner."

Anne sank into a chair. "Really? Because I couldn't have been more surprised, considering how he hates Tallulah."

"He misses you."

Anne smiled softly into her tea. "I actually think he does."

"And he's more concerned over losing his wife than whatever it is that has kept him from visiting Tallulah." Beatrice reached for a slice of lemon. "To tell the truth, I've been wondering about that myself."

"It has always been like pulling teeth to get him to talk much about his family," Anne said, stirring absently with a spoon. "I knew he had hard feelings toward his mother, but from the little he told me, I thought it was probably old-fashioned sibling rivalry, that Pearce was probably Victoria's favorite son and Buck resented it. That happens sometimes, doesn't it?" She looked up into Beatrice's eyes. "I was an only child, so I always imagined it would be wonderful to have a sister or a brother. And I would have been happy to share my parents, or so I told myself."

Beatrice smiled. "I think that's a pretty common fantasy for an only child. But you say he told you something tonight that puts a different face on it?"

"A cruel face." With her elbows on the table, Anne cradled her teacup in both hands. "What it boils down to is that when John Whitaker died, Victoria decided that Pearce was his primary heir. Which would have been okay with Buck, he tells me, as long as he could manage the cotton crop. He claims Pearce never had any interest in doing that."

"Buck is right," Beatrice agreed. "Pearce never cared a flip about Belle Pointe as far as farming it goes. He's a lawyer, first and foremost." She paused, stirring her tea. "Actually, he's best suited for exactly what he's set on now, a career in politics. It was Buck that folks expected to step in and manage Belle Pointe when John Whitaker died, but instead of doing that, he chose to pursue his baseball career."

"No, Beatrice. He didn't choose a career in baseball. Buck was in his last semester of college and, just as you thought, he planned to put his education to practical use running Belle Pointe, but Victoria had other ideas…and they didn't include Buck."

"What does that mean?" Beatrice asked, frowning.

"Victoria practically disinherited him. She flatly rejected the life he'd worked and trained for, essentially closing the doors to Belle Pointe in his face. That was when he turned to baseball."

"How is that possible? He's John's son, same as Pearce. John wouldn't have disinherited him."

"He wasn't written out of the will, but for some reason Victoria didn't want him at Belle Pointe. At least, that's the way Buck told it to me tonight. She wanted Pearce to run Belle Pointe and she wanted Buck to find his place in the world elsewhere." Anne set her cup down with a clink. "I was shocked. What kind of mother is she to do that?"

"One with her own private agenda," Beatrice said, looking thoughtful. "Or so it appears. Although I can't imagine what it could be. Buck would be an asset to Belle Pointe. Pearce lives in the big house, but it's only a house to him. His heritage as a Whitaker looks good on his résumé and now that he's in a full-fledged political campaign, you can believe he'll make sure the voters know it." She was shaking her head. "Shoving Buck out of Belle Pointe makes no sense."

"I know. But whether it does or not, Victoria now has changed her mind. With Pearce distracted by the demands of his campaign and Buck injured and out of baseball for the duration, she suggested that he could put his time to good use by managing this growing season."

"Really?" Beatrice blinked in surprise. "I thought Will Wainwright managed Belle Pointe."

"Not anymore. He's decided to retire."

Beatrice sat back and thought for a moment. "Well, I'm beginning to see why Victoria has had to change her game plan. She's up a creek without a paddle."

"Looks that way."

Beatrice heard something in Anne's voice. "So, what did Buck tell her?"

"A flat no." Anne fiddled with her spoon, then smiled at Beatrice. "He wouldn't admit it, but I think he's tempted."

They shared a moment of amusement as the sound of chimes striking the hour came from the front room. Then

Anne sighed. "Frankly, my head is just spinning with all this," she told Beatrice. "I always thought Buck was lucky to have such a big family, but of course it depends on the family, doesn't it?"

"Yes. Having a big family isn't always a blessing," Beatrice said. "I should know."

"At least you know," Anne replied. "You can look down a long line of relatives and see all kinds of interesting things, family likenesses, personality traits, body types. Dad must have told you that I was adopted. I know nothing about my birth parents and lately I've been toying with the idea of doing some research to try and find them."

"Are you really that curious?" As Anne thought, Beatrice chose her next words carefully. "There may be things you learn that hurt you…or someone else."

"I suppose so. On the other hand," Anne argued, "I might learn that there is some genetic cause that I didn't carry my baby to term."

Beatrice sighed and reached over, covering Anne's hand. "It's not uncommon for a first pregnancy to end in a miscarriage," she said gently.

"I know that. But I was told the accident didn't cause it, so I can't help wondering if there's something else. I remember once having a science project where we each had to draw a family tree and I didn't have one. Oh, I could have done my adoptive parents and I did but, deep inside, I really, really wanted to know how my biological family tree would look." She twiddled with a paper napkin, then smiled up at Beatrice. "My mother was very understanding about it. I don't think she would be upset to know I'm thinking of pursuing it."

"From all I know about Laura, she was a lovely person," Beatrice said.

"She was. And now that she's gone and Dad is remarried and so obviously happy, I can't see any reason not to pick up where I left off in the eighth grade." She grinned. "I know it won't be the same as being part of a family, that's not what bothers me. But I'd just like to *know.*" She paused, searching Beatrice's face. "Is that so wrong?"

"Of course not." Beatrice rose from the table with her cup in hand and went to the sink. "If it's troubling you so much, you have every right to search."

Anne got up to carry her cup to the sink. She stood for a moment watching as Beatrice opened the door of the dishwasher. "Do you think it will upset Dad when he finds out I'm doing this?"

"Maybe…" Beatrice smiled. "But he loves you too much to ever say no."

The lodge was a raised West Indies-type dwelling with wide steps ascending to a covered porch or gallery, as some called it, that encircled the house. Raised high off the ground to prevent the possibility of flooding, it overlooked the Mississippi River. The lodge was the place where he'd come of age as a Mississippi boy. Buck had found it a perfect escape from the conflicts that made life a misery at Belle Pointe.

It was the site of some of his best—and worst—memories. He'd learned to swim in the river at the lodge and he'd perfected the art of fishing, camping and canoeing. He'd hunted dove, turkey, quail and ducks here. He'd bagged his first deer when he was nine years old not fifty yards behind the lodge. And it had been here that he'd first seen death up close and personal.

Finding the door unlocked, he shook off memories, good and bad, and pushed it open, shaking his head at the arrogance of his family in thinking it unnecessary to lock the place as no one would dare vandalize Whitaker property. With his knee killing him after climbing twenty-six steps to the porch, he dropped his duffel just inside the door, closed it, and leaned back against it.

The smell of the place instantly took him back in time. The musty scent of a closed house, but overlaid with something lemony, whatever his mother ordered for the care of the pine floors and wood trim. Leather-upholstered furniture. Kerosene for the hurricane lamps, in case of an electrical outage. Candle wax. The past.

He took up the duffel and without looking much at anything, without turning on a light, went straight through the big front room to one of the smaller bedrooms radiating out from it. He reached for the tail of his sweatshirt and pulled it over his head, tossed it on the floor. Taking care to favor his knee, he took his pants off and without even checking to see if the bed was made with clean sheets—with any sheets—he elevated his knee on a pillow, grabbed the blanket folded at the foot of the bed and with a relieved groan, lay back. In less than a minute, he was asleep.

He came awake the next morning to the sound of a car. He was still for a beat or two, hoping that whoever it was wouldn't stop, then cursed under his breath when he heard footsteps on the porch. He guessed it was Pearce. He should have known his brother would waste no time trying to rope him into his campaign.

He rolled out of bed and on his way to the bathroom swept up his pants and duffel. It wouldn't hurt Pearce to cool his heels. Standing under hot spray, he found to his relief that his knee seemed okay. He could even put a little weight on it. Maybe he could make do with a cane instead of the crutch. Luckily, he'd brought a couple with him.

The visitor was not Pearce. It was his mother.

Victoria stood at one of the windows in the great room, which put bright morning sun at her back and in Buck's face. "Word reached us at Belle Pointe that you were here at the lodge," she said, making no move to cross the room and greet him. "I'm happy you changed your mind, but it would have been nice to let us know you were heading this way. How's that knee?"

"Coming along…with physical therapy daily," he told her. "I figured I can be tortured in Tallulah as well as in St. Louis." He spread his hands, moving toward her. "Don't I get a hug, Ma?"

It was Buck doing the hugging, but she tolerated it. "Did you get one from your wife?" she asked, smoothing her hair.

He ignored that, hoping her remark was a shot in the dark. "I apologize for not calling, Ma. It was late when I finally got here, so I just crashed."

She looked around the lodge slowly. "Here? Why not at the Marshes' with your wife?"

His mother was the last person he wanted to know about his marital problems. "I'd offer you breakfast, but I haven't had a chance to stock up on groceries yet," he said, reaching for a cane. "But if memory serves, there's always coffee. Join me in the kitchen?" At her nod, he swept out an arm for her to precede him.

The kitchen had always been his favorite room at the lodge. It was a fully equipped Viking showplace, but the brand and expense of the appliances weren't what made the place special to Buck. It was the hours—years—he spent as a boy in masculine harmony with the men who'd gathered at the lodge to hunt and fish and hang out. In this kitchen, he'd cleaned fish and dressed game alongside his father and his father's friends, men Southern born and bred and passionately devoted to preserving a way of life unheard-of beyond the boundaries of the Mississippi Delta.

He pulled out a chair at the round oak table in the center of the room. "Sit down, Ma. I'll have it ready in a jif."

He found the coffee can in the freezer and the coffee-maker tucked neatly in the pantry. When it was brewing, he turned and got a good look at his mother in morning light. She was sixty on her last birthday and for the first time, he saw that she was beginning to show her age. But not enough that she'd allowed herself to go gray or to get fat. As long as he could remember, she'd been a regular client at an expensive salon in Memphis, but no salon could give her that trim figure or that air of culture and class. It was discipline and a never-flagging determination to rise above her birth in a working-class family, a fact that she despised and was never mentioned by anyone who wanted to keep his head.

Leaning heavily on the cane, he pulled out a chair and sat down. "Is it wise for you to be up and about with your injury?" Victoria asked, frowning.

"It's okay. I'll be doing some physical therapy with a personal trainer while I'm here. You remember Ty Pittman, don't you?"

"Oscar's boy? Of course."

"He's a top-notch PT. I've called him and he's agreed to come out to the lodge and work with me as long as it takes."

"It sounds as if you don't plan on going back to St. Louis right away."

"I'm here until the knee is back to normal. Anne's keen on visiting with her dad and getting to know her new step-mother. Anyway, it looks as if I'm out for the season."

"What exactly is the situation with you and Anne?" she asked, watching as he elevated his injured leg. "Don't bother telling me everything's fine. If everything was fine, you wouldn't be sleeping here at the lodge. It doesn't appear that she's simply visiting her father and Beatrice. Is this a formal separation?"

"I don't mean to sound disrespectful, Ma," he said, "but I'm not discussing my personal life."

"That may be, but you'll soon find that everyone else in Tallulah will be doing exactly that. As I mentioned when I called you last week, it will look odd when people realize the two of you are staying in separate locations."

"Then it'll just have to look odd," he said shortly. "That's the way it is."

"Yes, yes." She waved away his irritation. "However, to keep gossip down, it would be best for you and Anne to come to Belle Pointe, I think."

"No, thank you," he said.

She gave him a familiar disapproving frown, the one he remembered from the time he was about four years old and then daily until he walked away from Belle Pointe. "You al-ways were too quick off the mark, Buck."

A glance at the pot told him the coffee was almost ready. He stood up. "It comes in handy when I'm pitching," he said.

"Do you want to be the object of gossip?" she demanded. "Are you trying to call attention to yourself? That's exactly what will happen if you're here at the lodge and Anne is with the Marshes. It'll create a firestorm of speculation. Gossips will say your career is over, that your marriage is on the rocks and that there's probably more scandal just waiting to surface. God knows, we have our share of gossips here."

"I'm not staying at Belle Point while I'm here, Mother. And neither is Anne." He opened a cabinet door. "As for gossip and speculation, bring it on. I'm used to it."

"But is Anne?"

Soft beeps from the coffeemaker saved him having to answer. "You still take yours without cream and sugar, I assume," he said as he took two mugs down from the cabinet. "There might be sugar, but—"

"Black is fine," she told him, watching as he poured. "And you're right, what's going on in your marriage is none of my business. Whatever the reason you're here in Tallulah, it's fortuitous. Now you'll be able to lend us a hand at Belle Pointe. It couldn't have worked out better. Also, I expect—"

"Ma, I told you before, don't count on me to do Will's job. I'll help you find someone to replace him, but—"

"You just told me your knee is fine. What will you do with yourself after your daily physical therapy sessions, pray tell? We need you at Belle Pointe. Mother Nature doesn't wait. The time to plant is now. If your father were here, he'd expect you to put aside hard feelings for the good of Belle Pointe."

"Hard feelings." He stared at her, wondering if she really expected that a few words wiped out years of bitterness and hurt.

Seeing his expression, she waved an impatient hand. "Take a few days to think it over, Buck. It's probably best for you not to put stress on that knee too soon anyway. Meanwhile, you'll also be able to participate in Pearce's campaign. Nothing physical in that. Anne's article in the *Spectator* should come out in the next edition. I'm not wholly supportive, as you can imagine. His—"

"You don't like the idea of Anne writing about him?"

"No, no, you misunderstand. Politics has a way of consuming an individual and Pearce's first responsibility must be to Belle Pointe. However, there are advantages. There's power in a senatorial seat. Doors are opened, opportunities present. But Whitakers have been planters first and foremost, so once he wins the seat I don't want Pearce to lose sight of his heritage."

No, we mustn't lose sight of Pearce's precious heritage. "You sound as if he's already won."

"Well, of course. He has the Whitaker name and the prestige that comes with it. I can't imagine his opponent giving him any real competition."

Knowing Pearce, Buck guessed he would trade heavily on that name, too, as well as the Whitaker wealth. Pearce's political philosophy aside, his brother looked good, he had a first-class education, a beautiful wife and with the blessing of their influential mother, he would probably make a formidable candidate. But so would Jack Breedlove.

"I take it you think there's no chance that his opponent will win?"

"Jack Breedlove? In the senate?" There was no mistaking the look of distaste on her face. "Hardly."

Like Claire's parents all those years ago, Victoria didn't consider Jack's blood blue enough when compared to Pearce. But Buck recalled Jack's tenacity and focus when they played baseball together. Raised by a single mom, he was forced to juggle practice and games around a job. It was still a mystery why he hadn't snagged a college scholarship. Instead, when they graduated, he'd joined the army. Buck had always wondered if Jack's decision had anything to do with the fact that Claire's folks busted up their romance.

"I wouldn't be so fast to write Jack off," he warned.

"He's a decent chief of police, I'll grant that," Victoria said, brushing at a tiny speck on her sleeve. "But he's simply not senatorial material and I'm confident the people in this jurisdiction will recognize that. So you see…" She touched a napkin to her lips, "it's important that you take care while you're here, Buck. If there's trouble between you and Anne, you must see to it that you keep a low profile so as not to give Breedlove a chance to throw mud."

"What if I decide to endorse Jack instead of Pearce?"

She gave him a cold look. "That is your idea of a joke, I assume."

He turned and poured the remains of his coffee in the sink. "Yeah, it was a joke, Ma."

"I wish you would stop calling me that," she said irritably. "When will you ever grow up?"

"Oh, I don't know…Mother. Maybe when I stop playing a game for a living and get on with life in a real job." They'd rubbed each other the wrong way for thirty-seven years. And still did.

"You can see that it's important to keep up appearances," she told him, ignoring his sarcasm. "If you and Anne won't stay at Belle Pointe, perhaps we could avoid speculation if you're seen coming and going." She tapped a finger against her lips, thinking. "Bring Anne to dinner on Sunday night. She and I have already discussed a visit to Belle Pointe. I've been remiss in not setting a day and time. Things are just so hectic right now."

"You've seen Anne?"

"Of course. I welcomed her to Tallulah the moment I heard she was here. But as I was saying, if you're together at Belle Pointe, people will see all is well in the family. And you will have endorsed Pearce by that time."

"Two things, Mother." He leaned against the counter with his arms folded across his chest. "If I endorse Pearce, it won't be because he's my brother or that you expect it. It'll be because I've decided he's the best man for the job. And as for bringing Anne to dinner at Belle Pointe, I can't promise that. I'll have to ask her."

"She's promised me and she's a woman of her word. And of course you'll endorse Pearce. Don't be ridiculous."

He sighed and changed the subject. "How is Claire these days? Is she looking forward to being Mrs. Senator Whitaker?"

"She could very well be Pearce's Achilles heel in this election," Victoria said with a small frown. "Lately she seems…well, without purpose. It's distressing."

"She's a wife and mother," he said. "That's purpose enough for many women. Paige is…what now, thirteen, fourteen?"

"Fourteen. And when you see her, you'll know what I mean. She's impossible. But I can't say I'm surprised. Pearce is extremely busy with his law practice, his responsibilities at Belle Pointe and his campaign, so he's simply unable to be father and mother to her. And, apparently, expecting Claire to become a responsible parent is like expecting a butterfly to morph into an eagle. She was a flighty teenager and she's a flighty woman. Why Pearce didn't see that before marrying her I'll never know."

"Maybe he was blinded by the fact that her daddy is president of the bank."

She gave an offended sniff. "Claire will settle down eventually. She knows the consequences otherwise. And Paige is already facing the consequences of her foolishness. After making a failing grade in honors English, she now spends three afternoons a week at the *Spectator* to bring up her grade."

"What can a fourteen-year-old girl do at a newspaper?"

"She can sweep floors, if nothing else," Victoria told him. "I don't care what tasks she's assigned. She must learn there are consequences for bad behavior."

Life at Belle Pointe was still just one big screwed-up mess, Buck thought wearily, unchanged from the time he was trapped there. Anne had always been fascinated by his family and here, by his mother's invitation, she'd get an up close and personal look at the Whitakers. No doubt, the meal would be a travesty of what a real family dinner should be, but he wasn't passing up any chance to be with his wife. All he had to do was persuade her to go with him.

Ty showed up later that day and after poking and prying, pronounced Buck in less than first-class shape for the demands that would be placed on him when he started practice next season in St. Louis. He outlined a punishing regimen and then left after arranging for the installation of the equipment he considered necessary and which he'd already bought with Buck's money. When he showed up at the lodge two days later, the room was outfitted and looked as professional as anything Buck would have access to back at the Jacks facility in St. Louis.

Now, sprawled flat on his back on a floor mat, sweating and in pain, he was barely able to lift one finger—his third—

to give his PT a crude insult. "And for this I'm paying you?" he muttered to the huge black man.

"Top dollar," Tyrone Pittman said, grinning. "And I'm worth every penny."

"Maybe," Buck snorted, "but it wasn't in the bargain for you to cripple me further before you whipped me back in shape."

"Shape?" It was Ty's turn to snort. "Shape I found you in, buddy, there could have been no treatment. Beats me how you were throwin' them fastballs to the competition. Muscles in your arms are plain mush. You want the Jacks in the Series next year, we gotta get that arm in shape."

"Hello? I hired you to fix my knee, not my arm." Wincing, Buck managed to roll into a sitting position. "Shit, man, I'm aching in places I didn't even know I had!"

"Keep that knee straight and that compress in place," Ty ordered, placing a hand on Buck's sternum to force him back down on the mat. "And tomorrow when I come out here for our session, I want to see you giving a hundred percent. You were out in space somewhere today, Buck."

He stayed down, knowing Ty was right. "I've got a lot on my mind," he told Ty, throwing an arm over his face.

"Then it's a good thing I'm here," Ty said, as he went about collecting towels and equipment. "You know how women tell everything to those hairdresser guys—so to speak—and when they leave the beauty shop, they're not only beautified, but they're rejuvenated? How about you think of me as your hairdresser and tell Daddy."

Eyes closed, Buck could only smile. Luring Ty away from his job in Memphis was the best idea he'd had since deciding to come to Tallulah. Better than being a fine physical therapist, he made Buck laugh. "Which is it, beautician or daddy-confessor?"

"Whichever." Ty shrugged. "You got trouble, I got time."

"Will Wainwright is retiring at Belle Pointe and Pearce is busy campaigning," Buck said, eyes still closed. "My mother wants me to manage the crews this season." He thought better of sharing his troubles with Anne.

With his back to Buck, Ty stood before an open cabinet to ask, "Did you forget how it's done?"

Buck gave a short laugh. "No. And I never met a cotton seed that I didn't want to plant. But I got over it."

"What does Pearce being busy campaigning have to do with anything? He doesn't manage Belle Pointe. Miz Victoria does."

"Not without Will." Buck was more alert now, noticing something about the way Ty stood at the cabinet, too still. Tense. Keeping his knee straight as ordered, he raised himself on one elbow. "Not being around during planting season for a number of years, I'm out of touch, but I could pick it up. That's not what worries me. Besides, I'd have folks like your daddy to see that I didn't screw up."

"Not my daddy, you wouldn't," Ty said, closing the cabinet with a snap. Turning, he met Buck's eyes. "Did you forget he doesn't work at Belle Pointe anymore?"

"Are you serious?" There wasn't a piece of equipment in use at Belle Pointe, no matter how sophisticated, that Oscar Pittman couldn't operate. "Where does he work now?" Buck asked, thinking he must have found a better job. He wasn't old enough to retire.

"He's a greeter at Wal-Mart."

"You're kidding me. Why?" Buck stared in amazement.

Nothing short of a catastrophic injury would have forced Oscar to leave Belle Pointe. "Did he have an accident on the job?"

"No accident," Ty said shortly. "Unless you'd call a run-in with Pearce an accident."

"What the hell are you saying, Ty?"

"Maybe you oughta ask Pearce, not me. I'm not exactly unbiased here."

"I'll ask Pearce, damn right, but later. I'm asking you now. What happened?"

"It was picking season last year. Pearce was working the crews long hours, which is nothing unusual. They go in at daylight, they're sometimes there after dark. Lights on those big combines are good as daylight now." He leaned against a contraption designed for torture. "Two things were happening. The price of cotton was falling in the market and it didn't look like Belle Pointe's yield was going to be graded top-notch."

Buck's frown grew darker. "Which is something I warned my mother about a few years ago," he muttered. "Smart planters are cooperating with scientists to develop new seeds, new ways to—" He stopped. "Never mind that. What happened?"

Ty gave him a hard look. "Are you telling me you don't know?"

Buck shrugged. "I haven't paid much attention to the goings-on at Belle Pointe since I left over fifteen years ago, Ty. Just tell me what happened."

"Shit happened," Ty said dryly. "To bump up the profit line for the year, Pearce stopped paying the men overtime. Come in at daylight, work fourteen, sixteen, eighteen hours for regular pay, they were told. My daddy didn't like it, so next thing, they all walked out, shut the place down and—"

"And Oscar was blamed," Buck guessed.

"You got it. Fired him outright the next day and told the rest of them that unless they got their black asses to work they'd be fired, too, that field hands were a dime a dozen in the Delta and he could pick up the phone and have every man-jack of them replaced."

"I'm guessing it worked," Buck said.

"Yeah, it worked. Put down the uprising pretty efficiently and my daddy was the only person not invited back to work as usual."

Buck raked a hand through his sweat-soaked hair. "Jesus, Ty, I never knew a thing about this. You should have called me."

"You said it yourself, Buck. You've been absent from Belle Pointe too many years. The men stopped expecting help from you a long time ago."

Buck winced, but let that pass. "You're saying my mother went along with this all the way?"

Ty's expression was priceless. "Pearce makes a decision and Miz Victoria disputes it publicly? What planet you been livin' on, man?" He straightened up suddenly, slapping his thighs briskly. "Hey, I'm supposed to be listening to your troubles and here I am unloading more shit for you to worry about. Let me get the hell out of here before I think of something else."

"I'm checking into this before the sun sets," Buck told him. "Anne and I are having dinner at Belle Pointe tomorrow night. I don't suppose Pearce has changed his overtime policy for this upcoming season, has he?"

"I don't suppose," Ty said. He put out a hand to hoist Buck to his feet. "You do those exercises I showed you today, five sets, between now and next session, okay?"

"Yeah, okay." Reaching absently for a towel, Buck draped it around his neck. "Funny thing, my mother asked me to help her out this season. With Wainwright gone, I've made a couple of calls trying to replace him, but this puts a different face on it. When she first mentioned it, I didn't think there was anything on the planet that would tempt me to do it...until now."

"I bet you the cost of a new BowFlex that she didn't clear it with your big brother," Ty said.

"I bet you're right." He rubbed the towel over his face, then looked up at Ty. "Speaking of family, how're you settling in? Is Lily okay leaving Memphis?"

"She is now that she knows it's for a good cause." Ty opened a bottle of water for himself. "Saving your rear just might turn out to be a nice opportunity for me. I've been talking to a couple of orthopedic people who'd refer patients if I set up a facility here. Tallulah isn't big enough for a full physical therapy operation, so patients have to travel to Memphis for treatment."

"Who's paying to set up all that expensive equipment?" Buck asked.

"Three guesses," Ty said with a grin. He screwed the cap back on the bottle. "Here's the way I look at it. After I've whipped you into shape, what'll you do with all this equipment?"

"Sell it and get some of my money back?"

"Yeah. To me. For about half what you paid for it. Then I'll move it into this sweet little space I've located near the hospital and be open for business."

"I've created a monster," Buck muttered, holding back a smile. But it would feel good to help Ty set up in business.

Ty began collecting towels. "By the way, where's your

pretty wife? I saw her going into the *Spectator* offices a couple days ago." He looked around the lodge, clearly absent of any sign of a woman. "I don't see anything telling me she's sleeping here."

"She's staying with her daddy."

"Oh, man, that's not good."

"No. It's another thing weighing on my mind." He handed Ty the towel. "I don't know which one will be easier to fix, the situation at Belle Pointe or my marital trouble."

"Get your priorities straight and they'll both be fixed," Ty said.

"How's that?"

"I'll leave it to you to figure out." Ty shrugged into a jacket and scooped up the duffel he used to carry some of his stuff. With his thumb and forefinger crooked like a pistol, he aimed at Buck and said, "I'll see you next time, my man."

"Yeah." With the use of his cane, Buck saw Ty to the door and stood watching thoughtfully as he drove away. It was no surprise that Pearce had a mean streak. No one knew Pearce's dark places better than Buck. But ousting an employee as valuable as Oscar Pittman was stupid as well as mean. Buck leaned back against the door and closed his eyes. If Pearce became a senator, could he be trusted with the power that came with the office?

Eight

"Don't expect anything like a normal family dinner," Buck warned Anne on Sunday night, as they headed for Belle Pointe. "My family is not even close to normal."

"You sound as if I've never met them, Buck. I'll grant you, they're a bit…unusual, but I think I'll be able to cope." In spite of Buck's dire predictions, she felt a thrill of anticipation as she caught sight of the big house through the trees. Its huge white columns were floodlit, standing tall and stark white against a sky darkening with an approaching storm. She didn't have to like the Whitakers to be interested in them, she reminded herself as lightning flashed.

Buck's reply was drowned in a mighty crash of thunder that rocked the SUV. He leaned forward over the wheel to inspect the sky. "Hey, this is perfect. A classic Delta gully washer to welcome us."

She flinched as another fierce flash lit up the world and the heavens suddenly opened with a vengeance. "Oh, my," she murmured, a little awed.

"I'm trying to tell myself the weather isn't a sign of worse to come," Buck muttered as the wipers swished back and forth furiously. "We arrive in a rainstorm, which could only be topped if it's followed by a tornado. With hail. Which, at this time of year, is entirely possible."

She gave him an exasperated look. "If the thought of an evening with your family is so awful, tell me why we're here."

He stopped the SUV before they reached the house and looked at her. "You want the truth? An evening with my family is bad, but I'm willing to tough it out for a chance just to be with you."

She considered that for a beat or two, then reached over with a playful smile and patted his shoulder. "Okay, grumpy. What if I promise to hold your hand all night and run interference for you? Oops, that was a football metaphor, wasn't it?"

One eyebrow shot up as he caught her hand and brought it up to his mouth. "Watch it, lady," he told her, smiling lazily. "We're stuck out here and I can think of several interesting things to do while it's raining. And talking about my family ain't one of 'em."

His mouth was warm and her palm tingled. "Then we'd better not wait. Frankly, I'm dying to go inside the lion's den and get a firsthand look at Whitaker family dynamics. Hopefully, all your relations are here tonight, otherwise, I'll be disappointed."

He gave a humorless grunt, but she could tell his mood had improved. At another wicked flash of lightning, he put the SUV into gear and pulled up to the front door.

Looking worried, Anne said, "If this doesn't let up, I may miss my chance to see anything because we won't be able to get out of the car."

He reached into the pocket behind her seat and produced

an umbrella. "Here, use this. The driveway curves close to the porch steps. I'll pull up so you can get out."

"You're not suggesting I go in without you?"

"Would you?"

"Buck—"

Eyes teasing, he held up a finger. "You'd miss an evening with the Addams family?" he said.

"Judging by your behavior tonight, I'm already married to Lurch."

He laughed. "Just wait for me on the porch and we'll go in together."

Before she could do it for herself, he released her seat belt, then handed her the umbrella. "It springs open when you—"

"I know how to open an umbrella, Buck." She took it and allowed him to reach across her lap to spring the door handle. Then, before she could avoid it, he kissed her, a quick, firm claim of her mouth that made her heart jump. Next, within a heartbeat, he had the door open and if she didn't want to get soaked, she had to pop the umbrella and make a dash for the porch. With the taste of him lingering…

Because Buck and Anne were delayed by the storm, Victoria extended the cocktail hour, which allowed Anne her chance to watch Whitaker family dynamics at play. Buck was wet from a mad dash to the door after parking the car, but even as he attempted to dry himself off, his mother pounced, peppering him with questions. Anne had to admire his skill in fending her off.

After a few minutes, she drifted away from Buck and his mother and was instantly corralled by Pearce's wife. Tucking her hand inside Anne's elbow, Claire steered her toward the baby grand piano in the room. With its top raised, it was a nice shield from the rest of the group. Claire watched as Anne took a sip of cabernet. "You want a refill of that?"

Anne glanced at what remained of her second glass of wine. "No. Thanks. I shouldn't have any more before dinner."

"I find it's the best way to cope." Claire raised her glass and took a hefty drink, letting her gaze drift around the room. "These family occasions can be devilish."

Anne followed her gaze. "I'll admit to being fascinated myself."

Claire's glance rested briefly on Buck standing beside his mother, his gaze fixed on the floor. "I bet fascination isn't what Buck's feeling right now."

Anne agreed, feeling a pang of sympathy for him, but thought better about commenting. "Tell me how it feels to be caught up in a political campaign, Claire," she said, searching for a topic of conversation. It struck her that her sister-in-law's classic blond beauty was a perfect complement to her husband's dark, somewhat wicked good looks. Anne thought they would photograph well as Senator and Mrs. Whitaker. "Are you looking forward to the day when you'll be Mrs. Senator Whitaker?"

"Not particularly."

Anne studied her cool profile. "A life in politics isn't appealing to you?"

"Not as Mrs. Senator Whitaker, no." Her gaze settled on Pearce across the room. "You want to hear something funny? Once I thought about marrying Jack Breedlove," she murmured. "Now, here he is in a dead heat with Pearce for the same political position. Isn't that a hoot?"

Anne coughed on a sip of wine. "Buck mentioned you and Jack had once been sweethearts, but that was in high school, wasn't it?"

She nodded. "About a million years ago."

"Sometimes those first loves can seem so sweet," Anne said. Secretly, she was appalled at Claire's indiscretion. Pearce's opposition would have a field day.

Claire turned to look at her. "Do you speak from experience?"

"About first loves?" Again, Anne's gaze strayed to Buck. "I guess so. Would you believe it? Buck was the first man I ever really loved. I never even had a steady boyfriend in high school. And when I was in college, between my course load and new experiences, I just never fell for anybody…until I met Buck."

Claire studied Anne's face thoughtfully over the rim of her wineglass. "So if he's the love of your life, why am I picking up on some marital stress? Buck's staying at the lodge, you're at your daddy's house. And nobody's talking." Then seeing the look on Anne's face, she hurriedly added, "None of my business, of course, but you're a lucky woman. Buck is a man in a million. Take it from me, you got the pick of the litter." She tossed back more wine and let her gaze drift to Pearce again. "He's nothing like Pearce."

More family discord. What was it about these people that there was so much discontent floating about, Anne wondered. Buck's whole outlook on family was sour and Paige never missed an opportunity to say something nasty. What was it that kept a family so screwed up when they seemed to have so many advantages?

"Speaking of my dear husband, has he made a pitch to you to stump for him on the campaign trail yet?" Claire asked.

"I think I'm safe. I hardly think I have the same clout as Buck."

"Well, that's where you're wrong," Claire said, patting her pocket for her cigarettes. "At least, half wrong. You won't have as much clout as Buck, but you're a pretty woman and a journalist to boot, therefore, an asset. Of course, Pearce will assume you're willing and, because you're family, all your write-ups will be positive. Read that as biased in his favor."

"It's not always an advantage having a journalist in the family. Let's see what he thinks after he reads the piece coming out in next week's *Spectator.*"

"He managed to get the *Spectator* to endorse him?" Claire looked astonished.

"It's not an endorsement. It's a feature article. In fact, I've interviewed both Pearce and Jack Breedlove."

Claire paused, the cigarette unlit in her hand. "How was he?"

"Pearce or Jack?"

"Jack, for God's sake. I haven't seen him in—" She stopped, her smile as sharp as a blade. "I shouldn't be talking about Jack, should I?"

"Probably not. But to answer your question," Anne said, "I was impressed. Jack is a very charming man, decisive and confident."

"Pearce is charming, decisive and confident," Claire said in a dark voice, "but the difference is that on Jack it's sexy, and on Pearce, it's…not."

"Maybe we'd better have some of those hors d'oeuvres," Anne suggested.

With a dry laugh, Claire said, "Meaning I'm drunk, otherwise I wouldn't say stuff like that?" Deciding against a cigarette, she signaled Miriam, Belle Pointe's longtime housekeeper, for more wine. "No, sugar, I'm not drunk, just depressed."

Miriam refilled Claire's wineglass, while Anne refused. "I spent some time with Paige this week at the *Spectator,*" Anne said. "She's creative and very precocious, but I'm sure you know that."

"Creative and precocious." Claire looked away toward a window, her gaze resting on the storm raging outside. "Is that a tactful way of expressing shock and awe?"

"Because of her Goth look? Not at all, although it is rather dramatic. No, I meant she's quick and funny and unique."

Claire leaned against the piano. "At least you recognized her outfit as a look. Dressed like that, she could be practicing to become the town coroner or at best angling to be public relations director at Knopf's Funeral Home."

"Is that what you think?"

Claire shook her head. "No, I think she's rebellious and creative and frankly, a little too smart for her own good."

Because that was essentially Anne's opinion of Paige, Claire went up a notch in her estimation. "Sounds like a daughter anybody would want. I know I would."

Claire's lips twisted in a rueful smile. "Yeah, I love her to pieces, not that she would believe it lately. I'm the Number Two Demon in her life. Her grandmama, of course, is Number One. At this point, I'm not sure where Pearce ranks."

"Age fourteen," Anne said, sighing in recollection. "It's painful."

"And she wouldn't believe this either, but I wish I'd had the guts when I was her age to do some of the stuff she does...and says." Claire glanced at the door. "You notice she's not here? Victoria gives strict orders that all members of the family attend these Sunday dinners, but Paige just loves jerking her chain. She'll probably be here, but in her own time…and she'll make an appearance with all the drama of a rock star! It's enough to drive me crazy."

If only. Anne looked down at her empty wineglass, wondering if she'd ever have a teenager. Even with the trials and tribulations that plagued Claire, she'd volunteer in a heartbeat.

"I remember thinking of my mama as a demon, too," Claire murmured, focusing again on the storm-lashed windows. Anne wondered, by the look on her face, if she was remembering her star-crossed relationship with Jack Breedlove. Whatever her thought, Claire blinked it away with a little shake of her head. "But I don't want to be seen that way by Paige. I'd like for her to think of me the way she thinks of Beady, but it's not likely to happen."

"Beady?"

"Beatrice, your stepmother." Seeing her surprise, Claire said, "She's practically a surrogate grandmother to Paige and has been ever since she was a little girl in Beatrice's Sunday School class. The woman is a saint to put up with her with so much grace and patience."

"I didn't realize they were friends." Anne frowned, thinking back. "I don't recall seeing Paige at the wedding. Why is that?"

"Spring break. We were skiing in Colorado. The trip had been planned for months, otherwise, nothing could have kept Paige away." Claire finished off her wine and set the glass on a small table just as a loud clap of thunder shook the house and a wind gust rattled the windows. "I hope Paige hasn't gotten it into her head to go out in this," she said, glancing at her watch. "I left her sitting in front of a mirror putting on that bizarre makeup. I'll wring her neck if she doesn't show up soon."

Miriam again appeared silently with a fresh glass of wine on her silver tray. Claire took it, smiled her thanks. "To hell with Victoria. I'm smoking."

Once the cigarette was lit, she opened the piano bench and found a tiny crystal ashtray. "I told Victoria that the reason Paige's grades went to hell in a handbasket was because she missed Beady so much. Before she met Franklin, Beady spent a lot more time with Paige. She'd take her shopping in Memphis, they'd go to the horse races in Little Rock, they'd go to the beach in Florida. When she went to Disney World the first time, it was with Beady. I swear those two are soul mates."

Once the cigarette was lit, she exhaled, blowing the smoke away from Anne. "It was great for Beady that she fell in love, but it was a major adjustment for Paige."

"Are you serious?" Anne asked in dismay.

"Well, I'm probably exaggerating a little, but whatever, it worked. When Beady saw how Paige screwed up, she stepped right in and arranged the 'punishment' at the *Spectator*." Claire made quotation marks with her fingers. "Paige acts like she hates it, but it's an act. Poking around in those old newspapers isn't nearly the trial she makes it out to be. She's always coming home and dropping some obscure fact about Tallulah's past."

"With five generations of her family in Tallulah's past, there is a lot for her to uncover. Actually, I'm looking forward to poking around in the archives, too."

Claire stared at her through a smoky haze. "Why, for God's sake?"

"Why not? I'm here for a while and when I'm not report-ing, I have the time." She smiled. "Let's face it, not a lot goes on here in Tallulah that's worth writing about."

"You're telling me." Claire tilted her head, thinking. "And I'd give my eyeteeth to do like Buck and shake the dust of the place off my feet forever."

"On the other hand, what if you had no roots at all?"

"Uh-oh." Something caught Claire's eye beyond Anne's shoulder. She groaned and ground out her cigarette in the tiny ashtray. "It's Paige, ready to make her entrance."

As soon as Buck got away from his mother, Pearce cor-nered him. "Where the hell have you been?" he demanded, drawing him apart from the group. "Man, you come into Tal-lulah under cover of night, not telling a soul and then you dis-appear. I've been all over this county looking for you. And while I'm thinking about it, before you leave I want your cell phone number."

"I'm at the lodge." Buck glanced across the room looking for Anne and was glad to see her talking to Claire instead of his mother. No matter that he was damp and soggy and that he felt hounded on all sides, it was worth it to spend an eve-ning with his wife.

"You think I didn't try the lodge?" Pearce replied. "That was my second stop…after your in-law's house. So unless you were under the porch steps or hiding in the azaleas, I couldn't find you there either."

"I don't answer the phone or the door when I'm with my trainer."

"Humph. And what's the big idea not staying at the Marshes' with Anne?"

He stared directly into Pearce's eyes. "It's a privacy issue."

After a beat or two, Pearce said, "Yeah, so how's that knee, man? I hear you're out for the season."

Buck nodded. "It may take a while to get back to a hundred percent."

"Rotten luck." Pearce studied his face, trying to read something he sensed. "Word is you've hired Tyrone Pittman."

Buck gave a short laugh. "I see the ol' grapevine is still dependable."

"Hard to keep a secret around here." Pearce glanced over his shoulder and moved a little closer. "Guess who I ran into yesterday at the Piggly Wiggly?"

"I don't have a clue."

"Bert Atkinson."

Buck looked at him blankly. "I don't know him."

"Yeah, you do. He's a few years older than you, but if you see him, you'll remember him. Went to law school with me at Ole Miss, but he's a Memphis State man, I think." He shook his head, giving up. "Anyway, here's why I mention it. He's Jack Breedlove's campaign manager."

Buck saw Miriam heading their way with a tray holding the drink he'd requested. "I've seen the signs around town."

Pearce cocked his head, eyeing Buck thoughtfully. "I don't know how you've managed to be all over town, checking out my competition, talking to Mama, cozying up to Tyrone Pittman and somehow or other I don't rate a measly phone call."

"Thanks, Miriam." He took the Coke and raised the glass in a silent salute to Pearce. "I've been busy."

"What's that you're drinking?" Pearce asked, making a face.

"Coca-Cola," Buck said, letting his gaze drift around the

room. Claire was entertaining Anne, which meant she didn't need rescuing yet.

"What the hell?"

"I'm off alcohol for a while."

"Huh." Pearce mulled that over half a minute. "Cleaning up your act, right?"

Buck's reply was a shrug, a brief lift of one shoulder.

"I hear you." He studied the straight Scotch in his hand. "I probably should cut back while I'm campaigning."

"Speaking of…how's it going, Pearce?"

"The campaign? It's going, but like anybody in politics today, I need money and good people working for me." He paused, still eyeing Buck shrewdly. "I know you and Jack Breedlove go way back. I'm not going to have a problem with that, am I?"

"I haven't heard from Jack since I've been here. He probably knows I'm not a political animal." Where's a distraction when you need it, Buck wondered.

"You don't have to be a political animal to do either one of us good and you know it. I'd just like to know where you stand."

"If that means you want me to get out and go glad-handing and kissing babies for you, I'd have to say not in this lifetime. But I wish you luck, Pearce."

Pearce studied him over the rim of his drink. "You mean that?"

"Why would I wish you anything else?" Buck noticed that Anne was still talking to Claire. His sister-in-law had a brittle look about her, reminding him of Victoria's disapproval. He wondered if being married to Pearce was as wearing as being his kid brother.

Pearce was talking again. "I mentioned Bert Atkinson because he couldn't wait to tell me not to count on your endorsement carrying enough weight with the voters to make a difference in the election."

"He was right. You shouldn't underestimate the voter."

"He was dead wrong," Pearce countered with a look of disgust. "He knows just how big a difference it'll make and he was ready to choke on the possibility." He set his empty glass on a table nearby. "Which is the reason I've been trying to find you all over this freaking town, Buck. Mama tells me you're here for the duration."

Buck finished his drink and looked around for a place to put it. He wasn't willing to chance setting it on one of Victoria's priceless antique tables as Pearce had done. His mother would be on him like a chicken on a June bug. "I know where you're going, Pearce. Save the pitch."

"What other plan do you have until that knee is fixed?"

"My life is baseball, not politics. I'm concentrating on getting back in shape while I'm here. I can't do anything to screw that up, which means I can't be out making personal appearances with you."

"Hey…" Pearce gave him a playful punch on the shoulder. "I know that, bro. But I need you to be openly supportive, you know? And when you're out and about, I need you to make positive statements about me, lie a little. Hell, lie a lot. It's what happens in politics. Your name is golden here, Bucko. You want to see your brother in the U.S. Senate, don't you?"

Buck caught Miriam in passing and set the glass on her tray. "I thought you were running for the state senate."

"Yeah, in this particular campaign." Pearce grinned and

winked. "But look out. Another couple of terms and I'm set to head for Washington."

Buck studied him for a moment. "Does Mother know this?"

Pearce heaved a sigh. He took Buck's arm and urged him over to a window well out of earshot of anybody. "If she did, she'd shit a brick, I don't have to tell you that."

"Yeah. And here I was having trouble believing she'd let you go off to Jackson," Buck said. "If she thought D. C. was your ultimate goal, she would probably be making contributions to Jack Breedlove."

"Which is why we aren't going to tell her, right?"

"It's a big hurdle for you to overcome, Pearce. She believes you should put Belle Pointe and your responsibilities here before anything else."

Pearce let out a hiss of frustration. "Yeah, and yet she wants to run things. It's her way or else. I try to tell her that we don't need to be so hands-on. We don't need to be hanging out with the hired help from daylight to dark. That's why we have hired help, for God's sake. But does she listen? No."

"She runs a tight ship."

"Tell me," he muttered with a twist of his mouth. "I don't have a clue how to operate a combine, Buck, and I don't care. You were the one who learned cotton farming from the bottom up. You were the one who was interested, for Chrissake! I never liked any part of it. But no…" He whacked his fist in his palm. "She wants me right here so she can continue to boss me around like a slave while she plays the chatelaine of Belle Pointe."

"She is the chatelaine of Belle Pointe."

"Big deal." He swore softly. "I'm tired of the stranglehold she has on my life. Sure, being born a Whitaker and living at Belle Pointe are definite assets. The Southern aristocrat role plays well with voters." He looked Buck keenly in the eye. "Do you realize how that stuff impresses people? It's a pain in the ass to me, but to other folks, the Delta and the whole mystique of plantation life, all this antebellum shit, it's irresistible…in a political sense. You know what I mean?"

"Tell me something, Pearce," Buck said, looking him in the eye. "If Mother has such a stranglehold on you and she makes all the decisions around here, how is it that she allowed you to fire Oscar Pittman?"

Pearce swore and rolled his eyes. "I see Ty's been talking. Got your ear while he's massaging that knee, so he's making hay while the sun shines, eh?"

"It was a low-down, dirty trick, Pearce. Oscar has been at Belle Pointe since we were boys. What were you thinking, firing a man like that?"

"He's a troublemaker, always stirring up shit. We don't need his type around."

"With Will gone, seems to me you need him more than ever."

"They can both be replaced. It'll just take some time. I'm working on it."

"In the meantime, I guess you're prepared to operate a combine and manage the hired help while campaigning," Buck said. He watched as Pearce tried to curb his temper, then lowered his voice and said very quietly, "I'm going to make it right with Oscar, Pearce. I'm going to see to it personally."

Pearce's dark eyes flared with temper, but he was prevented unleashing it when he spotted someone over Buck's shoulder. Instantly, anger morphed into a practiced smile. "Hey, here's somebody else you've been dodging. Joel, say hello to my brother, the town hero."

Buck turned, recognizing Joel Tanner. For as long as he could remember, Tanner had been the sole legal representative for the Whitaker family. "Joel, good to see you," he said, putting out his hand.

"Same here, Buck. You're looking good considering the garbage I'm hearing from the media."

"Don't believe everything you hear," Buck told him. Tanner was an older man with a distinguished look and keen blue eyes. "How're things with you these days?"

"Good. Better than good."

"Damn right," Pearce said jovially. "Joel's my campaign manager. We're headed for victory in November."

Buck managed to look interested. "No joke."

"Politics is nothing to joke about," Pearce said, then turned to Tanner. "So tell Buck how much we need him to take an active part in the campaign, Joel."

"Your endorsement would be helpful," Tanner said, looking hopeful.

Buck gave a noncommittal smile. Campaigning for Pearce was a non-starter, but he hadn't totally ruled out the possibility of endorsing him. He just wasn't sure yet that he wanted to and the incident with Otis Pittman didn't help. It told him his brother was still a ruthless SOB.

But it wasn't something he wanted to deal with tonight. He located Anne across the room talking to his niece, who had just made an appearance. He did a double take when he saw her all-black getup. Jesus, the kid was dressed like a mortician. He looked again. A mortician with orange hair.

"I see someone I need to hug," he told them and headed over to get a closer look. After tonight, it would be interesting to get Anne's take on his family.

Nine

Claire knew her daughter well, Anne thought. Paige, decked out in full Goth costume complete with wacky orange hair and bizarre makeup, had paused like a young Scarlett O'Hara midway on the stairs. Ignoring Victoria's disapproving scowl, she descended and strolled into the room with all the panache of a movie star.

Claire caught Anne's strangled laugh. "Whatever you do," she muttered, stubbing out her cigarette, "don't let her know you think she's cute."

Paige had foregone the clunky boots, Anne noted with amusement, and the long coat had been replaced with a long black leather vest over a black turtleneck and black jeans. Riding low over her flat tummy was a belt—black with silver studs. Where did she get the stuff, Anne wondered. It seemed unlikely that Tallulah would have a store catering to a fringe element of any kind.

But the little kid who still admired her sports hero uncle was somewhere underneath all that adolescent blackness. On seeing Buck, her eyes gave away her surprised joy. But surprise and joy were majorly uncool emotions, so her face quickly went deadpan.

Buck, mastering his astonishment, now abruptly left Pearce and the family lawyer and moseyed across the room. "Paige! It is Paige, isn't it?" he teased, greeting his niece with a big hug.

"I thought you said he wasn't going to come to Tallulah," Paige complained to Anne.

"I surprised her." Buck angled back while holding Paige's arms and giving her an exaggerated once-over. "I was missing my wife too much to stay in St. Louis without her." Then he glanced at his watch. "I thought this was a party, not a funeral. What time is the wake?"

Although Paige tossed her head with a sulky look, she had trouble hiding a smile. "I guess you're going to be like everybody else and try to cut me down about the way I dress."

"Well, just let me say this…" Buck lifted a strand of her neon-tinted hair, uncovering the row of studs in her ears. "I know a guy in St. Louis who owns a business salvaging scrap metal. He'll give you a good price for all this stainless steel."

In spite of herself, Paige giggled. "What about the ring in my navel?"

Buck's face showed mock horror. "You're kidding, right?"

"Uh-uh," she said with a gleam in her eyes. "And that's not the only place I'm pierced." She watched him clutch melodramatically at his chest, enjoying herself before adding, "But it's the only place I'm pierced that I can discuss…around here." She shot a wicked glance across the room at her grandmother.

"Paige, that's enough!" Victoria stood rigidly with her hand resting on the back of an elegant Queen Anne chair and frowned at Buck. "Do not encourage her, Buck. Her behavior is already a disgrace…as well as her style of dress. She does not have any piercing on her body." Victoria paused, giving Claire a stern look as she tapped ashes into the small crystal dish she held in one hand. "At least, I assume you haven't allowed any other atrocities, Claire."

"I didn't 'allow' the piercings she has now," Claire replied, drawing deeply on her cigarette. "You try keeping a fourteen-year-old from doing anything outrageous and if it works, tell me your secret. Short of tying her to the bedpost 24/7, I don't know how else it could be done."

"I have asked you countless times not to smoke in my house," Victoria snapped. "Go outside if you can't discipline yourself to give it up altogether."

With an ironic twist of her mouth, Claire's gaze went to the windows where rain still lashed at the panes and thunder rumbled. "Being struck by lightning is one way to quit, I guess," she said. But she ground the cigarette out in the crystal dish.

"I'll get rid of all my piercings," Paige said slyly, "when Claire quits smoking."

"Do not refer to your mother by her given name," Victoria ordered. Again, her disapproval settled on Claire. "Have you lost complete control of this incorrigible child?"

"I am not out of control, Gran," Paige said in a bored tone. She began ticking points off her fingers. "I'm not, like, doing drugs, I'm good in math, plus I floss every day and I'm not pregnant. In some families, I would be considered a model child."

Claire sighed. "Paige, please. You're just making things worse."

"How could they be worse?" Making wide eyes, Paige

poked one finger into her cheek as if thinking. "Oh, yeah. They could be worse if the bottom fell out of the cotton market and Jack Breedlove beat Daddy in the election."

"Paige," Pearce barked, finally noticing his daughter. "Knock it off!"

"It's a free country," Paige sassed, unfazed by his threat. "Or doesn't the Constitution apply here at Belle Pointe?"

Anne looked at the adults in the room, expecting someone to speak up before the evening spun totally out of control. To her relief, it was Buck.

"C'mon, brat," he said suddenly, catching Paige by the nape of the neck. "Let's go eat. Another round and you're gonna be in really hot water. Is dinner ready?" he asked his mother over his shoulder as he headed to the dining room. "I can't be the only one starving."

Buck's intervention wasn't any too soon, but Anne wondered why Victoria hadn't stepped in earlier to defuse the hostile situation. Still, she gave the signal to Miriam to start serving and everyone moved into the dining room.

It was at the table with Buck's family when Anne decided with a sigh that her wish for a better understanding of Buck's family was coming true…in spades.

Be careful what you wish for.

The conversation bounced from politics to Tallulah gossip to movies and books, to the demands of the planting season. Victoria, at the head of the table, was very much in charge. Pearce and Joel Tanner, the only person Anne had never met before tonight, concentrated on luring Buck into the campaign. Claire, she observed, kept her wineglass close at hand and was mute, for the most part. Very different from the chatty person she'd been earlier with Anne. It was as if she'd suddenly assumed another personality, the role of the quintessential politician's wife when Anne knew she was almost apolitical. And that she admired Pearce's opponent more than her husband.

Anne was taken by surprise when Victoria suddenly addressed her directly. "How does it feel to be a working journalist again, Anne?"

"I love it. There's not a lot of excitement in Tallulah, but I'm keeping busy."

Pearce looked up, breaking off a conversation with Joel. "When's my article coming out?"

"In this next week's issue." She didn't want him questioning her about it before it appeared in the press. "Meanwhile, I'm just poking around in the archives since it seems a good time to bone up on the history of Tallulah."

"Be still my heart," Paige muttered sarcastically.

"And I'm bound to find many references to the Whitakers," Anne said with a smile. Then, mostly to tease Paige, she added jokingly, "So if you've got any shocking family secrets, look out."

"There are secrets in every family," Victoria said quietly. "Pearce, would you please begin carving the roast? Miriam, we'll need another basket of rolls, please. See that they're warm."

"Yes, ma'am." It was a whisper from Miriam, the first sound Anne had heard the woman make all evening. Pearce rose obediently and began carving the roast. Anne met Buck's eyes and found him looking at her with an enigmatic expression. She thought nobody had picked up on Victoria's intriguing remark until Paige spoke.

"If I'd known there were Whitaker family secrets," she said, munching on a slice of cucumber, "I would've been looking harder. For about three weeks, I've been unloading a ton of stuff in boxes that came to Mr. Marsh from an old professor who died. So far, no secrets, only boring stuff about when Yankees came to Mississippi in the sixties and started stirring up black people."

"Yeah," Buck said, giving her a tolerant smile. "What were those folks thinking trying to give a black man the right to vote?"

"Well, I know it wasn't really stupid," Paige said, stung. "But it happened so long ago that it's hard to find anything fascinating about it now."

"I guess you'd have to be black," Buck said, still teasing her.

"Okay, Uncle Buck, I get it. I get it." She grinned. "Now, hold your breath because this is really riveting. It happened, like way before I was born. Some guy was arrested for operating a still out on Old Tucker Road and he was fined a hundred dollars."

"What happened to his merchandise?" Buck asked, deadpan.

Pearce snickered. "You can bet it wasn't busted up, not in that part of the county."

"I mean, it's just so not interesting," Paige said plaintively.

"Maybe not to you," Anne said, "but you're bound to find a lot of material relating to the Whitakers. They're a prominent family and they've been here for five generations."

"Hey, you may find the original source of the Whitaker's money," Buck drawled, twirling a water goblet. "Could be that guy operating the still was one of our ancestors."

Paige grinned. "My great-great-grandfather could have been a bootlegger. I love it."

Victoria sighed. "If you're finished, Paige, you may be excused."

"I haven't had dessert." Paige tipped her head to one side, studying Anne. "Were you really serious about writing a book?"

Victoria gave Anne a keen look. "You're writing a book?"

"I haven't decided definitely to do anything so ambitious, but I find the culture of the Delta pretty unique and even though Tallulah is small, history placed it in the center of things when a lot was happening."

"I get it," Claire said, slurring her words a bit. "You see Tallulah as a little Peyton Place, complete with scandals and secrets."

"No, not even close." Anne smiled. "But my journalism background probably does make me curious about…things. And since the paper has been in existence in one form or another since the Civil War, it'll be like a treasure hunt to sniff it out." She sent another smile across the table to Paige. "You're welcome to join me, Paige. You might learn a few things you don't know. And you might find yourself interested."

"Don't I wish," the teenager said, pushing green peas around on her plate. "But if I could discover interesting secrets, like a murder or a rape, now that would be interesting."

"Paige," Victoria snapped. "One more vulgar remark and you leave the table."

Paige gave an exaggerated sigh, rolling her eyes. "I can't believe you're poking around down there because you like it, Aunt Anne," she said.

"Blame it on my dad," Anne said, playing with a spear of asparagus. "I was telling Claire before dinner how Dad talked so much about Tallulah and the Delta when I was growing up, so I guess some of his obsession must have rubbed off on me."

"Everyone was amazed when Franklin moved here and purchased the *Spectator*," Victoria said.

"Including me," Anne said. "And I was even more amazed when he announced he'd met a nice lady and was going to marry her."

"Aunt Beady," Paige said, cutting a sly glance toward her grandmother. "Gran about had a kitten she was so surprised."

"What a ridiculous thing to say, Paige," Victoria said irritably. "It isn't true."

"I'd like some more wine," Claire said, looking around for Miriam.

Paige frowned at her mother. "You don't need any more wine, Mom."

"I didn't say I needed it, just that I'd like it," Claire said.

"It's a major advantage to have you working at the *Spectator*," Pearce said to Anne. "I've been hoping to get Franklin onboard in my campaign. With a positive article coming out this week and an endorsement from Buck, Breedlove will be toast from the get-go."

"Dream on," Claire murmured, motioning to Miriam, who circled the table with a newly uncorked bottle of wine.

Pearce gave her a hard look. "Excuse me?"

"I said, dream on," Claire repeated, enunciating clearly. "Which is what an endorsement of your campaign from Buck or Franklin Marsh is…a dream. A fantasy, my dear hubby."

"Our daughter's right, Claire. You've had too much wine."

"Whatever it takes." With a tipsy smile, Claire raised her refilled wineglass high. "Here's a flash, Pearce. The only way Franklin Marsh would stoop to anything as tacky as a political endorsement of you in the *Spectator* is if you figure out a way to apply a little pressure. Unfortunately for you, I can't see Franklin knuckling under the way everybody else does in this county when you put the pressure on."

Pearce glared at her. "You're drunk, Claire. Which means you stopped making sense about two hours ago."

Anne glanced uneasily at Buck, who sat stony-faced, still twirling his wineglass by its stem. Was anybody going to speak up before open warfare broke out? She gave a little start when Victoria suddenly struck the side of her glass with a spoon.

"It's time for dessert, Miriam."

"Yes, ma'am."

"I need more wine, Miriam," Claire complained.

"You won't get it," Pearce snarled, seething. "If you're angling to have me slap your ass in a rehab facility, just keep this up, Claire. You make the argument for me."

"That is enough!" Victoria repeated sharply. "I won't tolerate having dinner deteriorate into a crude sideshow. Claire, Pearce is correct," she said sternly. "You've had too much wine. If you can't control yourself, please leave the table."

Claire turned to Anne defiantly. "Anne, tell them I'm right that your daddy won't get involved in a sleazy political campaign."

"Here now," Joel Tanner said, taking the entire table by surprise. "I'm afraid I have to take exception to that," he said, using his courtroom voice. "There's nothing sleazy about Pearce's campaign."

"Oh, please…" Claire said with disgust.

"I don't know anything about my father's position on political issues," Anne said quietly. "Just as he had no input into the article I wrote. You will have to speak to him personally."

"You could work on him," Pearce persisted. "Remind him we're family. He'll listen if you push it."

Suddenly, Paige pushed back in her chair. "Leave her alone!" she shrieked. "And my mother, too!" With her arms straight at her sides, she glared at their astonished faces. "What is the matter with all of you? It's no mystery to me why Uncle Buck and Anne don't ever want to come here. It's because we're so weird. So mean to each other. So *screwed up!* If I had anywhere else to go, I wouldn't be here!" She threw her napkin on the table in disgust. "I'm just sorry I don't have a car or I'd take off right now!"

"Sit down, Paige!" Pearce roared.

Claire made a motion to stand up. "Paige—"

"I don't want to hear it, Mom!" Paige cried, her hands over her ears. "You don't make any sense when you're drunk. Don't worry, Dad. I'm going." Eyes brimming, Paige surveyed the faces of the adults at the table. "We're supposed to be a family here, people. Instead, it's like we're inmates at a halfway house full of crazies and we just live together because we have to." She dashed tears from her eyes. "Well, I don't care if I'm grounded for a month, or if I have to work another ten years at Mr. Marsh's newspaper for punishment, I'm leaving even if it's raining up a hurricane outside!" Whirling about, she ran out of the room.

In the shocked silence, Anne looked around, expecting someone—Claire, Pearce, Victoria, someone—to go after her, but Claire's face was buried in her hands. Pearce was white with rage and Victoria wore a chilly mask of disapproval. Anne looked at Buck and something in his face made her rise to her feet. "Excuse me, please," she murmured.

She hurried out of the dining room, heading in the direction that Paige had taken. She went first to the living room, but found it quiet and empty. The curving staircase was visible from the dining room, so she knew Paige hadn't gone upstairs. That left only one place.

She moved to the front door, opened it and looked out. Rain still came down, but the worst of the storm, it seemed, had passed. She hoped so, as Paige stood on the porch looking as if it wouldn't take much for her to dash out into it.

Something about the slump of the teenager's shoulders and the utter misery on her face caught at Anne's heart. After the scene at the table, she sympathized with Paige wholeheartedly. Stepping out of the house, she closed the door behind her. "Mind if I join you?"

With a shrug, Paige used both hands to wipe tears from her cheeks. "You probably need fresh air after all that."

Anne raised her gaze where rain dripped from the eaves. "There's not much fresh air out here, but if we stay in this spot, we'll get wet."

"I'm not going back inside," Paige told her stubbornly.

"Well, could we move over there? I'm already soggy after dashing from the car to the house." Not hearing a flat refusal, she slipped an arm around the girl's waist and urged her away and around the corner of the porch. "Now, isn't that better?"

Paige sniffed. "I guess." After a minute, she added, "You wanted to get to know the Whitakers so now that you've had a good look, I bet you can't wait to leave."

Anne chuckled. "Hey, you know how we reporters are. We don't back off from a story easily."

"You're just being nice. It was awful, Aunt Anne. Tell the truth!"

"I admit it was pretty dicey there once or twice, especially looking at it from your point of view. But mostly, I found it…interesting."

"To me, it was just plain horrible! Dreadful. It always is. My mother always gets drunk and Dad always gets mean. And Gran sits there like the queen of nice. I can't stand it!" She burst into tears again, hiccupping with the effort to talk. "I h-hate my life and this house and I hate that m-my mom is so wimpy and won't s-stand up for herself. If she doesn't get some g-guts, Dad really will send her off to rehab."

"Here." Anne offered the table napkin she'd brought with her, waiting while Paige wiped at her tears. Rehab might be the best thing for Claire, but now was not the time to say it, nor was Anne the right person to say it. When the girl had calmed a little, she said, "I wish I could think of something wise and wonderful to make you feel better, Paige, but I'm fresh out of advice."

"It's gonna take more than advice," Paige said flatly. "Like it'll take a miracle to fix all that's wrong in this house." She looked down at the napkin in her hands, then up into Anne's eyes. "You want to hear something funny? The Dragon is always telling me how to act, how to look, always nagging me about my manners and the way I talk and what people will think. Her big thing is that above everything I have to remember that I'm a Whitaker as if that's some kind of special honor or something." As she dashed tears from her eyes, her mouth twisted bitterly. "Well, I bet if somebody like Aunt Beady or your dad saw what happens around here, they wouldn't think we're special at all. They'd think we were white trash!"

Anne felt out of her depth. The girl's anger was scary. Kids did reckless things in the grip of rage. "Have you tried to talk to your mother? Or to your grandmother? Have you told them how you feel?"

"Are you kidding? Talk to my grandmother? It would be like talking to an android. Sometimes I wonder if she has blood in her veins like other people. And my mother is hopeless. Just hopeless."

Anne reached up and smoothed a strand of the girl's preposterously tinted hair. "Nobody's hopeless, Paige. I know your mother loves you and worries about you."

"Yeah? Well, she sure has a crazy way of showing it." Paige swiped at her nose and then used the napkin to blow. "Tonight, when I realized that Uncle Buck was here, I was so thrilled. You read about him all the time doing things for people, helping sick children, being like a real live hero. I used to dream that he'd come home to Belle Pointe and fix things." She folded and refolded the napkin, then looked up into Anne's eyes. "That's why it hurt so much that he didn't say something tonight. Why didn't he stand up and say something to stop my parents from tearing each other to pieces?"

Anne put an arm around the girl's shoulders. "I don't have answers for you, Paige, but I do know this. Buck can't fix what's making you so unhappy with your family. He's been gone from Belle Pointe too long."

"But I'm here now."

Anne turned to find Buck standing in the shadows. After a second, he moved forward, reaching out to Paige. "I'm sorry, kid. I let you down, didn't I?"

With her eyes swimming in tears, Paige scrambled out of his reach. "Hey, don't apologize," she said, looking at him with scorn. "It's nothing to you what happens here. It was dumb of me to even think it."

Buck took a step, intending to touch her.

"Don't you even," she said to him hotly. As she backed

away, it was to Anne that she spoke. "If he really cared, he would come here more than once every three years!"

With a smothered cry, she dodged Buck's attempt to catch her by ducking around a chair, then swept past them in a dash for the front door. Without looking back, she rushed inside and slammed the door hard behind her.

Buck muttered an oath and moved as if to follow, but Anne stopped him. "Let her go." She sensed the turmoil inside him, but the moment when he might have helped Paige was over. Shivering, Anne wrapped her arms around herself.

Buck turned and pulled her close. "Come on, I'll take you home."

It took but a few minutes to say their goodbyes and make a dash in the now drizzling rain to the SUV. Both were more than ready to leave and neither said much as Buck drove away from the big house and headed out Belle Pointe Lane toward the highway.

"You look shell-shocked."

"What?" Anne turned from her study of the SUV's busy windshield wipers. Buck was hunched behind the wheel, waiting to enter traffic.

"Don't say I didn't warn you," he said, staring straight ahead. "Warm and fuzzy, the Whitakers ain't."

"No, but it wasn't so obvious in the few times we visited before. Was it?" She thought not. Or maybe their visits had been so brief that his folks had been on their best behavior. "I already had a pretty good fix on Pearce from interviewing him, and Paige has been fairly blunt describing life at Belle Pointe. There was just so much…hostility."

"Pressure, I guess." Seeing a chance to pull out onto the

highway, Buck took it. "Pearce is caught up in his campaign and whether he admits it or not, he doesn't have the election sewed up, so the stress is building. And here's my mother facing a planting season without help. And Claire—" He stopped. "What the hell is going on with Claire?"

"You've known her a lot longer than I have," Anne said, unwilling to mention Claire's fixation on Jack Breedlove. "What do you think?"

"I think living with Pearce would make anybody drink too much." They drove in silence for a couple of miles, both thinking. "Hell, it's no wonder Paige went ballistic," he said.

"She's the one to be concerned about. She's so angry and frightened, Buck. That's what her bizarre look is about—the black clothes, the orange hair, the body piercings, the tattoos. She's saying, look at me. It's just a matter of time before she does something more reckless and crazy than dyeing her hair or piercing her ears."

By the time she was done, he'd pulled into the Marshes' driveway and stopped. "Tattoos?" he repeated.

"You don't want to know."

"Jesus."

They sat for a moment without making a move to leave, both caught up in their own thoughts. It struck Anne that they were more in tune tonight than they'd been in a long time. In spite of the chaos that reigned at Belle Pointe, she and Buck had somehow drawn closer. Maybe leaving their way of life behind in St. Louis, even temporarily, had been a good thing. Sad that losing her baby had been the motivation for leaving.

With a sigh, Anne reached down and unfastened her seat belt. "It's late. I need to go inside."

Before he could stop her, she'd opened the door and was

out of the SUV. Hampered by his cane, it took a minute to meet up with her on the sidewalk. "I'd ask you to come back to the lodge with me, but I don't think I can take any more pain tonight," he said, keeping it light. Taking a chance anyway, he wrapped his free arm around her and turned his face into her hair. "Damn, you smell good."

"Not smoky?" She slowed her steps to accommodate his shuffle with the cane. "Claire must have smoked half a dozen cigarettes while we talked. I thought I'd have to take a shower before going to bed."

He groaned, pulling her even closer. "Don't mention getting naked or going to bed unless you're inviting me in."

For a moment, she let herself enjoy the feel of Buck's strong, hard body pressed to hers. The scent of him was familiar and arousing. She was too honest to deny that. And it would be so easy to just unlock the door and take him straight to the guest room. Neither her dad nor Beatrice would blink an eye. In fact, she thought they were both secretly sympathetic to Buck. On that thought, she wiggled free and began rooting through her purse for a key.

Buck, giving up gracefully, propped himself against a small square column while she searched. "Have you rented a car yet?"

"No, I probably should, but Beatrice has been so generous about letting me use hers that I just haven't gotten around to it."

"I'll get you one tomorrow."

"Buck—"

His mouth set stubbornly. "You need your own wheels. Beatrice is nice to lend hers, but she's running a business, babe. It's an imposition, not that she'd ever tell you that in a million years."

He was right, of course. She'd thought the same thing a dozen times. "Okay, okay. I'll take care of it tomorrow."

"Let me do it for you, Anne."

She had the key out now. "What, you think renting a car is a guy thing? No, Buck, I'll go to the rental agency and pick it out myself," she told him firmly.

"I don't think it's a guy thing. But you're not in St. Louis now," he said patiently. "This is Tallulah. There's not even a car rental agency here. Do you want to take the time away from your job to locate one? C'mon, let me do this for my wife."

After a beat or two, she gave him a reluctant smile. "Okay, now that you put it that way. Thank you."

"You're welcome. More than welcome." He touched her face. "I miss you. I want to take care of you. I'd like to have you at the lodge where I can see you every day. And every night…"

He brushed his thumb over her cheek and then over her lips. Anne felt a little rush of desire…again. A part of her thought briefly about backing away and scooting inside. But now he was tipping her chin up and his lips were so close that she could almost taste him already. So she let her eyes close and her lips part. And welcomed his kiss.

All Buck's instincts urged him to take the kiss deeper and he was helpless to resist. He pulled her into a full embrace, pushed his sex against hers. Damn it, she needed to be reminded how it was between them. How it could be again. He heard the rush of her breath and let his fingers glide down the line of her throat…and then drop to her breasts. God, soft and warm and womanly. And his. Maybe communication was a problem in their relationship, but sex definitely wasn't, he thought with satisfaction.

He broke the kiss and spoke in her ear, "Let's go to the lodge," he said hoarsely.

"Oh, God, I didn't mean that to happen." She pushed with both hands on his biceps and stepped back. "I'm sorry, Buck."

He heard the breathy sound in her voice and he could tell she was tempted. Maybe if he pushed… But no, the next move had to be hers, he thought. When they came together, it would be because Anne was ready, not because he hustled her with sex. Even though he was hot and throbbing and ready. God, was he ready.

It took every ounce of control he could muster to nod and let her go.

Without looking at him, she ducked inside. And then, just before the door closed, she paused and raised her eyes to his. "Just one more thing…"

"Yeah?" Curt and one beat short of rude.

"I think—" Anne cleared her throat, knowing he had a right to be ticked off. "I meant to say this before, but—anyway, I think you should take your mother up on her offer to help with the planting season while you're here."

He looked at her with hostile eyes. "And why would I want to do that?"

"You've separated yourself from Belle Pointe, but you still love it, Buck. If you can't play baseball, what harm could come from spending a growing season doing something else that you love?" With only her face and one hand visible in the crack of the door, she held his gaze for another long moment. "Just…think about it, okay?" In a heartbeat, she closed the door and left him alone.

Ten

"That's a pretty fierce frown for someone who's been to a party," Beatrice said, peering at Anne over the rim of her reading glasses.

"Oh!" Anne slapped a hand to her chest, then sagged against the stair rail kicking off her shoes. "Lord, you gave me a fright."

Anne's head was spinning, not so much from her passionate response to Buck's kiss—he could always melt her down to her toes—but until they worked through their problems, resuming a sexual relationship would complicate things even more than they already were. What had her in turmoil was seeing the dysfunction in Buck's family. The evening had been an eye-opener.

Beatrice rose from the sofa in the living room. "I'm sorry, I thought you saw me from the front window." She set her book aside and removed her reading glasses. "How was dinner at Belle Pointe?"

"Interesting. And that's a mild word for all that happened tonight." Anne touched her forehead. "Wow, they're something else. Maybe it's a good thing that Buck keeps them at arm's length."

"You can't say something like that and go to bed leaving me agog with curiosity," Beatrice said dryly. "I know I'm supposed to respond politely with something like…" she pursed her lips primly, "'Well, dear, if you want to talk, I'm willing to listen.' Forget that! We're having a cup of tea and you're telling all."

Anne laughed. "I'd actually like a cup of tea. And maybe it won't sound so awful if I talk about it to someone who's neutral."

"Well, I don't know how neutral I can be, but I'm a good listener." And with that, Beatrice headed for the kitchen. Anne followed, still barefoot.

They chatted as Beatrice put the kettle on while Anne took cups and saucers from the cabinet. As she and her stepmother went about the familiar ritual of brewing tea together, she was struck by how quickly they'd gotten so comfortable. In a very short time she had come to look upon Beatrice as not just a friend—but more. If she had to lose her mother, as sad as that was, she felt fortunate to have Beatrice to fill the void. Almost.

"By the way," Anne said when they were both seated, "I told Buck tonight that while he's here I thought he should do as Victoria asked and lend a hand at Belle Pointe."

Beatrice's eyes widened. "Really. And what did he say?"

"I think he wanted to say 'mind your own business,'" Anne said with a wry twist of her mouth. "I could have chosen a better time, I guess. He was pretty ticked off at me about then."

"Was this before or after he kissed you? Because neither of you looked angry. Just the opposite."

Anne laughed at the teasing note in Beatrice's tone. "Were you looking?" she asked in mock accusation.

"Did you forget those two wide-open windows that front on the porch?" Beatrice said with a grin. "I was sitting on the sofa in plain view. Not that either of you noticed as you seemed to have eyes only for each other."

Anne released another sigh, softer this time, as her smile faded. "The problem in my marriage was never about sex, it was…other stuff."

"Well, talking seems a good start to working your way out of that…other stuff," Beatrice said mildly. "And kissing won't hurt either."

Amused, Anne said, "I think my dad has married a born romantic."

"Anybody can see the two of you are still in love, Anne," Beatrice said softly. She paused, stirring her tea. "But maybe you're responding to Buck's change of heart about sharing his feelings."

"Some of his feelings," Anne said, studying her cup with a thoughtful frown. "But I have a feeling there's more, Beatrice. I don't know what it could be or how significant it is— at least to Buck—but there's more. There's something he's keeping to himself and it's dark. I feel it."

"Then, because he's worth it and your marriage is precious, you can afford to give him time," Beatrice said mildly.

Anne smiled. "Is there a charge for your counseling services?"

"Yes, more frequent visits once the two of you are reunited." She turned serious and, with her elbows on the table, regarded Anne over the rim of her cup. "Claire was there, I assume?"

"Yes."

"How is she?"

Glad to get away from the subject of her own troubles, Anne launched into her impression of Pearce's troubled wife. "She was very friendly to me tonight, but I got the idea that she was there because Victoria demanded it, not because she wanted to be. For most of the evening, she behaved a bit outrageously, frankly. Underneath I felt she seemed...oh, fragile, I guess."

"That's an astute observation coming from someone who hasn't seen her in several years."

"Not really. She revealed quite a lot about herself when we talked. She seems unhappy, but she tries to mask it with a brittle sort of sophistication."

"Frankly, I'm worried about her. For Paige's sake as well as for Claire herself. Did she drink too much?"

"Well..." Anne hesitated.

"Never mind. I'm sure she did. And what was Paige's reaction? She knows her mother drinks too much."

"She was...upset." Anne described Paige's outburst. "Anybody can see why she's angry and confused. What with her mother drinking and her father blinded by his colossal ego and Victoria's rigid style, the atmosphere was just plain lethal toward the end." She stirred her tea furiously. "What fourteen-year-old wouldn't be upset?"

Beatrice stood up in agitation. "This is so unhealthy for Paige!" Hugging herself, she paced the floor. "For Claire, too, of course. When are they going to acknowledge that something's wrong? How long are they going to pretend that Claire can cope simply because Victoria expects her to?"

"Simply having the Whitaker name seems to be a big thing

with Victoria," Anne said, recalling Paige's outburst. "Paige mentioned it tonight, but she's far from honoring it in spite of her grandmother's dictates. As Paige sees it, she's forced to act in a way that's false and misleading."

"And she rebels by wearing those outlandish black clothes and painting her hair orange," Beatrice said. "It's so sad."

With a hiss of impatience, she turned from the window and faced Anne. "I'm sorry. I should keep my opinions about Claire and Paige to myself, but it's just so difficult knowing how unhappy they both are."

"I know. I feel the same way. And just for the record, Claire is aware of your positive influence on Paige and she's appreciative."

"Yes, I know," Beatrice said sadly, "but that's Claire talking. For me, there's a fine line to be walked there. Victoria will tolerate only so much."

Anne decided not to comment about her mother-in-law. Hesitantly, she traced the rim of her cup with one finger before looking up. "Were you aware that Claire and Jack Breedlove were high school sweethearts?"

"Where did you hear that?"

"Claire told me herself."

"Yes, I knew it."

Anne was no longer surprised by how much Beatrice knew of the goings-on in Tallulah. "Were they very much in love?"

"Maybe you should ask Jack that question."

"My interview techniques are pretty good, but I don't think I can get away with asking that, Beatrice. Besides, I've got enough material."

"I know he was crazy about her," Beatrice said, dabbing at a spot of tea on the place mat. "I knew Claire's parents well,

Bert and Madeline Schofield. Until just last year before he retired and they moved somewhere in Florida, he was president of the bank and Madeline was active in Tallulah society." She glanced at Anne with a twinkle in her eye. "You're looking skeptical, but there is such a thing as a pecking order around here and Madeline was at the top."

"And Jack was at the bottom."

"I see you already know the story." Beatrice took her cup to the sink.

"Buck said they disapproved and somehow managed to break them up."

"And Jack joined the army."

Anne studied the dregs in the bottom of her cup. "Star-crossed lovers," she murmured.

"Now who's sounding like a romantic?" After rinsing her cup, Beatrice turned to face Anne. "I'll just say this. Claire, as a teenager, was a handful for Bert and Madeline. The capers that girl pulled…well, I recall a few that make Paige's antics look tame. As they say, the apple doesn't fall far from the tree, so it's no wonder to me that Paige is a handful. Combining her mama's genes and Pearce's is enough to make anybody a little willful."

The subject of genes reminded Anne of her baby. "May I ask you something, Beatrice? It may be too personal and I won't be offended if you'd rather not discuss it."

There was an instant's hesitation, almost too brief for Anne to be sure it was there. Then Beatrice said with a smile, "Ask first and then I'll decide if it's too personal."

"I've been thinking a lot about my miscarriage, about genes and my own unknown genetic background. About Buck's reluctance to be a father. About my aging ovaries.

Maybe it's not meant for me to have a child at all." She brushed at a few grains of sugar spilled on the table, then looked into Beatrice's eyes. "You've never had children and you seem…satisfied with your life. Have you never wished it otherwise? Do you have any regret?"

She could see instantly that she had blundered. Beatrice was too still, too pale. "I'm sorry," she said, feeling color steal into her face. "Please, just—"

"No, no, dear. You just…caught me off guard."

Why would she have to be on guard, Anne thought. Oh, my God. A dark possibility occurred to her. Just because this woman had never married didn't mean she'd never been pregnant. Maybe she'd once had an abortion, or perhaps she'd given up a baby for adoption. No matter what, it would be private territory, personal territory on which Anne had no right to intrude.

"That was too personal, wasn't it? I'm so sorry," she repeated with genuine distress. Without waiting to hear a reply, Anne rushed on, "It's just that I'm so conflicted over all this. I'm not sure that Buck can overcome this…this problem he has with us having a baby. Which means that if we stay together, I may never be a mother. Of course, there's a chance that I will never conceive again anyway. That I can't…for some genetic reason. I'm just struggling with a lot of unknowns at the moment and—" She stopped babbling when Beatrice reached out and caught her hand.

"To answer your question," Beatrice said, giving her hand a firm squeeze, "which wasn't too personal, I just needed a minute to gather my thoughts." She released Anne and spent a moment fiddling with the place mat, picking up a spoon and napkin before looking into her eyes. "If you're asking can a woman be happy without having children, then I suppose it depends on the woman. There are other things to fill that…void—a solid marriage, career, friends, travel, other peoples' children…" She managed a smile. "All of which are available to you, Anne."

"Not all of them. I don't have a solid marriage."

"You can work on that. Of course, it takes two. And from all appearances, Buck is willing, even eager." Before Anne could argue, she added, "This is a man determined enough to patch up your differences that he's followed you to the last place on earth he wants to be. He knows why you left him. And he isn't acting like someone who dismisses your longing to have a baby."

"I don't want to make having children a condition of us staying together," Anne said quietly. "What kind of father would he be if he resented being tied down by a baby?"

"I think Buck would fall in love with his child the minute he laid eyes on him," Beatrice said softly. "He's that kind of man."

"I thought so once, but now I'm not so sure. I'll just never forget his reaction when I told him I was pregnant." Her eyes filled with tears. "I know he had a right to be angry. I'd tossed my birth control pills without telling him and that was bad. But I was so thrilled and happy that I put out of my mind the way I got pregnant and I guess I thought he should, too. Anyway, from the start, I adored being pregnant. I adored the baby. It didn't matter whether it was a boy or a girl." She grabbed her napkin and blotted her eyes. "I was just filled with the joy of it. The wonder of it. I want that again!" she cried.

"And you can have it again, Anne," Beatrice said firmly.

"Stop worrying about these things, especially about any genetic abnormality. It's so unlikely."

"Unlikely, but not impossible. Maybe there is something wrong genetically. I've taken the first steps on the Internet to try and find my biological parents. I don't think I can be at peace over this until I know. Not even if Buck and I work things out in our marriage. I need to know!"

Beatrice pushed her chair back and stood up. "It's late. You're tired. An evening with the Whitakers is enough to throw anyone into stress overload. And all these other problems will work themselves out, you'll see." She reached for Anne's cup and saucer and stacked them with hers. That done, she stood for a moment as if undecided about her next words. "As for the other part of your question, the part about regrets. Of course, I have regrets. Who doesn't?"

Claire always drove Paige to school—every day, rain or shine, come hell or high water. Or a hangover, even one as massive as the one she suffered today. Making it so much worse was the bone-deep self-disgust resting like lead in her stomach.

Last night, before coming downstairs and facing the ordeal of another of her mother-in-law's Sunday dinners, she had sworn to limit herself to three glasses of wine. But three minutes of exposure to Victoria's personality had unraveled her good intentions. And that had been before Buck and Anne showed up. By then, of course, she'd been well numbed. Which helped when Paige appeared in that god-awful getup. Once everyone was seated at the table, it was too late to be a lady.

Paige leaned forward and popped in a CD. Claire cringed

as 50 Cent blasted in full volume from all speakers in the Jaguar's sound system. "My God, turn it down, Paige!"

Paige scowled and crossed her arms over her chest. "It's no good unless it's played loud."

"Paige. Please…" Claire said between her teeth. "I have a headache."

"No, Claire. You have a hangover," her daughter sassed.

Claire reached over and angrily punched the CD off button. "I've told you a thousand times not to talk to me like that. It's only five miles to school. Can't we tolerate each other for five miles?"

"I don't have any choice," Paige said, gazing in extreme boredom out the side window. "You do. You could let somebody else drive me. But since I have no power around here, I'm stuck with you whether I like it or not."

Claire drew in a long-suffering breath. "Okay. Okay. I'm sorry. I apologize. That's what you want to hear, isn't it? You're mad at me for last night. I embarrassed you. It won't happen again."

"Oh, please…" Paige rolled her eyes. "It won't happen again until the next time it happens. Spare me your promises, Mom. Face it, you drink too much." Her voice rose in frustration. "Dad is gonna talk the Dragon into shipping you off to rehab if you don't stop. Don't you get it?"

Claire floored the accelerator to pass a slow-moving tractor. "Your father may think he's king of creation, but he doesn't have that much power. I'm not going into rehab," she stated. "I don't need it."

"He has all the power," Paige stated flatly, ignoring the denial, "except for Gran, but even she rolls over for Pearce the Precious. Better slow down, that's a cop coming this way."

Once the police cruiser passed, she turned abruptly and watched through the back window as it braked hard and executed a skillful three-point turn, reversed direction and headed their way. "Don't look now, but he's coming right up behind us with his blue lights flashing."

"Shit!" Claire muttered, then added hastily, "I didn't say that. And you didn't hear me." Sure enough, the patrol car was directly behind her now. If there was a God, she would not be his victim, but she sighed wearily when he gave a brief blast of his siren. Braking, she pulled to the shoulder of the road and stopped.

"Perfect start for the week," she said, giving Paige a bright, utterly false smile.

"It's your own fault," Paige said, but she was literally agog with excitement. "I've never met a cop up close and personal."

"Save your sympathy for someone who needs it, Paige." Leaning over, Claire popped open the glove compartment and fumbled for the car's registration. "My driver's license is in my purse. It's on the floor at your feet."

In the side mirror of the Jaguar, she could see the policeman—or rather half of him, chest to waist—as he made his way to her side of the car. "I can't believe this," she moaned. Only when he gave a rap of his knuckles on the window did she touch the button to lower it, still looking straight ahead.

"You're in a big rush this morning, Claire," he said.

She whipped her head around at the sound of that deep, low voice. Oh, God. Jack. With her heart doing crazy things, she managed a smile as she looked up into his face. Hard mouth, high cheekbones, square jaw. He wore sunglasses, the dark kind that obscured his eyes, but she knew them well, eyes as green as the fields stretching out behind him. Tall and rangy and fit, without an ounce of excess weight, he looked tough and uncompromising. And all too familiar. "Hello, Jack."

"'Morning." He shifted slightly with his hand on the car's window frame and as he bent at the knee to get a look at her passenger, she caught the scent of him, fresh shower, soap, subtle aftershave. Dizzy with memory, she still found it tantalizing.

"On your way to school?" he asked.

"Yes," Claire said. If he noticed anything about Paige's bizarre appearance, he concealed it.

"You're supposed to be buckled up, young lady," was all he said to Paige in his deep voice.

"Ah, okay." At fourteen, Paige was always ready with a sassy reply to her mother, or to anybody in her family, as well as her teachers at school, but apparently something about a direct look from Tallulah's police chief, told her not to try it with him. She buckled up.

"Your license, please, Claire," he said, holding a clipboard at the ready.

She handed it over, then fixed her gaze straight ahead again, anywhere except on that face. "Don't you have more important things to do as police chief than issue traffic tickets?"

"Not when a driver is doing seventy-eight miles an hour in a school zone," he said, scribbling something on his clipboard.

"Seventy-eight! Oh, come on. Are you sure?"

He touched the beak of his cap, pushing it up a fraction to give her a direct look. "Do you think I'd stop you otherwise?"

She flushed. "You know I didn't mean to imply—" She stopped, realizing that Paige was listening incredulously. "Just write the ticket and we'll be on our way, Jack."

Paige leaned toward the window to get a look at his face. "Hi, I'm Paige. Claire is my mother. It wasn't her fault that she was speeding. We were arguing, which like makes her so mad and she didn't realize I wasn't buckled up until just before you stopped us. In fact, that's what we were arguing about, me not having my seat belt fastened. She says all the time she'll, like, kill me if I don't buckle up."

Claire heaved an exasperated sigh. "Paige—"

"Pleased to meet you, Paige," Jack said, scribbling away without looking up. "I'm Jack, but you can call me Chief Breedlove. And I'm not citing your mother for either of you failing to buckle up." He scrawled his signature and carefully detached the citation. "I'm giving her a pass on that."

"But we're getting a ticket?" Paige demanded, eyeing the paper.

Without a word, Jack held it between thumb and forefinger and waved it in the air.

"Nobody's going to vote for you if you give people tickets all the time," she predicted darkly. "You should be trying to make people like you." Claire attempted to silence her with a fierce look. Paige shrugged, unfazed. "Well, it's the truth."

For a heartbeat, Jack Breedlove almost smiled. "I'll keep that in mind, Paige." To Claire, he said, "The instructions are on the reverse side if you decide to contest it."

"Whatever," she muttered.

"We won't have to contest it," Paige said with smug confidence. "My father will get it fixed."

Jack tucked his pen in a slot on the clipboard. "Since that's illegal, you be sure and let me know when it happens. It'll be a nice addition to the reasons I've listed on my campaign flyers why folks shouldn't vote for him."

"I was kidding," Paige said, glaring at him. "Don't you know a joke when you hear it?"

"Just give me the damn ticket, Jack," Claire said, sticking her hand out to take it.

"No ticket, Claire. It's just a warning," he said, handing it over. "But it'll go in the computer, so if you're stopped for speeding again, the fine will kick in double."

"Oh." She studied it without comprehending anything for a second or two, then looked up at him. "Well…ah, thank you. I don't usually drive so fast, but there was a tractor poking along and we're late, so frankly, I didn't realize…" She stopped. "Which is no excuse, is it? Anyway…thanks."

He shifted, resting his weight on his good leg. "I saw Buck a couple of days ago going into Walgreen's, but I didn't get a chance to talk to him. I understood from Anne that his injury was keeping him in St. Louis. I hated hearing he's out this season."

"Yes, he's really bummed over it."

Jack nodded a greeting to a passing motorist. "Gives us hometown folks a chance to enjoy a visit. How long do you think he'll stay?"

"Why?" Paige piped up. "Do you want him to endorse you in your campaign, too?"

"Paige, would you please be quiet," Claire begged.

Again that near-smile. "Uh-oh, does that mean Pearce has Buck working for him already?" He put the question to Paige, not Claire.

"No, not yet, but since he's family, he's almost obligated to do it." Paige had leaned forward so she could see Jack's face. "But even if he doesn't get Uncle Buck to endorse him, he thinks he can beat you."

Jack laughed outright. "Well, time will tell, little girl."

Claire's breath caught with the impact of Jack Breedlove's smile. God, she was still as susceptible as she'd been when she was sixteen and Jack had been the only reason she had for getting up in the morning.

Reading something in her face—or her thoughts—he nodded. "It's good to see you, Claire," he said quietly. "It's been a while."

"Something that could easily be remedied," she said shortly, the words out before she could stop them.

"What's changed? Am I now welcome in your world?"

She stared at him helplessly for a long, long moment, drinking in his profile as he focused on a freshly turned cotton field. A million words—feelings—clogged her throat. But before she said something else she couldn't take back, she turned the key in the ignition and started the Jaguar. It wouldn't matter what she and Jack Breedlove might say to each other anyway, she told herself. Thanks to her, it was too late.

Craning her neck, Paige looked through the back window and watched as the police chief made another three-point turnaround and drove away in the opposite direction. "Mom, you know him, don't you?"

"Of course I know him. He's the chief of police." With her hands gripping the wheel and her heart still acting crazy, Claire's face was grim as she drove. "His picture's all over the place."

"No, I mean…you *know* him. I heard all that. There's like *history* between y'all."

"Tallulah's a small town. There's history between nearly everybody you pass on the street. And please stop sprinkling the word 'like' in every sentence you speak. It's tasteless."

"Gosh, now I know you're upset because you sound just like the Dragon," Paige said, flopping back in her seat.

"And buckle up, for heaven's sake!"

"Oops, forgot." Paige busied herself pulling the strap over and snapping it into place. "Now, tell me what he meant by not being welcome in your world?"

"Obviously it was a reference to the fact that he and Pearce are political opponents."

"Nuh-uh," Paige said flatly. "It was a reference to something personal. I feel it. Gosh, he's like, really cool."

Claire knew Paige was capable of bugging her until her curiosity was satisfied, so she would have to come up with some explanation. Besides, what was the harm—after all these years—of giving an edited version of her history with Jack? "I knew Jack Breedlove when I was in high school. He was actually in Buck's class. We had a few dates. See, no big deal. Now you know."

"Not nearly enough. How long did you date? Were you, like, going steady?"

"For a while."

"A while. Hmm, let me think." She tapped her lips with a finger, looking for a second just like Victoria, Claire thought. "Was he…what's that old-fashioned idea? Was he 'of your class?'"

Claire didn't bother pretending she didn't know what Paige meant. "His mother was a single mom who worked two jobs and he worked, too. They all did, his brothers and sisters. They were a working-class family and they were nice people. The nicest."

Paige was silent, studying her mother's face. "You really liked him, didn't you?"

"It was a long time ago, Paige."

"And if he was the same age as Uncle Buck, you must have been in the…whoa, the tenth grade!" Her eyes went wide. "I bet you had to sneak around because Bert and Madeline—"

"Paige…"

"*Grandfather* Bert and *Grandmother* Madeline," she continued, "can be as stiff-necked as Gran, which means…" she paused dramatically, "he for sure wouldn't be welcome at the Schofields'. They freaked, am I right?"

On all points, Claire thought bitterly. She'd been sixteen and in the tenth grade when she fell in love with Jack. And her parents had been more than freaked that she'd fallen for "white trash." They'd been horrified. They saw none of Jack's work ethic, his fierce pride, his decency. As for sneaking around to see him, she'd done that, too, until they'd shipped her off to a school in Virginia to be "finished." "Our relationship was brief," she told Paige.

"How brief is brief?"

"A year," she said irritably, thinking she should have known Paige wouldn't settle for an edited version of anything that intrigued her. "And no more questions, because it's ancient history and here we are at school. Today's your day to go to the *Spectator* and Beatrice is picking you up. I'll be out front at five o'clock to drive you home."

Paige unsnapped the seat belt. "This is so interesting, Claire," she said, bending to pick up her backpack from the floor. "I do not know why Beady has never mentioned it, but you can bet I'll ask today when I see her."

"She's never mentioned it because it's ancient history," Claire repeated through her teeth. "And I forbid you discussing it with her!"

Out and on the sidewalk now, Paige leaned down and looked at her mother. "If it was really ancient history," she said, bent on having the last word, as usual, "you wouldn't be so freaked."

"Paige—"

"Bye, see you at five."

Eleven

Buck had had a busy morning. Up at daylight with a couple of errands in front of him—both done now—he was back to the lodge for a session with Ty, only a little late. Eyeing the twenty-six steps as if they were coiled snakes, he leaned on his cane and started up. Only then did he spot his PT waiting on the porch. "Don't jump me about being late," he growled at Ty. "I've been doing something you'll approve of…for once."

Ty was a fierce taskmaster. He had put Buck through some torturous sessions since taking over his rehabilitation. The good news was that his knee was vastly improved. The bad news was that Ty didn't show any signs of letting up on him.

With a couple of long strides, Ty was at ground level. With his big arm, he caught Buck beneath a shoulder and hoisted him to the top of the steps as if he weighed no more than Paige. "Like what am I going to approve of?" he asked when they were inside.

"For one thing, I've been to see your daddy." Buck dropped his cane into the holder at the door and made his way toward the workout room. "I wanted to hear from him exactly what happened at Belle Pointe. Turned out to be worse than you told me."

"Pearce plays hardball."

"Maybe. But I've got a plan." He smiled, showing a lot of teeth.

"Oh, man, you used to get that look when you were winding up ready to cream somebody at home plate."

Buck peeled off his jacket and tossed it toward a contraption that Ty claimed would work a miracle on his body, but up to now had only worked to put him in a state of extreme pain and suffering. "I've found a replacement for Will Wainwright."

Ty was watching him suspiciously. "And it is…"

"Oscar Pittman."

A loud laugh burst out of Ty. "Oh, that's precious. That's too much."

Buck grinned. "I figure your daddy is the perfect man to manage Belle Pointe."

For a minute, both men enjoyed the moment, chuckling, shaking their heads, grinning like two kids caught out in some fabulously creative prank and getting away with it.

Ty sobered first. "There's just one problem I see with your plan, man. Or maybe two problems. Pearce and Ms. Victoria."

"They're over a barrel, big-time, both of them. Even if Pearce wanted to, which he doesn't, he can't take time away from his campaign and his practice to farm cotton. And my mother is not up to the job physically. So they've got to have a manager." He grinned. "Oscar is the man for the job."

"You think you have enough power to make it happen?"

Buck's face set stubbornly. "I'm going to make it happen. It was a low-down, dirty trick and I mean to make it right."

Ty stood studying Buck for a moment, nodding. "Okay." He slapped him on the butt. "Now, get over there on that table. You've just done the only thing that saves your ass from a severe punishment by being late for your session this morning, buddy."

Buck grunted and swore under his breath, but he did as ordered and braced for the force of Ty's strong fingers on his thigh muscle. "Anybody else would show a little appreciation," he complained. "Like letting me off the hook today."

"I let you off the hook yesterday," Ty replied.

"It was Sunday!"

"God rested and so do I," Ty said and dug into a tender spot at Buck's kneecap."

"Ow!" Closing his eyes, Buck tried zoning into another sphere, a trick he'd developed over the years to help him cope with pain from injuries.

"Relax," Ty said. "Think about your pretty wife."

Buck laughed in spite of himself. "Then we can forget relaxing." But Anne was on his mind almost always now anyway. "We were together last night," he told Ty.

"Hmm." Ty gently rotated Buck's knee. "In that case, I would expect to see an improvement in your disposition."

Buck gritted his teeth against pain. "Do you have sex on the brain? I meant we had dinner."

"Progress at last."

"At Belle Pointe."

"La-de-da."

"You won't believe my wife's parting shot as I left her at the door."

"Was it before or after you propositioned her?"

Buck laughed. "Actually, I did proposition her and it almost worked. But as if she hadn't already tied me in knots, she tossed out a suggestion that I should rethink my decision about helping out at Belle Pointe this season."

"Smart lady." Ty applied pressure to increase range of motion in the knee.

Buck, in pain and sweating profusely, looked up into Ty's face. "And you say that because…"

"Because I happen to agree." He tossed a towel at Buck. "Plus, it's something you know is right and, face it, you want to do it, but you're just too damn stubborn to admit it."

"I must have overlooked that part in your résumé that says you're a freakin' shrink," Buck muttered with his face buried in the towel.

"Consider this. You're stuck here and you're bored. Instead of wasting time, you could do some good."

"I'm reinstating Otis. That'll do plenty good."

Ty gave him a telling look. "Your mama will be forced to accept Pop to replace Wainwright, but you could make the transition a lot smoother. You know she's going to ride hard on him, interfering, questioning his decisions, giving him grief wherever and whenever she can. Since rehiring him wasn't her idea, she'll almost make him wish he was back at Wal-Mart greeting customers." He had the grace to smile. "Almost, but not quite."

Buck sat up on the table. "Otis is tough. He can handle it."

Ty sighed. "Yeah, he can, but admit it, Buck. Deep down, wouldn't you like to be out there slogging around in that Delta mud? Instead of looking at these four walls, wouldn't you like watching those little green stubs pop out of the ground and start growing? Wouldn't you like to make a few changes now, this season, before it's too late?"

"Any bright ideas I come up with, I'll suggest to Otis and let him take the heat."

Shaking his head, Ty wouldn't quit. "In spite of the fact that you're a superstar in St. Louis, I'll bet you haven't been able to resist keeping up with new ideas in all the stuff that cotton farmers not stuck in the twentieth century are trying but that they ignore at Belle Pointe. Stuff you trained for and got a degree in. So here's a chance to play around with it a little."

"I take it back," Buck said, giving him a sour look, "you're not a shrink, you're a freakin' salesman!" He slung the towel around his neck and reached for a bottle of water, then sat for a minute considering. "I'd be lying if I said I hadn't thought about it. Hell, I've been tempted, but—"

"But you might like it well enough that you fear losing your focus on rehabilitating that knee, right? And losing focus could mean you won't be ready when ball practice begins next season. And if you aren't ready, your career's over. Where would you be without baseball?"

Hearing his fears spelled out with naked clarity made Buck's blood run cold. But he played it light. "Next you'll be making plans for me to start coaching Little League right here in Tallulah," he said dryly.

"Not a bad idea," Ty said, putting out a hand to hoist Buck to his feet. "'Specially when one of the kids would be mine."

Or mine. The thought startled Buck, coming like a sneak steal at second base behind his back. He must be picking up on Anne's obsession about having kids, which didn't make a lot of sense after the fiasco of that dinner last night. The nuttiness of his family should have shored up his resolve to keep from bringing more little Whitakers into the world, not putting images of Little Leaguers in his head.

"Don't we have work to do?" he growled and, for once, didn't put up any resistance for the rest of the workout.

On Wednesday, Anne waited at the entrance to Daddy Gee's, a popular diner on the square, when Buck cruised by in his SUV. Spotting her, he swerved quickly to the curb, zoomed his window down and gave her his best smile. "Hey, a beautiful lady and right here at high noon. How about lunch? My treat."

"I already have a date."

In the act of climbing out of the SUV, his smile froze. "With who?"

"Whom. I'm meeting Beatrice and possibly Dad," she told him. Even with the help of a cane, he moved with surprising grace and was beside her in a few strides. "Looks like your knee is a lot better," she observed.

"Ty's a miracle worker. He'll have me running a five-minute mile in a few more sessions…if he doesn't kill me first." He glanced at a news box and began to fish coins out of his pocket. "I haven't had a chance to read the *Spectator* yet. This is the issue featuring your first articles, isn't it?"

"Hot off the press," she said, wondering if he'd still be smiling once he read her profile on his brother. But that would be later. Beyond her shoulder, Buck spotted Franklin and Beatrice approaching, all smiles.

"Hey, folks, I was just trying to wheedle an invitation to join y'all for lunch."

"Buck." Beatrice's face lit up. "I've been wondering when we'd see you. How's that knee coming along?"

"Can't complain," he lied, jigging the cane. "At least not in public." Without looking at it, he tucked the folded newspaper under one arm and shook hands with Franklin. "I was just trying to talk my wife into having lunch with me, but she tells me she's already spoken for." He turned his whiskey-gold gaze on Anne. "I'm hoping she'll take pity and remember I'm doing my own cooking now and breakfast was—hmm, what was it? Oh, yeah, nothing. If I have to cook it, I skip it."

Anne, watching, rolled her eyes at his blatant effort to charm the Marshes. But a part of her admitted that she wasn't entirely immune to Buck's charm.

"Hey, does Daddy Gee still make the best fried green tomatoes in the world?" he asked.

Beatrice laughed. "Certainly the best in Mississippi."

"Considering we haven't had a chance to catch up since you've been back in Tallulah, we're willing to share," Franklin said. He seemed to realize belatedly that Anne might not be willing. Hastily, he added, "Of course, it's up to Anne…"

"Oh, for Pete's sake," she said, sending Buck a sparkling look. "Are we going to stand out here all day?"

By the time they'd ordered, Buck had them all laughing. He had a full arsenal of charm and knew how to use it. Even Anne had to admit that his inside baseball stories were funny. Her heart gave a little jump when he turned to her. "So, have you been busy uncovering Whitaker secrets in the archives?"

"I don't know if they're secrets or not, but I have uncovered a few interesting facts." She peeled the paper covering from a drinking straw and stuck it in a glass of sweet tea. "And I don't think they'll make you proud."

Holding her gaze, Buck frowned. "How so?"

"Were you aware that a thousand acres of Belle Pointe land used to belong to Beatrice's family?"

She expected a guilty look, but Buck's reaction was plain confusion. "No, I wasn't." He glanced at Beatrice, who was suddenly busy twiddling with her napkin. "What about that, Beady? It had to be way before the Civil War because that's when Buchanan Whitaker first bought the land." His grin included Franklin and Anne. "That would be my great-great grandfather and namesake."

"Yes, what about it?" Anne asked, looking at her stepmother expectantly.

Beatrice sighed. "It was a long time ago, dear."

"But not as long ago as the Civil War," Anne said. When she realized Beatrice didn't intend to explain, she gave a huff of impatience and turned back to Buck. "It was in 1989. The land belonged to Harvey Jones. Somehow, he fell behind on his taxes and John Whitaker loaned him money to pay them. As luck would have it, both of them died that year within weeks of each other, which meant the Whitakers then held a mortgage on the land. They quickly swooped in and foreclosed on land that should have gone to my stepmother as Harvey Jones's heir. So, instead of farming a total of four thousand acres of cotton, as they did before 1989, they then had five thousand."

Buck looked at Beatrice. "Is this true?"

"Of course it's true," Anne said, while Beatrice obviously struggled to come up with a tactful reply. "You don't have to try and pretty it up. It was a flat-out, old-fashioned land grab." She was shaking her head. "What I can't understand is how it could happen. Beatrice, was Harvey Jones your father or your grandfather?"

"Wait a minute," Buck said. Reaching across the table, he caught Anne's hand. "Calm down and give me a chance to ask some questions, will you?"

With a shrug, she spread her hands. "Go ahead."

"No, let me tell it, and then if you have questions, I'll try to answer," Beatrice said. She touched her napkin to her lips. "Anne has the facts straight basically. What isn't visible in a dry newspaper account is my father's stubbornness and stiff-necked pride. In his old age, his health failed and, rather than ask for help, he let the taxes go unpaid for several years and ignored the county's demands for repayment. Soon, the penalty and interest had reached a level that he couldn't pay." She shrugged. "And John Whitaker did float him a loan. They were friends."

"He had family," Anne said in distress. "You and a slew of relatives right here in this county. Nobody was destitute. Why didn't one of them loan him money?"

"They could have—probably would have—but Harvey Jones was too proud to ask." Beatrice cleared her throat, giving Franklin a quick look. "As for asking for help from me, he would have refused it even if I had known about his situation, which I didn't. My father and I were…estranged."

There had to be a good reason for bad blood between Beatrice and her father and Anne wished she could ask. The more she learned about her stepmother, the more fascinated she became. Someday, Anne vowed, she would ask.

"This is all news to me," Buck said, pushing his half-finished meal aside. "My dad died in 1989, so it had to be only a matter of months later that this happened. Maybe you think I'm making excuses and it sounds pretty lame, I guess, but I don't believe Dad would have condoned a land grab. It's way late, but on behalf of the Whitakers, I apologize."

Beatrice touched his hand. "It was a perfectly legal transaction. An apology is absolutely unnecessary, Buck."

"It is, Beady. After Dad died, I pretty much turned my back on everything pertaining to Belle Pointe. But it's one thing to distance myself from my family and another altogether to ignore my responsibility as part-owner." He reached for a glass of water. "I'm here now and as soon as my knee is stronger, I'm going to be looking at a lot of things. 'Course, Pearce may not even notice. He's never considered me much of a threat."

"Oh, I wouldn't say that," Franklin said. "Quite the opposite, in fact. I think if you stay around long enough you'll find your older brother is quite envious of you in a number of areas."

Buck gave a disbelieving snort. "Such as?"

"Your celebrity, for one thing. Why else would he aspire to political office if he didn't crave the limelight? For years, he's watched you in the public spotlight as a pro athlete. That's a life that many men can only fantasize about."

"Pearce never played any sport!" Buck argued. "He has two left feet. Hand him a baseball bat in the dark and he wouldn't know what it was."

"We're not talking logic here," Franklin said gently. "It's plain, old-fashioned sibling rivalry."

"It's plain, old-fashioned bull—" He stopped abruptly.

Franklin leaned forward to make his point. "Deep down, Pearce knows your achievements are a result of your own hard work, whereas, by sticking close to home, he's had the advantages of the Whitaker name to assist him in a variety of ways. In short, you're a big fish in a very big pond." He smiled as Buck actually blushed. "And Pearce is a big fish in a very small pond."

"Just one more thing about the transfer of that land from the Joneses to the Whitakers," Beatrice said with a soft smile. "It's funny the way things work out. In spite of the fact that the house, along with the land, could have been lost to me, Franklin bought it." She smiled. "Some women marry for money, but Franklin wonders if I married him for his house."

"In other words, what goes around comes around?" Anne wasn't even close to seeing anything funny about it. "Sorry, but I don't see it that way. I—"

She broke off as Pearce Whitaker suddenly appeared at the table, clearly furious, but smiling tightly for the benefit of the diners who recognized him. "Here you are, Anne. Buck. Since I'm family…" he said it with a sneer, "you won't mind if I join you."

"We were just finishing up, Pearce," Buck said in a dead-calm voice.

Ignoring him, Pearce gave Franklin and Beatrice a curt nod. "This won't take but a minute and it'll save me a visit to the *Spectator*." With that, he jerked a chair out and sat down.

His smile at Anne was lethal. "What the hell are you trying to do to me?" he hissed, slapping the current issue of the *Spectator* on the tabletop.

"I assume you're talking about the profile I wrote," Anne said.

He bared his teeth. "This isn't a profile, my *dear* sister-in-law, it's a hit piece."

"A hit piece?" Buck unfolded his copy of the *Spectator* and began looking for Anne's byline.

"It's on page three," Pearce told him helpfully. "I guess I should be grateful it's not on page one. How did that happen, by the way?" he asked Anne. "Then the whole world would have seen it instead of the limited number in Tallulah who can read."

It was just such remarks as that that had influenced Anne's profile of Pearce. "What is it that you object to in the article?" she asked.

"What the hell don't I object to," he snarled. "You led me to believe this was going to be a personality piece, an unbiased look at who I am, what I stand for, the good I want to do for voters. And instead I open the paper this morning and find I'm juxtaposed alongside my opponent and you portray Breedlove as God's gift to the voters and you throw out a bunch of lies about me."

"Specifically, where did I lie?"

"Hell, the voters now think I'm the next thing to Saddam Hussein! Thanks a lot, Anne. With friends—and relatives—like you, who needs enemies?"

Buck pushed his chair back and reached for his cane. "Let's take this discussion somewhere else, Pearce," he said. But as he made to stand, Pearce shot out a hand and clamped down on his arm.

"I can say what I need right here, Buck. And I'm wondering how much of this shit you knew about. I'm wondering whether you put her up to this."

Buck looked down at Pearce's hand, then lifted his gaze to meet his brother's eyes. Without Buck saying a word, Pearce withdrew his hand.

"This could ruin me," he said. "I want a retraction."

"Of what? So far, you haven't told me where I've erred." Anne folded her napkin and laid it beside her plate. "If you have anything else to say to me, you'll have to say it to me in my office at the *Spectator*."

"Are you working for Breedlove?" he demanded.

Anne sighed heavily. "I'm a journalist, Pearce. I'm not working for anyone."

"Yeah," he sneered. "Like the rest of the jackals in the media. Sure, you're neutral."

"That's it. We're out of here." Buck rose, tossed a fistful of bills on the table and caught his wife's elbow. As one, Franklin and Beatrice rose, too.

Pearce studied the group for a long moment. "I guess I am, too," he said, rising. On his feet, still holding his brother's gaze, he adjusted his cuffs, touched the knot of his tie. "I'll see you at the lodge," he told Buck, shifting his shoulders as if ants were inside his jacket. "And I'll expect answers."

"Hmm, that went well," Anne said a little breathlessly, when they were outside.

Buck was shaking his head. "I haven't made it past the first few paragraphs yet, but he looks like a loser when compared with what you said about Jack Breedlove."

"I thought we might hear from a few disgruntled folks," Franklin said in his gentle voice. "But Anne's the reporter and she had her own ideas about the piece. She felt it would have more…what was it you called it, Annie? Oh, yes, punch. It would have more punch if the two men were pro-filed side by side."

"It certainly has punch," Beatrice murmured, reading from Buck's copy of the paper. "And Jack does show up quite well."

"Jack Breedlove has a well-thought-out platform that will appeal to a broad base of citizens," Anne said, defending her journalism. "He came from an impoverished background, joined the army, was wounded, got a college education while still helping his younger siblings and from all accounts, runs a tight ship as chief of police."

"You learned all that in one interview?" Buck looked doubtful.

"No, I did a little research," she said, smiling softly. "I didn't have to do much. I just had to say his name and people loved to tell me what a great guy he is. He's going to win this race, folks."

"I guess nobody said my brother was a great guy?"

She gave a slightly awkward shrug. "Not really."

He released a weary sigh. "The Whitakers aren't looking too heroic today, are they?"

Beatrice patted his arm. "If you're thinking of that incident with the mortgage, please don't. It's a part of the past that's not worth wasting a minute worrying over. In fact, if you just stop and think about it, everything is still in the family." She smiled brightly at Buck. "I have the Jones house, thanks to Franklin, and you're a Belle Pointe heir, so your children will be heirs to the Jones land. I'm assuming the children will be yours and Anne's," she added.

In the small silence, Franklin cleared his throat. "I'll be escorting my wife back to her shop now. Come along, Beatrice."

"I guess that's one way to look at it," Buck said as the Marshes strolled away, arm in arm.

"The land grab? My stepmother is the eternal optimist. And we don't have any children."

"Yet." And with that, Buck walked off in the opposite direction.

Twelve

After leaving Anne and the Marshes, Buck went directly to the county courthouse to check the legality of the land transfer from Harvey Jones to Belle Pointe. His face was a grim mask as he climbed back in the SUV and headed out to see his mother.

He found her working in her rose garden. When she became aware of Buck at the ornate gate, she dropped her pruning shears into a basket and waited as he approached.

"Buck." She began removing her gloves, watching him walk. "Your knee is apparently much better. How long before you can discard the cane?"

"When Ty tells me." He glanced over at a bench situated beneath a tangled canopy of honeysuckle. "Can we talk?"

"Of course." Leading the way, she removed her hat and rolled up her shirtsleeves. She sat down, letting her gaze wander over the garden, and Buck did the same. It would be another month before the roses bloomed. One of his better childhood memories was the sweet scent of sun-warmed roses, even though the garden had been forbidden territory.

One surefire way to incur his mother's wrath was to accidentally clip a bloom from one of her prize hybrids with a fast ball. Or to cripple a rosebush with a bad throw.

"When do you expect that to be?" she asked.

"I don't know," he said, settling back on the bench. "I won't need the cane much longer, but that doesn't mean the knee can take much punishment. I won't be running any foot races, that's for sure."

He watched a dragonfly settle on the globe of a bright green gazing ball in the center of her rose garden. "That's what I wanted to talk to you about. Now that Will Wainwright has retired, I've reconsidered about helping out."

She gave him a quick, surprised look. "You just told me your knee can't take a lot of punishment. The work here is quite physical and the hours are long. It's nothing like playing a game a few times a week with panting fans cheering."

"Keep that up and you'll talk me out of it," Buck said. No point in reminding his mother that she'd literally pushed him into "playing a game" as a career, or that the constant competition he faced was more daunting than farming cotton would ever be. "I was under the impression that you needed help and I'm offering. Are you interested or not?"

"Well, of course I'm interested. We're in somewhat of a bind with Will quitting so abruptly, but the situation is not desperate. Although it would have been a challenge, I can run Belle Pointe without a manager."

"Or without Pearce's valuable assistance," he said, openly sarcastic.

"Yes, indeed."

He almost laughed. The way his mother's mind worked,

by helping her she would be doing him a favor. "I've got conditions," he told her.

"Why? Are you planning to make significant changes?"

"I want to hire and fire as I see fit. I want complete control of the crews and I want to see the books."

"Provided you discuss your actions with me before implementing them, I have no objection. Just remember, once you're gone Pearce and I will have to live with any changes you've made, or waste valuable time and energy dismantling them."

"If you fear my management style is such a disaster waiting to happen, why did you ask me to do the job?"

"I believe I explained. Will's departure was unexpected. It takes time to find a good manager and you know Belle Pointe. Besides the fact that you know what it takes to plant and grow cotton, men like you and will work for you. Finally, you're a Whitaker and you've arrived just at the right time here in Tallulah. I considered it almost…providential, if you will. Why wouldn't I ask you?" She studied her nails. "I'll be truthful and say I was disappointed when you refused."

It was the closest he'd ever come to actually receiving a compliment from his mother, even a left-handed one. "Then you shouldn't object to letting me do things my way. I don't promise to clear every decision with you."

"So long as you keep in mind that you're only here temporarily."

"Okay. Now, for my conditions. I'll be rehiring Oscar Pittman."

She turned her face away. "Terminating Oscar was Pearce's decision. You'll have to see him about that."

"Pearce is busy campaigning. Let's leave him to do what he does best."

"If you're suggesting again that he isn't capable of running Belle Pointe, you're quite mistaken. He simply has too much on his plate to devote the time it takes to do the job well."

"I'm not suggesting he doesn't know squat about farming cotton, Ma. I'm saying it flat-out. Regardless of what he has on his plate. It's a fact and you know it." He turned his head to watch a tractor plowing the field east of the house. It was dry from several weeks without rain and dust billowed out from behind the tractor. He was reminded of the countless ways that farmers were dependent on factors beyond their control.

"I had lunch today with Anne. She was with Franklin and her stepmother." He brought his gaze around to see her face. "Beatrice is Harvey Jones's daughter."

"There's no need to remind me of Beatrice's background. I've known her all my life." Still miffed by the insult to Pearce, Victoria's reply was cool.

"Then you remember that Harvey Jones farmed a thousand acres of cotton."

"What is your point, Buck?" Victoria's gaze was now on the tractor plowing the east acreage.

"He died deeply in debt. Did you know that?"

She brushed a leaf from her shirtsleeve. "Everyone knew."

"Couldn't pay his taxes, so he had to borrow money…from John Whitaker, a man he considered his friend. The upshot was that Belle Pointe then held a mortgage on Harvey's land. A thousand acres of rich Delta bottomland that just happened to border Belle Pointe's west property line."

"I see now where you're going with this. Yes, John loaned Harvey the money to pay a huge backlog of tax. Harvey was a stubborn old fool. He could have asked Beatrice for the money. He could have gone to his relatives. God knows, the Joneses are thick on the ground around here. He was a respected citizen in the town, therefore, the officials were extremely patient with him, but he simply let every tax year roll around and paid nothing. It was inexplicable." Her tongue clicked with impatience. "The town would have cooperated, but he was simply too stubborn to ask."

"Maybe you and Pearce could have offered help," Buck said softly. "Cut the man a little slack instead of foreclosing on the loan Dad made to him to add another thousand acres to Belle Pointe. Four thousand acres wasn't enough? You wanted five?"

"Is Beatrice responsible for filling your head with this drivel?"

"No, I heard about it from my wife," Buck said grimly. "And she got it from digging around in those archives."

"There was nothing illegal in what we did," Victoria said, with a defensive lift of her chin. "The land came to Belle Pointe in a perfectly respectable legal process."

"Yeah, but was it the right thing to do, Ma?" Without giving her a chance to reply, he added, "The only redeeming thing in the whole sorry mess is that now Harvey Jones's daughter lives in the house where she was born. I don't know how Franklin got it, I'm just glad he did."

"He bought it from me," Victoria said. "Or rather, from Belle Pointe Enterprises."

Buck frowned. "When?"

"Within a few days of moving to Tallulah."

For a second, Buck was struck by the coincidence of Franklin later marrying Beatrice, the woman who'd been born in the Jones house. He didn't mention to Victoria that he intended to see to it that Beatrice got the title to the Jones land, as well. But no sense signaling his next move to the opposition right now.

His mother sat a little straighter on the bench, balancing her hat on her lap. "Now I have a question for you," she said. "What do you think is Anne's purpose in rooting around in those old *Spectator* files?"

"Curiosity?" he guessed, shooing off a bee with his cane. "A carryover from her dad's obsession with the Delta? Research for the sake of research?" He glanced at the tractor, noting the neatness of the rows plowed by the operator. "I don't know, Ma. Why do you ask?"

"I would prefer that she put aside her research—if that's what it is—for the time being. The fact that she's reporting is a distinct advantage, as she's family. It will be helpful to Pearce to have a positive voice in the media…even though Franklin's newspaper is just a weekly."

Obviously she hadn't read Anne's article yet. Buck shuddered to think how she'd react.

"But there's a danger in poking around in the past," she went on. "Isolated incidents can be misleading when taken out of context. We want to avoid the possibility of embarrassment to Pearce as his campaign is getting underway."

"I get it. You wouldn't want the voters to know he grabbed a thousand acres from the Jones. Or that he fired Otis. Or that the crews at Belle Pointe are working for less than minimum wage."

She stood up abruptly. "I'm trying to discuss this reasonably, Buck, but you always make things so difficult. Must things always be stark black and white with you? I don't have to apologize for acquiring the Jones land, or for the decisions made in the management of this estate. And I expect you to keep your wife from blundering into sensitive territory as regards this family."

"The Whitakers aren't the only family in the county, Mother. And Anne isn't the kind of person who sets out to dig up dirt on anybody." He got stiffly to his feet. "To tell the truth, you aren't the only one who's concerned with what she might find. When I learned about the Jones land, I was ashamed, but all I could offer was an apology. God knows, I've done nothing to stay abreast of what's happening at Belle Pointe."

He brushed at a few dead leaves on his clothes. "As for asking Anne to stay out of the archives, I'd be wasting my breath. First of all, it would send a red flag up so fast she'd redouble her efforts. On top of that, she's a professional and she'd be insulted. As weird as it seems, she's interested in Tallulah history."

"That's all well and good," Victoria said, "but it's up to you to point out to her the impact that negative publicity can have on Pearce's campaign."

"I'll mention it," he said, on his way to the gate. With his hand on the latch, he looked back at her. "I'll start work here in a couple of days and I'll be bringing Oscar with me."

"All of this is contingent upon Pearce's approval, Buck," she called as he walked away.

Buck stopped, turned and faced her fully. "No, Ma, it isn't. Tell me now if the job is mine. With the conditions I laid out. I don't intend to dance to Pearce's tune and we need to get that straight right now."

He could see her struggling, needing him and hating it.

Worried that if she gave him an inch, he'd take a mile. Seeing him as a threat to Pearce's primary position at Belle Pointe. Troubled that Pearce was too preoccupied to deal with it. If the situation hadn't been so desperate, she would call his bluff.

She drew her mouth into a tight, hard line and nodded briefly. "You'll do me the courtesy of calling when you're ready to start," she snapped.

"Sure." He turned about before his face gave him away. He felt good. He couldn't wait to get started. It would be hard, hot work, at least until the cotton was planted. Then a period of relative calm before things got busy again and defoliating began. Then another period of calm as the cotton matured and burst ready to be picked. Not a lot different from a baseball season, he thought.

Hot *damn!*

His good mood took a dive when he found Pearce's big Lexus parked at the lodge. It hadn't taken his mother long to give his big brother a heads-up. Their conversation must have been a doozy, Victoria filling Pearce's car about Buck moving in and bringing Otis with him, and Pearce whining about the article. After considering it for a minute as he sat in the SUV, he decided to be amused.

Once out of the SUV, he strolled across the gravel drive with the help of his cane and stopped at the bottom of the steps. Pearce sat in a wicker rocking chair drinking a beer and smoking a cigar. Dreading the climb up the twenty-six steps, Buck said, "I thought you'd be out using the daylight hours to knock on doors and kiss a few babies."

"I've got volunteers for the first and I don't need to do any baby-kissing until the primary gets closer." Pearce ground out the cigar and tossed the butt out into the azaleas. "What I've got to do right now is use the media to introduce me, erase the impression of that goddamn article Anne wrote. We need to put a face with my name for folks in parts of the district who don't know me. For most of them, the only Whitaker they recognize is you. They need to know me." He jerked his thumb toward his chest.

"Hmm." Guessing what was coming, Buck paused halfway up the steps.

"So, I've got a date with an advertising agency tomorrow morning and I want you to go with me. I'm shooting a TV spot and I figure to get the most exposure if you're in it with me. They're suggesting a theme with me as a family man. I've laid down the law to Claire. She'll assume her political face. All she has to do is smile. Paige is the wild card. I want her to wear normal clothes and a wig, if necessary. And remove all that piercing shit. I want us to look normal, but special. I want to convince the voters they'll be lucky to have Pearce Whitaker working for them in Jackson. Which is where you come in."

"Excuse me?"

Pearce set his empty beer bottle on the floor beside him. "I want you to let them shoot some scenes with you and me. You know, give them a look at my life, my pretty wife, my charming teenage daughter, show some shots of Belle Pointe and—the icing on the cake—my little brother, the pro baseball great. Having you in the spot is better than a couple of towheaded kids. It'll be dynamite."

Painfully, Buck finished the climb, thinking his mother hadn't called Pearce yet. Or if she had, maybe his campaign was more important to him than the thought of Buck temporarily moving in on his territory at Belle Pointe. He took a seat on the porch swing and propped his cane against the wall. "Television ads are expensive," he said. "Isn't it a little early to be laying out that kind of money with the primary still so far away?"

"Right, but thanks to your wife's poison pen, I've got to do damage control. Which means you owe me. Besides, it's never too early for publicity, provided it's the right kind." Pearce stood up, slapping his thighs. "So, how about you showing up tomorrow morning around…oh, 9:30? We're filming at Belle Pointe. They get started early with the setting-up and whatnot, but no point in you hanging around while they shoot the house and grounds, or the stuff with Claire."

"Actually, I just left Belle Pointe, Pearce. Have you heard from Ma?"

He glanced at the cell phone clipped to his belt. "She's tried to call a couple of times, but I was tied up with these folks. I haven't picked up her messages yet. Why? What's up?"

"With Will retiring and you campaigning, she's in a bind. She asked me to fill in for this growing season."

"No shit? I guess you told her to go take a flying leap."

"No, I told her I'd do it."

His jaw dropped. "You're kidding."

"No. Her argument was that I'm here for the duration, I know cotton farming, she needs help and I'm a Whitaker."

"Shit!" Pearce wheeled about and began to pace. "Since when has she needed help? The woman can run Belle Pointe and the Pentagon at the same time. You don't want to pay any attention to her, Buck. You know how much time it takes to do what she's asking? You're up at daylight, you're up to your ass for ten, twelve hours. You've got crap going with the field hands. Trying to manage them is a full-time job in itself. You won't have any time left over to campaign. You can't do it, man."

"I can with the help of Oscar Pittman. I'm rehiring him as assistant manager."

Pearce stopped cold. "The hell you say!"

"Yeah, after spending most of his life farming cotton at Belle Pointe, I figure he's more than qualified for the job. I've already talked to him." Buck pushed the swing into gentle motion with one foot. "I found him at Wal-Mart working as a greeter. Did you know that?"

"I don't give a shit if he's working at Neiman Marcus! I fired him from Belle Pointe and I don't want his black ass back there. He's trouble. He's an agitator, always bellyaching about wages."

"He's the best equipment operator in the Mississippi Delta and Belle Pointe owes him after paying him peanuts for the past thirty-odd years. I gave him a raise and made it a condition of my taking the job. Ma agreed. It's a done deal, Pearce."

He got a long, hard stare from Pearce. "Who the hell do you think you are? You have ignored Belle Pointe and the family for fifteen years. Now you think being a big baseball star you can just waltz in and take over?"

"No. I think Ma gave me the job and I get to do it the way I want." It was a direct challenge and issuing it gave Buck more than a little pleasure.

"I guess you forgot who's in charge here, brother." Pearce stabbed a thumb at his own chest. "Nothing happens in Tallulah or at Belle Pointe if I don't say it does. And no fuckin' way I'm going for this!"

"I didn't get the feeling from Ma that she needed your approval," Buck said mildly.

"She for goddamn sure does. You just take care of that knee so you can get the hell back to St. Louis and the sooner the better. And take your wife back with you! Meanwhile, folks who know how to farm cotton can take care of the situation at Belle Pointe."

"Well, since you feel that way, you won't be too disappointed if I pass on appearing in your TV ad."

Pearce sputtered an oath and glared angrily. But when Buck merely stared him down, he turned and stalked off the porch, flung himself into his car and started it up with a roar. Buck watched him ram the Lexus into gear and spew gravel for a good twenty yards as he took off. When he realized he was smiling, he felt a little sheepish. Getting the best of Pearce for once might be juvenile, but it was past time for big brother Pearce to learn that the days when he could manipulate Buck were long gone.

Thirteen

Anne walked slowly between metal shelves of the *Spectator*'s archives studying labels on ancient cardboard boxes. She paused, suddenly spotting the year of Buck's high school graduation high up beyond her reach. She went to get a rickety ladder she'd noticed earlier.

A minute later, she was balanced on the topmost rung of the ladder. Upon opening the box, she found no microfiche, only old issues of the *Spectator*. She hadn't yet figured out why there was microfiche for some years and not for others. "1986 must have been a good year," she muttered, struggling with the weight of the box. Now the problem was how to get down without a mishap.

She had almost decided to give it up when she heard footsteps on the stairs. "Dad, is that you? Could you give me a hand with this box, please?"

With both hands occupied, she didn't turn to look at Franklin, but when strong fingers gripped her waist, she knew they didn't belong to her father.

"Leave the box," Buck told her. "I'll get it."

In a heartbeat, he was lifting her, letting her slide the length of his torso slowly. A part of her welcomed the rush of heat that was ever ready between them, but when she felt the brush of his lips on her neck, she resisted. "What are you doing here?"

"Looking for you." Reaching above her, he lifted the box and turned with it in his hands. "I found your office empty and guessed this is where you'd be." He shook his head looking at the dusty shelves. "Although it beats me why. Where do you want this?"

She noticed his cane propped on the shelf. "You aren't supposed to put any weight on that knee."

"So tell me where to get rid of this box and I won't."

"On that table over there." She headed for the space she'd cleared and waited while he set the box on it. "Careful that the bottom doesn't give way. Some of the boxes are overloaded. I spilled 1969 all over the floor a few minutes ago when the bottom split." He was frowning when she glanced up. "What?"

"You aren't supposed to be lifting anything either."

"I wouldn't get anything done if I kept running upstairs for help."

"What's to get done? Your real job is upstairs. Which reminds me. How's it going?"

"Well, Dad hasn't fired me yet. Even though a few subscribers may have suggested it. I seem to have hit a nerve with my twin profiles of Pearce and Jack Breedlove."

He looked alert. "Folks coming down on you?"

She smiled. "A few. Depending on their political persuasions."

"If anybody crosses a line, let me know."

She dusted off the top of the box. "I can handle it, Buck."

He glanced at the date on the label. "Why 1986?"

"Why not?" she replied, unwilling to let him know he had anything to do with her choice. With the flaps open, she lifted out several old newspapers.

"Take my advice and go to the sports section," he said, wagging his eyebrows.

"If you're suggesting I might find your name mentioned," she said, "here it is and it's not in the sports section. You're on the front page." She held up an issue with the headline, TIGERS WIN. WHITAKER SHINES.

Buck shrugged, managing to look modest. "What can I say?"

She had to laugh. "Surely there was something more important in the town news-wise than a victory for a high school baseball team. This is dated April thirteenth, so it was too early in the season for a playoff game."

He gave her a look of mock incredulity. "We're talking a defeat of Spring Valley, population ten thousand and some, woman. They were an awesome team. Beating them was an event."

"But news, it wasn't," she said, rolling her eyes. "Speaking of boredom, how's your physical therapy going?"

"Good. Ty's a real pro. Best choice I could've made." He took a cursory look at another of the old papers, tossed it aside and picked up his cane. Moving restlessly to the nearest shelf, he used the hook of the cane to pull out a box, seemingly at random, but with just a brief glance inside, shoved it back in place. Dusting his hands, he drifted back to the table where Anne was sorting the newspapers by date. "His daddy was working as a greeter at Wal-Mart until a couple days ago."

She tucked a newspaper into its proper date sequence and reached for another. "Didn't his father work at Belle Pointe? I seem to remember that you and Ty played together there when you were boys?"

"Yeah."

She leaned against the table to look at him. "Something on your mind?"

"Oscar was working at Wal-Mart because Pearce fired him," Buck said, beginning to pace. "We never had a piece of equipment at Belle Pointe that Oscar couldn't operate. And some of those big combines were monster rigs. When Ty told me what happened, I couldn't believe it."

"Was he fired for good cause?"

"No. Hell, no. The men's hours were mounting up in over-time, so Pearce decided to pay them for a straight work week only. Oscar didn't think that was fair and said so. Pearce fired him as the instigator of the uprising to bring the others in line."

Anne managed to conceal her satisfaction over Buck's newfound interest in Belle Pointe affairs. First, outrage over the Whitakers foreclosing on a mortgage to grab a thousand acres of land from Beatrice's family and now this. "I take it you didn't know," she said carefully.

"If I'd known, I would have hired a lawyer for Oscar and paid him out of my own pocket to sue the shit out of the family." He halted to look at her. "That man has been a loyal, hardworking employee at Belle Pointe for I don't know how many years. He knows more about equipment than any three men Pearce might have replaced him with. Firing him was mean and underhanded."

Anne thought it was interesting that he reacted so fiercely

on discovering his family's unjust practices. Since Belle Pointe was a family corporation, he had to have some notification of transactions. Had his need for emotional distance blinded him to what was going on?

"I'm trying to figure out why you didn't know about it," she said. "Your mother kept you from an active role at Belle Pointe, but you were still part of the family corporation. You must have gotten financial statements periodically."

"I got them," he said, shoving at a box on the floor with his foot. "But what I'm discovering now wouldn't show on a financial statement. Which is no excuse. I don't even read the damn things. Haven't for years. And I don't cash the checks."

She stared at him. "You tear them up?"

He was pacing again, eyes on the floor. "I endorse them over to a charity."

"Oh." There had been some pretty lean years after they were married and all along he'd been rejecting income that was rightly his? Did his resentment—or hurt—run that deep? "So, are you going to do anything?"

He poked at a dusty box with his cane. "I've done it. I took your advice."

She waved dust away from her nose. "My advice?"

"You said I should do what my mother wants. I decided the only way I could make any changes is by being right there. So after I left you at lunch today, I went to Belle Pointe and offered my services…with a few conditions. My mother hated it, but she's pretty much over a barrel." As if he couldn't help himself, he grinned. "I got the job."

Anne found herself smiling back. "Don't tell me, let me guess. You agreed contingent upon rehiring Mr. Pittman."

"No contingency. Whether I'm there or not, Oscar's back…replacing Wilcox. I took care of it a couple days ago."

"What about Harvey Jones's thousand acres?"

"As soon as I can find an honest lawyer around here, I'm drawing up a legal document reassigning title to Beatrice."

She blinked in surprise. "Can you do that?"

"I'll do it or pay the mortgage amount out of my own pocket. The family corporation won't be out a cent."

"Only a thousand acres," she said dryly. "But it's good of you, Buck."

He moved a little closer and her smile faded at the look on his face. She felt a rush of heat. She knew that look. When he put his hands on her waist, her heartbeat went into double time. She felt the strength of him through the layers of her clothes, warm, solid, sure, but at the same time, gentle. And blatantly male. There had always been something about Buck that spoke to all that was feminine in her.

Knowing he wanted to kiss her, she felt a tingle of anticipation. She stared at the hollow of his throat. If she let him, it would be a turning point. It would breach a barrier she'd put up to help her through this dark time. She had spent weeks working through her grief and loss, picking through the ashes of their broken relationship in hopes of finding something worth saving. She raised her eyes. "Buck…"

He pulled her close, wrapping her in his arms. With his face buried in her hair, he simply held her tight. It seemed like forever since she'd been surrounded by Buck's warmth and tough-tender masculinity.

"You feel so good, baby," he said, letting his lips move on the skin below her ear. When he bit her earlobe gently, she shivered with the delicious sensation. Encouraged, his breath turned heavy and hot as he kissed a trail down her throat to a spot where her pulse raced. He would leave a mark there, she thought dizzily, but instead of pushing him away, she tipped her head to the side and allowed it. It felt good and it had been so long…

Now his hands were beneath her shirt, tugging it up, seeking the softness of her breasts. Desire and need bloomed inside her as he nuzzled her wisp of a bra aside, abrading and arousing the sensitive flesh with day-old beard. And then he found her nipple, closing on it, his mouth wet and warm and wild. He was like a starving man. And Anne responded with a soft cry, clinging to him, wishing for the sheer power of raw lust to ease the pain that never seemed to subside. The pain of losing her baby.

"Come back to the lodge with me, Anne," he said, breathing the words against one breast. He was hard and fully aroused, locked against the softness between her legs. "I've missed you. I need you."

Anne struggled to resist the pull of her attraction to him. She had missed him, too. Buck was different here in Tallulah from the person he was when caught up in the fishbowl life they lived back in St. Louis. But to go back to it, nothing would be changed. And she knew that was Buck's plan. Baseball was his real life. He was only here because she'd forced his hand. So before going to bed with him, she needed to be sure that she could live that life again. That it would be enough.

With her hands braced on his forearms, she pushed him back. "Buck…no, I just can't."

He went still for a beat or two, breathing hard. Finally, he lifted his head, let her go, and with a sigh looked at her. "How can we fix what's wrong if we aren't together, Anne?"

"By being 'together,' you mean having sex, don't you?"

He made a frustrated sound. "Why do you say that, 'having sex'? Why can't you call it what it is? We'd be making love, Anne. I still love you."

"Whatever you call it, it won't fix what's wrong."

He drew in a long breath. "Then how about this. We'll make love…and we won't use any protection."

She felt a pang of anguish. Closed her eyes. He was offering what for years she'd prayed for, longed for, needed. When she could talk, she looked into his eyes. "In other words, now you agree to having a baby, but only to persuade me to come back," she said quietly.

"No!" He swung away from her, one hand slashing through the air. "It wouldn't be like that."

"Then tell me how it would be, Buck."

He stood with his back to her, taking time to be clear with his words. "It was never that I didn't want to be a father," he said. "We had something good, just you and me together. You've seen my family now. You've seen how they are. Don't you understand yet why I didn't want to trade what we had for that?"

"I suppose it's useless to argue that in having children, we would never have become like that. You're hung up thinking it's some kind of gene thing. Inevitable."

He turned back to face her. "I just think it's wise not to take the chance."

She picked up an old newspaper without really looking at it. "You make my point for me, Buck. Since that's so opposite from the way I think, I believe it's better to figure out whether we can be happy together and still be at odds about this," she said simply.

She expected a burst of temper. She knew from experience that when he was sexually frustrated, Buck was testy as a wounded bear. The Buck who'd rejected their baby and driven them recklessly into a ravine a few weeks ago would have gone on a tear. But he surprised her. Standing propped on his cane, with his bad knee cocked at an angle, he didn't appear furious. Instead, he seemed confounded. And very disappointed.

"I guess I jumped the gun there, huh?" he asked wryly.

"Offering to forget protection and chance another pregnancy if I'll stay with you at the lodge? Yeah, I guess you did."

"I guess I sleep alone again tonight, huh?"

She smiled, feeling for the first time a fragile hope that they might be able to work out their differences. With her eyes on the newspaper, she said, "I guess so…unless you can find a warm puppy."

He reached out and gently tugged a strand of her hair. "Smart-ass."

Still smiling, she shoved him back and resumed thumbing through the newspapers. Now in an orderly sequence, she scanned the headlines as she went along and picked up the conversation where they left off. "Since you've decided to make changes in the way Belle Pointe is being run, what makes you think Pearce and your mother will just roll over and let you?" she asked.

"Pearce will be too caught up in politicking to do much more than gripe. By the way, he did plenty of that when he turned up at the lodge yesterday. Of course, my mother will try crossing me at every turn, but I like a good fight."

Anne thought of the ruckus to come with some dismay. Franklin's insight was on the mark. Whether Buck realized it or not, his success in the highly competitive world of professional baseball had given him self-confidence he hadn't had fifteen years ago when Victoria had banished him from Belle Pointe. Oh, to be a fly on the wall at the moment when Victoria realized that.

Anne's mouth was curled with amusement as she turned up the next newspaper. September 1986, she noted. Front and center was a photo of several men dressed in hunting camouflage. Her smile faded at the headline. BUSINESSMAN KILLED IN HUNTING ACCIDENT. In the group photo were three Whitakers, John and Pearce and, standing between them, a very young, grim-faced Buck.

Buck leaned over to get a look. "What—" His question died as he read the headline. "Oh, shit."

Anne looked up at him in confusion. "A man was killed and Pearce was involved? Why have you never mentioned it?"

Buck rubbed a hand over the stubble on his chin. "What would be the point? It's just one more piece of garbage in my family. I don't like talking about garbage."

"It says here that the man who was killed—Jim Bob Baker—was forty years old. You and Pearce were on a dove hunt with older men? How does that work? I never understood this culture of young boys handling guns."

"Men have been hunting since they lived in caves, Anne. It's an ancient sport. You make it sound barbaric, but it's not. In fact, where I grew up it's not only a sport, it's a social thing."

"I know that. But—" She tapped the newspaper, repeating, "A man was killed while hunting and you were there. This surely must have made a major impression on you and it just seems...odd that you never mentioned it."

He was shaking his head. "Like I said, it's in the past. Why can't it stay there?"

She looked at him in silence for a long minute. "This is a good example of why we're in trouble in our marriage, Buck. I discover small pieces of your life that you claim are best left in the past, because you've decided they're meaningless. But I know they aren't. They can't be. You hate guns and you never go hunting, even though you've had dozens of opportunities. I thought surely you'd go on that African safari a couple of years ago with your friends, but you refused. Now that I've stumbled on this article, I understand why." She paused. "So, talk to me."

She saw that he was tempted to refuse. But then, with a heavy sigh, he pushed away from the table and went to one of the shelves stacked with boxes to the ceiling. With his back to her, he propped one arm high with his weight resting on his good leg, using his cane. "I was seventeen and Pearce was twenty," he said quietly. "From the age of ten—maybe even before—I knew how to hunt. Pearce, too. It was something we did in season, whether dove or deer or turkey…whatever. Dove season opens in early September, on Labor Day. But there's more to the pleasure of a hunt than the actual killing of your limit," he told her. "It's like I said, a—for lack of a better word—a social gathering of men.

"This happened the first day of the hunt. I was paired with Dad and Pearce was paired with Jim Bob Baker. It doesn't always happen that a younger hunter is paired with a more experienced one, but Dad always insisted, that for safety's sake, we do it that way. Baker was a businessman. He operated one of the largest cotton gins around here and Belle Pointe was one of his major customers. Which is why he was invited to the lodge for the hunt. It was an invitation that wasn't extended to just anybody. As I said, it's a social gathering as well as a sporting event."

He paused and looked back at Anne, who listened in fascination.

"The night before the hunt, there was a lot of drinking." As he expected, Anne looked unsurprised. "And eating. The menu is usually barbecue with all the trimmings. After, there's usually a poker game. Some of the men go to bed early, others late. As you know, there are a lot of bedrooms at the lodge and—"

"No, I don't know. I've never seen the lodge."

He gave a short laugh. "Say the word and you can have a tour right now. In fact, bring your clothes and you can move in. Separate bedrooms." He held up both hands, palms out. "Swear to God."

Shaking her head, she waved his invitation off. "Tell me what happened, Buck."

"We rolled out early, me and Pearce all paired up with grown-ups as Dad demanded. There were so many birds that it didn't take long to kill our limit that day. By midmorning, most folks had drifted back to the lodge. Finally, it was only Pearce and Jim Bob still out." His gaze wandered to the newspaper lying on the table with its dark headline. "We heard Pearce yelling before he reached the lodge. I remember running out to meet him. He was frantic. Pearce hardly ever got rattled, but he was more than rattled that day. He said there'd been an accident, that Jim Bob was back at a clearing near the river and he'd been shot.

"It was a pretty sophisticated group of Tallulah society at the hunt and a couple of the men were doctors. With Pearce leading, we all rushed out there." He gazed beyond her, as if seeing it all again. "There was so much blood…."

Anne put a hand over her heart. "You were only seventeen," she said, imagining the scene. "It must have been devastating, seeing a man die of a shotgun wound."

"I didn't see him die," Buck said stonily. "When we got there, Jim Bob was already—he'd passed away." He poked at the toe of his Nikes with the cane. "He'd been shot with his own gun."

"How exactly did that happen? If he was an experienced hunter—"

"Pearce said the two of them came to a fence," Buck said, interrupting her. "He climbed over and instead of Jim Bob laying his shotgun down or handing it over to Pearce, he was holding it when he climbed the fence. Somehow it fired and hit him in the throat. We're talking a twelve-gauge shotgun. A twelve-gauge can do some damage."

Anne knew very little about guns and even less about shotguns, but she had a vivid imagination. "He didn't have the safety on to climb a fence?" she asked incredulously. "Even I know you're not supposed to climb a fence without taking that precaution."

"It was the general consensus that he forgot. Pearce said they'd just taken a few shots at some birds."

After a long minute, Anne said, "The headline called it an accident. Was there ever any doubt?"

He gave her an odd look. "Why would you ask that?"

Her shoulders went up in a who-knows gesture. "Just—I don't know. I'm a reporter. And something about the way you look, I guess."

He hoisted himself onto the table and laid the cane across his lap. "I've never told anybody else this, but I didn't go to bed when most everybody else did that night before the hunt.

I was outside on the porch. There's a swing out there. I was lying on it, looking at the stars or doing whatever a seventeen-year-old kid does. Anyway, I heard voices coming from a footpath that's about twenty yards from the house. Since we had a bunch of guests, it wouldn't have been unusual, except whoever was doing the talking didn't sound friendly. It was two people and both were mad and cussing like crazy."

Leaning forward, he braced the heels of his hands on the edge of the table and stared at his feet, frowning, as if the memory still troubled him. "I could only hear bits and pieces, but I knew it was my brother and I recognized the man he was arguing with. It was Jim Bob."

"What was the argument about?"

"Money. Something about the cotton gin and the contract with Belle Pointe. And some other personal stuff that—" He stopped. "Personal stuff."

"What kind of personal stuff?"

He picked up the newspaper and tossed it in the box. "It never made any sense and it's—"

"Personal. Okay, I get the picture anyway." She wondered if Buck realized that keeping a part of the events of that day locked away from her was as hurtful as not telling her any of it. He either trusted her or he didn't. And it was plain he was a long way from seeing that.

Still focused on that day, Buck raised a hand and rubbed the back of his neck. "The police came...and the coroner...and the media." There was irony in the slant of his smile when he looked at her. "TV and newspaper. It was my first brush with negative publicity."

"What did Pearce say when you confronted him? When he knew you'd heard him arguing, he must have known you'd have a thousand questions. He must have known you'd be suspicious."

"He told me that the misunderstanding between him and Jim Bob had been cleared up while they were hunting before the accident. He told me to forget it." With his hand still at the back of his neck, he met her eyes. "And I did."

"You did? He expected you to just forget about it and you did?"

With a glance at his watch, he eased off the table, taking care not to put pressure on his knee. "Is there another box you want me to take down before I leave?"

"Because I don't see how you didn't press him for details. A man was dead. And under circumstances that seem suspicious, to say the least."

He moved to the stairs. "Did I mention I've arranged for your rental car? It's another Mercedes. I figured you'd want to stay with the same brand you're driving in St. Louis."

"At least, tell me you had a conversation with your father about this."

He stopped at the foot of the stairs, his gaze fixed on the crook of his cane for a long minute. Then he turned and looked directly at her. "I did. And I could tell he was troubled about the way Baker died. I don't know for sure, but I suspect something about Pearce's story didn't set well with him. Anyway, I got a feeling that he didn't want his suspicions confirmed."

Holding her gaze doggedly, he added, "How was I going to tell him something like that? What words would I use? Think about it. Once either of us said it out loud, it couldn't be taken back. I was thinking all this and before I decided one way or the other, he launched into a lecture about our responsibility to the Whitaker name. Being a Mississippi Delta Whitaker wasn't just about the land, he said, or the property or our roots going back five generations. No, he reminded me of the various family holdings that provide employment in the community. Didn't I realize that a scandal would jeopardize more than just Belle Pointe? After all, I was soon leaving to go to college and would not be around to suffer the consequences. So, as a Whitaker, I had a duty to the people of Tallulah that trumped all others."

She stared at him in disbelief. "So he knew—or suspected—what you were going to tell him?"

He was no longer looking at her. "I don't know what he knew or suspected. The subject was never mentioned again and I went off to school and tried never to think of it again. And don't assume I'm proud of weaseling out the way I did. I had a shitload of excuses—it would hurt my dad, it would damage the Whitaker name, it would open a can of worms and, yes, I admit it, although Pearce was directly involved, it might reflect on me and I had a baseball scholarship and didn't want to be tainted by suspicion of—" He stopped, refusing to say the word.

"Suspicion of murder, Buck. Say it." He was shaking his head, so she added, "The thing you haven't explained is why he did it…if he did."

"I don't know. I—"

When he stopped, she studied his grim profile and guessed he did know something. What was it he'd said earlier? That he overheard something when Pearce argued with Baker, but it was too personal to tell her. Was he going to tell her now?

"Actually, I think it could be something to do with my mother."

"Your mother? How? Why?"

"It was something Baker said," he told her, turning his head to meet her eyes. "This is something else I've never told anybody before."

"The 'personal' thing you mentioned?" She made quotation marks with her fingers.

"Yeah. I heard Baker say to Pearce, 'If I talk, your mother is going to get the punishment she deserves.'"

"But you don't know what he meant?"

"No."

"And you didn't ask?"

"No."

"I wonder if your father knew…or if he suspected something about his wife."

Buck started up the stairs. "We'll never know the answer to that, will we?"

She watched him climb the stairs thinking that in the litany of excuses he gave for keeping quiet, he hadn't mentioned protecting any secret his mother might have. "This is just so incredible, Buck," she murmured.

Buck, now at the top of the stairs, looked down at her. "I keep trying to tell you, I come from a screwed-up family."

Beatrice and Paige appeared within minutes of Buck leaving. As Paige clambered down the stairs in her combat boots, Anne quickly folded the issue of the *Spectator* that reported the hunting accident and tucked it out of sight.

"What was wrong with Uncle Buck?" Paige asked, big-eyed with curiosity. "He looked like he was really mad."

"What have I told you about asking personal questions, Paige," Beatrice chided, taking the stairs more cautiously than the teenager. She waved a hand in front of her nose and made a face. "Gracious, Anne, it's more dusty than usual in here. What have you been doing?"

"Digging up the past," Anne said with a vague look around the room. "That tends to stir up dust."

"It can stir up more than dust," Beatrice said, regarding her with a keen eye. "Is this a bad time? Paige is supposed to be organizing the material sent by the Vanderbilt professor, but she can always do something upstairs."

Paige wedged herself between the two women, her eyes fixed on Anne's face. "I was right! Buck is pissed off about something, isn't he? Wow, this week is turning out to be just full of interesting stuff. First my mom and now Anne."

"Paige…" Beatrice gave her a stern look.

Anne closed the flaps on the box. "There is something you can do, Paige. I picked up one of the cartons and the bottom split open. The contents spilled out over there in the second aisle. Would you find a new box to put it in, please?"

"Don't you want to hear what freaked out my mom?"

"Not really," Beatrice said dryly.

"Even if it's really juicy?" she said, giving them a side-long glance.

"Juicy usually means personal," Anne said, fighting a smile.

Paige appeared to consider that with her elbow resting on one arm, tapping her forefinger against her lips. "Hmm, is a love affair personal?"

"Yes!" Both Anne and Beatrice exclaimed together.

She grinned. "Just kidding. How about if it happened when my mom was in high school?"

"It's still personal," Beatrice said in a forbidding tone. "And those newspapers won't jump in that box all by themselves."

"I'm gonna pick the stuff up, Beady. In a minute." She backed to the table where Anne was working and hoisted herself up much as Buck had done a few minutes before. "Okay, here's the deal. Claire and I were on our way to school Monday and she was stopped for speeding in a school zone." Swinging her legs, Paige waited for a reaction. Undaunted at getting none, she continued. "Well, anyway, guess who stopped her?"

"The police?" Beatrice suggested.

"Jack Breedlove," Paige announced, with dramatic emphasis on the name. "Her old high school boyfriend."

"And your point?" Beatrice asked.

"Beady!" Paige put her hands on her hips. "You already know the story, don't you? Like, you know everything that ever happened in Tallulah." She switched her attention to Anne. "Mom and Jack Breedlove went steady for a whole year when she was in high school."

"Hmm, kids don't go steady nowadays?" Anne remarked mildly.

"She only told me that because I saw how freaked out she was when he was talking to us and I wasn't going to shut up until she told why. And get this. When he leaned down and looked at her with those sunglasses, she just about had a kitten! She was, like, so freaked."

"People do get nervous when they're stopped by the police," Anne said.

"It was more than nervous," Paige insisted. "It was way, way more than nervous. I mean, he looks a lot like Brad Pitt, so I can understand it in a way. He's hot." She waggled the fingers of her right hand suggestively. "Then they said a lot of stuff, back and forth, you know? And finally she just said,

'Give me the ticket, Jack.' Real snippy. Almost mean." Paige laughed. "So he, like, just gave it to her, not saying a word and boy was she the embarrassed one when he said it wasn't a real ticket, but just a warning."

"She must have been relieved," Beatrice murmured.

Paige hiked up a shoulder. "I guess. And then…the strangest thing. He said it was good to see her."

"That's strange?" Beatrice lifted an eyebrow.

"Then she said that was something easily remedied." Paige waited as if dangling a lure, then gave an impatient sigh when nobody bit. "Here's the kicker. He said, 'What's changed…am I now welcome in your world?' And Claire went, like…*white*. As. A. Ghost!"

"Paige, please do not refer to your mother by her first name," Beatrice requested.

"Okay, okay. So what I want to know is this." She paused dramatically. "Is Jack Breedlove my real father?"

Both women stared at her. "Of course not!" Beatrice said, recovering first. "You know who your father is."

Paige shrugged and bent to the job of stacking up the material spilled on the floor as if her question were a perfectly logical conclusion instead of something from outer space. "Well, it seemed kind of interesting—if it had been true. And Mom did act really weird while they talked. I wonder if my dad was the reason they broke up?"

Beatrice, who was leaving, stopped at the stairs. "Claire's parents were the reason they broke up. Your mother was sixteen years old when she dated Jack Breedlove. He couldn't be your father because he joined the army and was in Kuwait when Claire got pregnant. Do the math."

"See, you did know all this, Beady!" Paige said.

With one foot on the stair, Beatrice thought for a minute. "I'm only guessing, but I think Claire's parents were concerned since she was so young."

"And he was from the wrong side of the tracks!" Paige said.

Beatrice sighed. "Claire left Tallulah to go to an exclusive school somewhere in Virginia…I believe it was. She finished high school there."

"She was, like, banished from everything and everyone she loved. That was mean." Paige slid off the table and, after a moment, said with a thoughtful look, "I wonder if my mom would have been happier if she'd married Jack Breedlove."

Beatrice met Anne's eyes over the child's head. "I wouldn't jump to that conclusion, Paige," she said gently. "Things are not always what they seem."

"Maybe not," Paige said, "but my mom is definitely unhappy."

"I really must get back to the shop," Beatrice said, going up the stairs. "Anne, please don't start dinner before I get home. You're making me feel guilty cooking for us every night."

Anne gave a noncommittal wave as the door closed behind her stepmother and braced for Paige to continue to pursue the subject of her mother's unhappiness. But when Paige spoke, it wasn't about Claire.

"Hey, Anne, look at this," she said as she sorted through the contents of the broken box. Settling back on her ugly boots, she spread an old issue on the floor. "It's dated way back in the sixties. It's about a man from Tallulah who was killed in Vietnam. Here's his picture. It's sad, isn't it?"

Anne glanced briefly at the grainy photo before removing

the cap from a black felt pen to mark a box. "The Vietnam war was sad," she said.

"Rudy Baker, age twenty-one."

"Hmm?"

"The soldier. That was his name, Rudy Baker." With her head to one side, Paige studied the face in the photo. "He looks kind of familiar, doesn't he?"

Anne put a star beside the date—1985—on the box so she'd be able to find it again. She wanted to read about the hunting accident again later when she was alone. Now that Buck revealed the remark Baker made about Victoria, the incident had taken on the interesting aspect of a mystery. Pearce and John Whitaker—and possibly Victoria—may have been able to rationalize the circumstances of a man's death without guilt, but not Buck. Even now, years later, he still felt troubled at keeping their secret. More and more, she understood why Buck had chosen to distance himself from his family.

What was most interesting was that Buck suspected his mother of something—a secret or an act or an event—important enough that Pearce may have committed murder to conceal it. That alone was enough to alert any journalist, even one who was woefully out of practice.

Much later, as she lay in bed on the edge of sleep, she thought about the last name of the soldier killed in Vietnam. It was the same as the name of the man who'd died while hunting with Pearce. Baker. Sleepily, she wondered if they were related.

Fourteen

Lately, dinner at Belle Pointe had been a totally feminine affair. Paige was okay with that because when her dad came, he hogged the conversation. Between him and the Dragon, nobody else said much. Not that her mom seemed to care. Paige wondered what had been going on in her mom's head lately, but she didn't plan to bug her about it since Claire hadn't touched a drink in about five days—she didn't want to mess that up. Maybe this time she would stick to her promise. That would be nice.

Since she was now a vegetarian, Paige loaded her plate with an extra helping of broccoli and just a dab of corn casserole. No way was she going to eat one of those chicken breasts no matter how good they smelled. As for the rolls…maybe. Big-time carbs there.

"What's wrong?" Claire asked, looking at Paige's plate. "Aren't you hungry? Are you sick?"

"No, I'm a vegetarian now."

Claire laughed, her eyebrows raised. "A vegetarian? Since when?"

"Since this article I read. Did you know that you can add like, six years to your life if you give up eating anything that comes from an animal?"

"I wouldn't want to live that long if I could never have a steak," Claire said, slicing heartily into her chicken breast.

"This is only my first day, but I'm not quitting."

"Where is this new attitude coming from?" Claire wanted to know. "It can't be from anything at the *Spectator,* since only a week ago you considered the time you spend there cruel and unusual punishment."

"It's interesting now. Your finger is on the pulse of a community," Paige said, waving a half-eaten broccoli stalk on the end of her fork. "Journalists know everything that happens and everything that has already happened is in the archives. It's way cool."

"'Your finger is on the pulse of a community?'" Claire repeated with open amusement.

"Definitely."

"So, tell me something interesting that's happening."

"Well, for one thing, I've decided what to do as a career," Paige said, chewing broccoli. You were supposed to chew a long time. Chewing was a basic human urge and you didn't eat as much if you chewed a lot.

"And your career choice is…"

"I want to be a reporter. It takes guts and brains, but you get to go to a lot of cool places and be involved when cool stuff is happening."

"I don't know about going to cool places," Claire said, "but I know one smart reporter, who shall be nameless, who definitely has guts. Could that be where you're getting these ideas?"

One of Victoria's elegant eyebrows rose as she sliced a sliver of chicken. "I assume that's a reference to Anne. I'm very disappointed in the article she wrote. In fact, I wonder if she's a proper role model for Paige."

Paige was quick to defend Anne. "She's a perfect role model. And it's a lot more fun digging around in all that old stuff when Aunt Anne's doing it, too."

Victoria carefully balanced her knife on the edge of her plate and looked at Paige. "Anne is digging around in what, exactly?"

"Mostly family stuff," Paige said, eyeing a roll. "Are you still a vegetarian if you eat bread?"

"Beats me," Claire said.

"What kind of family stuff?" Victoria asked, passing the basket of dinner rolls over.

"Just Whitaker family stuff. Anything about Belle Pointe." Paige took two rolls and bit hungrily into the first. "And there's plenty of stuff about this place."

"Don't talk with your mouth full," Victoria ordered.

Paige gulped down peach tea. Milk she refused to drink, no matter how the Dragon nagged. "It's not only Uncle Buck either. She asks a lot of questions about the family in general."

Victoria looked stern. "I forbid you to discuss this family, Paige."

"She doesn't ask me, Gran," Paige replied patiently. "It's from the archives and Beady tells her stuff, too. She knows Tallulah history from way back." She turned to her mother, pointing with her fork. "For instance, Mom, Beady knew all about when you and Jack were lovers in high school."

"Paige!" Claire sputtered into her peach tea. "We were not lovers."

"And she said definitely not when I asked if Jack Breedlove was my real father."

"Omigod," Claire exclaimed faintly.

Paige grinned. "Aw, I'm just kidding. You have to admit, you acted really, like, so freaky when he stopped us."

Victoria turned a glacial look on Claire. "What is this child talking about?"

"Nothing, Victoria. Paige, leave the table if you can't behave yourself."

Paige reached for the bowl of garden salad, which was one of those all-you-can-eat-is-okay foods. "So where was I?" she said, settling back. "Oh, yeah, Aunt Anne poking around in family stuff. It's nothing for you to get your panties in a wad, Gran. She's just doing it because she's married to Uncle Buck and her daddy wrote a book about this place and she's just, like, interested." Paige gave Miriam her glass to refill. "She thinks I don't notice what she's reading, but I do. And the reason I know is that my job is organizing the old *Spectator* files that came from Professor what's-his-name who died. He used to be a *Spectator* contributor or something a long time ago."

Claire set her glass down. "Hey, maybe you have a reporter's instincts after all."

"Aunt Anne gave up her career as a reporter to be married to Uncle Buck. I don't know this for sure, but maybe that's why he's at the lodge and she's staying with her daddy. I mean, maybe she's tired of being arm candy."

"Arm candy?" Another faint response from Claire.

"Yeah, athletes have them—beautiful wives who don't have a brain. Only Aunt Anne's got a brain and she wants to use it. I think she wants to have a baby, too. She goes all mushy when we see babies or she reads anything about them."

"You certainly don't know that and do not repeat it to anyone else," Claire said. "Buck would skin you alive if he caught you gossiping about his marriage."

"I know that, Mom," Paige said. "I'm, like, totally cool with it."

"Since you appear to know so much," Victoria said, dabbing at her lips with a napkin, "maybe you can reveal Anne's purpose in collecting material about our family."

Paige forked up the last smidgen of corn casserole, chewed slowly and swallowed it. "She denied it before, but I think she's really writing a book. She's gonna tell all!"

Claire choked out a laugh. "What's to tell that the world doesn't already know? Anything that's ever happened to the Whitakers was always front-page news around here. We have no secrets, honey."

"That's not what Aunt Anne says." Paige eyed the banana pudding dessert that Miriam placed on the table and helped herself. Vegetarian didn't mean she couldn't have dessert, did it? "Aunt Anne says everybody has secrets."

Anne was on the point of leaving the house when she heard a car pull into the driveway and stop. Thinking her stepmother had probably forgotten something, she headed to the front door. But it wasn't Beatrice who emerged from the car.

Victoria Whitaker paused at the bottom of the steps. "I hope my dropping in this way isn't too inconvenient," she said with a frosty smile. "I wanted to try and catch you before you left."

Anne held the front door open. "Come in, please."

She watched Victoria climb the steps up to the porch, admiring her mother-in-law's style. Today, although there was

a trace of strain on her face, she was the quintessential Southern matron in sharply creased linen slacks and an Ann Tay-
lor cropped blazer over a silk shirt. As she crossed the
threshold, she brought with her the subtle scent of gardenias.
Once she was seated in the living room, Anne offered coffee.

"Thank you, no." Victoria glanced at her watch. "I had an
errand in town and I really should have called first, but—"

Anne waved away her excuses. "I'm just on my way to an
assignment. One of the perks of a reporter's job is not being
tied to a desk," she said with a smile, "which means my hours
are flexible."

"Hmm. I'll admit to some surprise that you've plunged into
your job with so much enthusiasm since I expect you will eventually return to St. Louis with Buck. I was also surprised and
frankly disappointed in your article about Pearce. As you carry
the Whitaker name, I expected more loyalty from you, Anne."

Anne felt some relief. She'd expected more express disapproval from Victoria. Instead, the rebuke was pretty mild.
"Can you point to anything specific? Pearce made his objections plain the day the paper came out, but he was unable to
tell me exactly where I'd been inaccurate…or biased."

Victoria made a dismissive gesture with one hand. "It was
the way you wrote the piece, side by side with Jack Breedlove." Saying the name, her mouth thinned with distaste.
"But I'm not here to tell you how to do your job. There's
something else on my mind."

Her curiosity on full red alert, Anne sat on the edge of her
seat.

"Paige tells me," Victoria said, "that you're using the *Spectator*'s archives as a source for considerable research on Belle
Pointe and the Whitakers."

Anne was a little let down. What had she expected from her mother-in-law, a bit of scandal or a juicy tidbit? "That's right, between the archives and Paige, I could write a book."

"This is genuine research? You're writing a book?"

Anne dismissed her concern with a laugh. "That was a joke, a figure of speech. Or, to be completely honest, I haven't yet decided against writing a book, but I know the difficulty in finding an agent and a publisher, in dealing with marketing and promotion issues. Frankly, it's all so daunting that I'm not sure I want to bother. All that aside, I still find it fun to read Tallulah's history."

"None of that explains your interest in Belle Pointe and the Whitakers," Victoria pointed out.

"No, I suppose not," Anne said, studying her hands. "I'll try to explain. I started by poking around in the archives only to satisfy a fascination I've had since childhood. I'm sure I was influenced by my dad's obsession, which as you know, resulted in a book. So Buck's background at Belle Pointe, as a fifth-generation Whitaker, is naturally of interest to me. Any family going back that far tends to make its mark in the area." Anne paused, considering whether to take the conversation to a more personal level. "Were you aware that I'm adopted?"

"No, I was not," Victoria replied with only a slight widening of her eyes.

"Well, I am a 'lonely only' and I've always fantasized about having cousins and aunts and uncles. I consider Buck so lucky to have that."

"I'm not sure he would agree with you," Victoria said dryly.

"And I admit I've never understood why." When Victoria went quiet at that, Anne sensed her caution. Curiouser and curiouser. She wasn't the type of mother-in-law to just drop in for a chat and keep the subject to generalities. Anne decided to wait her out.

"It's one thing to focus on the area itself," Victoria said. "Granted, the Delta has a colorful history. Your father's book was a balanced portrayal of the good and the bad, unlike any number of other books that have just savaged us Mississippians." She paused. "But I question what in particular you find so interesting about my family."

My family. Not our family. Was Victoria suggesting that Anne hadn't measured up as a Whitaker? "I'll say this one more time, Victoria," she said quietly, "I'm not researching a book. I'm simply looking at old issues of the *Spectator* because, frankly, I find Tallulah and Belle Pointe and the Delta interesting." So much for getting to the point. Their conversation had taken on a surreal air and she still hadn't a clue what the woman was getting at. "I'm puzzled as to what point you're trying to make, Victoria."

"Pearce is involved in a political campaign," Victoria said. "This is a small town but, as someone said, 'All politics is local.' It can get just as nasty here in Tallulah as it does in Washington."

Ah, Pearce. Back to the favored offspring.

"If information is taken out of context, the potential for disaster is great," Victoria said. "Such information in the hands of my son's enemies could wreck his candidacy. They'll seize on something and crucify him. I don't know how else to impress upon you what could result."

"I certainly have no intention of harming Buck's brother, Victoria."

"You've already done so in writing that article. My purpose is to request that you don't do it again."

"I said nothing negative about Pearce in that article!" Anne argued.

"One can be damned with faint praise, Anne," Victoria said, "which is what I think you did in that article. So we'll agree to disagree. But I'm still asking you to forgo further research in the archives until after the election."

Anne could not keep the astonishment from her face. "Excuse me? You're asking me to stay completely away from the archives?" She paused, waiting for a denial, but Victoria stayed stonily silent. "You want me to stop looking on the off chance that I might find something that could be potentially embarrassing, which might possibly be misconstrued and could conceivably fall in the hands of Pearce's opponent, who would perhaps crucify him and maybe wreck his chances at the polls? Do you realize how incredible that sounds, Victoria?"

"Buck has already mentioned the thousand acres that once belonged to Harvey Jones and is now part of Belle Pointe," Victoria replied stiffly. "There's one example of a perfectly legal transaction that could be misconstrued."

"I can see that you wouldn't want that to find its way onto the front page just now," Anne said dryly. "I take it there is other…ah, embarrassing stuff?"

Victoria stood up, no trace of a smile, not even a frosty one. "As Buck's wife, it's your duty to protect the family name. I hope that you'll remember your connection to the family if you must satisfy your curiosity about Tallulah, Belle Pointe and the Whitakers."

Oh, she was family now. "I will remember that," she promised. But she wasn't about to promise to cover up anything that smelled bad. And there must be something. Otherwise, Victoria would never have lowered herself to ask.

After writing an article for the next issue of the *Spectator*, Anne went to her stepmother's shop. She liked Beatrice's down-to-earth outlook and found herself drawn to her more and more lately. One look at Anne and Beatrice turned the shop over to her assistant.

Her stepmother's office was small and haphazardly cluttered. Half-opened boxes sat on the floor. Adding to the cramped floor space were cartons with bubble wrap and peanut packing spilling out. Papers that appeared to be invoices were a jumbled mess on her desktop. File folders were stacked six inches high on the only other chair besides the one behind Beatrice's desk. How she managed to run her shop so efficiently was a mystery to Anne.

Beatrice filled a mug with tea and handed it to Anne. "Something's definitely stolen your joy today. Is it Buck?"

"No, it's his mother." In the tight confines of the office it was difficult to pace, but Anne was unable to stay still as she described to Beatrice the gist of Victoria's visit. "She practically accused me of having a hidden agenda. Some kind of plan to discredit her precious Pearce. How ridiculous is that!"

Beatrice reached for the sugar bowl. "She's never been particularly perceptive."

Anne picked up a tin of organic tea, sniffed it and put it back. "All she's accomplished is to fire up my curiosity. Instead of persuading me to quit, I'm convinced there's something she doesn't want me to find."

Propping her elbows at her desk, Beatrice watched Anne move restlessly about the office, picking up, handling, poking into boxes, but with only vague interest in what she touched. Her thoughts were still locked on the interview with her mother-in-law.

"Put yourself in Victoria's shoes, Anne," Beatrice said. "Belle Pointe and her life there are everything to her. So, here you come along and start poking around in the past—her past. For whatever reason, she senses a potential for disaster. I don't know what she thinks you might stumble on, but surely her concern is understandable."

Frowning, Anne moved to the chair, transferred the stack of folders to the floor and sat down. "Maybe you're right and I'm overreacting. You went to high school with her, Beatrice. Tell me something that might help me understand her better. Right now, I'm just appalled and, frankly, offended by the woman's incredible arrogance."

"Maybe her protective attitude toward Belle Pointe and the Whitaker name is understandable when you consider her background," Beatrice said, settling back in her chair. "Remember, she came from a home where her father was the mechanic at Belle Pointe and her mother a waitress, so marrying John Whitaker elevated her social status to the most elite level in Delta society. Could be she's a bit sensitive to any threat to that, real or imagined."

Anne tapped a finger against her lips, thinking. "I've been wondering about that. Around here, there's obviously a gulf between the haves and the have-nots. And it isn't confined to race, as far as I can tell. So here's my question. If Victoria's social status was so much less than John Whitaker's, were his parents okay with his choice of a bride? Were John and Victoria just so passionately in love that they overruled any opposition? You were classmates. Wasn't there talk?"

"Isn't there always gossip?"

"Hello? That's why I'm asking. I know when I was in high school, if a girlfriend pulled off a coup like that, we would have been chattering about it like mad. C'mon, Beatrice, what was it like back then?"

"In the olden days?" Smiling, Beatrice settled again in her chair behind the cluttered desk. "You realize you sound like Paige, don't you? And both of us would be all over her for stirring the ashes of an old scandal."

"I won't repeat anything you tell me. So, was it a scandal?"

Beatrice released a sigh. "Maybe scandal is the wrong word, but it was a hot topic. It's been a long time, keep that in mind along with the fact that Victoria was three years older than I. Still, I do remember her as well as anybody at Tallulah High School would. She was a natural beauty. Striking amber eyes, honey-blond hair and a perfect figure. Not model slim, as girls want to be today, but…curvaceous." Beatrice moved her hands in an hourglass shape. "All the boys in school were mad about her, but when she was about sixteen, she stopped paying attention to them. And Rudy Baker was the reason."

"Who?"

"Rudy Baker's uncle owned a saloon, the Boll Weevil. It was a popular hangout because it had live music starting Thursday night and going through Sunday." Beatrice gave a little shrug as she met Anne's amused eyes. "You're thinking that sounds pretty tame considering what goes on nowadays, but back then—this was in the sixties—it was a little rowdy. My daddy would have skinned me alive if he caught me there."

"Rowdy?" Anne couldn't keep the smile off her face. "Live music, beer and what else?"

"Maybe you could get a little marijuana but, again, my daddy would have killed me. Anyway," she went on briskly, "Rudy Baker fancied himself a musician. Elvis was big then, you'll recall. Oh, I guess you wouldn't since you weren't born. Anyway, Rudy was tall and drop-dead handsome, he had coal-black hair and dark, dark eyes and a sexy way about him. He could pick and sing and Vickie Hinton didn't have time for any of those THS boys after she had a taste of Rudy Baker."

"What happened? She married John Whitaker in 1965 because I found the wedding announcement in the archives."

"Rudy was drafted and sent to Vietnam. Later, he was killed in action."

"Wait a minute." Anne frowned, thinking back. "I remember something about that. Paige found a write-up about a local man killed in Vietnam. There's a picture of him on the photo wall."

"Then that would be Rudy because he was the only soldier killed in action in the whole county."

Anne got up for more tea. "I think Baker was also the name of the man who died in a hunting accident involving Pearce," she said in a thoughtful tone. "Do you remember that, Beatrice?"

"I certainly do. That was Jim Bob Baker, Rudy's younger brother. He owned part interest in the cotton gin here in Tallulah. It was a sad thing, two sons from the same family dying young."

"Do you remember if there was much discussion about the accident?"

"What do you mean?"

"I found the story—again when I was digging in the archives—and I thought it odd that Buck had never mentioned it. Of course, it was Pearce who was directly involved, but Buck was there and he was only seventeen. When he realized I'd found it in the archives and wanted to talk about it, he got very agitated. I decided it was one of those links to Belle Pointe in his past that he tried hard to forget."

She returned to the chair and sat down again. "It's as if he's wary about telling me anything that touches him in a personal sense. I think he fears I might one day use it in some negative way against him. It's so frustrating."

"If he doesn't have a good relationship with his mother, it could be the root of his wariness about trusting any woman."

"Maybe," Anne said, thinking it made sense. "But back to Victoria. It sounds as if she was passionately in love with Rudy Baker. So how did she wind up marrying John Whitaker so soon after seeing the love of her life go off to Vietnam?"

"I couldn't say she was passionately in love with him or that he was the love of her life," Beatrice said. "I'm just telling you the way things appeared. She had no time for high school boys and she certainly spent a lot of time with Rudy. He was older than she was and, as I said, he had a way about him. And then he was gone. Not killed in action right away, you know, but absent from Tallulah."

"And *then* she took up with John," Anne guessed.

"Well, even though he was also four or five years older, she'd known him all her life because, as I said, her daddy worked at Belle Pointe. His name was Benny Hinton. She'd always been a bit of a tomboy and spent a lot of time there. She could operate the equipment that Benny worked on as well as any field hand. But if she had ever been romantically involved with John before that summer when they up and married, I never knew about it. Nobody knew."

"I see it now," Anne said, squinting thoughtfully. "John's a randy college student, home for the summer. The hometown girl that he's probably never paid much attention to has turned into this gorgeous, sexy siren. But she's forbidden fruit. Still, they play around a little—or a lot. It's a story as old as time."

"Maybe you should be a novelist instead of a journalist," Beatrice said. "But I see where you're going and I don't know that it happened that way at all. And Victoria will certainly never tell."

Anne held a piece of pottery in her hand. "Next is the surprise wedding and Pearce is born…how many months later?"

"I have no idea," Beatrice said. "They were away at Duke University for the next two years. John was in graduate school, I believe."

"How convenient."

"Even if it did happen that way, Anne," Beatrice said, her voice gently chiding, "it's ancient history. These things happen. In those days, a baby out of wedlock wasn't as easily dismissed as it is today. I shouldn't have told you. It's just that I thought you might—" She got up from her desk suddenly, sending her chair bumping against a stack of boxes behind her. "People make mistakes, mistakes that can sometimes have grave consequences. If that is what happened, Victoria was very fortunate that it was John Whitaker and not some irresponsible man or worse, a man who couldn't marry her because of…circumstances."

"Of course," Anne said with a pang of conscience. "I didn't mean to imply anything else. It's just that she's so…so full of herself and her position."

"She's earned it, hasn't she? She took over at John's death—actually before John's death—and Belle Pointe has flourished."

"And if it did happen that way," Anne went on, "I guess I'm envious of her ease in getting pregnant." There, she'd said the word. No more dancing around it. With a wistful look, she put the piece of pottery back in the box. "I'd take a baby under any circumstances."

"When you and Buck work out your differences, you'll have a baby."

"I don't know, Beatrice." She crossed the small room to the door. "There were times when I forgot to take the Pill for a day or two but I never conceived. I need to know for certain that there's nothing genetically wrong. I don't have time to waste. I'm not getting any younger."

"One miscarriage doesn't mean something's genetically wrong. I wish you would stop obsessing over that."

"I will once I know the facts of my background."

"What good will it do if you and Buck aren't reconciled?"

"That's a bridge I'll cross when I get to it." Anne moved to the door. "Thanks for sharing all that about my mother-in-law. I still don't like her much, but I do understand her a little better. I'll see you tonight."

Buck told himself he didn't have any particular purpose in stopping by the police department other than the fact that he hadn't seen Jack Breedlove in a number of years. Like Ty and Buck, Jack had been active in sports and they'd drunk a lot of beer and raised a lot of hell together.

Inside, he found the station looking the same as a thousand others in small towns across America. Smelled the same, too,

Buck thought. Old coffee, stale cigarette smoke—in spite of a No Smoking sign—and pine-scented disinfectant. A young rookie cop manned the front desk. He looked up without much interest, but did a quick double take upon recognizing Buck.

He scrambled up from his chair, tall and skinny with a buzz cut and significant ears. "Mr. Whitaker. Can I help you?"

Buck smiled and glanced at the name tag as he crossed to the counter. Daniel Peyton. "I'm looking for Chief Breedlove, Daniel."

"Yes, sir. He's right back there in his office. I'll show you." He started out of the counter area, then stopped and turned back, scrambled around on his desk looking for what, Buck hadn't a clue. He finally grabbed up one of Jack Breedlove's campaign flyers. "Sir, would you autograph this, please?"

"I'm Buck to anybody from Tallulah," he told him, taking the flyer. "Especially a cop." He scribbled his name, enjoying the irony of autographing the campaign flyer of Pearce's opponent.

"Hey, thanks, Buck." Daniel took the flyer and headed down the hall. "I saw that game last year when you pitched against Chicago. Put y'all two games from the play-offs. You think the Jacks can do that again this year?"

"Without a doubt." Actually, there was considerable doubt, but it was Schrader's problem this year, not Buck's. It surprised him that he didn't feel as miserable over missing out as he had before he left St. Louis.

"Here we are." Daniel rapped his knuckles on the open door and, without waiting for a response from the man behind the desk, went right up to him, grinning. "Look who's here, Chief."

Jack Breedlove sat facing a computer. Before turning to his visitor, he hit a key and closed out a program. Recognition dawned, wiping away his distraction. He rose from his chair and with genuine pleasure, stuck out his hand to shake. "Sonofagun, Buck, it's about damn time you showed up. Another day or so and I planned to arrest you just to say hello."

Buck found himself grinning. "Good to see you, Jack."

"Take a load off. Damn, Buck, it's great to see your pretty face." He dropped back in his chair, shaking his head, his smile wide.

"How's that campaign going?" Buck asked.

"Smooth as a sewing machine."

"C'mon."

"Okay, we both know it'll take a miracle to beat a Whitaker in this jurisdiction, but I'm giving it a shot. If Walter Birdsong hadn't retired, that seat would still be safe and secure, but now he's gone it's up for grabs. I think I can do the job as well as Pearce. Better, actually." He winked. "Especially with a little help from the wife of a friend."

Before Buck could deny having anything to do with Anne's article, Jack reached behind him for a campaign flyer. "Look this over and tell me what you think. I don't expect an endorsement. I figure your loyalty has to lie with your brother."

Buck let that pass without comment. "I never thought I'd see the day you'd get into politics, Jack. What'll you do if some of that stuff we did comes out? I mean, if I ever had a teenage boy, I'd hog-tie him to his bed for fear insanity was in his genes. It's a wonder we didn't wind up dead or in jail."

Jack chuckled. "Hopefully, other folks won't have your long memory." He shook his head. "You and me and Ty. We were crazy, weren't we?"

"And here you are chief of police." Buck was grinning, too. "Is this a great country, or what?"

"I hear you."

Neither said anything for a minute, reminiscing. Then Buck shifted, laying his cane over his knees. "Pearce is bound to try and discredit you, Jack. He was unhappy with Anne's article. Said it was tilted to you. He'll try and recover."

"And the mud will fly, I guess. But stop and think. I figure Pearce will be hesitant about it. You know that old saying, 'people who live in glass houses—'"

"Yeah, tell me." Jack Breedlove had been at the lodge the weekend that Jim Bob Baker died. Buck always suspected that Jack had his own suspicions about the accidental death ruling. Bud Breedlove, Jack's uncle, had been a deputy sheriff at the time. Even back then, Jack had been keen to get into law enforcement, so he'd followed every step of the investigation all the way to the ruling. Then Buck left for college and Jack decided abruptly to join the U.S. Army.

"How's that knee doing?" Jack asked. "An injury like that can be a killer. You think it's restored, start using it again and wham, it goes out again."

Buck rubbed the side of his knee which was, in fact, aching. "That's always a possibility."

"What if it happens, Buck? Would you consider coming back here?"

"Don't they say you can't ever do that?"

"That's what they say, but it can be done." Jack hitched his chair closer to his desk and leaned forward on his elbows. "Listen, this town—this area—could use someone with your charisma, Buck. Not only would Belle Pointe benefit if you took a hand in its management, but the town itself could use your name and benevolence."

It was disappointing to hear Jack hit him up for money. Buck got that often, but it was unexpected coming from Jack. He made to stand up, but Jack put up a hand to stop him. "I'm not hitting on you for cash, Buck. I imagine you get enough of that. I'm just saying—although the possibility is remote—that young athletes in Tallulah who might never have an opportunity to develop would sure benefit from mentoring by somebody of your stature. Just in case that knee puts you permanently out of commission."

"Jesus," Buck said, shaking his head. "Pearce better look out if he thinks he's gonna roll right over you in this election, Jack. You're either gonna make a damn fine politician or you should take up preaching. Another few words and I'd be shaking your hand and making a commitment."

Jack grinned and hiked a chin at Buck's injured knee. "You can't leave until that knee is fixed, so I have a little more time to work on you." He stood up as Buck got to his feet. "Before you go…"

At the door, Buck looked back. "Yeah?"

"How's Claire doing?"

Buck looked at him directly. "I don't see—"

Jack put up a hand. "I ask because I think she's got a drinking problem and if things don't change, she could hurt herself or somebody on these two-lane roads around here. One of my deputies stopped her a couple weeks ago and could have booked her for a DUI. It would have looked bad for Pearce and I didn't want folks thinking I was taking a cheap shot at my opponent by arresting his wife."

Buck moved a step closer to the desk, not wanting to be

overheard. "She's got her problems, like we all do, I guess." Claire's problems had been obvious Sunday night at dinner.

"I stopped her Monday morning for speeding in a school zone. She was going so damn fast—nearly eighty miles an hour—that I thought she might be drinking again. Turns out, she was just distracted. Her daughter was in the car with her. She needs help, Jack."

Buck studied the top of Jack's desk for a minute. "You're right. But frankly I don't feel right talking about it to you, Jack…" He looked up at him. "…considering."

"That happened over fifteen years ago, Buck." His gaze wandered to the window as if remembering. "We haven't had a conversation since."

Buck heard regret in his friend's voice. "And you shouldn't. She's a married woman."

"Yeah."

It was sensitive territory they were treading, Buck thought. The best thing would be to quit now, but there was something about the way Jack looked. His concern for Claire was genuine. "Her parents sent her off to that boarding school to separate you two. Did you know that?"

Jack laughed bitterly. "It worked. Out of sight, out of mind. I never got a postcard from her, let alone a phone call."

"She was only sixteen, Jack. She didn't stand a chance of holding out against powerful parents like the Schofields. You remember Bert Schofield. He was a mean SOB."

"So when she comes home, she goes right out and gets married?"

"If I recall," Buck said quietly, "you weren't anywhere around. You'd joined the army."

"If you recall, I didn't have a helluva lot of other choices."

No, but Jack had made the best of the choices he had, Buck thought, which was more than could be said about Claire. "You wouldn't still be carrying a torch for Pearce's wife, would you?"

"I got over it."

"Uh-huh." Buck studied the pattern of the ugly tile on the floor for about a minute before looking up to study the face of his friend. "I'll just say this, Jack. Claire's pretty fragile right now. Anne and I discussed it after having dinner with the family last weekend. The fact that you're aware of her problems concerns me. And it's none of my damn business. But she's pretty vulnerable and if you made a pass—" He put up a hand when Jack opened his mouth to object. "Hear me out. If you made a pass, she'd probably fall in your hands like a ripe peach."

"I wouldn't do that. You know I wouldn't do it, Buck." He paused. "But you and Anne could help. Nobody else in her life will."

"Did that just come to you out of the blue?"

"If you hadn't come in soon," Jack said, "I planned to give you a call. And before you refuse, there's her daughter to consider. Think of Paige."

Buck rubbed the back of his neck wearily. "The first step is for Claire to admit she's got a problem. I'm not sure it's totally a drinking problem, but I'd be out of line suggesting what else I think it is." Pearce was Claire's problem, but he could hardly say that to Jack. "Are we clear?"

"We're clear."

At the door, he added, "I hope I didn't offend you. Last thing I'd do, Jack. For what it's worth."

"Yeah. Okay."

He was halfway down the hall before he stopped and turned around. Leaning heavily on the cane, he made it back to Jack's office and found him standing exactly where he'd left him.

Jack looked at him. "What?"

"I'll take a few of those flyers. You just might be the man."

Shit. Buck stood on the sidewalk outside the police department with a stack of Jack Breedlove's flyers in his hand and scowled at a mud-spattered pickup rattling around the square. First Ty and his daddy, then Beatrice's family's land, then Belle Pointe's cotton crop and now Claire's problems. *Getting involved deeper every day, Whitaker,* he told himself with disgust. This was not the way to stay detached so he could be out of here as soon as he made things right with Anne. What he ought to do was hole up at the lodge and not come out, no matter what or who acted as if they needed him. Damn.

The pickup suddenly stopped with a squeal of tires. With his elbow hanging out, the driver grinned broadly. He was a carbon copy of Daniel, the young cop behind the desk at the police station. "Buck! Hey, man, my brother called me. I got my baseball bat here in the truck. Would you autograph it? I even brought my own Sharpie."

Buck laughed shortly. "Bring it on."

Fifteen

Anne had begun using the town library accessing Web sites dedicated to helping people find their birth parents. It had been two weeks so far and she hadn't had much luck. Without a single clue, it was proving difficult to locate a woman who wished to keep her pregnancy a secret. She was aware of the risks of showing up in some woman's present life, and she promised herself she would back off when and if it meant hurting someone.

Caught up in her thoughts, she took no particular notice of a car parked in front of the *Spectator* building until she realized Buck was behind the wheel. Her heart did a little dance at the sight of him climbing out of the driver's seat, his hair all windblown and his smile half-cocked. He wore faded jeans and a dark green golf shirt, which made him look a little too appealing and a lot too welcome. But she struggled to keep her feelings off her face, and watched him walk toward her without his cane.

While she was still gauging his gait, he walked right up to her and, in front of anybody on the street in Tallulah who might be looking, kissed her. It wasn't a quick hello kiss, but a slow, sensual, possessive greeting. "Hey, sugar," he said, letting his eyes roam her face. "You ready to take a spin in your new car?"

"It's a convertible," she said, when she finally managed to look at it.

"Nothing but the coolest for my honey," he said, gazing fondly at the car, not her.

"You said you'd rent the same car I have in St. Louis."

"No, I said I'd rent the same brand—a Mercedes—and I did." He dangled the keys in front of her nose, his eyes dancing. "Want to go for a spin?"

"I was just about to catch a ride home with Dad."

"I called your office, trying to reach you. Where were you?"

"Oh…around."

"Uh-huh." With their marriage on the rocks, he seemed hesitant about pushing her for a precise explanation. "Instead of a ride home with your dad, wouldn't you rather test drive your new wheels?" He put his arm around her shoulders and urged her toward the car. "You're gonna love this automobile, sweetheart." Because it was a neat car, she decided not to object that he hadn't consulted her on the model.

He made a big production of settling her behind the wheel and handing over the keys. While she checked the controls, he got in on the other side and sat sprawled against the passenger door, facing her. "Buckle up, sugar."

She glanced over at him. "You, too. I don't have to remind you what happened the last time you 'forgot,' do I?"

"But I was stupid and ticked off and you aren't either one." He did as she ordered anyway while she backed out.

"Where to?" she asked, merging with the traffic on the square.

"The lodge," he told her. "Two reasons. I had to leave my SUV there while I delivered the Mercedes to you, so I won't have wheels until somebody—" he winked at her "—drives me out there to pick it up. I'll need it to drive to Belle Pointe." When her eyebrows rose in question, he grinned. "A couple weeks on the job and Ma hasn't fired me yet."

"And the second reason?"

"You've never been to the lodge."

"Very slick, Whitaker. But don't get any ideas."

"I always get ideas when I'm with my wife."

"Aren't you farmers supposed to work from daylight to dark?" She glanced at the clock on the dash. "You have a couple of hours before the sun sets."

"That's just the point. You need to watch the sunset at the lodge. As for Belle Pointe, not to worry, Oscar has things under control…provided Ma doesn't butt in."

"It's not only Belle Pointe affairs that she sticks her nose into," Anne replied. "After reading my article about Pearce, she came to see me to express disapproval and to tell me to stop digging around in the *Spectator* archives. She warned me that facts taken out of context could sabotage Pearce's campaign."

All traces of his good humor vanished. "Tell me you're kidding."

She gave him more details of Victoria's visit. "She was dead serious, Buck, which tells me she thinks I may find something embarrassing to Pearce."

"Or to herself," Buck muttered.

"All she accomplished," Anne said grimly, "was to increase my curiosity. Until then, I'd been sort of casually interested in Tallulah and Belle Pointe, but now I'm wondering what she doesn't want me to find."

"Yeah," he said, frowning as he pointed left at an upcoming crossing.

She turned as he indicated and headed due west on a road that led directly to the Mississippi River. After a while, following his directions, she assumed they were close to the Whitaker lodge. Another turn and sure enough, there it was nestled in a grove of native hardwood trees. Built of river cypress and weathered to a silvery hue, it was a West Indies style structure with a wraparound porch her father would call a gallery from which she guessed the view of the river must be stunning. She caught her breath, wishing she was out of the car to get the full effect of the house, the grounds, the trees, the quiet setting.

"It's beautiful, Buck," she breathed. "No wonder you wanted to stay here."

"I knew you'd like it," he said, his eyes on her, not the lodge. "And I'd like staying here a lot more if you were with me."

She turned from the picturesque scene and looked into his eyes. He'd taken several opportunities to touch her and kiss her since showing up on her doorstep three weeks ago and, in this beautiful setting, he must surely have seduction in mind. But he surprised her by simply reaching for her seat belt, not her body. "Park under that oak tree," he said. "I'll give you a tour."

After she got out, he caught up with her as she rounded the front of the convertible, casually lacing his fingers with hers and falling into step beside her on the crushed gravel path leading to the house.

She stopped at the foot of the porch steps. "Wow, with your knee, how have you managed to climb these steps?"

"Painfully. Twenty-six of those suckers. But it's quiet out here and nobody knocks on the door asking for my autograph."

Once they were inside, he gave her the tour and they wound up in the kitchen. She refused a drink, but volunteered to make iced tea.

"Iced tea?" he said, raising his eyebrows.

"It's a Southern thing I've come to appreciate," she told him. "Have you bought any groceries besides beer, peanuts and nachos?" Left on his own, that was usually what he survived on back in St. Louis.

With a flourish, he threw open the pantry door and presented her with a box of tea bags. Knowing he never drank tea, hot or iced, she made a quick inventory of the shelves, then looked at him suspiciously. "Assorted teas, whole wheat pasta—my God!—oatmeal? Have you had a brain transplant? You've never tasted oatmeal in your life."

"I bought all the stuff you like hoping we'd wind up right where we are."

"In the kitchen?" she asked, smiling. "You surprise me."

His expression was wry as he leaned against the old-fashioned oak table. "Careful, sugar. I'm a man who's been deprived of my wife's company for a long time. You keep on lookin' at me like that and I might think of another way to use this old table. That kiss outside your daddy's building a while ago was supposed to whet your appetite."

And it did, but she couldn't afford to let him know it. Out here on the river, utterly isolated from anything except the power of her attraction to Buck, she was in more trouble than if she was caught in the hazardous undertow of the mighty Mississippi. While she still could escape, she moved toward the kitchen door. "Forget the iced tea. I'll just have bottled water."

While he rummaged in the refrigerator to get it, she asked, "Where's your exercise room? I didn't see anything on the tour."

He loosened the cap on the bottle and handed it to her. "What kind of exercise did you have in mind?" He grinned at the look she gave him and spread his hands, boyishly innocent. "Okay, I'll behave, but I can't promise for how long. First chance I get, sweetheart, I'm jumping your bones. Fair warning."

With his fingers again laced with hers, he led her through the lodge to a room that was outfitted with every conceivable physical therapy gizmo. She withdrew her hand and moved to examine an elaborate machine with a confusing array of weights and pulleys. Buck focused obsessively on a goal and it appeared he had everything needed to overcome his injury and be back on the mound next season.

"Is it working, Buck?" she asked, studying his sleek, six-pack abs in the golf shirt. He looked fit, better than he'd been since the season ended last year.

"I guess. Yeah, it's working. I tossed the cane yesterday." Avoiding her gaze, he gripped two tough elastic cords, stretched them to maximum length, then held to a count of ten before repeating the exercise. After performing the exercise a few times effortlessly, he dropped the cords with a clatter and looked at her. "What would you say if told you that since I got here I occasionally dream about something besides being out on the mound pitching?"

In the act of drinking from the bottle, she paused. "I would be surprised."

"Yeah, and I'm not talking about making love to you. I'll never stop dreaming about that." He moved to the window and looked out. Since they were at the rear of the lodge, the view was not of the river, but of woods, quiet and dark. Green. Peaceful. "The accident and the trouble in our marriage made me rethink a lot of things, such as, what to do with the rest of my life."

She took a seat on a stool. "Then that makes two of us."

"I don't have much to be proud of when I look in the mirror lately. Wrecking the Porsche, nearly killing myself and you, too, was just the last in a long list of dumb things. Add to that Casey Carlton dying in my house and I have trouble looking in the mirror. Casey was good, Anne, a natural. Another season and he would have been starting pitcher, not me."

"I think I know where you're going with this, Buck, but—"

"No. I need to say this. Maybe if I'd spoken up about the steroid shit going on, he would be alive today. Guys juiced up on that stuff can turn real mean real fast and some of them had been giving Case a hard time since he was signed. I could have stopped it that night with a word. Instead, I went inside and got another beer." He reached up and adjusted the blinds against the setting sun. "Next thing I knew, the kid was floating facedown in my pool."

"You weren't the only person who could have done something that night, but didn't, Buck. There's plenty of blame to go around."

"It was my responsibility. The kid drowned in my pool, at my house. It'll be on my conscience 'til the day I die."

"I didn't realize you felt so guilty."

"When I drive around here in Tallulah and see they've named a street after me or a ball field at the high school, stuff like that, I want to rip the signs down and tell them there are guys right here in Tallulah who are a lot more worthy of those honors than me."

"They're proud of you. It's perfectly appropriate to name a street and a ball field after a hometown hero. If they knew how tough it really is to be where you are and do what you do, they would probably name the town after you." She screwed the cap on the bottle of water. "Bucksville instead of Tallulah, how does that sound?"

"Pretty awful. Besides, I don't feel like a hero."

"Depends on how you define hero." She bent and set the bottle on the floor beside her. "You heard what my dad said when we had lunch at Daddy Gee's. You've been very successful in a highly competitive field. It takes courage to go out on that mound in front of thousands of fans knowing what the stakes are."

He stood looking at her for a long minute, then left the window and moved to a bench press opposite her. Throwing a leg over, he straddled it. "I had two goals in mind when I followed you back here to Tallulah. I'd work on winning my wife back and I'd get in shape to play baseball. I didn't count on being drawn into the stuff I left behind years ago. Now, not only am I reconnected with my family—and finding them as screwed up as when I left—but I'm actually working at Belle Pointe where I see them every day."

"Did you actually think you could just sit around and do nothing for several months?"

"I didn't think beyond getting here," he said.

She realized he was serious. Buck had more energy than two men put together. His motor was always running. In St. Louis, when he wasn't playing baseball, he was on the golf course. He played tennis, poker, hung out with his buddies, tinkered with his cars, kept up with the competition and made a lot of personal appearances to promote the Jacks. What he thought to do in Tallulah to fill up the hours when he wasn't engaged in physical therapy, she didn't know. Even if he thought to hang out with her—after talking her into it—it still would not have filled up all his days and nights.

"I guess I shouldn't be surprised that things had changed at Belle Pointe since I left," he said, making brief eye contact with her. "And I didn't like what had happened when I wasn't looking. First they grab a thousand acres from the estate of a man who was my father's friend. And then I find they fired Ty's daddy for daring to speak out about disgusting wage cuts. And this is a man who worked hard for the Whitakers for a lot of years, Anne." He looked down at the floor, rubbing the back of his neck. "Once I thought I could walk away from Belle Pointe and nobody would be hurt when I knew—I *knew!*—Pearce would only do the right thing if it didn't cost him in any way."

"Is it Pearce who's to blame for everything?" she asked. "Isn't your mother the guiding force at Belle Pointe?"

"I don't know which one to blame, maybe both. And I don't think it really matters so long as things change," Buck said, now rubbing a spot between his eyes as if to ease a dull ache. "My dad's got to be turning over in his grave. He was passionate about the land, about Belle Pointe. He knew its history from the journals kept by a string of Whitakers before him and he revered his birthright. I remember him sitting in his study meticulously recording facts and figures. Computers hold all that information now, but there's no computer program as meaningful as those journals."

"Where are they now?" Anne asked, her gaze following

him as he rose and moved to the windows again. The *Spectator* archives were interesting, but her heart beat faster at the thought of reading a hundred and fifty years of journal entries by Buck's ancestors.

"God knows. They're not in my mother's office. I've looked. Maybe the attic. I don't know. But I can't see Pearce or my mother keeping them anyway, not the way Dad did. I used to get a kick out of reading that stuff. He had an accountant keeping the books, but he still entered important events in his journal like all Whitakers before him, births and deaths of the field hands, marriages, divorces, baptisms. He was very paternal. He'd lend money at no interest and enter it in the journal. I can remember talking to him about it once when I looked at the books and found half of them never paid the money back. When I asked, he said it wouldn't hurt the company to carry a little debt."

She shifted on the stool and hooked both feet on a mid-level rung. "It's a stretch for me to believe your mother or Pearce have continued that practice," she remarked.

"Tell me. Considering everything I'm hearing that they've done since Dad died, it wouldn't surprise me if they've gone back to collect those old debts." With his palms in his back pockets, he turned to face her. "The journals were full of trivia for any particular year—crop yields, weather conditions, rainfall, the first frost, the first freeze. If a year was plagued by drought or was too wet, it was right there. You could page back to any year and find the last infestation of boll weevils, or any factor influencing the quality of the cotton, good or bad. And in any situation Dad could fall back on written accounts in the Whitaker journals going back a hundred and fifty years."

"Do you think that information is being kept on a computer now?"

"Births, deaths, marriages and divorces, no," Buck said, straddling the bench again. "Anything affecting the crop, yeah. First thing I did when my mother let me in her office was open up her computer. Belle Pointe is divided into sections and I need to know the status of each on any particular day or stage of planting." With one foot on the bench, he wrapped both arms around his knee. "Next, I'll get into the books, but so far I haven't had time."

"Do you think she'll be comfortable with that?"

"She has no choice now."

Anne believed he was genuinely concerned about putting right the dishonorable things he'd discovered, but it was difficult to believe that he was willing to pay the price to follow through. Change took time. Which would mean giving up baseball. Even when faced with a career-threatening accident, the loss of their baby and his marriage on the rocks, Buck had clung to his belief that baseball was his life.

"You're thinking I can't do it, aren't you?"

"You can't, Buck, not without serious commitment which will threaten your goal to return to baseball," she told him.

"Yeah, I know." He gave her his crooked smile. "Easier to pitch a no-hitter against the Yankees than to make changes at Belle Pointe, right?"

"When you're in St. Louis and the problems are here in Tallulah? Yeah."

When he shifted his gaze to the window again, his smile had faded. "Problem is, nothing will ever change at Belle Pointe as long as my mother and Pearce are in sole control."

"I think that's pretty obvious," she said.

He stood for a long time, simply studying the scene from the window. Finally, he gave a deep sigh. "Maybe it's time I stepped up to the plate."

The idea was so appealing that she was almost afraid to say the obvious. She slipped off the stool and bent to pick up the bottle of water on the floor. "Say you do decide to take a hand in changing things. And say you actually do succeed, what happens when it's time to go back to baseball next season?"

"The answer's obvious, isn't it? I would have to choose."

He reached over and took the bottle from her, set it on the window ledge and caught her hand. "C'mon, let's go out on the porch. The sun is setting and the view of the river will blow you away. Plus, I'm not done yet."

There were several chairs on the porch, but he led her to the old-fashioned swing suspended on a rusty chain. "Don't worry," he told her as she looked askance at the chain, "it looks in worse shape than it is. Humidity from the river is hell on anything that's outside and this swing has been hanging here since I was a kid."

"On the same chain?" she asked uneasily, as he brushed at a few leaves on the seat.

He chuckled, wanting her relaxed. The next few minutes were crucial in his plan. "No, it just looks as ancient as the original. I meant to replace it last week. Trouble is, I keep forgetting to stop at the hardware store." With gentle pressure on her shoulders, he urged her to sit on the swing. She looked surprised when he didn't take a seat beside her, but then turned her gaze to the horizon where the sun was setting.

She put a hand over her heart. "Oh, my, it's gorgeous."

Only a sliver of the sun remained, a brilliant orange crescent sinking fast in a pink-and-purple sky. As night fell, the cries of a flock of birds echoed faintly, flying high over trees on the levee that stood in stark black silhouette. In spite of the fact that Buck had watched the same sunset every evening since moving to the lodge, it felt good to share it with Anne.

"See, didn't I tell you the sunset would blow you away?"

Still looking at the stunning color display, she smiled. "You lied. There are two reasons why you like it out here, not just one," she said. "True, it's so isolated nobody asks for your autograph, but you're also treated to this fabulous sunset every evening."

But his gaze was on Anne, not the sunset. Holding the swing still, he waited until she looked up into his face. "Do you still believe that I don't care that we lost our baby, Anne?"

When she took so long considering her answer, Buck held his breath. For weeks, she'd been brooding over the baby and everything else she didn't like about being married to him. Now that he was asking straight out, was she going to tell him that she couldn't forgive him? That she'd made up her mind to cut him out of her life?

"I don't know what I believe, Buck. I don't know the person you are here in Tallulah. It seems every day I uncover some new piece of you I never saw or suspected. I'm still trying to figure who the real Buck Whitaker is."

While he still held the chain, she touched her foot to the floor and gave herself a tiny push, setting the swing in gentle motion. "As for not caring about losing the baby, I never believed that about you, Buck. You're not so heartless that you'd be untouched by the loss of a baby, any baby."

"Do you really mean that?" He felt cautious relief.

"Let me finish. But your reaction when I told you was…is…still hard for me to forgive. Instead of grieving over what we lost, you got all hung up in the way I became pregnant. That seemed irrelevant to me at the time, unimportant."

Now was not the time to argue whether she was right or wrong in what she did. He knew not to go there again…yet. Maybe never. "I just wish I could live that moment over again when you told me you were pregnant, Anne. I swear to God, I do. That mistake is up there on my list with the time Case Carlton died on my watch."

"You were so furious. Then when we got in the car—"

"I was in an unholy rage, yeah. I'll never know if the miscarriage was my fault or not. I'm just so thankful I didn't lose you as well as the baby. It's understandable that you couldn't stand the sight of me after it happened."

She looked quickly down at her hands so that he had only a second to see that her eyes had filled with tears. "You probably won't understand this—" her voice rose in a tight whisper "—but I had lost my *baby!* I was numb. I didn't feel anything except grief and despair. Nothing else mattered."

"If I'd been killed would you have cared?"

"The truth? No, not at that moment."

Buck was stunned by how much it hurt that he'd dropped off the radar screen of her heart. His fingers gripped the chain so tight that the links cut into his palms. Holding his breath, he finally managed to ask, "Does it matter now?"

She wiped at her tears with the tips of her fingers and gave a little sniff. "Oh, Buck, of course it matters now," she said almost briskly. "I didn't stop loving you. I just stopped feeling. It hurt too much."

He let go the chain and sat down beside her. Whether she pushed him off the swing on his butt or not, he was going to put his arms around his wife. He was aching to feel her snug up against his body. He was hungry for the taste and smell of her. But as he reached for her, she began to cry.

"I'm so sorry, Anne. You've got to forgive me."

"I wanted that baby so much, Buck!" Her shoulders were shaking with the depth of her despair. "I wanted to die with him."

He pulled her into his arms and held her fast, resting his chin on the top of her head. His chest was full of a need to comfort her, to ease her pain, when all he was capable of was murmuring a few meaningless words. He wanted to take her sadness into himself and find a way for them to start over. Most of all, he wanted to give her another baby. He was shocked at the sheer force of his need to fill her with his seed, and yet with fear that he'd waited too long to come to his senses—and it was now too late.

His heart turned over as she threw her arms around him and sobbed, holding on tight. He whispered endearments in her ear, incoherent words of reassurance and regret and promise. She felt warm and small in his arms, soft and womanly. With his face buried in her hair, he took a deep breath and closed his eyes, going almost dizzy with the familiar scent of her. Unable to resist, he caught her chin and tipped her face up, ran his lips over her eyebrows, her lashes, her wet cheeks. He traced the shape of her jaw and chin and stopped at the corner of her mouth.

"Ah, it feels so good to be with you like this. God, you don't know how much I've missed you."

His kiss had the flavor of desperation and Anne responded with a broken cry that opened her mouth to the thrust of his tongue. His need was urgent, raw and primitive, clawing at him, reminding him how long he'd been without her. He was hard and throbbing in his jeans, aching for release, but not now, he told himself, even as he kissed a wild and wet trail down her throat telling himself to go slow. Still, his hands were everywhere, moving with a life of their own, snaking under her shirt, finding her breasts, caressing them until the nipples pebbled and she whimpered with the pleasure of it.

He broke the kiss then and stripped her shirt over her head and dispensed with her bra in a quick, deft flick of his fingers. As he inhaled the fragrance of her skin, he fastened on one breast and drew on the sweetness of her as though he could never get enough. All he wanted was to taste and touch and thrill and react. For a few precious minutes, he blanked out any thought but the sheer joy of loving Anne. She'd always been the one woman above all others who could steal away all reason and caution in him.

With her hands gripping his hair to hold him in place she made soft, urgent sounds, then dragged his mouth back to hers in a kiss that was as hungry as any he'd given. Moving strictly on male instinct, he broke the kiss and lifted her astride his thighs, thanking God and the angels that she wore a denim skirt and not pants. He swept a palm over her belly, felt the quiver of her muscles at his touch, then moved down and down until he was cupping the heart of her.

"Buck…" His name ended on a moan as his fingers plunged. With his face caught in her hands, she took his mouth in a kiss that was deep and carnal, as if she wanted to eat him alive. And then, at his touch to her special place, she threw her head back and fell blindly into a rocking, age-old rhythm. Somewhere in the back of his mind, he realized she was too close to going over the edge for him to stop and try to make it to his bed. He wanted to be in her when it happened, but it was too late as with a cry, she tumbled into a fierce, hard orgasm.

Time ticked away then while Anne lay replete and bone-less in his arms. Mixed with the sound of their labored breathing was the nighttime racket of crickets and cicadas. Beneath his palm, the rate of her heartbeat was slowing, slowing as she came down. His lips moved in a lazy smile against her forehead, knowing the feeling, letting himself enjoy the gentle movement of the swing with his wife in his arms, all satisfied and submissive while somewhere near the porch rafters came the fluttering sound of an owl taking off to hunt. Buck still ached with the need to take his own satisfaction, but he could wait. For a few minutes, at least.

"That was nice, wasn't it, babe?"

"Omigod," she breathed.

"For starters." With his hands on her bottom, he pressed her against his erection, closing his eyes with the pleasure-pain of it. Anticipating the night ahead of them. "We'll go inside when you catch your breath, darlin'."

A long pause. One, two, three… "No."

Buck stopped the movement of the swing with his foot. "What?"

She pushed against his chest and made to scramble off his lap, but he stopped her with both hands clamped on her waist. "I've got to go now," she said, not looking at him. "What did you do with my car keys?"

He caught her by the chin, forcing her eyes up to his. "You can have the keys to your car just as soon as you explain why we can't go inside to my bedroom and finish what we just started. One of us…" He blew out a tortured breath and started again. "One of us is pretty frustrated right now."

"I shouldn't have let it happen," she told him, sounding as if she were ready to cry again. "I'm sorry. I didn't mean for things to go so far."

"You had plenty of time to stop before it did."

"I know, I know." As she felt for his hands at her waist to free herself, she put more force in her tone. "But I know what you had in mind to do, Buck. You planned for us to make love and not use any protection. You're thinking everything will be fixed if I just get pregnant again."

He let her go and watched as she stood up and began to straighten her clothes. In spite of himself, he felt a surge of lust at the sight of her beautiful breasts as she fumbled with the clip of her bra. He ought to be so damn pissed off, he thought, that nothing about her turned him on. But it was just the opposite. Everything about her turned him on. He wanted her and he wanted to yell it loud enough that it would echo across the goddamn river into the next state. "Here, I'll do it," he growled.

He surged to his feet, shoved her hands away and fastened the clip as deftly as he'd unfastened it ten minutes before. "You got one thing right, babe, I'll give you that," he said, as she jerked the tail of her shirt down and began tucking it into her waistband. "I was going to make love to you. But if you'd said anything about protection, I would have whipped out a condom so fast your head would swim. As for impregnating you on the sly, I'm not the one in this family who's that sneaky."

She went still with the accuracy of his shot, then moved over to the edge of the porch and leaned her head against a column. Something about the way her shoulders drooped made him want to go over and gather her close and take some of her pain on himself, share it. But damn it, he was the injured party here, so he kept his feet planted flat on the floor.

"I'm all confused right now, Buck," she said, speaking barely above a whisper. "I just need more time. Too much is happening. I don't know where we're headed. I don't know *you* anymore. I'm sorry."

"Maybe it's you that you don't know anymore," Buck said.

"I'm going to try and find my birth parents," she said.

"Huh? What?" He spread his hands, looking at her oddly. "Did I miss something here?"

She turned slightly and met his eyes. "You said I might not know who I was and you could be right. One of the things I did today at the library was to use the computer and look up Web sites that help adopted people find their birth parents."

"Your parents are Franklin and Laura Marsh, the people who raised you. Who fed and clothed and educated you, Anne. They're your parents."

"I know and I love them, but I need to know this."

He stood where he was another minute or two, struggling with a host of conflicting feelings. He couldn't see what the issue of her biological parents had to do with why she couldn't begin to fix what was wrong in their marriage. He damn sure couldn't see why they couldn't be together while she was working on it. Hell, he didn't know why he was surprised. Women had a way of complicating everything.

In the end, he turned abruptly and walked to the door. "I'll get the keys. They're inside."

"Thank you," she murmured.

He'd dropped the keys in a bowl just inside the door. Now

he swept them up angrily, turned and stepped back outside, resisting an impulse to toss them to her. Grimly silent and assuming she'd follow, he went down the porch steps, hardly noticing the pain in his knee until he got halfway to the bottom. "I need to show you how to operate the convertible top," he said tersely, pausing for a minute to rub at his knee. "You can't drive home at night with the top down."

"Can't I figure it out on my own? I can see your knee is hurting."

"My knee is fine. You just don't worry about my knee, okay?"

She shrugged. "Whatever, Buck."

He was gritting his teeth in pain when he reached the car, but he shot her a look that dared her to mention it and yanked the door open. "Get in."

She did as told and listened intently while he explained how to operate the mechanism that raised and lowered the convertible top.

"Any questions?"

"No."

"Then I'll see you around." Without waiting for her response to that, he closed the car door with unnecessary force before she could and stalked back to the dreaded steps. He was at number thirteen before succumbing to a need to look back. The taillights of the Mercedes were barely visible through the trees, meaning she was almost to the main road. Swearing, he gave in to the necessity of resting his throbbing knee, sat down on the steps and buried his face in his hands.

Back in Tallulah, Beatrice lay in bed waiting for Franklin. She heard him close and lock the front door, then move to the den and click the remote to turn off the television. He watched very little TV—mostly PBS—but he never missed the nightly news at bedtime. A minute or so later, he was in the kitchen noisily dispensing ice from the refrigerator door into a glass and filling it with water, which would sit on his bedside table although, as far as she could tell, he hardly ever drank from it. Next, the sound of lights being snapped off and then his footsteps as he made his way to their bedroom.

Beatrice wore her reading glasses and was holding the current bestseller from one of her favorite authors. In spite of the fact that she was on page eleven, she didn't have a clue what she'd just read, so she closed the book. She was holding it against her chest when Franklin appeared.

"If Percy Jenkins doesn't do something about that barking dog," he said, "I'll be forced to give him a friendly call."

She realized she hadn't noticed a barking dog until he mentioned it. "It won't do any good," she told him. "Percy has got to be one of the most cantankerous men in town. If you complain, I promise you he'll go out of his way to train that dog to bark all night instead of just half the night. Your best bet is to write an editorial."

He chuckled as he unbuttoned his shirt. "I accept that I'm no longer living in Boston, sweetheart, but my editorials will not sink to that level."

She rose up slightly and placed the book on her bedside table without bothering to mark her place. Next, she slipped her glasses off and put them on top of the book. "Do you miss it?"

"Boston?" He stuck his head around the bathroom door to look at her, toothbrush in hand. "I miss the museums and the cool summers, but not the snow, the crowds, the traffic and the taxes." He disappeared inside again, still talking. "And because of you, my darling, I gladly put up with the heat and the bugs and the sultry humidity of the Delta, even Percy Jenkins' irritating dog."

She heard him brushing his teeth, then shutting off the water. And in a minute or two, he was out of the bathroom and heading for the bed. As always, he slept only in boxer shorts. No matter the weather, cold or hot or in-between, just boxer shorts. She remembered before they were married and the first time she saw him without his clothes, which always looked a little too large and mostly mismatched. He looked a lot better without them than in them. Granted, she didn't see a lot of naked men, but it didn't take much experience to appreciate one like Franklin. Her greatest regret was that she hadn't been married to him when she was young and looked her best.

He climbed into bed and, instead of settling under the covers, propped on his elbow, sensing her mood. "Something bothering you, love?"

Beatrice turned onto her side to face him. "Anne."

His glance shifted to her clock radio. "She's not a teenager, Bea. She's probably with Buck. And she has a key."

"I wasn't suggesting a curfew." She put out a hand and cradled his jaw, letting her thumb caress his lips. She loved the shape—and taste—of Franklin's beautiful mouth. "I didn't mention it to you, but Victoria stopped by for a private word with Anne. It was a week or so ago. Anne was very upset."

"What was on her mind? Victoria's mind, I mean. Let me guess, Anne's article that didn't portray Pearce as God's gift to Mississippi."

"That, too, but she seems more worried about Anne looking into the archives and possibly stumbling on something that

Pearce's opponent could use against him in the campaign. She actually asked Anne to stop, which only fired up her curiosity."

She made to withdraw her hand, but Franklin brought it to his mouth and pressed a sweet kiss into her palm, then held it against his heart. "And then what happened?"

"Exactly what anybody but Victoria would expect. Anne's nose for news is now twitching like mad. Her interest was purely casual before Victoria's visit, but now she's wondering what her mother-in-law doesn't want her to find."

"If that's so, why hasn't she spent more time at the *Spectator* scrutinizing those archives? She turns her assignments in days before deadline, giving her ample opportunity."

Beatrice settled back on her pillow and looked up at the ceiling. "She has something else on her mind besides her job and Whitaker family secrets, Franklin. She's determined to find her biological parents."

"Ah."

"Mildred Pinkston called me."

He blinked. "The librarian?"

"Yes. Anne has spent a good deal of time using the library computer lately."

"Huh. I don't know what concerns me more, the fact that Anne is surfing the Internet at the library instead of using one at the *Spectator,* or that Mildred Pinkston felt compelled to tattle something that's absolutely none of her business."

"It wouldn't happen in Boston, would it?"

He laughed softly. "No, it wouldn't. Add that to the list of things I admit I miss."

"Anne is not going to let this go, Frank. At least twice she's mentioned a fear of something in her genetic background that may be a factor in her difficulty to get pregnant. I keep telling her she has nothing to worry about, but nothing I say makes any difference. She's determined to open Pandora's box."

"She was always as stubborn as a little mule." He glanced at his wife. "Now, genetics may play a part there."

"Stubbornness is learned behavior," Beatrice shot back. "She picked it up from you."

"I'm reasonable, not stubborn," he said with a wicked light in his eyes.

She sighed. "Oh, Frank, it's just a matter of time before she comes to you and begins asking all sorts of questions. In fact, I don't know why she hasn't. I just hope—"

He shushed her by laying a finger on her lips. After a moment, he lay back, his arms behind his head. "I'm not surprised that she's fired up about this again. I assume it's that miscarriage driving her this time, but she's always had a keen curiosity about her biological parents. Actually, I think her mother encouraged her interest."

"Her mother."

He turned his head and smiled at her. "Laura."

"Why, do you think?"

"Why encourage her? I'm not sure, but Laura knew, because of her illness, that she would not live a long life. Multiple sclerosis was going to take her and there would be many years when Anne would be without family except for me. Laura was simply delighted when she married, thinking Buck with his roots going back five generations would fill the void. Of course, she knew nothing about Victoria Whitaker's personality."

Beatrice set her teeth and crossed her arms over her breasts. "Sometimes I think the woman was a saint."

"I assume you refer to Laura and not Victoria," Franklin said, still smiling.

"I certainly wouldn't refer to Victoria Whitaker as a saint."

"Hmm." He rose slightly and leaned over to kiss her, then settled back and said deadpan, "Just for the record, I'd rather be married to a beautiful, sexy, slightly jealous Southern woman than to a saint."

"I am not jealous."

"Oh, did you think I was referring to you? Heck, I was just speaking hypothetically."

Beatrice suddenly yanked his pillow out from under his head and hit him with it. Laughing, he fended her off, then caught her and pulled her over on top of him. She made a brief, halfhearted pretence of trying to wiggle off, but when she realized the effect it had on him, it was her turn to laugh. "Gotcha," she said softly.

"You are so right, love." Franklin wrapped both arms around her and sighed with satisfaction. "You feel so good, soft and womanly." He buried his nose in her hair. "Smell good, too. God, I am the luckiest man alive."

She raised her head. "You better believe it, buster."

He spent a moment simply looking at her, letting his eyes wander over her face. "I do, my darling."

She settled back with her head tucked beneath his chin, a hand on his chest. "What will you say when Anne tells you what she's doing?"

"What would you like me to say, Bea?"

"The truth. Tell her the truth."

Sixteen

Anne was reading a *Spectator* account of a drought in the fifties when Claire appeared at the top of the stairs.

"Am I interrupting?"

"No, of course not." Anne waved a hand at the uninteresting array of shelves, boxes and *Spectator* memorabilia. "What's to interrupt down here?"

Midway down the stairs, Claire paused with a look of amazement. "Well, kiss my grits! Paige was right. You have transformed this place." In smart black gaucho pants, a honey-gold sweater and boots, she sauntered on down to the bottom of the stairs. "Honey, you're wasted in the archives of this musty ol' paper. Anybody who could organize a hundred years of pure crap like this should be on TV. What's that show on the Home and Garden channel, something about organizin' stuff? That's where you would shine."

Because she was familiar with the show and actually liked it, Anne smiled. "Anybody with a broom and dustpan, a roll of paper towels and spray cleanser could accomplish the same result."

"That would only clean it up," Claire said, scrutinizing date labels. "I'm talking about the absence of chaos. Your daddy's gonna hate to see you go back to St. Louis." She turned in time to catch Anne's grimace. "Aw, don't get that look on your face. Buck'll wear you down. He'll sweet-talk you into going back and next thing you'll be swallowed up in his career again. Might take him a while, but he'll do it."

"We'll see," Anne said.

For a second or two, Claire simply studied her face. "You've got him mad as a sore-tail cat, you know that? He walks around lookin' mean and gettin' things done."

"I wouldn't know. I haven't seen him lately." He hadn't called or dropped in to see her at the *Spectator* or at the Marshes' in the two weeks since she'd refused to have sex. Which was the way she wanted it, she told herself. Often.

Claire laughed. "Maybe I'll revise the timetable. I thought he'd stay in Tallulah ten days max. But it's going on…what? Five or six weeks now. I don't know what y'all are at odds over, but my money's on him dragging you back to St. Louis…as soon as you bring him around to your way of thinkin', that is."

Anne sighed. "Is all of Tallulah discussing Buck's marital problems?"

"Not so much Buck's problems, but your contrariness." Claire strolled across the floor to inspect the neat working station Anne had set up for herself. "He's Tallulah's favorite son, their hero. So of course, they're discussing what's gone wrong with the crazy woman who luckily finds herself married to him and doesn't want to kiss his feet every day."

Anne laughed out loud at that. "I guess I shouldn't be surprised that it's all my fault. Have you been sent to bring me to my senses?"

"Moi?" Claire spread the fingers of one hand over her breastbone. "Bite your tongue. No, I'm the last person they'd send to knock sense into anyone." She moved to a shelf loaded with neatly labeled boxes.

"Lordy," she murmured, then turned to look at Anne. "This place was an unholy mess. And now look, neat and organized. You know what? You and Buck really are a matched pair. He's stepped in and done the same thing at Belle Pointe."

"Things at Belle Pointe were an unholy mess? Considering what I've heard about Victoria's ability to manage, I find that hard to believe."

"And don't forget she's a control freak, too."

"Which is why I'm skeptical."

"Actually, Victoria's not young anymore, not that she'd admit it even if you put a gun to her head. In fact, I think she's looking downright peaked lately." She stopped, looked around. "Is smoking allowed down here?"

"I'm sorry, no. The place is full of old paper and aging artifacts. In a fire, they'd go up like tinder."

"Sure." Claire slipped her fingers into the front pockets of her slacks and sashayed over to a wall of photos. "Where was I? Oh, yeah. Victoria and Belle Pointe. Well, she wouldn't admit that lately production has been slipping, as has the quality of the cotton, which is trouble with a big T. Poor Will Wainwright tried to keep up, but with Victoria's constant interference—she called it guidance—and Will being nearly seventy with diabetes and high blood pressure, it was hopeless. Anyway, along comes Buck who, thanks to you, is stuck in Tallulah whether he likes it or not and with a proven knack for farming. Don't think my mother-in-law didn't seize on that like a hungry cat on a bird."

"Frankly, I don't think she had to try very hard. He was bound to be bored without baseball to focus on."

"He could have focused on you."

"And I'd have to be willing. As you see, I have other fish to fry."

Claire chuckled delightedly. With her hands clasped behind her, she bent to study a few of the framed photos on the wall. Pausing before a 1975 Chamber of Commerce gathering, she pointed to a tall man. "Look, there's John Whitaker. The older Buck gets, the more he looks like him."

Buck was so much like his father that Anne could have guessed who he was without the identifying caption.

"And here's Victoria," Claire said, picking out the lone woman in the group. Her tone went noticeably flat. "Chamber President. She only quit last year."

"I was struck by the number of photos of Whitakers and their ancestors in the archives," Anne said.

"Not just ancestors," Claire said, peering at a series of baseball photos of Buck from middle school to recent shots in his Jacks uniform.

"Dad pulled those out of the archives after we got married and framed them," Anne explained. "Buck was a little embarrassed when he saw them."

"Who's this guy? He looks familiar." Claire gazed at a uniformed soldier.

"Paige said the same thing when she found the write-up in an old issue in the sixties." Anne looked at the youthful face. "He was Tallulah's only casualty in the Vietnam war."

Claire peered closely at the caption under the photo. "Rudy Baker. Hmm, don't know why I thought—" Catching sight of another more recent photo, she moved on to study it.

"Here's the ribbon-cutting ceremony when they dedicated the Whitaker Library."

"The family figured so large in the community that the *Spectator* is practically a repository for their history," Anne said. "Paige has become very interested in her family's past."

Claire turned to look at Anne. "Paige is the reason I dropped in to see you, Anne. I wanted to thank you for all you've done for her. Since spending so much time with you, she's had a major attitude adjustment. I don't know your secret, but whatever it is, please don't stop."

"I don't know that I've done anything." Anne leaned against her makeshift desk thoughtfully. "We get along fine now, but when I first came, she was—"

"Rebellious, call it what it was," Claire said. "Not that she's an angel now, but she used to refer to time spent at the *Spectator* as torture, only one step up from working on a chain gang. Now, I honestly think she'd come here anyway. She likes poking around in this old stuff. She likes finding connections to a past that's pretty unique. And she really admires you."

"It goes both ways. She probably has a very bright future, Claire."

"My other prayer," Claire added in a heartfelt voice, "is that she'll soon get over needing to shock folks, including me. Do you know what she said one night at the dinner table?"

Knowing how Paige delighted in getting a rise out of adults, Anne wouldn't hazard a guess.

"She asked was it possible that Jack Breedlove could be her real father."

"And everyone reacted with...let me guess, shock," Anne said laughing. She could easily imagine Victoria Whitaker's reaction.

"I'm just thankful she didn't ask Jack outright," Claire said, almost moaning with the memory. "He stopped us one morning because I was speeding in a school zone. I was pretty rattled that it was Jack. And Paige picked up on it instantly. She's so...so..."

"Observant?"

"Yes, she saw right away that Jack and I...that we..."

"Had history?"

Claire met Anne's eyes squarely. "Which you already knew. That's another reason I wanted to see you, Anne. The night you and Buck came to dinner, I'd had too much wine and I said things I shouldn't have. I'm sure I shocked you." She made a face. "Maybe that's where Paige gets her smart mouth. Anyway, I just wanted to set something straight. I'm not having an affair with Jack Breedlove."

Anne blinked in surprise. "I never thought you were, Claire. My goodness, have I said something that—"

"No, no. It's just that I was..." She looked away with a nervous laugh. "This is really embarrassing, but I needed to be sure you didn't get the wrong idea."

"I didn't get any idea, Claire," she said quietly.

"Except that I drink too much, right?"

"Well..."

Claire rushed on, "Pearce wants to force me into rehab, not for the desire to help me, but to prevent the possibility of me embarrassing him during the campaign. But I'm not going to let him do it. I've been going to an AA group since, although nobody in my family knows it. And I haven't had a drink. It'll take a while—a long while—before I can regain the respect and trust of the people I care about, especially Paige, but I'm working on it."

"I'm very happy to hear that, Claire."

"And about Jack…I just wanted to…" She swallowed hard. "I just wanted to clear that up."

"Consider it cleared up," Anne said in a gentle voice.

Claire nodded as if a difficult chore was completed and slipped the strap of her purse on her shoulder. "Thanks for listening."

Anne, still smiling, said, "What are friends for?"

As Claire climbed the stairs, Anne smiled faintly as she stored away the microfiche and closed out her laptop. It was strange and incomprehensible the things that pushed people to finally make life-changing decisions. She snapped off the lights and climbed the stairs. Franklin's small staff was already gone and as she passed his desk, Anne saw that he was on the phone. He waved to her, mouthing, "See you at home."

Claire was still on the sidewalk when she got outside. "Can I give you a lift?" Claire asked, jangling her car keys in her hand. "Or did Buck finally manage to get a car for you? I know how—"

When she stopped short, Anne looked to see why. A few feet away, a man stood propped against the door of a police vehicle. He straightened as they approached and Anne recognized Jack Breedlove.

Claire's surprise was quickly overcome. "Well, what have we here?" she said, sauntering over to him. "Am I illegally parked?"

"You were," he told her, "but since you left the keys in your car, I took the liberty of moving it."

"You towed my car?" She looked outraged.

"No, I moved it," he repeated.

A step or two behind Claire, Anne had time to observe the

two former high school sweethearts. They were like wary an-
imals, both sniffing danger. Anne found it interesting that
Claire was almost taunting him. More intriguing was the
look on his face as he watched her. No, she decided, they were
not having an affair, but it wasn't because they weren't
tempted.

Neither noticed as Anne left.

Except for two hours of physical therapy, Buck's days
were spent getting a handle on the situation at Belle Pointe.
He started early and stayed late. It was physical work, dusty
and exhausting and hard on his injured knee, which let him
know it when he got back to the lodge at night. Pain and fa-
tigue helped to keep him from thinking about his headstrong
wife. It had been two weeks since he saw Anne off in her new
car and he swore she would have to be the one to pick up the
phone and make the next move.

The crews were overjoyed to take orders from him and his
mother was oddly restrained in her interference. He'd expected
major opposition from her, but after the first couple weeks, she
gave him a free hand. Without trying to analyze her—and he'd
never been able to in thirty-seven years—he did what he thought
best for the crops and the crews and Mother Nature did the rest.

It surprised him to discover how much he'd missed Belle
Pointe and the sheer satisfaction of growing cotton. Sometimes he got in his SUV and simply drove the boundaries of
Whitaker land, imagining the changes he would make if he
stayed. But the fields had already been planted this year when
he decided to step in and he would be leaving before the crops
were harvested. He had to keep reminding himself that baseball was his life. Not Belle Pointe.

He was sitting on the steps of the lodge nursing a root beer and brooding when he heard a car coming up the road to the lodge. Forgetting his aching knee, he stood up thinking Anne had finally come to her senses. But it wasn't a Mercedes that stopped. It was a large, powerful black Lexus. Pearce.

"Shit," he muttered, watching his brother. With the door still open, Pearce paused and stretched languidly, releasing a loud sigh. Then, taking his time, he lit up one of his big cigars. Apparently, he wasn't carrying a grudge over their last encounter.

After a day of campaigning and who know what-all else, he was dressed to the nines in suit and tie. To Buck, tired and dirty, his brother looked as fresh as a spring morning. It struck him that Pearce had inherited their mother's knack for neatness. Buck, on the other hand, was like John Whitaker, casual about his appearance. Resigned to hearing another sales pitch, Buck turned and hobbled up the rest of the steps, taking the first chair he reached.

Pearce spoke from the bottom of the steps. "Wasn't that your wife I passed a while ago driving that sweet little convertible?" He peered in the direction of the river as if pondering a troubling problem. "Hell, bro, it's bedtime. Shouldn't she be heading this way instead of going in the opposite direction?"

The thought of Anne tooling around at night doing God-knows-what hit him in the belly. And it was irritating that Pearce knew it and he didn't. Damn it, what in sam hill was she doing? "It's late, Pearce," he said. "What's on your mind?"

"Hmm, a little testy, are we?" He started up the porch steps at a leisurely pace. "You know, that's the trouble when one of us Southern boys marries a Yankee gal. They're stubborn up north, they think too much. They want to run the show. Now those are complications I don't tolerate well. Me, I picked a pretty hometown girl, educated at Ole Miss. Maybe you should have looked around closer to home, Buck."

"I repeat, was there anything on your mind other than my wife's personality?"

"Yessiree, definitely testy," Pearce said, grinning through a smoke cloud. "And I wouldn't be out here in the woods at this hour if you'd answer your goddamn phone. Middle of the day all I get is your voice mail, so this was the only time and place I'd be sure to find you." He was at the top of the stairs now. "I guess being in the public eye you learn how to make yourself scarce when you want."

"If you had serious business with me, you could have found me at Belle Pointe." Buck rubbed at the ache in his knee, anticipating a headache. "I'm there at daylight every day."

"But not up at the big house. I don't need to see anybody bad enough to chase 'em around five thousand muddy acres." He strolled across the porch and sat down in the swing. "I never liked mucking around in the fields."

Buck finished off his root beer and set the can on the step beside him. "With Will Wainwright gone, you should be glad I don't have the same problem."

"The damn cotton will get planted and picked and ginned whether you manage it or somebody else does. Plenty of people around who could do the job, but Mama has a bug up her ass now you're here. Whitaker pride and all that shit. Naturally, you rolled right over for her. Damn, Buck, I thought you were smarter than that."

"Was there anything else on your mind, Pearce?"

He fumed a minute. "Two things. I heard you visited the chief of police. I know y'all were friends back when you were kids. I hope the only reason you dropped in was to talk about old times."

"We talked about our rowdy pasts, yeah."

"And what else?"

Knowing it would rile Pearce, Buck allowed himself a half smile. "He might have mentioned his campaign."

His brother nearly lost the tenuous hold on his temper. "You think that's funny? Let me ask you this." He pointed his smelly cigar at Buck. "Why would you avoid your own brother, then stroll into my opponent's office giving the impression that Breedlove is your man? Why would you do that, Buck?"

"I don't expect you to believe this, but I dropped in to see Jack because he and I are old friends and I haven't seen him in years. I'm not responsible for whatever interpretation anybody puts on that."

"I don't want you going near him again!" Pearce got up abruptly, sending the swing jerking wildly on its chains. "And I want you to put down the rumors that you're supporting him. I want you to get active in my campaign. Be visible."

"We've discussed this before, Pearce." Buck stuck out the leg with the bad knee. "You see this? Until I'm able to walk without taking a chance on tearing something loose again, I wouldn't be much good stumping for you."

"You don't seem to have any difficulty walking around in a fucking cotton field!"

"I'm riding around in a pickup out there and you know it."

"Okay. Okay." Sensing he was getting nowhere, Pearce

struggled to calm himself. "So tomorrow come to my office and talk about stuff you could do…like calling some of your influential friends with big bucks." He glanced at the front door. "Better yet, let's go inside and discuss it now. Firm up a plan."

Buck stood up, not to fall in with Pearce's plan, but to let him know he was done talking. "It's late and I'm tired. One of the reasons I don't want to get involved is just what you're suggesting, calling people and asking for money. It's not gonna happen, not from me. And frankly, right now, I've got too much going in my life to have time for that."

"Like what? You aren't playing baseball." The sparks from his cigar arced across the porch steps as he tossed it. "You're on a fucking vacation, Buck!"

Buck sighed and opened the door. Sooner or later, he'd have to tell Pearce flat out that not only was he not going to campaign for him, but he wasn't going to endorse him either. But for tonight, he'd had about as much of his brother as he could take. After those remarks about Anne, the only thing he might share with Pearce was a brief discussion of the weather. And even that was iffy. As he made to step inside, Pearce caught his arm.

"Hold on, I'm not done. I didn't get to the second reason I'm out here in the sticks."

Buck paused, going stone-still as he looked at Pearce's hand on his arm. In the dark, his reaction could only be felt, but it was enough for Pearce to hastily remove his hand.

"Ah, it's about Anne."

"If you speak my wife's name again, Pearce, I swear to God, I—"

"No, no. Just hear me out. It's nothing like…you need to listen to this."

With the door still open, Buck folded his arms across his chest. "What?"

"Word is Anne's all fired up over Tallulah history."

The damn archives again. "And your point?"

"Is she really writing a book?"

"I suppose it's a possibility, provided she can hit on a theme."

"What kind of a theme?"

"Hell, I don't know. She's been fascinated with the Mississippi Delta since she was a little girl. Her daddy wrote a book, remember?"

"How's she going about doing her research?"

"She works at a newspaper, Pearce. The archives are right there, she has a free hand and a journalist's curiosity. Seems obvious." He gave a shrug of his shoulders. "She's doing what journalists do. What's the big deal?"

"The big deal is that I'm in a serious political campaign," Pearce said. "I don't want to give Jack Breedlove any ammunition to hurt me."

Buck paused, studying his brother's dark profile. "What does that have to do with Anne?"

Pearce bent his head, as if weighing his words, before looking directly at Buck. "Does she know about the hunting accident?"

A scuffling, fluttering sound came from under the eaves. A nesting female, the owl was probably agitated by interlopers on her territory. Buck knew the feeling.

"Well, does she?"

"Hmm?"

Pearce ground his teeth. "Does Anne know about Baker?"

"Yeah. It was on the front page of an old issue of the *Spectator*."

"Did she ask any questions?"

He looked at his brother. "Yeah, she asked questions. She's a reporter, did I mention that?"

Pearce rubbed the back of his neck. "It's ancient history, Buck. I hope you told her that." When Buck failed to reply, he went on, "Look, I've got enemies, people who would love to dredge up that old story and get some political mileage out of it."

Buck studied him for a minute, thoughtfully. Then, his decision made, he closed the door to the lodge and faced his brother squarely. "Since you're the one bringing it up, Pearce, there's something that happened the night before Jim Bob died that I've been curious about for a long time."

"I'm telling you, it's ancient history."

"Yeah, you said that. But humor me. And remember, you brought it up."

Pearce grunted. Not looking at Buck, he studied the horizon with an inscrutable expression.

"You clammed up when I asked about the argument you and Jim Bob had that night over Baker's contract with Belle Pointe to gin Belle Pointe cotton."

"He was overcharging us."

"I didn't care about that then and I don't care about it now. But the one thing that's bothered me all these years is what he said about our mother."

Pearce's head lifted, like an animal sensing danger. "I don't remember anything like that."

"Then let me refresh your memory. I may not have his exact words, but it was something like, 'If I talk, your mother will finally get the punishment she deserves.' What did he mean by that, Pearce?"

"Did you hear me? I don't remember that, but hell, everybody was drinking that night, you too, so you can't rely on memory after all these years."

"Just answer the question, Pearce."

"My argument with Jim Bob was about him gouging Belle Pointe on ginning our cotton. He had this too-sweet deal going and I'd just found out about it. I told him Dad might be okay with it, but I wasn't. I don't remember anything about Ma."

"I don't believe you."

Pearce glared at him. "Are you calling me a liar?"

Buck returned the look without flinching. "I'm saying I don't believe you."

After a beat, Pearce shrugged. "Believe what you want. I know what happened."

"And I heard what I heard. To this day, I don't have a clue what he meant by that crack about Mother. I was seventeen, and even though I didn't get along with her, I didn't want to look too hard at anything that might be embarrassing to her. So between my own concerns and you letting me know I was treading on delicate ground by pushing for an explanation, plus Dad lecturing me about the Whitaker name, I let it go. But now I've decided I want an answer. Whatever it turns out to be, I'm not going to embarrass Mother, but you won't be able to stop me this time."

Pearce's tone vibrated with rage. "I'm telling you now like I told you then, Buck. Leave this alone. With this campaign, the eyes of the whole fucking state are on me! You go dragging old skeletons out of a closet, it could be a disaster. I want this senate seat. The next step is D.C. Do you know what that means? Don't you get it?"

He moved in agitation to the porch railing, keeping his back to Buck. "I admit we had words that night, me and Jim Bob, but it was about the contract to gin Belle Pointe cotton, nothing else. An argument like that could have happened anytime, but then the next day he was dead. If you'd told what you overheard, it would have turned into a major scandal."

"As I recall, that was your argument to shut me up before, Pearce. Everything you're saying now, you said then. But what I'm asking about now is the part about our mother that I didn't mention then. Why are you so hot? Why deny it? Who knows, it may not mean anything. What Jim Bob said may be the words of a man who had too much to drink. Hell, maybe he had a thing for Mother, I don't know. But you do know and I think that was what the argument was really about."

"I don't remember anything about Mother," Pearce repeated stubbornly. "And you go stirring up old shit, you may not escape getting some of the stink on you. Any scandal touching the Whitakers at Belle Pointe or me in my campaign is bound to reflect on you, too. Did you think of that?" He gave Buck a hard look. "I don't believe you're in a position to take that chance. You've already stepped in it a couple times lately. What's to keep the Jacks from deciding you're more trouble than you're worth?"

"That sounds like a threat to me," Buck said very softly.

"It's whatever you want to call it. And while you're thinking it over, you need to have a talk with your wife and rein her in. Another hit piece like she did on me at the *Spectator* and I'll begin to think you're working for Breedlove. I won't stand for it."

Buck cocked his head. "Excuse me?"

"You heard me. If she can't write something damn good about me, I don't want her writing anything."

"First of all, Anne has a mind of her own. Any attempt to—as you say 'rein her in'—has the opposite effect. You may be able to bully Claire, but Anne's made of different stuff."

"I want her to stop nosing around in family stuff that's none of her business!" Pearce said belligerently.

Buck refused to be riled. "Actually, my wife is family now, but if you're aiming to discourage her, you're sure going about it in a strange way." He watched Pearce puff up, ready to argue. "Think about it, Pearce. Between your heavy-handed threats and Ma's visits to call her off, she's now convinced there's something in those old issues of the *Spectator* you don't want her to find. And I'm thinking she's right."

Narrow-eyed, Pearce balled his fists in a threatening stance. "First you show up after fifteen years of ignoring Tallulah and Belle Pointe, strutting around and playing up your big-time baseball career, then next thing you finagle your way in at Belle Pointe agitating for change. And somehow, Mama caved. I don't know how or what you said that she went for it, but it's bullshit and it smells."

"Maybe she believes I've got Belle Pointe's best interests at heart," Buck said mildly. "We both know you always put your own interests above all else."

"So now you're ready to derail my campaign and sully the name of Whitaker over something you imagined you overheard fifteen years ago! You think I'll just sit back and let you do all that?" He gave a short, humorless laugh. "Hey, bro, you think you've seen hardball before, but you cross me on this it won't be hardball, it'll be a goddamned bloodbath."

Buck's eyes glinted as he shrugged and spread his hands. "So bring it on…bro."

Seventeen

Buck waited only long enough after Pearce left to take a quick shower before heading off to try and catch Anne at the Marshes'. It worried him that Pearce believed Anne might somehow damage his campaign, because when Pearce was scared, he was dangerous. Buck had seen that once before and he didn't intend to stand by with the possibility of his wife being in harm's way.

After ringing the doorbell at the Marshes' he dropped his gaze to his feet as he waited. Best case scenario, Anne would answer the door. He'd done all he knew to let her know he was sorry for his initial reaction about her pregnancy. But now it was time—past time—for her to be a little less stubborn, to show that she was willing to work with him to save their marriage. He straightened abruptly as the door was opened by Franklin Marsh.

"Buck! By golly, glad to see you, son!" His father-in-law's smile was warm with welcome. With his reading glasses at half mast, his finger marking his place in a *Delta* magazine, he stepped back to let Buck in. "It's about time you gave us a visit. Come in, come in." He called out over his shoulder, "Beatrice, we've got company!"

Buck stepped inside…reluctantly. "I know it's late—"

"Not a bit. I hear you're taking over at Belle Pointe. How's it going?"

"Right now I'm just trying to keep ahead of boll weevils and budworms. Kill off a few million and double that number come back."

"Delta farmer talk," Franklin said, smiling. "And here I thought you were a professional baseball player."

Buck realized he didn't think much about the Jacks lately. His gaze moved beyond Franklin, scanning the stairs. "Is Anne here? I need to talk to her for a minute."

"You just missed her." He turned as Beatrice approached, drying her hands on a tea towel. "Bea, here's Buck wanting to see Anne. Did she say where she was going?"

Beatrice's face lit with pleasure. "Buck! What a nice surprise." Without missing a beat, she walked over and kissed his cheek. "How's that knee?"

He gave himself a pat on the thigh. "Around this time of day I sure know it's there," he admitted.

She gave him a chiding look. "I can't imagine that Tyrone approves of the long hours you put in at Belle Pointe, does he?"

Did everybody in Tallulah know the details of his life, he wondered. "No, he nags me worse than my—" He stopped, realizing his wife didn't nag him anymore. About anything. "I was wondering if you knew where Anne was."

"She went to the *Spectator* offices to get her laptop," Beatrice said. "I think she has her cell phone with her. If you call, she'll let you in, otherwise—"

"She went alone?" He frowned at the thought.

"Well…yes. She—"

"It's past ten o'clock. They roll up the sidewalks in Tallulah at night." He pictured the *Spectator*'s dark and empty offices and his blood ran cold. "She's alone in an empty building? Did you think to tell her what a reckless idea that was?" he said to them. "Anything can happen."

Franklin cleared his throat. "Actually, I didn't know what she had in mind when she left. She didn't tell me where she was going and…" He coughed delicately. "To tell the truth, I assumed she was going to meet you."

Buck already had the door open. "I'll head that way now. If you reach her, try to talk some sense into her. How long has she been gone, Beatrice?"

"Not ten minutes. You could very well catch her before she gets there."

"Call her anyway," he ordered before thinking to add, "Please. And tell her I'm on the way and to be sure those damn doors are locked."

"Yes. Yes, I will," Beatrice said in a faint voice, but he was already making for his car in long strides and never heard her. That poor knee was never going to heal, she thought. But she was almost smiling as she watched him peel out from the curb in his SUV. It appeared that Buck had taken just about as much of Anne's rebellion as he could stand. Those two might be estranged, but if she were any judge of human nature, they wouldn't be much longer.

She glanced up to find Franklin wearing a bemused look, too.

"About time, eh?" he said to her.

"Finally." Beatrice picked up the phone to call as she'd been instructed.

* * *

Buck made it to the town square in six minutes flat. He spotted Anne's empty Mercedes parked in front of the dark and deserted *Spectator* building. He stopped beside it and got out, primed to give her hell for pulling such a foolish stunt.

At the door, he swore fervently as he realized he'd forgotten to ask Franklin for an extra key. But it wasn't necessary. With a start, he realized the door was unlocked and ajar. His frown went darker. She hadn't even locked the damn door. He gave it a furious shove with the flat of his hand and that was when he smelled smoke.

A burst of terror caught him in the chest.

His heart pounding, he peered into the building, but could see no flames. A few steps inside and he realized the smoke seemed to come from offices in the rear. As he made his way around desks and down the hall, he fumbled with the cell phone on his belt. Pulling it out, he sent frantic looks right and left, trying to locate the fire. Trying to locate Anne. Choking and coughing, he looked around for something to cover his mouth. Nothing. He tugged at the tail of his knit shirt and held it over his mouth and nose.

"Anne, where are you?"

No answer. And no light. Thinking the fire must have tripped the master switch, he felt his way further down the hall. The office was dark except for a dim reflection of the outside streetlight through the front windows.

With dread in his heart, he dashed toward the rear of the building, making for the door to the basement. If she was here to get her laptop, it had to be down in the archives. She wouldn't head into a basement that was on fire just to retrieve a laptop, would she?

Hand shaking, he punched out 911 on his cell phone. Then, holding the phone at his ear to wait for a response, he stepped through the door to the archives and stopped at the top of the stairs. "Anne, are you down there?"

"Here! I'm back here. We need help, Buck. Paige is hurt."

We? Paige?

"Nine-one-one," said a calm voice in his ear. "What is your emergency?"

"I'm at the newspaper office on the square, the *Spectator,*" Buck shouted. "There's a fire. And we might need an ambulance. Hurry." Without waiting for a reply or punching off, he clicked the phone back on his belt and took the stairs down two at a time. He was vaguely aware of pain in his knee, but his only thought was to get to Anne.

Smoke was thick and heavy, and in the pitch darkness it was impossible to get any bearings. He dropped low near the floor to avoid the worst of the smoke and moved deeper into the basement. He still hadn't spotted any flames. "Anne, where are you? Call out so I can find you."

"Here…we're here."

He made a half turn at the sound of her voice, took a few steps and crashed into one of the metal shelves, almost knocking it over. Remembering they were arranged in straight aisles, he put out a hand and used it to guide him toward the rear of the basement. Now he could see flames, but so far the fire did not appear to be out of control. The danger in a situation like this, he thought, was smoke inhalation.

Then, by some miracle, he almost ran right into Anne.

She sat crouched on the floor and by the light of fire, he could see that she was cradling Paige in her arms. His niece was not moving.

"Jesus." He went down on his good knee beside them. "Is she…"

"She's inhaled a lot of smoke. We have to get her out of here, Buck, but I don't know where the stairs are. I tried to—"

"I do." *With luck.* He gave her shoulder a reassuring squeeze. "We'll be okay. We just need to follow this set of shelves. They end right at the stairs. Don't stand up. Just keep low where the air is better."

"What about Paige?"

"I'll carry her. You catch hold of my back pocket and don't let go."

He bent and lifted the teenager, who weighed less than some of the weights Ty had him lifting. But in his therapy, he didn't put weight on his knee as he was now forced to do. "Hold on, here we go."

Low to the floor, he took a second or two to inhale deeply and stood up. Keeping the set of shelves on his left, he hurried along the narrow aisle until the shelves ended. Light from the flames behind them offered no illumination here. Praying that he remembered about where the stairs were, he left the security of the shelves and headed blindly across the empty floor. Three strides, four, five. And he bumped into the stair rail.

"Thank God!" Anne said on a strangled cough. Slipping in front of him, she scurried up the stairs and held the door for Buck as he carried Paige through.

"Close it," he ordered when they emerged in the hall. "Confine the fire to the basement." He was breathing hard, coughing and wheezing, and his knee was throbbing painfully. Outside, they heard sirens. And in seconds someone bellowed, "Anybody in there?"

"Here!" Buck shouted. "In the back. The fire's in the basement."

Two firemen outfitted in full gear and carrying flashlights materialized out of the smoky darkness. Behind them, two more firemen appeared. Buck refused to give Paige over to them, but carried her through the office to the front door.

Outside, he stood with his niece in his arms and inhaled deep gulps of fresh air. Beside him, Anne coughed and gasped as two EMTs appeared with a stretcher. Buck gently placed Paige on it and then reached for his wife.

With his arms tight around Anne, they both watched as one of the EMTs slipped an oxygen mask over Paige's face and another covered her with a blanket. Instantly, she began to cough and claw at the mask to tear it off. The female EMT at her head leaned close and spoke quietly to calm her.

"She has a head injury," Anne said, pushing against Buck to get to Paige, but just then Claire's Jaguar screeched to a stop and in a heartbeat, she was out and running toward the ambulance. Close behind, a police unit pulled up, blue lights flashing. Jack Breedlove climbed out and, with a quick glance at the group huddled around Paige, headed to the door of the building.

"Paige! Omigod, Paige!" Claire dashed toward the ambulance where the EMT was securing the teen to the stretcher with a safety strap.

"Mom!" At the sight of her mother, Paige burst into tears.

Claire bent and tried to take her into her arms, but was hindered by the oxygen mask on her face and the security strap holding her down. "Oh, Paige, baby, what happened? Are you hurt?" She looked up anxiously at the EMT. "Is she okay? Does she have any burns?"

"I don't know the extent of her injuries yet," he said. "She appears to—"

"I'm okay, Mom. I never got close to the fire." Paige's momentary spate of tears was done as abruptly as started. Her spunky spirit was back. "It was just the smoke. And I hit my head on something when the lights went out. That's all I remember until Uncle Buck picked me up. I remember thinking I should walk because I didn't want him to hurt his bad knee carrying me, but I couldn't."

"You don't need to worry about my knee," Buck said, fighting an urge to give her a good shaking for scaring the hell out of him. "What you need to worry about is why you were here at this time of night."

Anne heard the edge in his voice as he shifted his gaze to her. "Both of you."

"Aunt Anne didn't know I was here," Paige said meekly.

"I came to get my laptop," Anne explained. With everyone looking on, she didn't add the reason she wanted to get on the Internet. Paige's close call made her search for her biological parents seem somehow insignificant. If Buck hadn't arrived when he did, she wasn't sure she could have gotten Paige out in time to avoid a tragedy.

Jack Breedlove approached with a fireman at his side. "Fire's out, folks," he said. "Sykes here has the status."

Sykes removed his helmet and rubbed a hand over his face. "Not too much damage. More smoke down there than fire. We'll know more after daybreak. Can't see much now."

"I'll have the premises sealed off," Jack said. "And, Sykes, you'll launch an investigation as to the cause?"

"You bet, Chief." He looked at Anne. "Tell your daddy we tried not to do too much damage with the water hoses. Newspaper and microfiche can go up like tinder, but those old metal file cabinets acted like a barricade, so it was confined for a spell…which accounts for all that smoke."

"You have any idea what started it?" Jack now stood at Claire's shoulder, looking as if he wanted to touch her.

Sykes gave a definite nod. "Looks like somebody set it. Several clues telling me it was an amateur, but yeah, I'll go out on a limb and say somebody wanted the *Spectator* burnt up."

Jack's expression was fierce. "You say clues. Such as—"

"He used an accelerant," Sykes said. "It's dark down there now, but you can smell it. What with the metal file cabinets and that old tarpaulin draped over the artificial Christmas tree—they're fire retardant, don't you know—it was more smoke than fire, but sooner or later it would have turned nasty. Good thing it was caught when it was." He looked at Paige. "You had a close call, missy. Lucky Buck was around to rescue you."

"She's lucky Anne spotted her down there," Buck said grimly. Anne recognized the signs. He never showed fear. It came out as anger. From the glint in his eye, she knew he would have a few pithy questions for her.

Paige gave her mother a wary look. "I know you're gonna, like, ground me for doing it, but it was necessary, Mom. I had a good reason."

"There is no good reason for you being in a deserted building alone at ten o'clock at night," Claire said sternly.

Paige fumbled with the strap that confined her to the stretcher. "Can I please get up?"

"Not until I'm told you're okay."

Paige's mouth set stubbornly. "I said I was fine. I just—"

"Listen to your mother, Paige," Jack said in a tone similar to Buck's.

To everyone's surprise, Paige subsided. She looked from Claire to Jack. "I thought you were at the mall in Memphis," she said to her mother.

"Is that why you thought you could sneak out of the house?" Claire asked. "Where's Miriam?"

"Still asleep in front of the TV, I guess. That's where she was when I left."

"How did you get here?" Buck asked. "What were you doing in the archives at this time of night?"

"I wanted Aunt Anne to have the journals and I knew I'd have to sneak them out of the house because nobody at Belle Pointe would let her have them except maybe Mom, and I didn't figure she'd go against Gran to let Aunt Anne look at them." She sent a quick, sideways look at her mother. "So I took them and hid in the back of Mr. Pittman's pickup and I got out when he stopped at the red light at the square. He never even knew."

"I'm going to kill you when we get home," Claire threatened.

Jack's eyes narrowed. "Paige, are you saying you were in the building when the fire started?"

"Uh-huh. I was looking for a place to hide the journals so nobody else would, like, stumble on them or something and I heard this loud whooshing sound. Just suddenly, you know? There was this explosion. So I was way back in the archives and I knew I had to save the journals. If they got burned up, everybody would really kill me."

"You could have died in that fire!" Claire cried.

"Aw, Mom. I didn't even come close to dying."

"You did, Paige." Buck's profound relief was quickly changing into something hard and stern. "And Anne would have died, too. You were overcome with smoke and she couldn't find the door. The two of you could easily have died tonight."

"I'm sorry," Paige said, eyes down, shoulders drooping.

Jack touched Claire's shoulder. "I need to talk to Milton Sykes for a few minutes. If the EMTs think Paige is okay to go home, I'll drive the two of you. You're probably too shaken to be driving." His gaze shifted to Anne. "I have a few questions for you, Anne, but they can wait until tomorrow morning. Can you come down to the police station?"

"Yes, of course. But I need to call my dad and tell him—"

"I've already done it," Buck told her. "He's on his way. Beatrice, too. They were pretty upset." He saw the look on her face and added, "Don't say it. After a close call to his newspaper and his favorite daughter, you can't expect him to wait until morning to check it out."

"I just can't believe this happened." Anne took a deep breath. "Who would want to destroy the *Spectator*? It's the town's history, records of facts and events that would be lost forever. It's—"

She stopped at the look on Buck's face. "We can talk about that later," he told her. "Right now, I think that's your dad and Beatrice heading this way. If not, Jack's sure to ticket the driver since he just shot through the red light."

"Oh, Lord…" Anne put her hands on her cheeks and said to no one in particular, "Just let me get through this night."

"I'll be glad to help you there." Buck growled the words in her ear. She didn't realize he'd been standing so close. She took in a deep, deep breath and turned to face her father and Beatrice.

Her stepmother was almost as upset as Franklin. Spotting Anne, she rushed over and pulled her into a fierce embrace. Anne felt her trembling and realized with a rush of emotion that she'd come to feel deep affection for Beatrice and hated the thought of distressing her.

"Oh, Anne, what a close call! Buck was right. You shouldn't have come here at night alone. I shouldn't have let you. What was I thinking? What if Buck—"

Anne squeezed her hand. "I'm sorry for giving you such a scare, Beatrice. Because Tallulah's so small, and I feel so safe here, I just didn't consider it being in the least risky. Paige and I were lucky that Buck showed up when he did."

She hadn't yet had a chance to ask him why he'd decided to talk to her after avoiding her for two weeks.

Beatrice touched Anne's cheek with a shaky hand. "I don't know when I've been so scared. Don't ever do that again."

"Not if I can help it." She turned to her dad. Franklin opened his arms and she walked into his embrace. With her throat tight, she held on to him. Here was someone who wouldn't scold or berate her for her foolishness. But she could tell that he was as shaken as Beatrice and unable to say a word for a long minute.

"You are so precious to us, Annie-girl," he whispered.

"I'm sorry, Dad. I just didn't think."

"You couldn't have waited until morning to get that damn laptop?" It was a rebuke, but a gentle one.

"I could have. I should have." She dropped her gaze, unable to meet his concerned gaze. Unwilling to explain the urgency that drove her to try and find her birth parents. She felt ashamed and guilty, but even now she knew deep down that she would not quit.

"I need to talk to Melvin Sykes about the fire," Franklin told her. "Beatrice, why don't you take Anne back to the house in our car? I don't know how long I'll be here tonight."

"I'll take her," Buck said. "There's something we need to talk about. If it's all the same to you, I'll drop her at your house later…" His gaze moved to Anne. "That is, if you don't have a problem with that plan."

Beatrice spoke before Anne could. "That's good. That's fine. I'll just check on Paige before I leave. That girl has a lot of explaining to do." Unable to resist, she gave Anne another heartfelt hug, kissed her on the cheek and reluctantly let her go. "I love you, Anne."

As Anne hesitated, looking into her stepmother's eyes, Buck caught her elbow. "My car's there," he said, already steering her away. "Next to yours. Is it okay to go to the lodge?"

Her chin went up and her voice was as cool as his attitude as she freed her elbow. "I've been scolded enough for coming here alone tonight," she warned, primed to resist.

He held up both hands. "No scolding."

She gave him a narrow-eyed look. She had been far too happy to learn he'd been looking for her, but his curtness since rescuing her was a chilly reminder that for the past two weeks he'd avoided her. "Can whatever you want to say be done without throwing in a lecture as to how foolish I am…"

"No lectures." Hands still up, he added, "I promise."

It was her call. Without another word, she got in the car.

They were well on the way to the lodge when he turned to look at her. "Are you really all right?"

"My throat is a little raw from inhaling smoke, but other than that, I'm fine."

"I've got some Gatorade in the fridge at the lodge. Drinking that'll probably help."

"Okay. Thanks."

"No wine."

"I'll try to make it through the night without it." She gazed straight ahead.

"There's something else a lot better than wine to help both of us make it through the night."

She turned to look at him. "I thought you had something urgent to talk to me about."

"Getting you in the sack is urgent to me."

"Buck—"

"Just kidding. Well, I'm not kidding, but it's hard not to make a pass when we're alone together and it's midnight."

"Just tell me what's on your mind."

"Let's get to the lodge, then we'll talk."

A brief glance at the set of his jaw and she let it go. As she forced herself to concentrate on the look of the dark world outside, all she wanted was to move over and be close to him. To be warmed by his body. To be comforted by his strength. She was still shaken by how close she'd come to losing her life in that basement tonight and how sad it would have been because she and Buck were barely speaking. While she struggled in panic and fear trying to save Paige and herself, she had known a deep, despairing regret that she would miss living out her life with Buck. The thought had filled her with anguish.

"Where's the damn laptop?" Buck asked as he made the turn that led up to the lodge.

"What?"

"Your laptop. Isn't that why you went back tonight?"

"Oh. Yes." She lifted one shoulder. "I don't know. I forgot all about it when I got inside and realized there was a fire." She pushed back her tousled hair and caught the smoky scent. "Ugh, my hair smells like smoke. I need a shower."

"Not a problem. I think I can find a clean T-shirt."

Her mind veered away from the thought of being naked in the shower with Buck nearby. "I hope Paige doesn't have a concussion."

He pulled up at the lodge and cut the engine. "I'd be surprised if she did. I've had a few and she was way too sassy."

Fumbling at the unfamiliar door handle, she got it open before he reached her side of the SUV, but he was there to catch her on the long step down to the ground. That was the trouble with these huge gas hogs, no ordinary woman could exit an SUV gracefully. They were made for men, tall men.

She drew a shaky breath as she felt him brush a kiss to her temple. It was silly, but she felt the quick start of tears in her eyes and her throat went tight. Now that she was standing so close to him, she gave up the battle. Slipping her arms around his waist, she buried her face in his chest. "I was so scared," she admitted in a whisper. "I thought I'd never see you again."

For a minute he was silent, holding her tight. "I almost had a heart attack when I knew you were inside and all I could see was a solid wall of smoke."

"I couldn't even remember the reasons I had for leaving you."

"I can help you out there." With her body molded to his, he smiled against her temple. "I'm grumpy, moody, egotistical and I cuss too much."

"And pigheaded with a bad attitude."

He laughed, low and rough, tickling her ear. "Okay, as nice

as it feels standing here, we still have to climb those freakin' porch steps." Giving her a final hug, he turned, settled his arm around her waist and started the climb.

It was slow going. Buck's knee had been sorely abused and as much as he hated it, he needed to lean a little on Anne to make it to the top.

"Ty's not going to be happy when he looks at that knee tomorrow," she predicted, as he unlocked the door.

"I get a break. He's not coming tomorrow. He's at some kind of seminar in Memphis for two days." He reached for one of several canes in a tall umbrella stand just inside the door. "By the time he gets back, it'll be okay."

Anne wrapped her arms around herself. "What did you want to talk to me about, Buck?"

He didn't say anything for a minute, just looked at her. Then, using the cane, he pushed away from the door and headed to the kitchen. "Let's get you that drink, then we can talk in the den." He made a motion toward the fridge, but she stopped him, knowing he needed to get off his knee.

"I'll do it. Why don't you get settled someplace that's comfortable?"

"I'm okay." He propped against the door facing and watched while she filled a glass with ice before pouring the bright yellow-green drink.

"I hope this isn't as vile tasting as it looks," she said, wrinkling her nose.

"We must have had gallons of that stuff on hand at home," he said with surprise. "You've never tasted it?"

"No. I'm not the one who needs electrolytes. You're the athlete."

"Yeah. C'mon, let's get out of here."

In the great room, she watched him ease down on the leather couch and reach to drag over a large ottoman as a prop for his leg. She picked up a cushion and offered it to him. Although he tried to conceal it, she saw a flash of pain on his face as he elevated his knee on the cushion. She recognized the act: grit the teeth and bear the pain. No whining.

Shaking her head, she set her own drink on the coffee table and walked into his bedroom, going straight to the bathroom medicine chest. Scanning the contents, she found one narcotic for pain, but she knew he wouldn't take that since he hadn't yet gotten around to telling her what he wanted to say. Since he was having trouble spitting it out, it couldn't be good news. As she shook four tablets from a bottle of ordinary aspirin, her hands were unsteady, a dead giveaway that she was nervous, too. Whatever it was, the good news was that he wanted to share it with her.

Eighteen

When she returned bearing aspirin and a bottle of water, he was stretched out on the couch with his knee elevated. Without even a grunt of protest, he took the aspirin, tossed all four back at once and washed them down. "Thanks."

She reclaimed her own drink, which wasn't as bad as she feared, and sat on the edge of the ottoman facing him. "Last chance," she said. "Talk to me."

"The hell of it is I don't know how to say this. There's no way I can make it sound anything but dreadful."

"Is it that bad?"

"I don't know. I'm not sure." He raked a hand through his hair, looking trapped. She knew only his bum knee kept him from jumping up to pace. "Pearce came over last night. It was late. He's made it plain he wants me to get active in his campaign, but I've been dodging him. Except for the sessions with Ty for physical therapy, I'm up at daylight and on my way to Belle Pointe and I don't get back until late. On purpose. He tries calling my cell, but when I see it's Pearce, I just don't answer."

"Why are you so reluctant to tell him you aren't going to support him?"

"I've been thinking about that. It sounds dumb, doesn't it? Or spineless. I guess it's family loyalty, something bred in me, in all us Whitakers. By not supporting Pearce, he—and my mother—would see it as out-and-out betrayal." He rubbed the back of his neck wearily. "The thing is, I know Jack Breedlove, and not Pearce, will be the better representative for the people in this area."

"I agree."

He sent her another quick sidelong glance. "By the way, did you see the way Jack looked at Claire tonight?"

"Like he wanted to grab her and disappear? Yes, I saw it. What's more, I think Claire would fall back in love with Jack in a heartbeat. I don't think she ever really got over that teenage love affair all those years ago, Buck."

"Seems like Jack didn't either. My God, what a Pandora's box if they aren't careful. She's a married woman, Anne," he said, frowning.

"An unhappy married woman," Anne said.

"With a drinking problem. Talk about a recipe for disaster."

Anne settled in the corner of the couch. "She's sober right now, two weeks and counting."

"How do you know that?"

"She dropped in at the *Spectator* today to talk about Paige's new and better attitude. She wanted to thank me, claiming I had something to do with it, which I doubt. Paige's turnaround makes a lot more sense to me when Claire mentioned she'd quit drinking and had joined AA the day after that awful Sunday-night dinner at Belle Pointe."

He did a double take. "Alcoholics Anonymous? No kidding?"

"I don't think I'm betraying a confidence telling you. She said Pearce planned to lock her away in some rehab facility to keep her from embarrassing him, but she's not going to let him." Anne took another sip of the sports drink, made a face and gave it up. "It's not Jack and Claire you wanted to talk about, is it?"

"No. Pearce wanted to know what you were really up to by fooling around in the archives. He's worried about what you'll find and possibly misconstrue."

"Then there must be something to be found, because that's essentially the same thing his mother said when she tried to warn me off."

He studied the label on the water bottle. "Finally he got around to asking if you'd found an account of the hunting accident."

"I can see why he wouldn't want people to be reminded of any tragedy with his name attached. But it was ruled an accident and accidents happen. Voters are pretty forgiving about stuff like that."

"I think I'm the wild card in this," Buck said, setting the bottle aside. "Since I didn't tell everything I should have when the accident happened, he's afraid I might decide to talk now, maybe tell you." With a lift of one shoulder, he met her eyes. "Especially since I won't endorse him in this campaign."

Anne was frowning, still confused. "So you wanted to bring me out here to say…what? That Pearce is antsy about what I'll dig up and possibly reveal in another article? He wants you to tell me to stop?" Her face changed as the answer came. "That's it, isn't it? You're supposed to tell me to find some other way to pass the time while I'm in Tallulah. What did you have in mind, Buck? That I should take up quilting? Or pottery? Maybe learn to make organic soap? Or hey, I could start clerking in my stepmother's store."

Now it was Anne who felt a compulsion to spring up and pace. Instead, she took in a calming breath. "Read my lips, Buck. Nobody's going to keep me away from my job as a journalist or those archives."

Buck turned his head and looked out the pitch dark window. A long, long minute passed. Finally, releasing a tired breath, he said simply, "I wish."

"You wish?" She gave a ladylike snort. "You wish? Well, make another wish because no matter what you say, I'm sticking!"

Heedless of his knee, he shifted on the couch to be able to face her squarely. "I wish you had it right in everything you said because that would make it so simple. And ordinary. What I suspect is a lot worse." He paused, looking away. "I went over to Franklin's house tonight to tell you that you needed to be careful poking around in those archives. I was going to ask you to be discreet in discussing what you found, and not because I worried over you misconstruing anything about the Whitakers or Pearce or…or anything personal. Frankly, I worried that Pearce seemed desperate enough to do…something."

He seemed to find it difficult to look her in the eye. "And whatever he did, it would be made to look like an accident."

"What are you saying?" Eyes wide, she pressed her fingers to her mouth. "Is Pearce the person who set the fire tonight? Did he do it to destroy the *Spectator*'s archives?"

"Pearce is at a fund-raiser," Buck reminded her in a flat voice.

It was a minute before she got it. "Someone else did it for him?"

"Considering what's at stake, I think he'd get one of his stooges to do it."

"What if Paige had died?" She was horrified. "His own daughter."

"And my wife. He would have attended the funeral looking grief-stricken and made all the appropriate gestures of sympathy to Claire. And me." Eyes closed, he leaned back against the couch. "He's done it before."

Jim Bob Baker.

Now Anne did get to her feet. Hugging her arms, she stood over him, struggling to take it all in. "And you know all this…how, Buck?"

"I don't know it. What I have are strong suspicions because of the way he reacted last night. I think what spooked him was that I asked about that remark Baker made about our mother."

"Something about getting what she deserved, wasn't it?"

Bucked turned his head on the couch to look at her. "'If I talk, your mother's going to get the punishment she deserves.'"

"Do you know now what he was talking about?"

"No, I don't. Pearce claimed he didn't remember anything like that. I told him I didn't believe him, but he stuck with his original story. He went on about Baker gouging Belle Pointe in a contract to gin the cotton crop, same as he did all those years ago. But I don't think Pearce would have killed him over something like that."

"Are you convinced now that he actually did murder him? You know what that means, Buck?"

"I don't know what to think. What I heard last night when

he warned me about stirring up trouble for him was a definite threat. Then, just to be sure he had my attention, he threw in your name. Now, there's a fire that would have destroyed the archives but for a stroke of luck. If I'd been fifteen minutes later, you and Paige—" He dropped his head in his hands. "My own brother. His young daughter. It's just so freakin' crazy!"

"It's criminal, Buck. You have to go to Jack Breedlove."

He lifted his head and met her eyes. "And tell him what? I don't have a shred of proof, only suspicion. And they're political opponents. What if I'm wrong? It would destroy Pearce's candidacy. I don't want him to win, but I don't want to be the one to bring about his destruction. I have to get the facts and I have to do it on my own, Anne."

"Maybe your mother—" But she stopped, shaking her head. "I can't see her telling you anything that has even a remote possibility of damaging Pearce. You're right, you'll have to do it on your own."

"I was thinking I might get some help from you."

"Me? How could I help?"

"As a journalist, you're trained to look beyond the obvious. And there's just nobody else I can trust."

"Thanks, I think," she said dryly. "If you're really scraping the bottom of the barrel and I'm all you've got to choose from, I guess I'll do it."

Before she finished, he was sitting up straight looking at her in exasperation. "You once told me I didn't trust you. I denied it then and now in telling you all this, I think I'm demonstrating the deepest kind of trust between a man and a woman and still you don't like it." For a second, silence stretched between them. And when he spoke again it was plain that he was baffled trying to please her. "I can't win with you, Anne."

Her heart turned over at the bleak look of him. It dawned on her that their relationship had changed. Buck had changed. Somewhere along the way, with her pregnancy and miscarriage, her flight to Tallulah, his attempt to follow and bring her home, some subtle shift in power had occurred. Buck was more attuned to her needs, not so blindly focused on his own.

She sat down close and reached out, cradling his jaw in one hand. He immediately covered it with his own. "We keep messing up, don't we?" she said in a soft voice. "You trust me with a deep secret and I try to find some flaw in why you'd do that. I'm sorry."

He caught her hand and kissed her palm. "I'm just so tired of being without you. I've run out of ways to convince you to work with me to fix what's wrong. We have to be together to do that. I don't know why you can't see it."

She sat silent and unmoving for a long minute, considering. "Okay."

He went still, eyes narrowed as they searched hers. "Okay... what?"

"Okay, we'll try to fix things and we'll be together while we work on it."

He was still suspicious. "Can we sleep together?" He waited a beat, then said, "Oh, shit. Forget I said that. You're not ready for that yet, are you?"

Smiling, using her finger to trace the shape of his mouth, she asked, "Do you think we could stay in the same house—" she looked around "—or lodge—and still sleep in separate bedrooms?"

He angled his head back to get a good look at her face. "That's a trick question, right?"

She laughed and launched herself over into his lap. Startled, it took a split second before his arms came around her, hard and tight. And with a sound that came from his heart, he pressed his face in the sweet hollow of her throat. "Am I dreaming?"

"No." Carefully, keeping in mind his damaged knee, she straddled him. "Am I hurting your knee?"

With his arms locked around her, he mumbled, "What knee?"

Another soft laugh. "My hair smells like smoke."

"Your skin smells like heaven." His tongue came out and he licked the hollow of her throat. "And you taste even better."

She rocked against his pelvis and even through the rough thickness of his jeans, she could feel his arousal. "Better than heaven?"

"Has to be." With his hands he framed her face, needing to look in her eyes. "If we get started here, it may be hard to stop. Maybe impossible. I'm that hungry for you, Anne."

"I don't have a problem with that," she said quietly.

Still holding her gaze, one hand went to the front pocket of his jeans and with a thumb and one finger, he pulled out a condom and waggled it before her. "Just so there's no misunderstanding," he told her.

She looked at him. "How long have you had that?"

"Since the day I reached the city limits of Tallulah."

"Oh." She watched him tear it open and set the foil pack on the end table within reach. "Okay…"

And if there was some doubt in her voice, he told himself they would talk about it later. Not now. God, not now.

Holding her gaze, moving at a pace she could easily block,

his hands went to the buttons on her shirt. He stripped it away and then with a deft flick of his fingers, he had her jeans open. "We can do this here or somewhere else," he said, his voice sounding to his own ears a little unsteady as if he had some kind of obstruction in his throat.

Without a word, she was on her feet and kicking off her jeans. Only her bra and bikini panties left. Wanting to entice him, she slipped the straps of her bra off one shoulder slowly. Buck simply lay back against the couch and watched. But he was breathing hard, praying he would be able to make this last long enough to at least give her what she needed.

His jeans were unsnapped and the zipper down now, but all she could see was a strip of white underwear. Just to look at him made her mouth go dry and her heart race. She wiggled out of her bra and tossed it toward the fireplace. The bikinis she eased down and kicked away without taking her eyes off Buck. There was color in his face and a stillness about him that was almost predatory as his gaze roamed over her, from her throat to her breasts and waist and further, his whiskey-gold eyes darkening with heat.

And then with a curl of his body that was almost violent, he reared up and reached for her. Again she was astride him, this time his hands framing her face and his kiss devouring her. There was nothing gentle in the way his tongue plunged, his need so fierce that the sounds coming from him were almost animal-like. And there was nothing shy in the way Anne returned the kiss.

Ah, the familiar taste of him. She'd needed this, she'd craved it. And while she drowned in sensation, she was unable to recall why she'd denied herself all these weeks.

Breaking away, Buck left a trail of openmouthed kisses

until he reached her breasts. He wanted to smile as he drew a nipple into his mouth, heard the tiny sharp breath she inhaled, felt her sigh as he teased the other until it peaked and she cried out with the sheer pleasure-pain of it.

Suddenly he set her aside. "Out of this chair," he muttered, rising. "We've got to get out of this chair." And then he had her on the floor, the delicious weight of him warm and familiar, so wonderfully familiar. She wasn't sure how he managed it, but somehow he'd shucked his jeans and the condom was on and he was probing, finding her wet and ready. As she whimpered, he made a like sound and drove into her, plunging deep and true.

For a few blind minutes, he held her still, his forehead against hers, his breath harsh and strained as he forced himself into an unnatural disciplined pause. "I love you, Anne," he told her in a voice that was unsteady and oddly strained with the effort to hold off. But she was mindless with a greedy need for satisfaction and battled back a momentary urge to give him the words he wanted to hear. Instead, she made a plaintive sound and arched her body to force him into movement. But he was stubbornly still, rigid with tension. Waiting.

"Tell me," he managed, his mouth at the corner of hers, his shaft deep inside her, unmoving. "I need to hear you say it, Anne."

After a heartbeat when she finally managed to focus, she felt something inside her give over. Yield. She gave a shaky, strangled laugh and shifted so that she could look in his eyes. "This is blackmail," she told him.

"Yeah." He nipped at her chin. "Whatever works."

"I guess it works," she said, pulling him down until her lips were just barely touching his, "because it's easy to say now. I love you, Buck."

She could say it, she realized, because it was true. She loved him and she forgave him.

He shuddered like a man reprieved from the gallows. For Buck, the long, long weeks had built up a need that would not now be denied. Claiming her mouth in a kiss that was lush and deep, he fell blindly into the ancient rhythm, taking Anne with him, both lost in the delicious choreography of two who knew each other well, who were perfectly attuned. And when he felt the convulsive tightening around him, he was buried to the hilt, glorying in the feel of his wife in the throes of her climax. Then, with a shout, he let himself follow.

Spent, she lay boneless and satiated beneath Buck, resisting when he made to shift his weight from her. Only two fingers were capable of moving anyway, lazily sifting through the hair on the back of his neck. With his face pressed to her throat, she could feel his raging heartbeat finally slowing. The whole thing had taken less than seven minutes.

Somewhere outside an owl gave a soft hoot. "She lives here," Buck managed to say.

"Who?"

"Owl."

"Oh."

"She's a mommy with a nest under the eaves. She's very territorial."

Anne imagined the female owl protecting her precious eggs. "I know the feeling," she murmured.

His nod, after a long minute, was gentle with understanding.

Anne frowned with a sudden thought and her fingers stilled. "Did we do any damage to your knee?"

"I guess we'll know when I try to get up off the floor."

She pushed at him to get a look at his face. "Are you serious?"

He grinned. "Nah, it's fine." He sighed expansively and eased off her. "Trust me, everything is fine. Or it will be once we make it to my bed."

A few seconds passed as he helped her sit up, catching her chin so that their eyes met and he could search her face. "You are going to stay with me tonight, aren't you?"

"Yes. But I need to call my parents—" She stopped, realizing her mistake. "Rather, I need to call my dad and Beatrice. I find myself considering them as my parents without thinking."

He scooted so that he rested against the couch, pulling her with him. "Easy to understand," he said, fitting her in the crook of his shoulder. "It's plain that Beatrice loves you. Tonight when she realized you'd had such a close call, she was every bit as distressed as Laura Marsh herself would have been."

"Sometimes I feel a little guilty that we've drawn so close and it seems so natural."

"I bet your mama would be happy that you and your stepmama are so close. Laura wouldn't want you to feel guilty."

"She was so generous-hearted, I know she wouldn't." But Anne still felt a niggling sense of disloyalty. She shifted a little and gazed thoughtfully up at the ceiling fan. "Beatrice has been so sweet to me from the day we met. I don't think it's due so much to me in particular. It's a natural extension of her affection for my dad. She loves him so she loves me." She paused, still puzzling it out. "Maybe another woman might not be so…loving, but Beatrice has a lot of love to give and because she's never had any children of her own, I happen to be the lucky recipient. Paige, too."

Buck made a disgruntled sound. "Don't remind me of my headstrong niece. When I think of what could have happened tonight, I swear I want to lock that kid in the attic at Belle Pointe and not let her out until she's about twenty-five years old."

"You'd have to lock me up, too," Anne said, "because even though this is a small town without much crime, I shouldn't have gone to a deserted office building at night alone."

"Locking you up is not an option." He bent and pressed a kiss on one breast. "But tell me this. Where did Paige get the idea that she had to sneak the journals to you? If you'd asked, I would have taken you to Belle Pointe with me any day you wanted."

"That's the funny thing. We never discussed it. Did you know where they were?"

"Now you mention it, no. I assumed they were around somewhere."

She settled back. "Even so, Buck, I don't see your mother just handing them over in view of the fact that she's warned me off snooping into the Whitaker family's past."

"Too bad." He angled his head to look at her. "You're mine and you're a Whitaker and she'll have to get over it."

"Maybe easier said than done for her. Victoria has a very proprietary attitude toward all things Belle Pointe," she said dryly. "I don't think she's convinced that I've quite measured up as a 'real Whitaker' yet."

"Then I guess we'll just have to have a baby. Will that be real enough?"

She went still. "Just like that?"

"Just like that." His gaze was steady as she searched his face. And after a minute when she was still silent, he said, "How about we get started now?"

Nineteen

The next morning, Buck was up and out of the house at daylight without waking Anne. Before leaving, he'd made a couple of calls and was easy in his mind about leaving his wife alone. With what he planned, he was convinced it was the last easy moment he'd have that day.

Sunrise was still just a pink promise in the sky when he stopped at the big house at Belle Pointe. Pearce would be in a dead sleep. Buck was counting on that. It paid to have the advantage when confronting his big brother.

As he expected, the front door was unlocked. He opened it and went straight to the stairs. He had a foot on the first step when his mother appeared. Clad in a blue dressing gown, she carried a cup of coffee in one hand and the newspaper in another.

"Buck. This is early, even for you. I'm surprised you left your wife. How is she?"

"You heard about the fire?"

"Of course. Everybody in Tallulah heard about it. She's well or I assume you wouldn't be here." She frowned, noting that he was on the verge of heading upstairs. "Where are you going?" she asked sharply.

Upstairs, all was quiet. Nobody stirring yet at Belle Pointe except his mother and, of course, Miriam. Good. He hiked a chin at the coffee she held in her hand. "I'd like a go-cup of that when I'm done, if you've got it to spare."

"See Miriam in the kitchen," she said faintly, still frowning. "You didn't answer. I can't imagine what reason you have to go upstairs at this hour."

It had been years since he'd seen Victoria before she was made up and outfitted for the day. Now, he was struck that she suddenly looked every year of her age. Without makeup and her hair not perfectly styled, he saw that her skin had a sallow cast and there were circles under her eyes, dark circles. He had a fleeting thought that she looked downright unhealthy. Maybe she'd had a bad night after Paige's close call.

"Actually, Ma, I thought I'd pay Pearce a little visit."

"You will do no such thing," she said with shocked disapproval. "Why, he's not even awake at this hour."

"I know." He grinned and took the first half of the stairs in two strides. "I was counting on that."

"Buck! You come back here this instant."

But he was already up the sweeping staircase and headed for the double-door entrance to the wing occupied by Pearce and his wife. Only once had Buck been in this renovated section of the big house and that had been after Pearce's wedding when he'd hired an architect to add on to the rear and reconfigure the original floor plan. Fortunately, he'd done nothing to change the look of the front of Belle Pointe, but he'd forever altered the antebellum credentials of the place. Buck wondered about John Whitaker's reaction and imagined their father turning over in his grave. He wondered, not for the first time, why Victoria had allowed it. She'd always had a thing for Belle Pointe's heritage.

But Pearce's carelessness in ignoring the historical significance of Belle Pointe was not on his mind as he crossed an elegant sitting room with long strides to reach another set of double doors. Had to be the bedroom. Without bothering to knock, he threw them wide and walked right in.

Only one person occupied the king-size bed and he was motionless, still sleeping. Where was Claire, he wondered, then found himself unsurprised that she didn't sleep with his brother anymore. Couldn't blame her.

His footsteps made no sound on the deep carpet as he crossed to the window and pulled hard on the cord that opened the drapes. The room was instantly flooded with early-morning sun.

Pearce made a disgruntled sound and rolled over, away from the shaft of sunlight that struck his face.

Behind Buck, Claire appeared in the doorway. Already fully dressed, she looked surprised and then slightly amused to find Buck in their bedroom. "What's going on?"

Buck put his finger to his lips and shook his head. Reaching over, he caught the expensive comforter in one hand and yanked it off. Pearce, buck naked, rolled over in a temper and spotted Buck. For a second, he blinked in sleepy confusion.

He reared up in stunned shock. "What the hell!"

Buck stood with his back to the window. "Claire, you might want to leave us now," he said calmly. "You may find what I've got to say to Pearce embarrassing."

"Get the hell out of my house!" Pearce ordered. "Claire, you stay right where you are."

With a casual lift of one shoulder, Buck crossed his arms over his chest and leaned against an antique armoire. "Fine. Suits me. I just thought you might want to keep our conversation private."

"We're not having a conversation in my bedroom, private or otherwise. How'd you get in here?"

"Through the door. And yeah, we are having a conversation, Pearce," Buck said quietly. "One that's way overdue."

Pearce paused a long minute to study his brother's face and found something that cooled his outrage. Without taking his eyes off Buck, he said in a milder tone, "Go downstairs, Claire."

She had moved from the door to stand at the window and appeared to have no intention of leaving. "Don't mind me," she said and perched on the edge of an elegant chaise. "I'm dying to know what this is all about."

"Nothing that concerns you," Pearce said, not taking his gaze off Buck's implacable face. "Buck, tell her to leave."

"C'mon, hon." Buck walked over to Claire and took her hand. "He's right. This is between me and my brother. Go have some coffee and I'll be down in a minute."

"I'm holding you to that." With her face full of curiosity, she allowed herself to be led to the doors.

Pearce was out of bed when Buck strolled back to take up where they left off. "You've got me at a disadvantage here, bro. How about I take a piss and put on my pants?"

"My wife was at a disadvantage last night when she found herself trapped in a burning building. The SOB who set it left your unconscious fourteen-year-old daughter on the floor to die." Buck snatched a pair of pants folded over a clothes caddy and threw them at Pearce. "They both survived, but only by the grace of God."

With his pants shielding his privates, Pearce's dark brows snapped together in a fierce frown. "Now you wait just a goddamn minute, Buck. I don't like what you're insinuating."

"And I don't like what I'm thinking, Pearce. So tell me something that will convince me my own brother isn't a full-fledged sociopath."

"That's a helluva thing to say, man. You've had a bug up your ass about me since you got here and I'm sick of it. I was at a fund-raiser last night! Somebody said there'd been a fire at the *Spectator,* yeah, but I was told it was put out before any harm was done. I didn't know Paige or Anne were involved until I got home."

Buck's smile was wolfish as he watched Pearce put on his pants. "Did that disappoint you, Pearce?"

"Disappoint me?" Pearce looked up with one leg in his pants, genuinely baffled. "That Paige wasn't harmed? What do you take me for, man?"

Buck was shaking his head, looking weary. "I'm working on that, Pearce. At this point, I'll be goddamned if I know. When Jim Bob Baker died I gave you the benefit of the doubt. I'm wondering what other low-down stuff you've done since. Stuff I might have prevented if I'd done the right thing then."

"And I'm wondering if you have some brain damage from that last concussion." Pearce gave a hiss of exasperation and began to pace the room. "Just listen to yourself. You're talking like an idiot. I am a respected individual in this town. I'm going to win that senate seat and in four years I'll be in Washington, D.C. You are not going to screw it up for me, Buck."

"You almost killed my wife, you bastard!"

Pearce swung around, eyes blazing. "That's a goddamn

lie! You go around saying crazy stuff like that, my campaign is toast. You've gotta get a grip." After a beat or two, he gave a sickly smile as if trying to sooth a fractious four-year-old. "We're family, Buck. When you get right down to it, I'm a Whitaker. You're a Whitaker. We can't lose sight of that."

"What's in those archives that you wanted destroyed?"

"Listen to yourself!" Pearce yelled, losing patience again. "Read my lips. There's nothing there I would need to kill anybody over. Your wife is a pain in the ass, yeah, but I wouldn't try to kill her. And Paige…Jesus, man, she's my little girl. I'm her father. What's the matter with you? Why are you all over my case after fifteen goddamn years of ignoring me and everybody else at Belle Pointe?"

"That could be the problem here, Pearce. For fifteen years, I haven't cared enough to even think about you or Belle Pointe. But now I'm here and you've trespassed on my territory by endangering my wife and that young girl and I'm going to see you pay for it."

Pearce sat down heavily on the bed. "Man, this is crazy. I don't know what else to say to convince you. I tell you, it beats me where you're getting all these bullshit ideas. It's paranoia, that's what it is. I'd expect it from Claire, she's about half-nuts nowadays. But you. Hell, you disappoint me, bro. I tell you, I don't know anything about that fire."

"You made a special trip out to the lodge to grill me about Anne's purpose in digging into those old files at the *Spectator.* You told me to call her off. Think. Weren't those your exact words? 'Call her off,' you said. When I wouldn't promise, you threatened to give me grief. Well, it would have grieved me to lose my wife in a fire. As for damaging my stock with the Jacks, have at it. As you said to me a while ago, when you throw mud, some of it sticks on yourself. See how far your campaign gets after that."

It sickened him to think his own brother would deliberately try to damage his career, but it was a thousand times worse that his vendetta would harm Anne and Paige. "I can't prove anything yet, but I'm here to tell you that I'm going to find proof. I'm going to be all over your ass like white on rice, bro." His lip curled on the word. "As for making it to the U.S. Senate, it'll be a cold day in hell when that happens if I have any say in it."

While Pearce sputtered, Buck turned in disgust and left

Victoria was waiting when Pearce stormed down the stairs a few minutes later. "What was that all about?" she demanded as he shouldered past her on his way to the front door.

"That sonofabitch accused me of setting the fire at the *Spectator* last night! Like I give a freakin' nickel about all that old shit Franklin Marsh plays guard dog over." He shoved a hand in his pocket and swore viciously when he came up empty. "Shit, the bastard rattled me so I forgot my car keys. Claire!" he bellowed up the stairs. "Bring me the keys to the Lexus!"

"You're not going anywhere until you explain what happened with your brother," Victoria stated. "Now, what about the fire?"

"That's just it. I don't know a damn thing about the fire," Pearce said, pacing restlessly while keeping an eye out for Claire, who suddenly appeared from the vicinity of the kitchen.

"I'm waiting to be told what's going on," she said. Moving to the door, she peered out to catch sight of Buck. "Where's Buck? Did he leave?"

"Go back upstairs with Paige, Claire," Victoria ordered. But her expression changed as she realized Claire was not in her nightclothes, but a trim suit and heels. And obviously on her way out. "Where are you going? Do you know what time it is? Where's Paige?"

"She's in the shower. I offered to let her stay home today, considering the circumstances, but she's so full of last night's adventure that she can't wait to milk it for all it's worth at school." Seeing no trace of Buck outside, she turned back to them. "I wanted to catch Buck before we left for school. Is he gone?"

"I'm sure I don't know," Victoria said frostily. "He appeared this morning at an indecent hour and barged upstairs with absolutely no consideration for anyone's privacy. I don't know what's come over him since he returned to Tallulah."

"Superstardom, that's what," Pearce muttered. "He's a goddamn hero elsewhere, but he's nobody here at Belle Pointe. By God, I want him off the property by nightfall."

"We won't even go into why you can't order him off Belle Pointe," Claire pointed out in disgust. "He has as much right here as you. But why would you want to do that? With Will gone, he's saved our asses by stepping in to supervise the crops this season. As to being a hero, he saved the lives of his wife and our daughter last night. If that's not heroic, I don't know what else you'd call it."

Both Victoria and Pearce stared at her as if she'd suddenly turned into a stranger. "This is none of your concern, Claire," Victoria snapped. "Go back upstairs and see to Paige."

"Paige is fourteen years old and doesn't need me to dress her, Victoria." She shifted her attention back to Pearce. "What did you mean when you said Buck accused you of setting the fire? Why would he think that?"

"Beats the shit out of me, but that kind of loose talk can destroy my campaign. Which I believe is what he's been after all along, to blacken my name and throw the election to Jack Breedlove."

Claire huffed in disgust. "That is so ridiculous, Pearce. He was totally uninterested in the fact that you were in a campaign until he got to Tallulah, and the only reason he's here now is to try and reconcile with Anne. Get it out of your head that he has some kind of vendetta against you."

"It sure as hell seems like a vendetta," Pearce said. "And try making yourself useful, Claire. I need my car keys."

She reached over and plucked them out of a bowl on an antique library table within arm's reach of where he stood. "These car keys?" She tossed them at him.

Surprised, he caught them in midair, then frowned at her, catching what appeared to be a gleam of temper in her eyes at his rudeness.

"Anything else I can do for you?" she asked him sarcastically. "Can I bring you a cup of coffee? Tea? Arsenic?"

He glared at her. "What's the matter with you?" He threw up his hands, looking genuinely confounded. "What's the matter with everybody around here lately? Am I the only sane person left in this fucking house?"

"I'm sane, Pearce," Claire said quietly. "Finally. And I'm sober." She looked at him for a long moment and then gave a deep sigh. "I guess this is an awkward time to announce it, but I don't think there ever is a good time for something like this."

Pearce made a sound of disgust. "I've got things to do, Claire. Spit it out."

"I want a divorce, Pearce."

After ten minutes of heated argument, Pearce stormed out of the house leaving Claire to face Victoria's reaction to her decision. "With all due respect, Victoria," she said, "this is a personal matter that doesn't concern you. So whether you think a divorce is wise or not, my mind is made up and I've already seen a lawyer."

"It's too early for this," Victoria said, touching her forehead.

Claire noticed a tremor in her hand and frowned, studying her face narrowly. She didn't want to be responsible for the woman having a stroke. "Are you okay?"

"I'm fine," Victoria snapped. "And if you won't listen to reason about your very foolish decision to divorce Pearce, perhaps you'll explain why you're overdressed for driving Paige to school. You must have other plans."

"I don't believe you're okay, Victoria," Claire said, avoiding a reply. "In fact, Miriam mentioned she was worried that you haven't been yourself lately." She moved to use morning sun to study Victoria's face. "You're pale and those are dark circles under your eyes. Something is wrong, isn't it?"

"Absolutely not!" With a lift of her chin, Victoria's gaze was fierce with denial. "I'm sixty years old and I've had no work done on my face to disguise that fact. And indiscretion by Miriam will not be tolerated. I'll speak to her immediately."

"What, you're going to fire her after thirty years?" But knowing sarcasm was no way to reach her mother-in-law, Claire gentled her tone. "Please don't even think of disciplining Miriam, Victoria. She's not telling tales, she's expressing concern about you. And I think she's right. Your color's off and you've definitely lost weight."

"My weight has remained unchanged for forty years. As

for my color, I'll remind you that you've seldom seen me at this early hour. Furthermore, you've just made a distressing announcement. It's no wonder I'm looking less than my best."

Still unconvinced, Claire had to let it go. There was no prying confidences from her mother-in-law if she didn't want to talk. "It was just a thought. To be honest, I thought it was odd that you gave Buck a fairly free hand managing the crops this season when you're usually breathing down Will Wainwright's neck. On top of that, you let him bring Oscar Pittman back without protesting. But if you promise nothing's wrong, then I guess I added two and two and came up with five." With a determined smile, she made a move to get to the door.

"Just a minute, Claire," Victoria ordered, catching her arm. "You didn't say where you're going. You know it's irresponsible to take off without revealing your plans. What if there's an emergency involving Paige?"

"I'm not leaving. I'm going outside to talk to Buck. I've told Paige to meet me at the car and I'll drive her to school as always."

"What have you decided as punishment for that really outrageous caper she pulled last night?"

"She's grounded for a month except for school. And she has to forego her precious Goth look. When she comes downstairs, you'll be happy to see that she isn't wearing anything that's black."

"Humph. Doesn't sound like much of a punishment to me."

"She'll be bored stiff. And after being trapped in the house with her for a month, you'll be glad I didn't make it longer." She hesitated a moment and decided to lay it all out. "Actually, you may not be subjected to that torture. I've made arrangements to rent an apartment. Paige and I will be moving out, but it won't be available until the end of the month." Again, she tried edging toward the door, but Victoria stopped her with a hand on her arm.

"What are your plans after dropping Paige at school?"

Claire sighed. "I'm going to Jack Breedlove's campaign headquarters, if you must know," she confessed. "I'm volunteering a few hours this morning."

Victoria's hand fell away as if bitten by a snake. "You cannot be serious."

"I can and I am."

"I won't have it, Claire! It's preposterous. Do you realize—"

"And just so you know," Claire said, unfazed for once by her mother-in-law's disapproval, "I believe Jack is the best man for the job. He's honest and honorable and he'll represent everyone in his constituency, not just a choice few. You know as well as I do that Pearce is obligated to a few powerful financial interests. Unlike Jack, Pearce only wants to win the senate seat to use it as a stepping stone to the U.S. Senate in Washington."

"Wherever did you get that idea?" Victoria asked with genuine outrage. "Pearce's first loyalty must be to Belle Pointe. It *is* to Belle Pointe. He'll be in a position to do good for Tallulah once he's a state senator. He doesn't need to go to Washington. He won't turn his back on his heritage."

"Then you'd better have a talk with him...and soon," Claire said as she opened the front door. "And while you're at it, you might ask him a few questions about that fire at the *Spectator.* I don't believe whoever set it intended any harm to Paige or Anne, because it was a fluke that they were there, but someone damn sure wanted those archives destroyed. And Buck believes it was Pearce."

The only word for Claire's mood as she left the big house was euphoric. The confrontation with Pearce and her announcement to divorce him made her literally vibrate with relief. She wished for a heartfelt minute that she could go straight to Jack and tell him what she'd just done. But she intended to conduct her divorce and any relationship that might develop with Jack on the up-and-up.

Buck was talking to Oscar when she got to the equipment barn. She still felt bad that she had not spoken up in Oscar's defense when she knew that Pearce was wrong in firing him. Taking a stand against Pearce and her mother-in-law would have been doomed to fail, but it still didn't change the guilt she felt over the shameful way Oscar was treated. Rehiring him was only one of the much-needed changes Buck had instigated.

"You left your brother foaming at the mouth, my mother-in-law apoplectic, and me agog with curiosity, Buck. I just wanted to come out here and thank you."

Grinning, he shook his head at her impertinence. "How is Paige?"

"Oh, you thought I was thanking you for saving Paige's life?" Eyes dancing, she shook her head. "Uh-uh, although I do. You left shock and awe in your wake at the big house just now, Buck. It was the most entertainment we've had since the day Pearce found out Jack Breedlove was his opponent."

In a beat or two, her smile gentled, her face grew soft and her eyes became suspiciously bright. Stepping close, she threw her arms around him for a quick, hard hug. "Thank you for saving my little girl, Buck. I would have died if I'd lost Paige."

"I know the feeling," he said huskily, returning the hug. Then, angling back, he held on to both her arms to look her over. "That is one spiffy outfit you've got on this morning. If this is the way you dress driving Paige to school, it's no wonder Jack stopped you for speeding."

She shook him off and twirled about. "Like it? I figure all eyes will be on the only Whitaker volunteer in Jack's campaign headquarters, so I should make a good impression."

He stared, unsure whether she was serious. "How about we go inside the barn and have some of the worst coffee ever brewed? Ma promised me some of the good stuff up at the house, but she reneged after I pissed everybody off. We need to talk about this."

"No, no coffee, but I'm up for talking." She glanced at her watch. "Paige will be ready to go in ten minutes. Is there any place private around here?"

"Not much, but I've got some space I call my own. Paperwork I take to the big house and use Dad's library." Falling into step beside her, he walked with her into a corner of the barn near the entrance. When she was settled in a chair, he sat on the edge of the desk.

He was smiling faintly when he said, "If Jack has recruited you to work in his campaign, I guess some of the shock and awe you left behind you just now came from your husband."

"He won't be my husband much longer, Buck. I've filed for a divorce."

"Jesus, Claire."

"I'm going to marry Jack."

Buck's eyes widened more. "Whoa, even for Jack, that's fast work."

She laughed softly. "He doesn't know it yet. He's still working on trying to hold on to his resentment for the way he thinks I treated him when we were kids."

"Well, you did stand him up the night of the prom," he said with his tongue firmly in cheek.

"Yeah, because my parents locked me in my room, which was on the second floor. I couldn't sneak out without breaking my neck."

"No kidding? They really locked you in?"

"They were determined I wasn't going to get involved with a person who was 'beneath me,' socially speaking." She bracketed the words with her fingers. "And because they sensed there was something special between Jack and me, they decided to pack me off to that awful school to be 'finished.'" More bracketing of a word with her fingers. "I was so young and easily intimidated that I let them get away with it, Buck. Then, when I was finally allowed to come home, Jack was gone."

"Fifteen years is a long time, Claire. Don't do anything hasty."

"You think I'm making a mistake divorcing Pearce? After what you suspect he's done, you think I should stay married to him?"

He put up both hands. "My suspicions are just that. And I don't have insight in to what goes on behind closed doors in your marriage. I just say you should proceed with caution."

"Because he's dangerous when he's crossed." She managed a smile. "I know him better than you do, Buck. And I'm sure I'm doing the right thing. I'm taking Paige and getting out."

She gave a brisk pat to his desktop as if a thorny problem was solved. "But that's not the only reason I wanted to talk to you." She paused. "I think Victoria is sick."

He frowned, recalling that he'd thought the same thing. "Anything specific making you think that?"

"Mostly that she simply looks bad. This morning when I noticed, she denied it, but I don't believe her. Not that she'd tell us anything. She's not a person to curry sympathy…even if she was dying."

Buck studied the horizon beyond the entrance where a field of cotton now stood knee-high, an endless sea of green. He wondered if Claire could be right and made a mental note to try and find out. Even if Victoria didn't want sympathy, the family needed to know if she was sick.

"Just thought I'd mention it." Claire stood up and moved to the door looking out. After a long moment, she said, "There's so much you could do here, Buck. Not just at Belle Pointe, but in Tallulah."

He eyed her suspiciously. "You been talking to Jack about that?"

"Jack?" She frowned. "No."

"Okay, Ty."

"Neither," she told him, looking at him oddly. "But Ty would definitely know a lot of kids in this part of the state who'd benefit not only from your celebrity as a sports superstar, but just from the force of your personality."

Buck grunted, then moved to stand beside her. "I see two problems. First of all, Pearce won't be the next state senator from this district because I'm convinced Jack's a far better man and I'm doing all I can to help him win." When she lit up, he lifted a hand to shush her, adding, "When the time is right."

"Oh."

"When that happens, I can't see Pearce stepping aside to let me move in on his territory here at Belle Pointe. And second point, I have a life in St. Louis. It's no secret that I'm only here because of Anne. My knee is improving daily…as long as I don't screw up, which means I'll be going back to baseball. Have you forgotten that baseball is my life, not cotton farming?"

She looked at him. "Is it really, Buck?"

With a wry half laugh, he shook his head, rubbing the side of his neck. "Well, it was my life until I found myself caught up in a rash of shit in Tallulah that I never counted on. I admit I'm struggling trying to decide what I want, Claire."

"Do you think Pearce set that fire?"

"Damn. I thought the door was closed when I jumped him this morning. Did you hear everything?"

"Did you think I was going to go downstairs like a good girl when I knew something pretty serious was going down with you and Pearce? Not likely. And I got an earful. I have a right. I almost lost Paige in that fire."

Buck's gaze focused on a slow-moving combine in the field. "I know Pearce pretty well, warts and all. When we were kids, I could tell most of the time when he was lying. He was good at it. And as he got older, he got better and better. Today…" Buck shook his head. "…today he seemed truly insulted when I accused him of setting the fire. Actually I knew he didn't set it, but I thought one of his stooges had probably done the deed for him. Now I'm not so sure."

"I think you're right," Claire said.

He gave her a quick, surprised look. "Just based on overhearing our conversation?"

"I know him, too. But if he didn't do it, who did, Buck? And why? Was this person downstairs when Paige showed up, or had he set the stage, so to speak, and gotten out?"

"Did you ask if she heard anything or saw anything?"

"I did. She told me no, nothing." She pushed at a pebble with the toe of her pointy shoe. "Those archives are full of years and years of Tallulah history. What could he want down there? And did he find it? Did he take it? How would we know? It's like trying to find a needle in a haystack, isn't it, Buck?"

"Yeah. But I'm working on it. With Anne. And we'll figure it out."

"Good. I want to know everything, so keep me posted, you hear me?" She glanced again at her watch and they fell into step together, heading for her car. "Promise me, Buck."

"Yeah, okay. But you can't tell Jack anything we've discussed here, Claire. Just think. It's a helluva situation. As a cop, I'd like to keep him abreast of everything we do, but he's Pearce's opponent. What we're talking about is merely suspicion, but to Pearce it's deadly. Talk about a conflict of interest! If Pearce isn't guilty, the scandal would destroy his campaign and his law career."

"Jack wouldn't do that," Claire said loyally.

"Maybe not, but I need to hear your promise that you'll keep everything you've heard confidential until we prove something."

"Promise," she said, raising a hand. "Think about it, Buck. My situation as Pearce's estranged wife, as of today, is even more of a conflict, so my lips are definitely sealed."

"Good girl." He gave her a quick, sturdy hug. "And who knows, maybe we'll get lucky and the cops at Tallulah PD will solve the crime without us."

Twenty

While Buck and Claire were stirring the pot at Belle Pointe, Anne was still sleeping. The ring of her cell phone woke her. Not moving, she lay in Buck's bed with the scent of him all around her. On her. In her. The night had been one long loving reunion. After taking a shower together, they'd fallen into bed and slept hard until he woke her again. Making love with him that time had been slow and easy, an erotic middle-of-the-night dream. Back to sleep again and then again in the darkest hour before dawn. Neither could seem to get enough.

But he was gone now. She vaguely remembered the sound of the shower and then next thing, the smell of him fresh with aftershave and vibrating with male energy as he dropped a soft kiss on her naked breast and murmured, "I love you." Eyes closed, she'd smiled and burrowed back under the covers.

Wrapped in a sheet, she stumbled out of the bedroom and followed the sound of the cell phone to her purse lying on the table at the front door. "Hell—" It was a croak. She cleared her throat and tried again. "Hello?"

"Anne? Oh, dear, I woke you up, didn't I? I'm so sorry. I apologize."

Beatrice. "Ah…it's okay. Past time to be out of bed anyway." She glanced around looking for a clock, but there wasn't one in sight. "Is everything all right? Is Dad—"

"He's fine. Look, I'll call you a bit later after you and Buck have had your breakfast and then—"

"Buck isn't here, Beatrice. He was up very early heading for Belle Pointe. I'm not even sure when it was."

"You were exhausted. Anyone would be."

Feeling her brain finally kick in, Anne headed to the kitchen, holding the sheet in place with one hand. "What time did Dad get home last night?"

"Late. You know how he feels about that newspaper. He was so relieved that there wasn't too much damage. I know this sounds harsh, but whoever did this is a despicable person. I just thank God both you and Paige were spared."

"Buck did appear in the nick of time," Anne said, reaching for a can of coffee. His suspicions about Pearce's involvement were better left unsaid until they found proof.

"You say he's at Belle Pointe?"

"Yes." Anne smiled, spotting a sprig of honeysuckle stuck in a wineglass in the center of the table. She picked it up and sniffed it. It was particularly thoughtful since he had to descend those beastly porch steps to get it and then climb back up to leave it on the table. At this rate, his knee would never heal.

"I was wondering," Beatrice said, "if there was anything on your schedule for the next couple of hours."

Anne's gaze roamed around the kitchen and finally spotted a clock. Ten-fifteen. Lord. "No, nothing special. Did you need me to do something for you?"

"Actually, I'd like to come out there if you don't think Buck would object since I know he likes his privacy."

"Of course. You're welcome here. You should know that." Anne frowned. "Are you sure everything's all right? Is Dad—" She was struck with a horrible thought. "Dad isn't sick, is he? Did the fire—"

"Franklin's fine. In fact, he'll be coming with me."

It all sounded very casual, but Anne heard something in Beatrice's voice that wasn't at all casual. Something was up, she decided, as nothing short of an emergency kept her stepmother from opening Hodge-Podge. And in the hour it took the Marshes to get to the lodge, her mind raced with a dozen questions.

She opened the door as soon as she heard their car and went out on the porch to greet them. A quick search of their faces told her nothing, but Beatrice's smile as she climbed the steps seemed a bit off.

"Blueberry muffins and some fruit," her stepmother said, handing over a basket after kissing Anne's cheek. "I know Buck wasn't expecting company and I wasn't sure he'd have much in the way of breakfast food that you like."

"Surprisingly, he did," Anne said, giving a heartfelt sigh as she inhaled the aroma of warm muffins. "But nothing as delicious as fresh muffins."

After a hug from Franklin, she ushered them inside. "Fortunately, there is coffee, but I need to make a fresh pot, so let's go to the kitchen. It's my favorite place."

"It's beautiful out here," Beatrice said, looking around, "the lodge, the grounds—the *view*—just beautiful. It's easy to understand its appeal to Buck, considering how he must live constantly in the public eye in St. Louis."

"It is quiet and peaceful," Franklin said and added, "maybe a little too quiet and peaceful."

Anne turned from the counter with the coffee carafe in her hand. "I bet I know what you're going to say."

Franklin met her eyes directly. "Someone set that fire last night and we don't have a clue as to the reason. You've been the only person interested in those archives since I've been associated with the *Spectator.* Maybe it wasn't intended to hurt you—or Paige—then again, maybe it was."

"Oh, Dad—"

"And just now, your moth— Ah, Beatrice and I passed a man parked in a pickup at the turn from the main road onto this lane. I think you should call Buck and tell him. Or Jack Breedlove. I don't like it that someone's hanging about."

"Are you serious?" Anne went to the window and looked out toward the levee. "I don't see anyone."

"He's out near the main road. And he didn't seem inclined to move on in spite of the hard look I gave him as we passed."

"He's a huge man with a shaved head." Beatrice gave a distasteful shudder. "He looks like a thug."

Anne picked up her cell phone and dialed Buck's number. It rang several times before he finally answered.

"Hey, sweetheart." His tone was low, suggestive. "Did you finally wake up?"

"Buck, someone's parked on the main road. Dad says he seems to be watching the lodge."

"Franklin is there?"

"Yes, with Beatrice. We're...ah, having coffee. Should I call Jack Breedlove to send someone out? The man's not exactly trespassing since he's not on lodge property, but couldn't Jack—"

"No, he couldn't." Buck chuckled. "All of you just relax. It's Pug Morris, one of my men here at Belle Pointe. I called Oscar before I left this morning and he sent Pug. He's your bodyguard."

Still holding the phone, she turned and found Beatrice and Franklin anxiously watching her. "Do you think that's necessary, Buck?"

"Better safe than sorry. If you're alone at the lodge, Pug is on duty."

"We'll talk about this when you get home tonight," she stated.

"Yes, ma'am. Gotta go. Love you."

"You, too." She was frowning as she broke the connection and faced Beatrice and Franklin. "Buck has decided I need a bodyguard."

"Good idea," Franklin said, clearly approving.

"Yes, indeed," Beatrice agreed, "even if he looks like a terrorist."

When nobody spoke for a minute or two, Anne was more convinced than ever that something was up. "The coffee will be ready in a few minutes."

Franklin touched his wife's waist gently. "Here, Bea, you take this chair. We'll all be more comfortable sitting down for this."

Watching them dither, Anne released a breath of exasperation. "What? What is it?" She looked from one to the other. "Just tell me straight out, Dad."

Franklin turned a troubled gaze to the window as if to search for words. "It's something that will be easier to understand if I give a bit of background, Annie-girl."

She watched him rub the side of his face with an unsteady hand and was filled with a deep foreboding. Still, he seemed unable to find words.

"Franklin," Beatrice said, gently prodding.

"Yes, yes. You know I came to Tallulah in 1970 with that PBS crew out of Boston, Anne. I was fascinated with the Mississippi Delta, not just because of the civil unrest but, oh, lots of other things. Some of our great novelists were born right here. I guess you could say I was in a state of mind to be enchanted."

He rose out of the chair abruptly and moved to the window. "I was enchanted all right," he said, almost to himself, looking not at Anne, but at the peaceful scene outside. "It wasn't just the place, but the people. One person in particular." He took a breath. "I was a married man. My wife—Laura—was sick. Multiple sclerosis is a cruel disease. I loved her, but there were parts of our relationship that—" He stopped. "That's no excuse. I was young. I was healthy. Maybe it was inevitable that I would be unfaithful."

"Oh, Dad…"

He tensed at the way Anne said his name. "So when I met this beautiful young woman who was home for the summer from college, so bright, so talented—so *healthy*—I was enchanted." He cleared his throat, still facing outside. "I'm ashamed to say that I took advantage of that darling girl. We had an affair. She was nineteen and I was twenty-four. Some might call it a summer fling, but it was more than that to me. My God, it was everything to me. I fell so hard and fast in love with her that I lived in hell wondering how I was going to live without her. And I had to live without her, do you understand? I couldn't divorce Laura. She was sick. She was…" With his hands clenching on the rim of the sink, his voice grew rough and almost inaudible. "She was sick."

Anne pressed hard against her mouth with the fingers of

her hand. She felt an oily lurch in her stomach. Her father—
Dad!—her knight in shining armor, the rock of her childhood,
had betrayed her mother. With another woman.

Beatrice spoke up in a quiet voice. "Franklin, let me—"

"No. It's for me to tell." But he seemed enveloped in his
thoughts. A minute passed. Two. Then, as if gathering courage, he turned around and faced Anne squarely. "I wish that
was all that I had to tell you. I wish I could finish right there.
Tell you that after being so dishonorable, that I'd gone back
to Boston and not too much harm was done. But it wasn't to
end that way, Annie-girl."

He paused as the coffeemaker gave off three beeps signaling it was ready, but nobody noticed. All three were frozen in
place.

"I did go back to Boston and about two months later I received a letter. There were consequences to our affair. She
was pregnant. Her family was sending her to live with an aunt
in Atlanta. She would have been disgraced if she'd stayed in
Tallulah. In those days—well, her father never got over it. He
died without forgiving her."

Anne's heart was beating fast now. She stood up abruptly,
moved to the coffeemaker. She had no desire for coffee, but
she couldn't just sit and wait for the second shoe to fall. Dear
God, this couldn't end the way she was thinking.

Franklin moved to Beatrice and rested a protective hand
on her shoulder. She instantly reached up and covered it with
her own. "I responded to that letter, of course, but only after
I confessed to Laura what had happened…and told her the
consequences. I wanted to be punished. I wanted her to yell
at me, to call what I'd done despicable and vile, but she simply asked what I intended to do about the baby. My God, as

if it was in my power to do anything about the baby. And then Laura said the words that changed everything. She said, 'The baby is your child. Your responsibility. Of course, we'll adopt the baby.' And so we did."

Motionless at the window, Anne felt as if she stood before an abyss. One step and she would fall into an empty, bottomless pit. She turned and met the eyes of her father. Her *father.* She knew the shock of it was on her face. With a hand braced on the counter behind her, she asked, "Are you going to tell me the name of this woman?"

"I think you've already guessed who it was, Anne," Beatrice said softly.

"You," Anne whispered, staring into eyes as blue as her own.

"Yes."

A tumult of emotion roared through Anne. Denial. Betrayal. Fury. Franklin and Beatrice were her birth parents. Not some unknown teenage couple who found themselves in dire straits, forced to give up for adoption a child they couldn't properly care for. And not some promiscuous woman whose lifestyle was screwed up by an unwanted pregnancy. Not an overloaded single mom who couldn't afford another illegitimate baby. Lord, there were a dozen scenarios she had conjured up to explain how she'd come to be given up by her birth mother, but never had she expected anything like this. But she should have, she told herself. It was all so disgustingly obvious now. Everything that had perplexed her about her father's bizarre decision to move to Tallulah was suddenly crystal clear. Beatrice's inexplicable opening of her heart to a stepdaughter almost sight unseen was plain now. Shamefully so.

Watching her struggle to take it in, Franklin said, "Any negative thing you're thinking about my behavior I've already called myself a thousand times over, Anne."

"I knew he was married," Beatrice said in a voice that quivered slightly. "I'm as guilty as he."

Anne stared at them. She had been a fool not to guess. She'd been trusting and naive. And they'd played on her naiveté, played her like a violin. She'd been completely taken in by the spectacle of two people their age finding love. Being so obviously in love. Oh, it was disgusting.

"Did you continue to betray my mother on those business trips you took before she finally, conveniently, died?"

It was a cruel jab, but Franklin took it standing straight and unflinching. "No. I never saw Beatrice again until three years ago. I never wrote her. Never called her."

Beatrice, visibly shaken, rose from her chair, looking every year of her age. "That's true. Franklin never did, but Laura did. I'll tell you about that when you decide you're ready to listen. When you've decided what you want to do."

Anne stood silent, simply shaking her head.

"I know you went to get your laptop last night because you're using the Internet to try and find your biological parents. You can imagine how we felt—Franklin and I—when you almost lost your life over a mystery we could have cleared up with a word." She gave Anne an imploring look. "But when should we have spoken up? At the wedding? I wanted a chance to get to know you before telling you something that was bound to upset you. I was afraid your loyalty to your m-mother would be a barrier between us that we might never overcome. And then you called to say you were coming to stay with us. It was like a gift from the gods. I couldn't believe it. I wanted to tell you everything, most of all how much I love you. Have always loved you. But you were all caught up in your problems with Buck. I couldn't add any more stress to your life."

"Thinking I might have some genetic reason for miscarrying added stress to my life," Anne said bitterly. "You could have eased my mind with a word."

"Don't think I haven't lain awake night after night since you arrived thinking just that," Beatrice said with a sad smile. Her eyes were suspiciously bright, but her chin came up. "I've loved your father all my life," she said quietly. "I could never be sorry for that summer. You asked once if I had any regrets for a life lived without children. Now you know the greatest. That I was denied seeing you grow up. But I have one other regret. I wish we'd been able to spare Laura knowing."

"As you say, behavior has consequences," Anne said, wanting to lash out and hurt them as they'd hurt her.

Franklin stood looking shattered by her reaction. What had he expected? That he could tell her of his infidelity and the twisted circumstances of her birth and adoption and she'd shrug and say, Oh, well, you're happy now, so all's fine?

"Franklin," Beatrice said, tugging at his sleeve, "we'd better leave now. Anne will want to be alone."

"Yes, I certainly do," Anne said, skirting the table to avoid the possibility of touching either of them. She stood with her back against the counter. "Thanks for the muffins."

Franklin put out a hand. "Annie—"

She wrapped her arms around herself, unaware that it was exactly the way Beatrice stood. "Please, Dad, just go."

* * *

Anne didn't move until she could no longer hear the sound of their car. The minute she was sure they'd had time to get far ahead of her, she flew through the house, collecting her purse and car keys before dashing out onto the porch. Down the steps at a reckless pace, she reached her car and literally threw herself inside and behind the wheel. Without a thought for her seat belt, she roared away from the lodge, startling Pug Morris by missing the front bumper of his pickup by a hair.

All the way to Belle Pointe, her mind teemed with the shock of it. Her blood boiled at the injustice of it. She thought of a childhood missing so many things. Ordinary, kid stuff that her friends took for granted. Many times her mother had simply been too sick to listen to adolescent chatter. Or tolerate the noise of teenage music. Or attend her piano recitals. Or sit through her high school graduation ceremony when Anne, as valedictorian, had spoken. But she'd accepted it all because she loved her mother. Had accepted that it was simply a cruel fate to be saddled with an incurable, mean-spirited, fatal disease.

It was no excuse that her father was shortchanged as a husband, she told herself. It was one thing to be resentful, another to have an affair! Having an affair was selfish and despicable.

She shot through the gate at Belle Pointe in a cloud of dust and drove the lane that led to the house in under a minute. Although she never noticed, Buck was in a pickup bouncing along off-road in the distance. Spotting the Mercedes, he came to an abrupt stop.

She wasn't sure what bothered her more, that Franklin had been unfaithful to her mother or that there'd been secrets in her family intentionally kept from her. Everyone who'd been important in her life had known but her. She felt stripped and exposed. Was this the way Buck's mother felt at the possibility of her secrets being laid bare for the world to see? Did everybody have secrets but her?

She stopped the car and only then realized she was crying as the beautiful facade of Belle Pointe blurred in her vision. Struggling to get hold of herself, she fumbled in her purse searching for a tissue. She'd come instinctively to Buck, but not to cry on his shoulder, but just…just because, she told herself. Compared to the loss of her baby, this was a mere bump in the road. And she'd made it through the miscarriage and a very rocky patch in her marriage, so she could make it through this.

Hands trembling, she reached for the ignition to restart the car and leave. And go where? Back to the lodge? It was too lonely and isolated. Certainly not to Franklin and Beatrice's house. And the *Spectator* was cordoned off. Maybe she would just pack up and go back to St. Louis. Buck would probably drop everything he was doing here and come back with her. He'd asked her over and over to do just that.

She was startled when the door was wrenched open suddenly. "What's the matter?" Buck demanded, looking shaken. "What's happened?"

All her defenses crumbled like a sand castle in the path of a tidal wave. The keys fell with a clatter at her feet as she launched herself into his arms and burst into tears with all the abandon of a six-year-old betrayed by her best friend.

"Oh, B-Buck!" she wailed.

"What's the matter, baby? Are you hurt?"

She shook her head, clinging to his shirtfront. "No. Yesss…"

"Jesus. What? Where? Did someone—"

"Nooo, n-not that."

"What then?" Buck angled back to get a look at her face. "Is it Franklin?" All he got was more mute movement of her head. Holding her arms, he gave her a little shake and spoke sharply. "Tell me what's happened, Anne."

"Dad. It's D-Dad. And—and B-Beatrice." With that, she dissolved into a new spate of weeping.

He looked confused. "You just told me it wasn't Franklin. Are they hurt?"

"No." She moved back into his embrace and pressed her cheek to his heart. "Oh, Buck. It's... I just...n-never thought—"

With a sigh, Buck looked around and made a decision. Slipping an arm around her waist, he guided her to the front door. "Let's go inside and you can tell me what this is all about."

She shook her head vehemently. "No, I don't want your mother—"

"Ma's gone. She has some kind of appointment. Claire's working at Jack's campaign headquarters and Paige is at school. Miriam sees nothing, knows nothing." He opened the door. "Come on, let's go inside now."

He went with her through the foyer, past the formal living area on toward the back to the room that had been his father's library. "Here, we can talk in here." With a gentle push on her shoulder, he urged her down on a leather couch and stepped to a credenza against the wall.

While he poured her a drink, she rested her head against the back of the couch, her gaze roving over the books lining the shelves of the bookcases. For years, she'd wanted to explore the library at Belle Pointe, but now she found she had no interest whatsoever in Buck's heritage. Only her own.

"Here. Drink this." Buck put a small glass filled with brandy in her hand and watched her take a gulp. "Whoa, easy."

Making a face, she coughed and patted her chest, but finally managed to croak, "That was awful."

"Uh-huh. Now," he said, "tell me why you're so upset."

She looked at him sadly. "Dad and Beatrice are my parents."

Twenty-One

Buck eased himself down on the couch beside her, keeping his gaze on her face. "Franklin and Beatrice are your parents. Didn't I know that?"

"No, Buck, I mean they're really my parents. My biological parents."

He stared at her. "Get out."

"It's true." Her voice rose and she teared up again.

He instantly reached over and gathered her in his arms. Tucking her beneath his chin, he began rubbing her back. "Come on, honey. Don't do that. Just give me some details here. You know this because...?"

Nestled in Buck's embrace, she still felt blindsided and angry, but somehow it wasn't the shocker it had been an hour ago. "I know it because they confessed everything."

"Well, I'll be damned."

"They felt guilty. They knew I've been trying to get a lead on my biological parents through the Internet. The reason I went out last night was to get my laptop. If they'd been honest with me from the start, I wouldn't have needed it."

"Yeah, but Paige wouldn't have stood a chance in that fire if you hadn't shown up to get your laptop."

"That's the only good thing I can think of in this whole mess."

"Oh, I don't know." With just a trace of a smile, he tipped up her chin to look into her eyes, still running a soothing hand up and down her spine. "I can think of at least one other pretty good thing."

"They had an affair, Buck!" she said, pushing away in exasperation. "Dad was unfaithful to my mother. Then, when Beatrice came up pregnant, they had the nerve to somehow talk my mother into adopting *their* baby."

"Their baby. That would be you."

She was quickly recovering. Moving away from him, she sat up straight on the couch, wordlessly accepting the handkerchief he held out. "I feel like such an idiot. I should have been suspicious when he left New England to move to a small town in Mississippi. I was suspicious, darn it, but my relationship with Dad was so solid that he could have told me the world suddenly went flat and I would have believed him. So when he gave me those smarmy reasons for retiring early to manage an obscure weekly after a stellar career in the most prestigious location on the east coast, of course I believed him."

"Smarmy?"

"What would you call it if you found out circumstances in your family weren't what you'd been told all your life?"

"You want the truth?" Buck said dryly. "I'd trade my screwed-up family for parents like Franklin and Beatrice in a heartbeat."

"Well, I can see I'm not going to get any sympathy from you," she said huffily.

"Just so I'm clear here, when do you think they should have told you?"

"Right away," she said indignantly. "Before they got married."

"Yeah, I can see how that would have set up a lovely relationship between you and your new stepmother…mother." When she opened her mouth, he reached out and shushed her with one finger. "How long did this affair last?"

"They claim only the one summer." She jumped up and began prowling the library. "He swore he never got in touch with Beatrice again after that, although she said she and my mother corresponded."

"I bet she sent pictures."

Anne paused at that, reluctantly imagining the way a childless Beatrice would have felt seeing the baby she'd given up grow from infancy to adulthood without ever touching her or hugging her or hearing her voice. Without ever having the right to do any of that.

"And why did Beatrice give up her baby?" Buck was asking.

"Hmm?" Distracted, she studied the spine of a book. "She was nineteen and a college student. Her father sent her off to a relative somewhere."

"Hmm, pregnant and in disgrace. Must have been tough."

She replaced the book and looked at him. "How about my mother whose husband admitted he'd been unfaithful?"

"I see her as a good person, too."

"Too?" She put her hands on her hips. "You don't see anything dishonorable in what they did?"

"I know how it feels to love somebody so much that nothing else matters if you aren't with that person."

Disarmed, she went back to the couch where he still sat.

With her head cocked, she said, "I sound like a self-centered, spoiled rotten, only child, don't I?"

"Maybe just a little." With a grin, he tugged her down on his lap and linked his arms around her. With his chin resting on her shoulder, he said, "Let's think about this for a minute. Beatrice didn't have to tell Franklin she was pregnant. But she knew as long as he was married to Laura, he'd never have a child of his own. And if she lived long enough, even if he married again, he might have been beyond siring more children. It sounds to me as if Beatrice wanted him to raise their child."

She stroked the backs of his hands as he held onto her. She always felt so warm and secure with Buck's arms around her. "It does, doesn't it?"

"Pretty generous of her, too…especially since it meant she sacrificed any chance of contact with you. Couldn't very well call them up and ask to come to your next birthday party, could she?" He kissed the nape of her neck. "Without wishing you any unhappiness, she must have seen the trouble that sent you here to Tallulah as an ill wind bringing a rainbow."

A gift from the gods. With a pang, Anne recalled the words.

They sat in silence for a while. "All things considered," Buck said finally, "they paid a dear price for that summer affair."

With Victoria occupied with an engagement elsewhere and the rest of the family out of the house, Anne was persuaded to stay at Belle Pointe. In John Whitaker's library, Buck sprawled on the leather couch and watched his wife's fascinated scan of the bookshelves. "We can leave together after I've wrapped up a few things with Oscar and his crew.

Meanwhile, you can explore Belle Pointe. Start with the journals."

She closed a book and replaced it where she'd found it. "Did you forget? They're impounded behind police tape at the *Spectator* until the investigation's over…along with my laptop."

"Nope. I swung by and told Jack Breedlove that they were priceless Whitaker heirlooms. He agreed and I've got them in my SUV. But I'm not sure I want to leave them here at the big house. I'd like to keep an eye on them, but no matter where I stash them, they're yours to examine to your heart's content."

"Really? With or without your mother's approval?" she asked.

"I'll tell her, sure, but I don't need her permission, sugar. The journals are as much my property as hers, more if you want to get technical about it. I was born a Whitaker. My mother is a Whitaker by marriage."

At last, she thought gleefully, trying to keep a straight face. A chance to read Belle Pointe history written by people who knew it, lived it, loved it. She would need her laptop to make notes. "Did you think to pick up my laptop?"

"They didn't find it, so I don't have it."

She paused, forgetting the book in her hand. "It was in plain sight on that table I was using for a desk. You couldn't miss it."

"I was all over your tidy little work station." He watched her carefully replace the book. "It's not there. I was hoping you might have locked it up somewhere."

A tiny frown drew her eyebrows together. "It has to be there."

Buck let out a breath and got to his feet. "Is there a particular reason why you need it? I mean, other than your adoption notes."

"That wasn't the only thing I have on it," she told him. Then her eyes widened, meeting his. "Buck, someone took it because of my notes from the archives!"

"I think it's a possibility."

"This is getting more and more bizarre. Mostly I entered stuff I simply found interesting…for the book I haven't decided to write."

"Such as the accident where Jim Bob Baker died?"

"I included that, yes. As well as the death of his brother. Mostly it was all like that, bits and pieces that don't mean much and certainly don't shape up into any kind of theme."

Buck was frowning. "I didn't know Jim Bob had a brother."

"You wouldn't have known him as you weren't born when he died. He was Tallulah's only Vietnam casualty. It struck me as one of those cruel twists of fate, you know? A mother loses both her sons. How sad is that?"

"One of those little nuggets that authors tuck in the pages of a book about a town that's pretty unremarkable otherwise," he guessed, smiling at her.

"But who'd want to steal it?"

"Best guess? The person who decided to destroy the archives. The person who took the pictures off the walls."

She stared at him. "Someone removed the pictures?"

"Actually, Jack noticed it. He mentioned it this morning when I contacted him about the journals. Seems before he announced for the senate, he was down in the archives doing research about other campaigns in Tallulah. He didn't pay much attention to the photos on the wall, but he noticed they were there. And now they're gone…at least some of them."

"You think Pearce took them? Old photographs?" Her face was blank with confusion. "Why would he do that? As a record of the town's history, they're spotty at best. Plus, duplicates probably exist somewhere." She shook her head in bewilderment. "My God, Buck, why would Pearce take such an awful chance? He knows you suspect him. Has he lost his mind?"

He sat on the corner of the desk that had belonged to his father and several Whitakers before him. "I'm not sure Pearce is behind all this," Buck said thoughtfully. "I had a come-to-Jesus talk with him this morning and either he's become a helluva lot better liar than he used to be or he's as baffled as I am."

"This is so unbelievable," she murmured.

"Yeah, more than you know. He flipped out when I mentioned the hunting accident. I still think there's something fishy there. I meant to take a look at the books before now, but I haven't had time."

Suddenly a thought struck Anne. Buck could sense something, and asked, "What is it?"

She moved across the room to a window. "It's probably nothing, I mean, there's no way—"

He straightened, watching her gaze out. "Tell me and we can both puzzle over whether it's something or nothing."

"It's about the pictures on the wall," she said, turning to look at him. "Generally speaking, they were taken of events that had relevance to the town. For example, if there was a huge rainstorm and the front page ran a picture of kids playing in high water in the street, that wouldn't have been considered significant enough to frame. Such discrimination doesn't exclude you, however," she added dryly. "As the town's only world-class athlete, you were up there right along with a dedication of the Whitaker Library, the swearing in of every mayor, a rare visit by the Governor once upon a time—that kind of thing. But what I just remembered was a picture of Rudy Baker."

"Who?"

"Pay attention. The Vietnam soldier I just told you about. Jim Bob Baker's brother. His picture was on the wall."

"Oh, yeah."

"Because he was the only Tallulah soldier killed in action, his death was covered in the paper. Paige actually found it. I recall she commented on his looks. He was very handsome in a dark and wicked sort of way."

Buck gave a dismissive shrug. "I don't see any connection…"

"Well…I'm getting there. It's kind of far out, so don't laugh."

"I'm not laughing. I'm listening."

"Your mother and Rudy Baker had a fling that ended when he was drafted and sent to Vietnam."

"No shit."

She had his full attention now. "Wait'll you hear the rest. His uncle or somebody, anyway a relative, had a bar called the Boll Weevil."

"Oh, clever."

"Your mother's name was Vicky then, not Victoria. She seemed smitten with Rudy, who was—get ready—a musician. In the style of Elvis. But all good things must end and Rudy was drafted and wound up in Vietnam."

"Where he was killed," Buck said.

"Yes. And here's the interesting part. It was shortly after— I'm talking a few months later as I don't know the exact time frame—Victoria began dating John, who happened to be home for the summer from college. In just no time, they were married." She stopped, squirming a little under his gaze. "I told you it was far out."

After a long minute, Buck said, "Are you thinking what I'm thinking?"

"Whatever we're thinking, it happened a long time ago. I just found it…interesting what with Jim Bob Baker's death and your mother's affair with Rudy, his older brother. Then she ups and marries John."

He shifted his gaze from her to the window, thinking. "I never knew much about my mother's life before she married Dad," he said, almost as if he was talking to himself. "She never wanted to talk about the fact that she'd—as they say—married up." Moving away, he tucked his hands in his pockets, his eyes downcast. "I wouldn't have known that her father was a whiz of a mechanic who worked at Belle Pointe except that Oscar mentioned it not too long ago. We had a complicated problem with one of the engines and he fixed it."

He'd moved back to the window. Pulling a cord, he let in a sliver of sunshine. "Oscar laughed and said I could probably have fixed it myself since I had Benny Hinton's genes, who just happened to be the best mechanic in the Mississippi Delta. He could see I didn't know what he was talking about."

He turned his head to look at Anne. "That's who trained Oscar—Benny Hinton—my grandfather. I swear that's the first I ever knew about that."

"She never spoke of her parents, not ever?" Anne asked with an incredulous look.

"I guess once she was a Whitaker she felt her background didn't go with her elevated status." He spoke with a bitter twist of his mouth.

"We don't know that," Anne said gently. "It's not fair to judge her. Maybe there were…circumstances. When Beatrice told me all this, she made it a point to caution me about assuming gossip to be true. So, until I hear the story from your mother herself, I'm reserving judgment."

"Then you'll wait a long time, sugar. If she's kept her secrets all these years, she's not likely to tell all now." Moving from the window, he rested a hip on his ancestor's desk. "So, where were we before we got sidetracked by my mother's past?"

"Trying to figure out why anyone would want to destroy the archives and steal my laptop."

"Maybe my mother did it," he said dryly.

"Be serious. We've agreed we don't have a single clue. And since you suspect Pearce might be responsible for the death of Jim Bob Baker, it's worth doing a little digging into the lives of both brothers, don't you think?" She was warming to her theory, pacing again, her eyes on the floor. "We've got to start somewhere. In the absence of any other lead, that's where an investigative journalist would start." She swung about and shot him a brilliant smile. "You did ask for my help, remember?"

Arms folded, he smiled faintly.

"What?" she asked.

He reached out and pulled her between his legs. "Looks like I made a smart choice when I asked my wife for help." He drew her closer. "You feeling better now?"

"About my big discovery?" She gave a little shrug and stroked hair from his forehead. "I guess I have to. I can't change anything, can I?"

"Would you want to?"

"I would want my father not to have been unfaithful."

He gave her a little squeeze, not quite a shake. "He's a good man, darlin'. Don't judge him too harshly. Think of it this way. Since Laura appears to have forgiven him, what would she want you to do?"

That very thought had been in the back of her mind, but the shock of discovery was too fresh. With a sigh, she linked both arms around Buck's neck. Tomorrow. She'd think about it tomorrow.

"Hmm, you smell good," Buck said, sniffing behind her ear.

She tilted her head with a smile. "I should. It's Joy. You bought it."

He stopped, angling back to give her a hard look. "You were mad enough to leave, but you remembered to take a hundred-and fifty-dollar bottle of perfume with you?"

Framing his face, she leaned close so that he was able to catch the scent she'd applied lightly between her breasts. "So what are you going to do about it?"

"This...for starters." He snuck a hand beneath her sweater and found her breast. Anne made a little sound, recalling that Miriam was in the house and could easily walk in, but as Buck nuzzled her tingling breasts through her sweater, warming her with his breath, it was hard not to give in to a moment of pure pleasure. After all, she'd had a bad morning.

"And this..." he murmured, reaching for the zipper on her jeans.

"Buck—" She looked back in agitation at the door, wide open. "I was just teasing. We can't—"

"Didn't your mama tell you that a girl can get in a lot of trouble teasing a man?" His hand was inside her jeans now, nipping at her throat while he worked his way into her bikinis. Eyes dreamy and heavy, Anne did nothing to stop him until she heard sounds of footsteps nearing the library. She glanced back at the door just as Miriam appeared, beet-red and apologetic.

"I'm sorry, Mr. Buck," the housekeeper said, sending an anxious look over her shoulder. "Ms. Victoria just came in. I thought you'd want to know." With a last flustered look at Anne, she scurried away.

"Omigod!" Anne batted at Buck's hand; Buck grinned wickedly, but she had no chance to say more—or do anything—as he gave her a quick, hard kiss on the mouth and as neatly as he'd invaded her jeans, he had them zipped and her sweater straightened when Victoria walked in.

Nobody spoke for a beat or two. Victoria's gaze sliced from one to the other, then settled on Buck, who showed not a trace of embarrassment. "Buck, that is a very valuable antique you're sitting on."

"Ma. Back from Memphis already?" He took his time straightening up, using a minute to study his mother's face. He'd seen her looking better, he decided. Claire could be right.

"I was never in Memphis." Victoria's look shifted to Anne. "This is a pleasant surprise, Anne. Has Miriam been told to set an extra plate for lunch?"

"It was a spur-of-the-moment decision," Anne told her, managing a polite smile. "And thanks, but I'll just pop over to the square and get lunch." Anne had skipped breakfast, but lunch with her mother-in-law was not a pleasant prospect. And she'd be safe enough on her own in the middle of town.

"Uh-uh, you're staying," Buck said flatly. "She shouldn't be popping around anywhere on her own…under the circumstances," he told Victoria.

"The circumstances," his mother repeated. "That would be

the fire, which I understand has been declared a case of arson. I got details from Chief Breedlove when I dropped by his office a while ago. I'm shocked, truly appalled that you and Paige had such a close call, Anne. Criminal activity in Tallulah. It's incredible." With a click of her tongue, her gaze narrowed on Anne's face. "How are you feeling?"

"No lingering effects. Mostly I had a good scare."

"That's basically what Paige said." Victoria's gaze shifted to Buck. "It's fortunate you came along when you did, Buck. Of course, there will be severe consequences for that girl's outrageous behavior. She's simply out of control."

"She's a normal teenage kid, Ma. And we came damn close to losing her."

"And the journals," Victoria said. "Which reminds me. I stopped at the *Spectator* intending to pick them up. I expected to encounter resistance since they were on the premises during the fire and might be impounded, but they're Belle Pointe heirlooms. They could be damaged in careless hands. However, I was told by Jack Breedlove that he'd turned them over to you." Her gaze roamed around the room. "Where are they?"

"In a safe place." He moved to stand close behind Anne.

"But not here where they belong? Why not?"

"Just haven't gotten around to it," he said, shrugging. "By the way, Ma, where were they all this time? I've done paperwork here in the library since I've been on the job and they weren't here."

"That's a very good question. It's a mystery to me how Paige found them and I intend to ask the minute she gets home from school. Nobody has written in them since John died, nor has anyone had a chance to write in them. I know

I haven't. As it falls to me to officially record activity here at Belle Pointe, I personally prefer using the computer."

Buck frowned. "You're saying the journals haven't been seen since Dad died and yet somehow Paige got hold of them?"

"That's exactly what I'm saying." She moved to the door. "I'm heading to the kitchen to give Miriam instructions for lunch. When I return, I want to see the journals returned to their proper place. There." She pointed to a glass-front cabinet against the wall opposite John Whitaker's desk.

"Now what?" Anne asked Buck in a hushed tone after Victoria left. "I don't think your mother is going to stand by and let me read those journals."

"I can see how it wouldn't be any fun with her breathing down your neck," he said, looking thoughtful. "I wonder where Paige got hold of them."

"I wonder why they were hidden in the first place."

He looked at her. "You, m'dear, have a suspicious mind."

Her expression turned gloomy. "But not suspicious enough to guess my parents' secret."

"Hey, we're making progress," he said, giving her a quick hug. "You're calling them your parents."

"Do we really have to stay for lunch?" she asked. Since she'd gone to the lodge with Buck after the fire, she didn't have a change of clothes. "I need clothes and it's a good time to go to their house and get my luggage."

Standing close, he stroked the side of her arm. "We could go back to the lodge and get naked and you wouldn't need any clothes."

She laughed. "In your dreams."

"Yeah, so what d'you say?"

"I say Beatrice will be at her shop and Dad's probably

hanging around the scene of the fire, so it's a good time to take my things to the lodge."

He went still. "You're moving in?"

She looked at him. "Well…yeah."

"Sounds good to me," Buck said after a minute, "but just so we're clear, are you moving in to avoid your folks or because you want to be with me?"

She shifted to look at him directly. "I thought we cleared that up last night. We made love with no protection. For me, that's as complete a commitment as I can give."

He caught her hand and brought it up to press a kiss in her palm. "I guess I need to hear you say it a lot before I'm totally convinced. You scared the hell out of me in St. Louis when you left."

She leaned her head on his shoulder. "I never stopped loving you and last night was an epiphany for me when I thought I might not be able to tell you that ever again." She sighed. "As for grabbing an excuse for avoiding Dad and Beatrice, I'm just chicken enough to admit it, yeah."

Buck lowered their laced fingers to his thigh. "I'm supposed to be the partner in this relationship who doesn't like to talk things out. The longer you dance around the problem, the more time you give for grievances to fester."

"I can't believe I'm being counseled on the value of communication by Mr. Buttoned Up himself," she said grumpily.

"That was then, this is now," he said virtuously. "I've learned the error of my ways."

She ignored that. "I've thought of another reason we should go now," she told him, casting a sideways look toward the house. "It's a legitimate excuse to skip lunch with your mother."

"Good thinking." He caught her hand to hustle her toward the door. "I guess putting off resolving your differences one more day won't matter."

Twenty-Two

Some differences were to be resolved that day whether planned or not. Just as Anne unlocked the door of their house, Franklin and Beatrice pulled into the driveway behind Buck's SUV. "So much for sneaking in and grabbing my luggage on the sly," she muttered.

"Best laid plans and all that," he murmured in her ear before turning to greet his in-laws.

As Beatrice approached them on the sidewalk, her smile was strained. She looked as if she'd had a bad night. "This is a nice surprise," she said, her blue eyes—so like Anne's—watchful. "You're just in time to have lunch with us."

"Thank you, but I only came to pick up my luggage," Anne said, noticing how alike she and her birth mother were. Now that she was aware of it, the similarity was striking. Flustered at the discovery, she looked down at herself and added wryly, "I don't think this outfit is good for another day."

Franklin was close behind Beatrice carrying three bags of groceries. "Here, let me give you a hand with that," Buck said.

"Good to see you, Buck." Franklin handed over two of the

bags and looked beyond Buck to Anne and said heartily, "Well, this is good timing. I'm glad we didn't miss you, Annie-girl. I told my wife you'd be coming for your luggage. No talking her out of it, I said." Head cocked, he gave her an openly affectionate look. "We'd sure like you to have lunch with us."

She glanced away to find Beatrice standing with her hands clasped tightly together, almost as if in prayer. *Oh, God, what a nightmare!* Her eyes bounced to Buck and away again. "We still need to drop my stuff off at the lodge and Buck needs to get back to Belle Pointe."

"Maybe a glass of iced tea?" her father wheedled. "It's turned out warm today."

"Iced tea sounds good," Buck said, slipping an arm around Anne's waist and nudging her inside. "My wife isn't used to these sudden turns from chilly to hot yet." He glanced down, meeting her eyes. "Right, sugar?"

What, was he a facilitator for intervention now, she wondered. It was a sneaky trick, but if she refused now, she would come off looking bitchy and spiteful. "Iced tea sounds nice," she said, forcing a smile. "I'll just get started packing my things and have it when I'm done."

Beatrice closed the door. "Franklin, do you think you and Buck can manage to brew tea? And I'll give Anne a hand collecting her things."

"Oh, that's not—"

Beatrice lifted her hand without a hint of diffidence. "You can grant me just this few minutes, Anne," she said firmly. "And then you won't have to talk to me again…ever, if that will make you happy."

Anne flushed at the rebuke. She was the wronged person

here, she reminded herself righteously. "I really don't have anything else to say, Beatrice. And I'd rather not—"

"You don't have to say anything. You just have to listen." Beatrice was careful not to touch Anne as she moved past her, one arm extended to usher her toward the bedroom. "Come along now."

Without much choice, Anne gave a tiny huff, but she did as asked and was stonily silent as they headed for the bedroom. At the door, she stopped short. Her suitcase lay open on the bed, neatly packed. The room, emptied of her things, had a sterile look. The top of the dresser was cleared off, as was the chest of drawers except for a chintz-covered box that Anne didn't recognize. Beatrice had even packed her hanging bag with toilet articles collected from the guest bathroom. It now lay on the bed, zipped and ready to go.

She turned to look at Beatrice. "It seems you're eager to get rid of me."

"I won't even dignify that with a reply. Frankly, your father and I were hoping you'd reconcile with Buck and move in with him at the lodge, but whether or not that happened, we knew you wouldn't want to be here."

"It would be too uncomfortable. This was a major shock to me. I need some time…."

"Of course." Beatrice again shushed her with a lift of her hand. "We—Franklin and I—have had thirty-four years to come to terms with what we did, whereas you've had only a few hours. In your place, I'd need some time, too. You really don't have to explain your feelings. We understand." She paused with a faint smile. "Well, at least I understand. It's a bit of a struggle for your father."

Anne sat down on the bed. "Are you trying to make me

feel guilty? If so, it's working." Her voice rose with emotion. "I have a right to be upset. My whole life has been lived around a lie!"

Beatrice sat, with Anne's luggage between them. "You'll get no argument from me on that," she said sadly as she looked around the room. "I could paper these walls with the letters I've written to you since Laura died where I confessed everything, but of course they were never mailed. I hoped—prayed—there'd come a day when I could tell you in a straightforward, honorable way."

Anne touched her forehead, feeling a headache coming on. "I don't know what you expect from me. If you agree it's okay that I need more time, why did you force this conversation? I just wanted to come here and get my things without seeing you. Or talking. If that's cruel, then I'm sorry. It's the way I feel."

"It hurts," Beatrice said softly. "I don't deny that, but it's not cruel. We can't help what we feel, you any more than I. And there is a reason I wanted this conversation…forced it, as you say." She nearly winced on the word *forced* as she rose. Moving to the chest, she lifted the chintz box. Rectangular shaped, the lid was secured with a bow of rose-colored ribbon.

"When you take your things, I'd like for you to take this, too." She untied the ribbon and opened the box. Anne saw it was divided into two parts. On one side were letters, fifty or sixty, she guessed at a glance. On the other side were photographs. Dozens of photographs, the top one a studio portrait of Anne when she graduated from high school.

She looked, but didn't touch. "What is this?" Her voice was a whisper.

"I think you know." Beatrice closed it up, retied the ribbon and set it on top of the suitcase. "I don't know what your reaction will be when you finally get around to sorting through all this, but please do be careful. I treasure everything I ever received from Laura Marsh. She was a gracious and loving and forgiving woman. You were lucky—I was lucky—to have her as your mother."

"You don't think I'm anything like her, do you?"

Beatrice smiled on her way to the door. "I'm hoping."

In the end, they stayed for lunch. When Anne emerged from the bedroom pulling her suitcase and carrying the chintz box under her arm, a lunch of cold cuts and fresh French bread was already on the table. One look at her father's hopeful expression and Buck's single raised eyebrow—an outright plea—and she mentally threw in the towel. To refuse would have been tacky.

"See, that wasn't too bad now, was it?" Buck wanted to know as soon as they pulled out of the driveway.

"You never think anything's bad as long as it comes with a square meal," she shot back. "You ate so much I was embarrassed."

"You forget I missed dinner last night and breakfast this morning." When she gave a ladylike snort, he added, "I have to keep my strength up if you expect a repeat tonight of my incredible performance last night."

"I don't plan to be caught in another burning building tonight." Slanting him a sideways look, she pretended surprise. "Oh, *that* performance."

Coming up to Tallulah's only red light, he stopped and made a grab for her. As much as her seat belt allowed, she scrambled out of reach, hugging her door and laughing. He grinned back. "Just wait, I'm punishing you for that."

"Hey, it's tough being a hero."

"Aw, shucks."

"I mean it." When he sputtered a denial, she suddenly released her seat belt. Leaning over the console, she plucked off his sunglasses and tossed them on the dash, then pulled his face toward her and kissed him. "You really are a hero, you know that?" she said softly before turning him loose.

His look turned suspicious as he retrieved his sunglasses. "That's another trick question, right?"

She chuckled. "Let me count the ways. Just lately—" she began ticking off her fingers "—you've rescued two females from a burning building, you've had a hand in reuniting a pair of star-crossed lovers—"

"Me and you?"

"Don't interrupt. No, Jack and Claire, even though it's crazy. You've reinstated an unfairly terminated employee at Belle Pointe, you've stepped in this growing season when your mother would have been up the creek otherwise—not that she'll ever admit it—and finally, I'm halfway reconciled with Franklin and Beatrice because you've personally nagged me into it."

"Speaking of Claire," he said, "she told Pearce she wants a divorce."

"No. Really?"

"Cross my heart. Just this morning."

"And you didn't tell me until now?"

"Too much going on. I forgot." He accelerated as the light changed. "And I meant to ask you this, too. Do you think my mother looks sick? Claire's convinced she is."

"Actually, I have noticed that she's looking her age. And today I thought she seemed tired. It could be she has too much on her plate. After all, she's sixty, not forty. There's Pearce's campaign not going well, disapproval of just about everything Claire does, your unexpected return. And then there's Paige flaunting her disregard for Victoria's rigid standards. As for being sick, I never thought to consider that possibility."

"Yeah, I know what you mean. I've always thought of her as almost indestructible. The idea that she could be sick comes as a shock." He waved at a couple of teenagers passing in a souped-up pickup. "I'm cornering Miriam tomorrow. If anybody noticed a change, she would. She's the only person allowed in my mother's bedroom and that's only because it's her job to clean it."

When he turned the opposite way from the road that led back to Belle Pointe, she asked, "Where are we going?"

"I thought I'd drop in on the family lawyer."

"Joel Tanner? Why?"

"I've got questions, he'd better have answers. Let's see what kind of reaction he has if I get too close to anything that might reflect on my big brother." He shoved his sunglasses on his face. "I'm also checking that old ginning contract with Jim Bob Baker."

"There may be something about it in John Whitaker's journal for that period." Suddenly, she remembered to check for the journals. Craning her neck, she surveyed the back of the SUV and found nothing but her luggage and the chintz box. "Speaking of which, I don't see them. What did you do with them?"

"I asked Franklin to hold them for the time being."

"Buck! Why did you do that? You know I've been dying to look at them." With a scowl, she flopped back against the seat, crossing her arms. "Now if I want to read them, I'll have to go back there to do it."

"Uh-huh."

"You did that on purpose! Is this another one of your ideas as a facilitator?"

He barked a laugh. "A what?"

"An intervention facilitator. Someone who pushes people into doing things they don't want to do…for their own good."

Still grinning, he dipped his head to eye her over the top of his sunglasses. "Well, hell, I didn't realize I was so damn smart."

"You want me to have to be around Franklin and Beatrice, don't you?"

"Franklin and Beatrice," he repeated, gently chiding. He let a bit of his smile go. "You're calling your parents by their first names now? Didn't I hear you scolding Paige for doing that?"

She let out an exasperated breath. "When you work out your problems with Victoria Whitaker," she said loftily, "then you can give me advice."

"I hope it won't be that long," he said with feeling.

"Then stick to your own family problems," she said, looking stonily ahead, "and I'll handle mine."

"Here we are," he said, pulling up in front of a renovated Victorian. Joel Tanner was one of only two names on a tasteful green-and-gold sign set unobtrusively on the landscaped lawn. The other was James Tanner, CPA.

"James just happens to be Joel's brother and the Whitaker accountant," Buck remarked. "That job used to be Harmon Jackson's, but I guess he retired."

"Or, since James is Joel's brother, Pearce decided to keep things all in the family," Anne said.

With his hand on the door handle, Buck turned to look at her. "Like I said, m'dear, you have a suspicious mind."

"Takes one to know one."

The sight of Buck Whitaker, pro baseball star, flustered Tanner's receptionist, who was no doubt trained to head off individuals who had no appointment. She made an exception for Buck.

As Pearce's campaign manager, Anne expected to see evidence of the campaign strewn about Joel's office, but it was uncluttered, as tastefully and expensively furnished as suggested by the building and landscaped grounds.

Once they'd all shaken hands cordially, Joel's practiced smile included them both. "You two must be looking forward to going back to St. Louis."

"I'm entertaining myself at Belle Pointe," Buck said. "And my wife's getting a chance to polish her journalistic skills at the *Spectator.* Neither of us can complain. At any rate, we're here until the cotton's picked and processed."

Joel made a sympathetic sound. "That knee is still not up to par, eh?"

"It's fine." Buck gave his knee an affectionate pat. "As long as I don't overdo it, I'm right on schedule, according to my PT."

"That would be Tyrone Pittman, wouldn't it?"

"It would."

"I heard he's considering setting up a full facility here in Tallulah. I suspect you had something to do with that."

"The way I see it," Buck said, settling back in the comfortable leather wingback, "we Whitakers owe Ty and his family for the years Oscar put in as a loyal employee at Belle Pointe. Still, in spite of considerable hardship, Oscar and his wife managed to educate every one of their children. Reinstating him at Belle Pointe and helping Ty set up his own shop seemed the least we could do."

"It was unfortunate that Oscar was so openly defiant of the established system at Belle Pointe. If he'd only—"

"Knuckled under? Worked from daylight to dark for straight pay?"

"What can I do for you today, Buck?" Joel's smile was tight. Lawyerlike, he knew when to fold up.

"Couple things." Too irritated to stay in his chair, Buck stood up. "First, I want to see the books, current and past, plus the complete Whitaker and Belle Pointe files. You probably have appointments scheduled today, so I won't impose on you while I look them over." He glanced toward the door. "I assume you have a conference room we can use?"

Joel, who had been kicked back in his chair, straightened and rolled close to his desk. "You must know that's impossible, Buck."

"Why?"

"Well…" Joel cleared his throat, politely discomfited. "First of all, about the books, I'm not the accountant of record for Belle Pointe."

"I'm aware that James, your brother, has taken over from Harmon Jackson. And since I noticed his office on the other side of the house, I don't see the problem. I'll just step over there and tell him what I need. I don't recall ever meeting James, but you can vouch for me being who I am." He paused and looked Joel directly in the eye. "A Whitaker with equal standing to Pearce."

"Look here, Buck, I can't just turn over my files without first consulting Pearce. You know that." He reached for the phone.

"No, I don't know that, Joel. Hear me on this, my man. I'm up to my eyeballs in the affairs of Belle Pointe. Examining the books would seem perfectly logical. You can consult with Pearce, of course, but I expect to have everything brought to me in your conference room. As for other Whitaker documents, I don't see the problem in letting me access them…seeing as I'm family."

He watched Joel's hand ease away from the telephone, guessing the lawyer was calculating a way to stonewall. "And another thing, Joel. From now on, no matter what town I'm in, St. Louis or Tallulah or Timbuktu, I'm playing a major role in the affairs of Belle Pointe. Your position as legal counsel for the family isn't necessarily a lifetime appointment. And managing Pearce's campaign is actually a disadvantage. Some might say it looks bad for you professionally, smelling of conflict of interest."

"That sounds like a threat," Joel said, but he seemed unfazed. "So if I were you, I'd consult with Victoria before taking any drastic action."

"There'll be no drastic action so long as I get what I came here for today," Buck said, wondering at the man's confidence. What did he know that gave him that kind of confidence? "But I think I heard a message somewhere in there. Would you care to be more specific?"

"I haven't lasted thirty years as Victoria's lawyer without being privy to certain matters that could be embarrassing, to say the least. You might want to be careful digging around in the past. You may turn over a few nasty stones that would be better left in place." Tanner paused with a gleam in his eye as Buck processed his words. "Consider that free advice. I won't bill you for it."

Buck moved over to a world globe on a stand near a window. He touched it, watched it rotate for a minute before turning to face the lawyer again. "Since you claim to be privy to family secrets, maybe you'll be able to give some insight into the second matter I'm here to discuss. It's a bit more delicate."

Joel was silent, but spread his hands as if to say, go for it.

"It's about that hunting trip when Jim Bob Baker was killed by a blast from his own shotgun," Buck said. "You recall that, Joel?"

"I'm not sure—"

"You were in that hunting party. I was seventeen years old but, as I recall, you were partnered up with a cousin of the Watkins'. Kid was visiting from somewhere on the coast, Biloxi I think it was."

"No one forgets a tragedy like that, Buck. Of course, I remember. I was going to say that I'm not sure where you're going with this. It happened twenty years ago. Pearce has worked diligently to erase the cloud of that accident. You must know that his campaign would take a hit if folks were reminded of it."

"Well, you see…" Buck rubbed the back of his neck, looking somewhat apologetic. "It's a funny thing. My wife—" he smiled at Anne "—is purely fascinated with Tallulah history. She's writing a book, isn't that right, honey?"

Anne acknowledged that with a cautious lift of her shoulder, uncertain where he was headed, but fascinated with what she'd heard so far.

"And in doing her research down in the archives, she stumbled across the *Spectator*'s account of that accident. Naturally, having a reporter's instincts and training, she had a few questions. Anne probably wasn't thinking about the effect it might have on Pearce's campaign if she dug up this old—what did you call it?—tragedy, which is sure enough what it would have been to Miz Baker, Jim Bob's mama. With Jim Bob gone, that makes two of her sons dead, Jim Bob in that hunting accident and his big brother, Rudy, in Vietnam."

"His brother? Vietnam?" Joel looked ready to laugh. "Please tell me how a war casualty forty years ago is relevant."

"Patience," Buck said with a purely false smile. "I was just dropping that bit about Rudy as an aside, don't you know? What I want from you are the details of the deal to gin Belle Pointe's cotton that Jim Bob had going."

"This is ridiculous!" Joel rose abruptly, his patience gone. "Even if I recalled the details of a transaction that happened back then, I'm bound by attorney-client privilege. Your status as an heir might be equal to Pearce's, but I'm not free to discuss personal matters entrusted to me."

"As the attorney for the family, you represent the entire family and if any member of the family has entrusted personal information that affects any one of us, Pearce, myself or my mother, there is no privilege, Joel. You are required to share it." Buck gave him a few moments to digest that. "So I'm asking, did he discuss the Baker-Belle Pointe contract with you?"

Joel sighed. "It was so many years ago that I'd have to pull out a file to refresh my memory. And I'm not discussing it with you until I talk to Pearce. You can threaten all you want, but I'm not doing it."

Twenty-Three

The house at Belle Pointe was quiet when Anne and Buck let themselves in after leaving Joel Tanner's office. With Victoria's signature approving the outrageous terms of the agreement to gin Belle Pointe cotton with Baker, Buck figured she was the logical person to question.

"Let's go upstairs," he told Anne. "She's probably in the master bedroom suite where she has an office of sorts. The only reason I know about it is that a few days ago she needed me to install a new ceiling fan. For some reason, she's never claimed Dad's library-office. Too masculine, maybe."

"Or it could be that she has too much reverence for Belle Pointe tradition to disturb what's existed for over a hundred years," Anne said.

"Yeah, probably worried that the ghosts of Whitakers past will haunt her."

"I don't think we should just barge in on her," Anne said, lagging behind. "Let's call her first."

"We're right here in the house, sugar." He caught her hand and pulled her along with him up the winding stairs.

"What if she's not in her office, but is resting?"

"In the middle of the day? Never happen. C'mon, actually she's likely to be more polite at being questioned if you're along."

"She doesn't like me very much as it is," Anne said in a tense whisper. "Now she'll hate me."

"That'll make two of us she hates. No, three. Claire thinks she hates her."

But he slowed as they approached the area of the house that was exclusively his mother's. Even as a kid, he never dashed in to his parents' bedroom. The rules Victoria laid down left no room for kids' spontaneity.

At the door of her office, he had his hand raised to knock when he saw her. In the plushness of the carpet, she had not heard his approach with Anne. She sat at her desk, leaning back in her chair with her eyes closed. Was she asleep, he wondered in sudden concern. Then he realized she wasn't sleeping. One hand was pressed to her middle and her face was—God, it was awful. Pale, strained and ravaged with pain. Serious pain.

He knew that feeling.

Reaching behind him, he stopped Anne and silently backed out of sight of the open door. Turning, he put a finger to his lips and caught Anne's hand to lead her back to the stairs. "Maybe we should call," he whispered.

"What? Why?"

He reached for the cell phone at his waist, pressed a programmed number and waited. In his mother's office, he could hear the ring. Once, twice. On the third ring, she answered.

"Hello."

"Ma, it's me."

"Buck." She cleared her throat. "Yes, what is it?"

"We're in the house, Anne and me. We need to see you for a minute. Can we come up?"

"Well, of course. I'm in my office."

He clicked off his cell, stood without moving for a full minute with Anne's questioning gaze on his face. "Okay, let's go."

She hesitated, debating whether or not to go along, then fell into step beside him. "I want to know what that was all about as soon as we're done here," she told him in an irritated whisper. "And just for the record, I'm against this."

At his mother's door again, he tapped politely, even though it was still wide open. "Hey, Ma. How's it goin'?"

She gestured to a sheaf of paperwork on the top of her desk. "As you see. Hello, Anne." With a tip of her chin, she indicated the settee against the wall to her left. "Sit down. Would you like tea, coffee? I think Miriam has lemonade, too. It's so warm outside and early for it, too."

"Nothing for me," Anne said politely. "But thank you."

"You feeling all right, Ma?"

She gave an irritated click of her tongue. "Why is everyone so concerned about my health lately? Yes, I'm fine." She glanced at his knee. "I could ask the same of you. How's that knee?"

"I think I'll keep it," Buck said.

Her tight smile was for Anne. "You should have heard the jokes he made when he was ten."

"Jeff Foxworthy he isn't," Anne said.

"Ma, we've got a couple of questions, if you don't mind."

"I may or I may not. It depends on the questions."

He had the original of a 1975 contract rolled up in his hand. Leaning forward from the settee, he pushed it toward her on the desk. Ten minutes ago, he'd have demanded an explanation outright. Now that he'd observed her obviously in pain, some of the steam had gone out of him. "Do you remember this document, Ma?"

She donned reading glasses and glanced at the heading. "It appears to be an old contract with Wilson Enterprises and Belle Pointe."

"Which you signed."

She lifted her shoulders in a casual shrug. "Apparently. I don't recall."

"I was wondering why Dad didn't sign it."

"The same reason he didn't sign any number of business documents. He was far more interested in papers generated by his friends in academia."

"Did you have power of attorney?"

"I did."

"Did you ask for any guidance when negotiating the terms of the contract?" He hurried on when her eyes flashed with indignation. "I'm not suggesting you needed help, but the terms are pretty one-sided, to say the least. Wilson overcharged Belle Pointe for almost ten years, starting with this contract."

"Why are you concerning yourself with this, Buck? Until recently, your baseball career consumed your life. You neglected to show any interest in the business affairs of Belle Pointe. I find your curiosity unseemly now."

"I think we both know why I didn't show much interest in the business affairs of Belle Pointe or any other aspect," he said in a neutral tone. He didn't want to fight with her now. "But whether I did or not, this contract was costly and inefficient. It amounts to highway robbery. You'll note that as of the date of this contract Jim Bob Baker became a new partner at Wilson's. Ma…" his tone dropped to an even quieter level "…the really weird thing is that the contract was rescinded in 1985 on the Monday following Baker's death."

"What are you suggesting?" she demanded coldly. The hand she brought up to her throat was not quite steady. Lined with a tracery of blue veins, it looked very fragile and showed her age more than her face. How had he not noticed that before today?

"I'm not suggesting anything. I'm asking if you can explain what to anybody is a questionable business agreement."

"What does it matter?" she asked wearily. "It was so long ago." She moved to collect some of the papers on her desk and shuffled them. Reaching for a clip, she pinned them, moved them aside and picked up another bunch. "I have a lot to do, Buck. I need to get back to it."

"That's what I'm here for, Ma," he said quietly. "I'll be glad to take a lot of that stuff off your hands."

She instantly straightened up in her chair. "I'm perfectly capable of handling paperwork. You volunteered to see to the crops, nothing else."

Buck didn't dispute what she said. Both knew he'd told her up front that he intended to have access to all aspects of Belle Pointe, books, crop management, employees, everything. He was troubled that she was stonewalling.

From the moment they'd entered the office, Anne had watched Victoria's attitude grow more and more uneasy. This was Buck's business, but it was difficult to sit still while his mother grew steadily more tense. Perhaps even afraid. Why? Of what?

Buck settled back on the couch. "I went to see Joel Tanner today," he said quietly.

"I assumed that was how you came into a copy of the contract," Victoria said. "I hope you didn't burden him with your suspicions."

"I don't believe I've mentioned being suspicious, just curious," Buck said.

"Joel is in a delicate position."

"He's a lawyer. They live for delicate positions. And as Whitaker legal counsel, he was obliged to answer a few questions. He wasn't happy. I eventually convinced him that I was within my legal rights as a Whitaker to ask whatever I damn well pleased."

She lowered the papers and looked directly at him. "What questions?"

"I wanted to know why he hadn't advised against signing a contract that gave Wilson—and Baker as a new partner—a license to steal from us."

"Why do you keep harping on that, Buck?" She tore her reading glasses off and tossed them on the desk. "What possible relevance does an ancient contract have to do with anything today?"

"My question exactly." Buck stood up and Anne thought with relief that he was done. As she started to get to her feet, with one hand he motioned for her to stay. "Ma, a six-year-old can see there's a connection between Baker becoming a partner at the gin and the lucrative contract he negotiated with Belle Pointe. He dies on Friday and on the following Monday the contract is renegotiated. I hate what I'm thinking here, but it makes his accidental death look not so accidental."

Victoria was now on her feet. "I don't have to listen to this."

"It's not only the link between his death and the contract that worries me," Buck said, pushing on. "I've never mentioned what I'm going to say now to anybody but Anne and Pearce," he said, letting his tone go even more gentle as his mother's agitation grew. "I overheard Pearce and Jim Bob arguing the night before the hunt."

"I know this," Victoria said in an unsteady voice. "Pearce told me. If you think you're revealing something ugly about your brother that will discredit him, you're sadly mistaken."

"It wasn't only about the contract that they argued, Ma. It was about you."

Victoria sat down abruptly, her hand at her throat as if she couldn't breathe. Anne leaped up, thinking she was near collapsing. "Victoria, are you all right?"

"I'd like a drink of water," Victoria said in a weak voice.

"Yes, I'll get it." With a severe look at Buck, Anne rushed out.

Buck was on his way around the desk, when Victoria put up an imperious hand. "Wait," she ordered in a clear voice. Buck realized she wasn't anywhere near collapse.

"What did you hear?" she asked when Anne was safely out of earshot.

"Not much. At least, not much that made sense. Just that it was a threat. He said if he told what he knew, you would get the punishment you deserve."

"Did you tell your father what you heard?"

"Dad? No. I didn't tell anyone until now, not even Anne." He gave a humorless laugh. "Even though I hadn't a clue what it meant, I had some idea that it might damage your reputation, Ma. Whatever it meant, it couldn't be anything good."

"I don't want to speak of this again, Buck. I have only your word for it that anything of the sort happened between Jim Bob and Pearce. Now, please leave me. You've created enough havoc for one day."

Again, Buck ignored her and pushed on. "You said Pearce confided in you about his argument with Jim Bob that night. Did he tell you that Jim Bob had threatened you personally? Do you know what it meant?"

She swiveled away from him in her chair, her chin set stubbornly. "I've said all I intend to say."

He studied the back of her as she faced the window, head and shoulders ramrod-straight. Whether she admitted it or not, Buck felt sure she knew what Baker's threat meant. "I'm going to find out, Ma. I believe that man's death was no accident. I believe that fire last night was meant to keep Anne away from the archives because of what she might uncover. And I believe it's all related."

Anne rushed in carrying a bottle of water, breathless from taking the stairs at a run. "Is she all right?" she asked Buck.

Catching her arm, Buck prevented her from going to his mother. "She's recovered," he said dryly. He took the bottled water from her and set it on the desk, then nudged Anne toward the door. Just before closing it, he looked back at Victoria, who still faced the window. "We'll talk later, Ma."

Anne managed to contain herself until they were on their way downstairs. Then she lit into Buck. "That was awful! That was horrible! She's your mother. How could you?"

"I guess it was pretty pathetic, wasn't it?" He looked around for a sign of life in the house, but saw nothing and no one. "But you and Paige almost died in that fire, Anne. As long as the people who know aren't talking, I don't see how we'll get to the bottom of this without ruffling a few feathers."

"You didn't just ruffle your mother's feathers, Buck. You nearly gave her a heart attack."

"She was fudging."

Anne stared at him, dimly aware that her mouth was hanging open. "Have you forgotten? I was there. I saw how her hands shook."

"It was an act, a way to get you out of her office so you wouldn't hear any more."

Anne was ready with more outrage, but after a moment considering it, she realized that Victoria was capable of just such a ploy. "Are you serious?"

"As a heart attack," he said. "Which reminds me. I think she's sick. When we first got to her office, she was leaning back in her chair with her eyes closed. I know what someone looks like when they're in pain and she was definitely in pain."

"Do you think she's seriously ill?"

"I don't know and we won't either until she's ready to tell us. I plan to ask Miriam, first chance I get. She'll know." With a hand under her elbow, he guided her across the foyer to the front door. "Here's the interesting part. She wanted to know if I'd told Dad about the argument between Pearce and Jim Bob. Makes me think she and Dad may have had a conversation about it."

"Wow, wouldn't you like to have been a fly on the wall for that one," Anne said, big-eyed at the thought.

"You don't know how much," he said.

Just then, the front door burst open and Paige dashed inside, narrowly avoiding a crash when Buck put out his hands and caught her.

"Whoa! The fire was at the *Spectator,* little girl." Holding her by the arms, he looked at her pink T-shirt and skintight jeans. "Hey, don't I know you?"

"Let me go put on my Goth stuff," Paige said cheekily. "You'll probably recognize me then. Hi, Aunt Anne."

"Cute T-shirt," Anne said, guessing that the very unoriginal outfit was part of the precocious teen's punishment. Overall, she appeared amazingly normal, including her naturally dark hair with most of the neon-orange tint gone.

"I could use some help here, Paige!" Outside, Claire was struggling up the steps carrying a cardboard box. "Go back to the car and get the other."

"Oh, I forgot!" Paige dashed out to the car and returned with another box. "Jack Breedlove campaign stuff," she explained to Buck and Anne. "We're gonna be volunteers in his campaign. It's neat! My dad is gonna go ballistic."

Claire met Anne's eyes and muttered, "Now there's an understatement."

Buck took the box from Claire. "Where d'you want these?"

"All the way upstairs in my bedroom, which is not the master bedroom. Show him, Paige. And thanks, Buck. If I left them lying around in plain sight, they could very well go the way of the *Spectator* archives."

With a grim smile, Buck said, "Hold that thought. When I get back, that's what I want to talk about."

Claire waited until Paige was out of earshot. "Did Buck tell you I've filed for a divorce?"

"Yes. You're making so many personal changes I can't keep up."

"I haven't told Paige yet, so don't mention it." She made

a face. "I know I should have, but she was in such a good mood I hated to throw a damper on it, but I'll have to say something before Pearce comes home tonight."

Anne marveled at the difference in Claire. There was a glow about her. She looked younger, almost like Paige's older sister instead of her mother. "I wish you well, Claire. A divorce is a big step, especially with a child involved. If I can do anything…help in any way, all you have to do is ask."

"Thank you," Claire whispered, squeezing Anne's hand.

Buck spoke coming down the stairs. "Did you say you'd seen Jack today?"

"Yes, remember, he wanted to question Paige." She looked at Anne. "He mentioned you were supposed to drop by and give a statement, too, Anne."

She gave a squeak of dismay. "I completely forgot. Buck, we need to do that now."

"Wait, first let me fill you in." Claire moved to the third step of the stairs and sat down. "Jack doesn't have any leads on who might have started the fire, but he told me how it was started. It appears that the arsonist didn't know there was anybody inside. He'd made a sort of wick by soaking a piece of rope in something flammable. When it reached the area where the accelerant had been poured, it ignited. Jack said it was pretty primitive, but it worked. It gave him time to get out and, unfortunately, time for Paige and Anne to get in."

Buck was frowning before she finished. "How did the arsonist get in a locked building in the first place?"

"The lock on the front door was pretty flimsy. Jack said it was easily jimmied open."

"Jimmied open?" Buck looked at Anne. "You would have arrived after that. Didn't you notice?"

"Frankly, no. The door was wide open and I could smell smoke. I didn't think about it. I just ran inside to see if I could save anything."

"Me, for instance," Paige said, appearing at the top of the stairs.

Buck looked up at her. "I've got the same question for you. How did you get inside to leave the journals?"

"I had a key, but I didn't need it because the door wasn't locked. Which I now know was because the guy who set the fire left it unlocked." She gave Anne an apologetic look. "I just thought your dad forgot to lock up when he left."

Buck was looking at her. "You had a key."

"Well, duh. Everybody who works there knows Mr. Marsh has a spare hanging on a nail, so that afternoon when I left, I just took it with me because I knew I'd need a way to get inside later that night to leave the journals."

"I know what you're thinking," Claire said, looking at Anne and Buck. "She needs a firmer hand. And you're absolutely right. Jack deals with a lot of adolescent mischief. When she made her statement, even he was impressed by her audacity."

"I couldn't think of any other way to get those journals to Anne," Paige said. "And it would've worked, too, if there hadn't been a fire."

"We have a saying in baseball," Buck said. "We would've won the game if the other team hadn't."

"Huh?"

"Ignore him." Anne sent Buck a speaking look.

He grinned and chucked Paige beneath her chin. "I've got another question for you, brat. Just how did you manage to get your hands on those journals? They've been missing for years. Nobody, not even your grandmother, knew where they were."

"Simple," Paige said, brightening. "They were in the secret hidey hole."

Buck gave a surprised laugh. "I forgot all about it. How'd you find it, Paige?"

"I used to spend a lot of time in the attic," she said, with a quick look at her mother. "And one day I was just fooling around and I found it. It was really neat the way it was designed. Anyway, when Gran would go on a tear or Dad started yelling, I'd just go in there and you couldn't hear anything." She shrugged. "So…like, forever I've known the journals were in there. I was just not much interested in reading them until I started working with Anne in the archives."

Anne's expression was thoughtful. "I assume there's a secret room in this house, which doesn't surprise me. Many antebellum houses have one. But wouldn't everybody know about it? And Victoria didn't know where the journals were. Wouldn't she have looked there, first thing?"

"Actually, Ma might not know," Buck said. "It's a room behind a room that opens with a concealed spring lock. It's incredible that Paige figured it out. And its purpose is just what the name implies, a hiding place for runaway slaves. Dad told me about it when I was around eight years old and he swore me to secrecy. I never told anybody and it's been years since I thought about it."

"But wouldn't John have told his wife?" Anne asked.

"He didn't tell Pearce," Buck said. "I know that, because we were in the original room many times as kids, but it was plain to me that he didn't know about the secret panel that led to the hidey hole. So it's possible Dad didn't tell her. As to why he didn't tell either of them, I don't have a clue."

"How odd," Anne murmured. It was inconceivable to her that the life John Whitaker lived with Victoria was so void of intimacy. With only their relationship to influence him, it was no wonder Buck's image of marriage was skewed.

"That still doesn't shed any light on why the journals were hidden away instead of being in the library where a cabinet was built especially for them," Anne said.

"Reading them may explain that." Buck took her arm and steered her toward the door. "Meanwhile, Claire, you might want to go upstairs and check on Ma. You were right thinking she could be sick." He told her about seeing Victoria looking ill and in pain. "If she won't talk, see if you can get anything out of Miriam and call me."

"I'll do it."

"Good. And now I'm taking my wife home."

They weren't able to go straight home. There was still Anne's statement about the fire to be given to Jack Breedlove, which took another hour. The pavement glistened from a light drizzle when they finally headed for the lodge. By then, both were more than ready to call it a day.

"Tired?" Buck asked, looking over at her when she gave a weary sigh.

"Yes." The events of the day were catching up with her and Anne realized she was looking forward to the quiet isolation of the lodge…so long as Buck was there with her. "This has been the longest day of my life. I just want to go to sleep and forget everything."

"That was a pretty stunning discovery…I mean, about Franklin and Beatrice being your parents.

She sighed again. "Tell me."

With his eyes on the road, he said, "You think you might bring yourself to go see them tomorrow?"

She sat without moving for a long minute. "Facilitating again, are you?"

He gave a shrug and grinned at her. "Hell, why not? It seems to be my new role in the family."

"If you can facilitate harmony in your family, you should give up baseball and put out a shingle," she said dryly.

He was silent too long.

"That was a joke, Buck."

"I'm thinking about that," he said. "Giving up baseball, I mean."

Her mouth dropped. She was speechless.

"I guess I shocked you. But just think, at my age I can only play another couple years, best case. I wouldn't admit this to anybody but you, but my pitching arm has been giving me trouble. Just a matter of time and I blow it out."

It was no surprise to her that his arm was not up to par, but she'd never expected him to admit it. She'd known that he didn't want to hear any wifely questions of concern from her, which had only added to the list of things they couldn't talk about...then.

"So what next, I'm asking myself," Buck went on. "Until I came back to Tallulah, the time when I wouldn't be playing just stretched out in front of me, a long line of nothing. But now that I'm here, I see a lot of good things I could do with my life, starting with whipping myself into shape as a good husband and next, becoming a father. It's like my eyes are open now, when before I was walking around with blinders on."

"Oh, Buck..." Seat belt unbuckled, she reached over and

kissed him on the mouth. "This is so incredible. You are one wonderful man. Are you serious?"

"I am." He grinned at her. "I have to admit Ty's been working on me and so has Jack. There's a lot of good I can do here, Anne. First of all, I intend to have a real role in the affairs of Belle Pointe, but after growing season, I'll have time. I can use my name and influence, whatever it amounts to, to doing something good for kids around here that wouldn't have a fair shot otherwise."

She felt a surge of pleasure and relief. And anticipation. There was so much they could do together here. Her enthusiasm faded as they turned in at the lodge and saw the big black Lexus parked in front.

Buck groaned. "Seems like my big brother considers the lodge his meeting place of choice when he wants to talk."

"I'm just surprised he hasn't managed to corner you before now," Anne said. "In fact, I thought he'd show up at Joel Tanner's office while we were there. Tanner surely called him."

"Campaign took precedence. Joel said he was in Jackson sucking up to the party bigwigs. He needs financial commitment from the party."

"His supporters there must be wondering why you haven't endorsed him."

"Not gonna happen." Buck threw open his door. "This is one race he'll have to run on his own."

As Buck had done in his struggle from baseball's minor leagues into the majors, Anne thought as they made the long climb up the lodge steps.

Lights blazed as Buck ushered Anne inside. Unlike Buck's other encounters with his brother, it appeared this one wouldn't happen on the porch.

Pearce stood in the center of the great room. "This is Diet Coke I'm drinking, bro," he said, rattling ice in the tumbler. "I don't how long it's been since I've hung around cooling my heels without the benefit of good scotch. Turned the place upside down and couldn't find a bottle. No booze in the lodge. Seems a desecration somehow." He raised the drink to Anne. "Evening, Anne."

"Hello, Pearce."

"Sorry to keep you waiting," Buck said, closing the door behind him. "If you'd shared with me the time of our appointment, you might not have had such a long wait."

"That would probably have been a good plan," Pearce said, "but I was in Jackson and you know how it is trying to corner a politician. They make you hang around, then leave you feeling like crap. It's a bitch." His practiced smile included both of them. "But we're here now and…hey, let's talk."

Anne blinked with confusion. Pearce should be seething with rage. Instead, he was in full politician bonhomie. Maybe Tanner hadn't told him.

"It's been a long day, Pearce," Buck said, "especially for Anne. Whatever's on your mind, let's have it. And if you're thinking of suggesting my wife might want to go to bed without me, not a chance."

Pearce lifted his glass again, a silent acknowledgement that Buck had the upper hand. "Can we at least sit down?"

With a touch to Anne's waist, Buck steered her to the big leather couch and sat down beside her. As soon as Pearce took the large armchair opposite them, he said, "Okay, what's on your mind?"

"What else? Your visit to Joel's office."

"Sweet setup he's got there," Buck said, "exclusive handling of all Whitaker family matters and Belle Pointe, too. And his brother doing the books. I can see why you'd want him to manage your campaign. Who better to keep a lid on your secrets than someone with a vested interest?"

Pearce didn't rise to the bait. "According to Joel, you're still bent on reminding people that I was involved in Jim Bob Baker's accident. There's no secret, Buck, but if you keep going around talking about it, pretty soon folks will begin to think where there's smoke there's fire."

"I'm not talking about it with anybody except you, the family lawyer and Mother. And since they're both in your pocket, why're you so nervous?"

"Stuff gets out, man!" Pearce glanced at Anne. "Your wife's listening right now. Next thing, Franklin Marsh gets wind of it and runs a story in the *Spectator.* I can't afford for that to happen."

"I have no intention of discussing you or your past with my father," Anne told him. "Or anyone else."

"Then what's all that nosing around in the archives about?"

She sighed. "It's about Tallulah history. It's about the Whitakers and the role they've played in this town…" She paused. "Before you were born, Pearce." Did the man think everything had to be about him?

Buck stood up. "Are you done?"

"Deny it all you want, but you're killing me, Buck. You've got to know that. I haven't cottoned on to your game yet, since you'll be out of Tallulah as soon as that knee is a hundred percent. Yet you're going around stirring up shit right and left. It's doing damage, man. I hear people whispering, wondering. And suddenly Jack Breedlove is coming on strong…out of nowhere. Deny it all you want, but you're with him. What can I do to persuade you to back off?"

"How about telling me what Jim Bob meant when he made that crack about Ma? I might back off then."

With an oath, Pearce slammed the half-full tumbler on a table and stalked to the door. "I can see it doesn't do any good trying to reason with you," he said, wrenching it open. "Just tell me the date you'll be heading back to St. Louis so I can throw a farewell party. And do me a favor. Make it soon."

With a quick wink at Anne, Buck grinned. "You'll be the first to know."

As soon as the taillights of the Lexus faded, Buck pulled Anne into his arms and smiled down at her. "Looks like I've got my big brother in a sweat."

She looked at him with one brow arched. "Should you be enjoying it quite so much?"

He hiked one shoulder. "I'm only human, darlin'."

She pushed her hips against him and laughed. "I can testify to that."

He made a growling sound and nipped her on the side of her neck. "Can we go to bed now? Finally?" Before the last word, his cell phone rang. He groaned. "I'm ignoring that."

Ignoring him, she plucked the phone from his belt and looked at the caller ID. "It's my dad, so okay we'll ignore it."

Buck's smile faded as he took the still-ringing phone from her. "I don't think he'd call at this hour unless it's something urgent. Your frosty attitude at lunch was pretty discouraging."

"I was polite," she said coolly.

The phone, still in Buck's hand, beeped to signal new voice mail. "I'm checking the message," he told her. "What if one of them is sick? Telling you their secret was pretty heavy-duty stuff and they're not exactly young anymore."

Anne was chilled at the thought. Listening to the message didn't mean she had to return her dad's call. "Okay, listen."

Buck punched the numbers to retrieve voice mail and frowned as he listened. "What is it?" Anne asked when he closed the phone with a snap.

"It was Franklin and he sounded upset. He asked me to call him."

"Oh." Anne told herself it wasn't fear she felt, just a natural concern. After all, her father was still her father, even though she hadn't known how much of a father until today. Of course, he could be calling because Beatrice— "Okay, call him back," she said.

He smiled. "That's my girl." He dialed, using his thumb. While it rang, he reached for Anne and pulled her close, so that when Franklin answered, she could hear his voice.

"Is that you, Buck?"

"Yeah. What's up, Franklin?"

"Well, I know it's late…and you and Anne have probably just gotten settled for the night, but Bea insisted I needed to call."

"Ask if she's sick," Anne whispered to Buck.

"No, no, it's nothing like that," Franklin said, apparently overhearing. "It's about the journals. The Whitaker journals."

Buck met Anne's eyes and gave a beats-me shrug. "What about them?"

"Well, maybe we shouldn't have, but you know both of us have a special interest in the history of the Mississippi Delta and of course the Whitaker journals are pretty irresistible dating back, as they do, over a hundred and fifty years. So we took the liberty of opening them and reading a while. I hope—"

"Franklin, it's okay. Be my guest. But your message said it was urgent."

"We're thinking you might want to come over and read one of John Whitaker's entries, Buck…considering all that's gone on lately."

Buck looked at his watch. "Right now? It's nearly midnight, Franklin."

"I'd rather say no more on the cell phone, don't you know. But the entry is dated around the time that fellow, Jim Bob Baker, was killed in that hunting accident. It relates to that, Buck."

The receiver went slack in Buck's hand. He looked into Anne's stunned eyes. "We'll be right over."

Twenty-Four

The drizzle had cleared by the time they pulled into the driveway of the Marshes' Victorian and patches of fog were developing. The moment they were out of the SUV, the door opened and Franklin beckoned them inside.

"Muggy weather, isn't it?" he said as they wiped their feet in the foyer.

"Good for the crops," Buck said, nudging Anne forward. Beatrice stood in the arched doorway of the dining room. Behind her, on the fine antique table, were several of the Whitaker journals. "Hi, Beatrice."

"Buck." She managed a smile, then shifted it to Anne. Her gaze was anxious. "This was not a ploy to get you back over here."

Anne had to smile. "At this hour? I never thought it was. Besides, I was coming around tomorrow anyway." Three faces registered surprise. She shrugged. "I needed a while to overcome the shock."

"Oh." Beatrice put a hand on her heart. "Please believe we didn't mean to give you such a shock...ever."

"You could say it set the stage for the rest of the day, which has been…interesting. Right, Buck?"

"You could say." Buck rubbed his hands together. "So, how about those Whitaker journals? Let's have a look."

With Beatrice leading the way, they went into the dining room. Franklin put a hand on one of the ancient books and stroked it reverently. "I just couldn't resist reading a bit," he said. "I went right to the early days after the Civil War. Beatrice, now, she wanted some insight into John Whitaker." He winked at Anne. "I've always suspected she had a bit of a crush on him."

"Franklin!"

"Just teasing, Bea." He slipped his spectacles on and opened a journal that looked less aged than the others. "This would be the last journal and Bea found the entry you'll want to read." He glanced up, looking over the spectacles. "At least, I hope we're doing the right thing in bringing this to your attention at this particular time. You'd have found it on your own, or I know Anne would as she's been so keen about reading them."

"What is it, Dad?"

"See for yourself." He pushed the journal across the table where Anne and Buck stood, then waited while they read the entry he'd marked with a sticky note.

"Oh, my God," Anne whispered, clutching at Buck's arm.

"Yeah. I guess this explains everything. I was hoping—" With thumb and forefinger, Buck rubbed his eyes wearily. "Read it again, Anne…out loud."

Anne read, "Today I betrayed every ethical standard I've been taught to revere as a Whitaker. I'm deeply ashamed. Buck came to me voicing suspicion of his brother in the death of Jim Bob Baker. In spite of Pearce's quite cunning account of the 'accident,' I suspected the moment he told us Baker was dead of a bullet wound from his own gun that it might be a lie. Pearce may have killed the man in cold blood. So instead of telling Buck that I shared his suspicions, I lectured him about family honor and his duty to the citizens of Tallulah and sent him off to university hoping he'd put it out of his mind. I blame myself for this tragedy. I was suspicious of the terms of the ginning contract with Wilson's. Since Victoria is an excellent businesswoman, she would never accept terms so unfavorable to Belle Pointe without good reason. I suspected blackmail. If I'd spoken out earlier, confronted her openly, all would have been revealed and Pearce's motive for murdering Baker would possibly have been removed. I knew, and I'm convinced Victoria does, as well, that the contract had everything to do with Rudy Baker. As did the murder of his brother."

Anne looked up into Buck's eyes. "We were right," she whispered.

"*You* were right. Keep going."

"Confronting her now is too late. The time to tell her what I suspect is long past. I've known ever since Pearce was a small boy that he was not my son, but Rudy's."

Anne pushed the journal aside. "I don't want to read any more." She put a hand on Buck's shoulder. "Why do you think John didn't tell this to the police when it happened?"

"Protecting the almighty Whitaker name," Buck said bitterly.

Franklin spoke quietly. "There could be another reason." When all three were looking, he said, "For love. Maybe he loved her."

Beatrice moved her finger down the page and read, "I daresay I'm not the first man to be made a fool of by a beautiful woman. And Victoria is that, beautiful, intelligent, sensual, seductive."

"She sounds very much like that sixteen-year-old girl you remember from high school, Beatrice," Anne said in a hushed tone. What was more amazing was how that girl could have reinvented herself into the woman Victoria was today.

"So what we think," Buck said, "is that Baker was blackmailing her, demanding exorbitant terms for ginning Belle Pointe cotton. But here's the thing. Since there was no DNA then to disprove paternity and with Rudy long dead, I don't see how someone as shrewd as my mother could be victimized."

"Only Victoria can tell us that," Anne said.

"And she won't," Buck said. "You can take that to the bank."

Buck balled up his shirt and tossed it at the clothes hamper. With a sigh, Anne crossed the room and picked it up. "Are you going to ask her about it?"

"Hell, I don't know. Like I said, I have one screwed-up family." His jeans he managed to hurl accurately into the hamper. Naked now, he stalked into the bathroom. "I need a shower."

Anne watched him go. Although he'd suspected his brother, she knew Buck had held out some hope that he was wrong. His father's journal entry wiped out that hope. Maybe even worse, his mother's dark secret was revealed. It didn't appear to make him happy that he, and not Pearce, was lone heir to Belle Pointe. Anne recalled Joel Tanner's words about poking around under the rocks of the past and getting a nasty surprise.

She wandered into the bathroom. Buck stood in the shower

with one arm braced on the wall, his head bent under the spray. Her heart twisted. Hesitating only a minute, she stripped, pulled the door open and stepped inside.

For one startled moment, he was caught off guard. Then, with a groan, his arms went around her, holding on as if he would never let her go.

"I love you," she said, burying her face in his neck.

He raised his hands and sank his fingers in her hair. His kiss was fierce, hot and desperate. It exploded into her senses, pulling her deep into the same vortex of feeling where he was. No cascade of water could ever wash away the pain of what he'd learned tonight. Or the shock of what Anne now knew. Nothing could do that. In the rush of need that consumed them both, there was no panacea to be found, only pleasure fraught with forgetfulness and greedy lust.

On an incoherent sound, he changed the angle of the kiss and took it hot and deep again, both hands fisted in her hair. Without breaking the kiss, he caught her up, bracing against the wall so that she instinctively locked her legs around him. One thrust and he was inside her, oblivious of the water cooling rapidly as it sluiced over them. Another and he shuddered in a violent release.

"Damn." He fumbled for the faucet to shut off the water. Scooping her up, he shoved the shower door open and stepped out into the bathroom. "Towel," he muttered. "We need a towel."

"Your knee."

"I deserve to have you kick it black and blue." He sat on a vanity stool and, with Anne in his lap, began to dry her off. "I'm sorry, darlin.'"

She leaned up and kissed his jaw. "For what?"

"You didn't get a damn thing out of that. But, lord, when you appeared in the shower all warm and soft and sexy, one kiss and I lost it."

"Two."

He paused with the towel at her breasts.

"Two kisses. And do you hear me complaining?"

He rested his chin on her head. "I've been thinking about making love to my wife all day. I wanted to take it slow. I wanted it to last all night long. But it was one thing after another today. Then tonight getting that glimpse of my parents' twisted marriage—" he shook his head "—it shot my plans to hell...until you opened the shower door. I'm sorry."

"You're saying you're finished for the night?"

He angled back to bring her face into focus. "Oh, shit. That's another one of your trick questions, isn't it?"

Laughing, she untangled herself and, grabbing him by the hand, led him over to the bed. "Now, it's my turn."

The next day, Buck put off heading to Belle Pointe. He wasn't sure what he should do with what he'd learned from John Whitaker's journal. Somehow it still felt disloyal to tell the world what Pearce had done. And he damn sure didn't feel good about revealing his mother's secret. First thing, he wanted—needed—was to talk to his mother. By midmorning, he'd worked it all out sitting on the porch swing. Anne was skeptical, but supportive.

His strategy was doomed from the get-go. Miriam met them at the door carrying a tray with a carafe of water and looking very distressed.

"Oh, Mr. Buck, I'm glad it's you. I've been trying to talk

your mother into letting me call the doctor, but she just won't allow it. Maybe you can reason with her."

"What's wrong?"

"She will not allow me to discuss it." Miriam sent a fearful look up the stairs which threatened her hold on the tray. While she flailed, trying to rescue the carafe, Buck headed up the stairs, taking them two at a time. Anne rescued the tray, then nudged the shaken housekeeper up, carrying the water herself.

"Where is everyone?" she asked.

"Ms. Victoria wouldn't let me tell anybody she was too sick to get out of bed this morning, so they all went their separate ways."

"Everyone?"

"Mr. Pearce, of course, is at his campaign headquarters. Ms. Claire took Paige to school and—" her voice lowered "—afterward, I think she's working the phones on behalf of Jack Breedlove."

They were in the upstairs hall now. "What is wrong with Victoria, Miriam?"

"You should ask her," she whispered. "She won't listen to me."

Indeed, Victoria was in bed. Buck was at the window adjusting the blinds to let in some light, but it was still possible to see at a glance that she was ill. Her skin had a sickly pallor and her eyes appeared sunken. Dark circles gave her the look of a cadaver. Anne was horrified. Yesterday she hadn't looked well. Today she looked dreadful.

"Ma's in bed," Buck said to Anne unnecessarily. Like many men, he was uncomfortable when confronted with illness.

Anne went inside the room to remove Buck. She was certain that Victoria would not welcome visitors at her sickbed under any circumstances. Not even her own children. Buck could help by calling her doctor…or an ambulance. But even as Anne reached to tug him to the door, he shook her off.

"Claire said you were sick, Ma, and it looks like she was right."

Closing her eyes, Victoria turned her face to the wall. "Go away, Buck."

"No. Hell, no. Not 'til you tell me what's wrong."

Anne stepped in front of him. "Victoria, I apologize for barging in like this. Buck means well. Is there anything we can do for you before I drag him away?"

"I'm not leaving until I get an answer," he said stubbornly.

With a halfhearted laugh, Victoria turned and looked at Anne. "My dear girl, it puzzles me why you persist in apologizing for Buck when he misbehaves. You heard him. You can't drag him away now. He's as stubborn as his father."

It was hard to tell, but Anne was sure she saw a suspicious brightness in Victoria's eyes. Her mother-in-law near tears?

Buck elbowed her aside. "It's not misbehaving to ask why my mother's in bed in the middle of the day looking half-dead!"

"I have a touch of flu," she said wearily.

"I don't believe you," he said flatly. Glancing around, he spotted a collection of pill bottles. He walked over and read a few labels. The technical names were meaningless, but the instructions for dosages were clearly spelled out. "This is for pain, this is for nausea, this is a sleeping pill. No antibiotic in the lot." He was scowling. "That doesn't sound like flu to me, Ma."

She met his eyes directly. "And you got your medical degree…where?"

"Enough, Buck," Anne said, catching his arm. "We're going now."

"You should tell them, Ms. Victoria." Both Anne and Buck were startled when Miriam spoke at the door. The housekeeper was wringing her hands, but she stood straight, looking gamely at her longtime employer.

"Tell us what?" Buck demanded.

Victoria's face was a stony mask.

With a sigh, Miriam moved to stand at the foot of Victoria's bed. "It's cancer." She flinched slightly under the fierceness of Victoria's gaze, but she stood her ground, "You can't expect to keep it a secret forever, Ms. Victoria. You need to let Buck call your doctor."

"I'll decide when I want my doctor," Victoria said coldly. "And now that you've disobeyed my instructions, Miriam, you'll find your paycheck docked of two weeks' wages."

Miriam stood even straighter. "Yes, ma'am," she said with a trace of the dignity her employer displayed.

"Wait for me downstairs, Miriam," Buck said.

"Yes, sir," the woman murmured and with one last imploring look at her employer, she left quietly.

"And there will be no undermining my authority," Victoria ordered.

"What kind of cancer, Ma?"

She released a weary sigh. "Ovarian. And I've declined the use of chemotherapy, so don't start planning a program that I've rejected."

"How long have you known about this?"

"A few months." She reached up and rubbed her face. "You'll have to get details from my doctor. I don't want to discuss it beyond what I've told you."

"When were you planning to tell us, Ma?"

"I don't consider my personal aches and pains to be anybody's business."

"Meaning never. You'd suffer with a fatal disease and one morning we'd come in here and find you dead?"

She sighed again. "Why are you here this morning, Buck? You're usually in the fields at this hour."

Anne looked at Buck with alarm. Whatever he planned to say about what they'd found in the journals would surely have to wait. His mother was far too fragile to be reminded of what had to be a dark period in her life.

"It's nothing, Ma. It's…nothing."

Victoria studied him thoughtfully for a moment, then shifted her gaze to Anne. "Have you had a chance to look at the journals?"

Anne considered trying to dodge the question, but something in her mother-in-law's demeanor told her she would see through any ploy. "Yes, a little," she replied cautiously.

"My husband's entries?"

Anne glanced at Buck, who answered for her. "It was late, Ma, so we didn't get a chance to get too far—"

"You know, don't you?" Victoria said quietly.

There was silence in the room for a long, long minute. When neither Anne nor Buck spoke, Victoria laughed weakly. "Incidentally, where did Paige find the journals?"

"There's a room in the attic," Buck said.

"I searched that room. They were not there."

"The room has a secret panel concealing a small space that was once used to hide runaway slaves. Dad told me about it."

"But he didn't tell me." Victoria's laugh was weak with irony. It brought on a spell of coughing. Anne moved to her side and put a glass to her lips. When she'd taken a sip or two, she leaned back against the pillows, exhausted.

"You need to rest, Ma." Buck turned to leave.

"Wait." Victoria lifted a shaky hand. "There are...facts you need to know. Sit down." Anne eased toward the door, but Victoria gestured to a place beside Buck. "Stay, Anne. Please."

"Ma, are you sure—"

Again, she stopped him. "I don't know exactly what John wrote in his journal and what I'm going to tell you I'll deny afterward if you plan to take any...legal steps. But for the sake of accuracy and the Whitaker heritage, you should know the truth."

She turned her gaze to an artist's rendering of Belle Pointe painted in 1890. "My father was a master mechanic. In another age, under different circumstances, he would have been an engineer. I grew up on the premises of Belle Pointe spending as much time as I wished in the equipment sheds at the plantation. I could drive a combine or a tractor as well as most field hands at Belle Pointe. I guess you could say I was a tomboy."

She fell silent for a moment. "John never saw me," she said with a bitter twist of her mouth. "Like his parents, most of the people who made Belle Pointe work were invisible to him. But that one summer when I was eighteen, he did finally notice me." She gave them a proud look. "I intended for him to notice me. I'd learned from experience how to attract a man. A woman who uses her female assets wisely can usually get what she wants. And I wanted to marry John."

She raised her left hand, fragile with spidery blue veins and spotted with ill health, but still bearing a gold wedding band. "It wasn't as easy as I anticipated. His parents naturally wanted him to marry within his class. That would have been one of the beautiful, well-bred girls at Ole Miss, not a trashy tomboy girl whose daddy's fingernails were permanently dirty with grease, and whose mama had run off years ago. In spite of their disapproval, John was besotted. The only problem was that I didn't love John, I loved Rudy Baker."

As if seeing her own nails blackened with grease, Victoria tucked her hands out of sight beneath the embroidered border of a first-quality percale sheet. "Before my plan to marry John Whitaker, I'd been seeing Rudy, but suddenly he was drafted and ordered to Vietnam. Two men couldn't have been more different. Rudy was a musician. He was wickedly handsome, dark-eyed, hair as black as coal. He could charm the birds out of the trees and he was a born liar. He was dangerous when angry, but I was mad about him."

Anne met Buck's eyes and knew he was thinking of Pearce. She remembered him saying his brother often lied just for the sake of lying and everyone knew to be wary of Pearce's temper.

"John, on the other hand," Victoria continued, "was quiet, attractive in his way and gentlemanly, carefully reared to revere Belle Pointe and his place in the long line of Whitakers before him. So, in spite of the fact that there was passion in my relationship with Rudy, John was far better husband material." Her expression was suddenly bitter. "He was easily seduced, but he didn't want to marry me. He just wanted to sleep with me. Every chance he got. Often. And on the sly."

She turned her face to the wall and spoke in a dull voice. "About that time, Rudy came home from boot camp and wanted me to go out with him that last night, as he was going to Vietnam and might be killed. Of course, I didn't believe that. Rudy was too vital, too alive to be a war casualty. But I was angry with John. So I went out with Rudy. And six weeks later I knew I was pregnant."

"Ma, you don't need to say any more."

"I do, Buck. Just hear me out." She smoothed a hand over the embroidery on the sheet as if taking pleasure in the feel of it. "I told John I was pregnant and since he didn't know about Rudy, he naturally assumed the baby was his. Frankly, it could have been. I didn't know for sure myself. His parents were outraged, of course, but we married anyway in a discreet, perfectly respectable ceremony. The guest list was very small, nothing like the wedding the Whitakers' only son would have had had he married within his class."

Coughing again, she reached for a tissue and delicately patted her lips. "I think they suspected Pearce wasn't John's child when he was about four years old and looked nothing like John or me, but they were too genteel to ever call either of us on it. You were a baby when they died within a few months of each other, Buck." She smiled bitterly. "As you were a clone of John and other Whitaker babies in the family photo gallery, they died satisfied that I'd produced a true Whitaker."

Buck was moving about the room restlessly. "Why are you telling this, Ma?"

"To cleanse my soul?" she said, arching a single brow ironically. But her irony faded as quickly as it flared in another bit of coughing. When she recovered, she appeared thoughtful. "I suppose it was because of respect for Belle Pointe and five generations of Whitakers, Buck. Pearce has been a disappointment to me. Perhaps breeding does matter, who knows? In spite of the example I've set, he simply doesn't have the best interests of Belle Pointe as his primary focus in life. He's on his way to becoming a politician and he's well suited to that ambition. He plans to eventually wind up in Washington."

"Have you told him you're aware of that?" Buck asked.

"No. Claire shared it." Another ironic laugh. "He's too arrogant to think it matters one way or the other. He assumes he'll get around me when the time comes." She paused, as if considering what she would say next. "Whereas, you, Buck, do have the best interests of Belle Pointe at heart. I refuse to admit sending you off to a career in professional sports was a mistake and, by the same token, welcoming your return to take up the reins in my place is now the right thing."

"I'm flattered," he said dryly.

"Yes, it is a compliment." She drew in a deep breath. "Now, I'm tired and I want to be alone. That includes Miriam. Do not send her up. Do not call the doctor. I've been in this state several times in the past few months and I've managed. Here's the one last thing I want to say."

Her hand was shaky as she dropped the tissue into a tray on her bedside table. "I've been disturbed by Anne's fascination with the town's archives. Before, with the journals lost, there was little risk. But you would eventually have found all kinds of things, Anne, and with your journalist background, eventually the family—and Belle Pointe—would be embarrassed. One obvious example was the hunting accident. Following the trail would have uncovered a link to that evil contract I was forced to sign and eventually you would have connected Jim Bob Baker and Rudy. I wanted to prevent that, so I set the fire."

"Jesus Christ, Ma!" Buck stared at her in disbelief.

"Yes, it is shocking, isn't it? I'm just grateful that I'm a poor arsonist. You can't imagine what I felt knowing I'd almost caused the death of Paige and Anne. I'm sorry. I hope you can find it in your heart to forgive me someday."

"You're sorry." He studied her with an expression of shock and bewilderment. "It wasn't only two lives you endangered, but Tallulah's past would have been destroyed. That alone was criminal, Ma."

"Yes, it pained me that I was forced to do it. And by the way, Anne's laptop is in that armoire." She waved a hand toward the tall antique.

For a moment, he was speechless at her bloodlessness. "We'll have to tell Jack Breedlove," he told her dully. "He's launched a full-scale investigation."

"Whatever, Buck."

Having said she'd deny everything, he wasn't sure she comprehended what was in store. "Ma, we're talking arson and probably reckless endangerment."

"Yes, I think that's most likely. But with a fatal disease," she informed him, "I probably won't survive long enough to cost the taxpayers a trial."

Buck waited a beat or two, studying his mother as if she'd come from another planet. Then, shaking his head, he turned to his wife. "Are you ready to go?" He'd clearly heard all he could take.

"As for telling Jack Breedlove," Victoria said as they headed out, "do whatever you feel you must. And remember,

I don't want Miriam up here fussing for a while. I'm exhausted and I want to rest. Oh, don't forget Ann's laptop."

While Buck had a word with Oscar Pittman, Anne waited in the SUV, still reeling from Victoria's confession about the fire. Her laptop appeared undamaged, but it held no interest for her at the moment. She watched Buck break away from Oscar and noticed that he favored his knee. No surprise there considering how he'd abused it lately. It dawned on Anne that if it had been his intent to continue playing baseball, he would have been more disciplined in the rehabilitation process. Maybe he'd been looking for an excuse to retire. Or a new purpose in life. Anne touched her abdomen. For her, it was a no-brainer.

Buck climbed in the SUV. "Okay, that's taken care of. I'm off to see Jack at TPD. Do you want me to drop you at your mother's house? You still planning to talk to her today?"

Her mother's house. The Victorian where Beatrice was born. Where several generations of Joneses had lived and died. Anne's own ancestors, her blood relatives. She felt a little thrill. It was no longer a mystery where she came from and who her parents were. Maybe she'd always known who she was, but it was nice to be able to fill in all the blanks.

"Hello?"

"Hmm?" She blinked at Buck. "Oh, yes. I think so. Drop me there."

"Good girl." But his smile had an edge. "I'm glad something's going right for somebody today."

"What're you going to do, Buck?"

"Hell if I know." He rubbed the side of his jaw as he slowed for a stop sign. "How about we stop for some lunch before I drop you off? I have to tell Jack how the fire started and why and he'll have to take it from there. But I don't have to do it on an empty stomach."

"Just out of curiosity, does anything kill your appetite?"

He looked over and gave her an air kiss. "Only when my wife threatens to divorce me."

They took their time over lunch at Daddy Gee's. "At this rate," Anne said, watching him polish off a dish of peach cobbler, "you should consider buying into this place. I hear restaurants are big items with retired sports figures."

"Can't do it. Thanks to Ty and Chief Breedlove, I'm already into a physical therapy facility, a teen center, a baseball camp for promising athletes and I'm farming cotton. You like restaurants, I'll spring for you to open one."

"I can't. I'm going to be too busy being a mother."

His mouth dropped. "You're pregnant?"

She laughed. "How could I be, Buck? We've only been trying two days."

He stood up, grinning, and pulled her chair out. "But we had multiple possibilities in those two days," he said in a sexy drawl near her ear. She felt a rush of heat, hurrying out ahead of him. How had she ever thought she could leave Buck?

"Okay," he said, driving out of the square. "No more procrastinating. I'm dropping you at the Marshes' and then I'm heading for Tallulah's top cop."

Anne's gaze was fixed on a line of cars at the town's single red light, but her thoughts were elsewhere. "I know your mother has a reputation for being rather aloof, but don't you think it was odd how remote she appeared telling us what she'd done? It was almost as if she was relating someone else's story…sort of like John Whitaker's journal entries. Except that John's words had a lot more emotion."

"Because he was a better person," Buck said grimly. "That's an ugly thing to say about my own mother, but the calculating way she set about her plan to seduce my dad into marriage was ugly. And then when he didn't propose and she found herself pregnant—without being sure whose baby it was—she had what she needed to trap him. It's disgusting!"

"I think what my dad said is probably nearer the truth," Anne said quietly. "John was passionately in love with her—no doubt about that—and there was a good chance the baby was his. Whether she was 'of his class' was irrelevant, but it's plain that that's been a sore spot for your mother all these years."

"You're saying he would have divorced her otherwise."

"I think so, don't you? There was no stigma in divorce in the sixties, which is when all this happened. Still, she was one cool lady today, wasn't she?" Her gaze narrowed, thinking about it. "Maybe a little too cool, Buck."

"What do you mean?"

"I think we should turn around and go back." She glanced at her watch. "How long ago was it that we were there?"

"It's been a couple hours. Why should we go back?"

"Well…" She rubbed her nose, thinking. "It's just a thought, but what do we know about Victoria all these years? She's always nagging Paige about the public image of the Whitakers. She harps on Claire for failing to measure up as a proper Whitaker. And yet she tells us the details of the disgraceful way she tricked John into marrying her, she admits to an affair with a redneck and she confesses to committing arson. I know she's sick, but being sick doesn't suddenly change an individual's personality."

At a stop sign, Buck signaled to turn toward the Marsh house. "So why did she do it?"

"Don't turn here, Buck."

"Because she's not going to be around to cope with the scandal," he said suddenly. "I see where you're going." In the next breath, he released his cell phone from its clip and punched the programmed number for Belle Pointe. "It'll take us twenty minutes to get back there. I'll call and tell Miriam to keep an eye on her whether she likes it or not."

With his fingers dancing restlessly on the wheel, he waited for Miriam to pick up. After five rings, the answer machine clicked in. He swore and disconnected. "I'm trying again. Miriam's there, she's gotta be."

He keyed the number again and waited through four rings.

"Whitaker residence."

It was Miriam and she sounded strange. "Miriam, Buck here. I want—"

"Oh, Mr. Buck! Oh, thank God. Mr. Buck, it's—" She broke down in a storm of weeping, trying to talk, but Buck couldn't make out anything she said.

"Miriam," he said in a firm tone. "Listen to me. Calm down and tell me what's wrong."

"I've already called 911, Mr. Buck. It's your mother. Oh, this is terrible!"

"What is terrible? What's happened?"

"I don't think I should tell you this on the phone."

He set his teeth. "Tell me."

She blew her nose and drew a fortifying breath. "She's gone, Mr. Buck. Ms. Victoria has killed herself."

Twenty-Five

The curved drive at Belle Pointe was crowded with automobiles. At first glance, Buck recognized Claire's car, Pearce's Lexus and Jack Breedlove's police unit. An ambulance was parked close to the front door and further along the drive were two more cars. "One of those will be Bill Armstrong," he told Anne, "Ma's doctor."

As he stepped down to the ground, Buck looked up at the house and his stomach did a slow roll. It dawned on him that the last hour he'd spent with his mother would probably haunt him forever. Drawing in a deep breath, he put out his hand to Anne and together they went up the steps.

He recognized the rookie cop posted at the door. "Daniel," he said, "is the chief inside?"

"Yes, sir. Upstairs. The EMTs are in there, too. Uh, I'm sorry for your loss, Buck."

"Thanks, Daniel." Still holding Anne's hand, he gave it a squeeze. "Stay here, sweetheart," he told her. "No need for you to see this."

He took the stairs at a fast clip, barely pausing as he passed two men he didn't recognize in the hall. When he reached his mother's bedroom, he slowed, swallowing down the queasiness in his stomach.

A knot of people were gathered at the bed. Two EMTs, Victoria's doctor, Pearce and Claire, Jack Breeedlove. His gaze fell on his mother's face. When he left her that morning, there'd been circles under her eyes and her skin had a sickly pallor. Now it was as pale as marble and oddly peaceful. The EMTs, he saw, were readying her to make the transfer from her bed to a stretcher. On the floor and scattered about the bed was evidence of medical apparatus that told him they'd tried to revive her. For the first time since hearing she had died, he wondered if he and Anne had been wrong fearing she was suicidal. Maybe it was a heart attack. Or a stroke.

Claire looked up as he stepped into the room. "Oh, Buck!" She moved to meet him and hugged him wordlessly. When she let him go, she was wiping tears from her eyes. "I knew she was sick, but she shouldn't have had to die this way!"

Over her head, he met Pearce's eyes—remote and empty of emotion. "She was in a lot of pain," Buck said to Claire.

"There are meds for pain. She could have had the best of care. It's not as if we couldn't afford it," she said bitterly. "I talked to Miriam yesterday like you told me. She was nervous, but she didn't give me any hint that Victoria was eaten up with cancer!"

"You need to go downstairs," he told her in a gentle tone. "Anne's there. Find Miriam, between the two of you, I bet she could use a little comforting right now. Okay?"

"Okay." At the door, she looked back at Pearce. "We'll need to tell Paige together, Pearce."

"No, you can do it."

She gave him a long look. "Do you want to go with me to pick her up from school?"

He shook his head. "I need to see about arrangements."

Her eyes went to Jack, standing straight and stern near the window, as if she'd like—needed—some sign from him, but his gaze remained fixed on the EMTs dealing with the body of her mother-in-law, now draped in a blue sheet. After watching the body transferred to a stretcher, Claire left and Buck turned his attention to his mother's physician.

Bill Armstrong had treated Victoria for as long as Buck could remember. A tall man, thin as a result of his addiction to marathon running, he was unsmiling now as he shook hands with Buck.

"I'm saddened over this, Buck. I tried my best to get your mother to agree to chemotherapy, but she was determined to refuse."

"I know. She told me the same thing today." He stepped back as Victoria was wheeled out of the room. "We talked a little over two hours ago. She was sick, but she wasn't at the point of death. Was it a heart attack?"

Armstrong held out a sealed plastic bag. "No, I'm afraid it was an overdose of this medication. I prescribed it for sleeping, but it looks like she saved up a couple of months' supply and took them all at once."

Anne punched the off button on her cell phone after telling Beatrice of Victoria's death. Between them, she and Claire had decided to ask Beatrice to pick up Paige at school. Even before Anne got around to asking, Beatrice's first thought was of Paige and she volunteered to pick her up. Anne was satisfied that the delicate job of telling the girl about her grandmother was in the right hands with Beatrice.

She chose the servant's route to the kitchen with a thought to making coffee for the crowd that had somehow materialized out of nowhere just in the short time since word of Victoria's death got out. If she were busy in the kitchen, she might avoid being cornered and pumped for information. Suicide was being whispered and she didn't want to find herself in a position to confirm or deny it. Not that she could do either at this point.

Nearing the butler's pantry, she stopped short at the sound of a man's voice, an angry voice. Pearce. She paused with an idea of letting him know he could be overheard.

"You know all her secrets, Miriam, don't try to tell me you don't. And I'm warning you to keep your mouth shut."

Was he threatening Miriam? Anne frowned, unable to hear the woman's reply, but the tone was apprehensive. And fearful?

"Did she tell you where she put it?" Pearce again.

Another brief, low-toned reply from Miriam. What? Anne wondered. Put what where?

"Don't lie to me!" Pearce again. "She's gone now and you screw me over on this, there's nothing says you get to stay on here for the rest of your life. You do that, you'll be lucky to live as nice as one of the field hands."

Furious at his bullying an old woman, Anne cleared her throat loudly and stepped to the butler's pantry. She blinked at Pearce in shirtsleeves, his tie askew and his hair sticking up as if he'd been running his hands through it. She'd never seen him so agitated, but she dismissed any concern for Pearce. Miriam, looking fearful, was backed in a corner.

Anne shouldered past Pearce. "Miriam," she said, slipping

her arm around the thin shoulders. "I've been looking everywhere for you. I thought we'd make some sandwiches for the crowd." She looked at Pearce and said coldly, "There's a crowd gathered and they're bringing your mother down now."

For a moment, he seemed ready to have a go at her, too, but with a growl of frustration, he turned on his heel and stalked off.

Anne cocked her head, watching him. "I've never heard a person growl before, have you, Miriam?"

To her surprise, Miriam giggled. "Only Mr. Pearce…and he makes a habit of it."

With her arm still about the woman's shoulders, Anne walked with her to the kitchen. "There's no need for you to make sandwiches for any of these people, Miriam. You've had a stressful day and the next couple of days will be difficult. I only said that because you looked as if you needed rescuing."

"Thank you, Ms. Anne. That Pearce was a bully as a boy and he's still a bully. As for sandwiches and food for people as they crowd in, several women from my church circle have already volunteered. They'll be here soon and they'll stay until we get past this terrible time."

Anne gave her a reassuring squeeze. "What in the world was that all about? It sounded as if Pearce was threatening you."

Miriam sniffed and put her nose in the air. "I'm not afraid of Pearce Whitaker. More likely he's afraid of me."

Buck guessed Pearce was bursting with a need to light into him. Something had him upset, big-time. With the house full of people, it wasn't like his brother to appear looking as if he'd been pulled through a knothole backwards. To avoid the crowd avidly watching, Buck strolled around in search of privacy for the confrontation. But instead of being cornered by Pearce, it was Anne who clamped a hand on his arm.

"I need to talk to you," she said urgently. "Privately."

"I guess we could go to the equipment barn," he said dryly.

"No, here." Dragging him by the arm, she led him down the hall to the small powder room. Once inside, she closed the door and locked it, then flipped the switch that turned on the exhaust fan.

He was stressed out, grieving over the shock of his mother's suicide and conflicted about what to do regarding his brother, a killer, but at the moment, with his pretty wife standing close to him in a very small room, looking like a female Sherlock Holmes with incredible blue eyes, he suddenly realized all was right in their world, his and Anne's.

"Buck, you—"

"Wait." He put a forefinger on her lips.

"Buck, this is important!"

He caught her face between his hands. "Can I kiss you first?"

She looked at him like he was crazy. "They just took your poor dead mother away in an ambulance. There are at least thirty people milling around just outside this door. Claire's a basket case and Pearce is—mmfftt."

His mouth was on hers, hot and fierce and needy. She was so soft and sweet and the taste of her was everything good, he thought, reveling in the leap of his libido. With Anne fitted to him perfectly, head to toe, she completed him on some elemental level that he didn't understand and didn't need to. It was enough just to know that she was his. And when she sighed and opened her mouth, yielding to his need, he wanted to smile. Inside, he was smiling.

"What was that all about?" she asked a minute later with her head resting on his chest.

"I just needed it, darlin'." He stroked her back lovingly. "So, what did you drag me in here to tell me?"

"It's about Pearce. I just overhead him threatening Miriam."

Buck's hand went still. "Explain," he said grimly.

And she did.

Buck had no trouble locating Pearce when he left the powder room with Anne. He was pacing just outside the door.

"We need to talk," Pearce said. "Somewhere private."

Buck looked unenthusiastically at the tiny powder room. It was one thing to be in there with his wife, another entirely with his brother. "I hope you can suggest a better place."

"My bedroom," Pearce ordered and with a shrug, Buck agreed. Soon enough his brother would have to come to grips with not being in charge, but since it suited Buck to have this talk, he went with him up the winding stairs to the sumptuous suite.

Pearce closed the double doors with a thwack. "I know you spent an hour with Mama this morning. She had to've taken those pills right after you left. What happened? What upset her?"

"I didn't upset her, Pearce. Just the opposite."

"What do you mean?"

"I mean, I was the one who was upset. In my shoes, you would have been, too."

Narrow-eyed, Pearce demanded, "What are you talking about?"

With a glance in the bedroom beyond to check that they were alone, Buck went to the window and faced Pearce with the advantage of light at his back and in his brother's face. "Anne and I read some of Dad's entries in the journal last night." He watched as Pearce went still, scenting danger. "I'm not sure what his purpose was. It could have been a secret he took with him to the grave, but for whatever reason, he decided against that."

Pearce made a strong effort to look unconcerned. "Is there a point here?"

"The reason I went to see Ma this morning was because Dad mentioned Jim Bob Baker's death. I had some idea of—"

"That again! Whenever the hell are you gonna let that go, Buck? I swear to God, I can't figure you out. You—"

"If you let me finish, I promise you will figure it out." He waited until Pearce grunted reluctantly. "Anne and I found Ma sick in bed, really sick. One look and I changed my mind about mentioning the journals, but she knew I had them and she guessed I'd read them. You know how she can be once her mind is made up. She would talk about it."

"So…"

"Apparently she'd worried what Dad wrote in the journals and had searched for them for years."

"The damn things should have been burned."

"As it turned out, that was her plan for the *Spectator* archives," Buck said. "Tallulah's history was expendable, in her view, but I think she would have balked at burning a hundred and fifty years of Belle Pointe history. She had too much reverence for the Whitaker name."

Pearce assumed a look of outrage. "You're not suggesting Mama set that fire at the *Spectator*?"

"Cut the crap, Pearce. Anne overheard you threaten Miriam a few minutes ago. You wanted to know where Ma had stashed the laptop, which tells me you knew she set the fire. As to whatever else you might want to coerce from an old woman—one who changed your diapers and wiped your snotty nose, I'll remind you—knock it off or I'll knock something off you that won't be easy to fix."

"Big talk," Pearce said with a sneer.

"Not talk, Pearce. That was a promise." Buck waited a beat and, getting no more sarcasm, continued. "As for the fire, Ma admitted she set it, simple as that. She apologized for endangering Paige and Anne, but she needed to keep Anne from digging up secrets from the past." He paused, watching his brother closely. "Your past, Pearce."

"You're back to Jim Bob Baker, I assume," Pearce said in disgust.

"Actually, I'm back to Rudy Baker," Buck said softly. "And I don't think you want to go there."

Pearce was silent for a stunned minute. Buck let him stew. He didn't know in his own mind what he could do—should do—about the Whitaker lineage. Maybe there was no harm in keeping his mother's secret and letting Pearce go on claiming to be John Whitaker's firstborn son, but it stuck in Buck's craw to let Pearce get away scot-free with cold-blooded murder.

"You can't prove anything," Pearce said finally.

Buck looked at his feet with a wry shake of his head. "That you killed Jim Bob because he was blackmailing Ma? That pesky contract does keep rearing its ugly head, doesn't it? Or was it because you didn't want the world to know that you were sired by a rowdy country-western musician instead of an aristocratic gentleman planter?"

Pearce couldn't quite prevent a quick glance at the doors of the suite to be sure they were closed. "You can't prove anything," he repeated.

"About your paternity? Not without DNA, I can't. About Jim Bob's murder?" Buck shook his head. "Again, it would be hard. It was a long time ago and it was an accidental death. Maybe that's the way it should stay. And I'm willing to let it stay, but only on two conditions."

Peace gave him a look of patent disbelief. "I don't see how you're in a position to dictate conditions, bro. You just admitted you can't prove anything and I've warned you before about stirring up family shit. You are in no position to be tainted by scandal again. Your hopes for another sweet contract with the Jacks will go down in flames with my reputation."

"I've already resigned from the Jacks, Pearce. I won't be playing baseball again. I'll be running Belle Pointe."

Pearce stared at him. "What kind of bullshit is that? You live and breathe for baseball. I grant that you didn't have it easy at first in the minors, but you've got it made now. And you want me to believe you're going to settle down and grow cotton in a one-horse town? Do you realize you have to drive to Memphis to get sushi?" He gave a grunt of disgust. "Get real, Buck."

"You haven't heard the conditions yet," Buck said, unfazed.

"Doesn't matter what the goddamn conditions are."

"One, you drop out of the senatorial race. You're gonna lose anyway once I start openly campaigning for Jack." While his brother sputtered, Buck added, "Two. Move. Leave Tallulah. Go to D.C. You've probably made some useful connections there. You're a lawyer and a liar. You're well suited for the D.C. scene."

Pearce vibrated with rage. "You're a sonofabitch, you know that?"

Buck left the window, heading across the room. "Watch your mouth. That reflects on our mother and the ambulance carrying her to the funeral home is barely out of sight."

He made to shoulder past him, but Pearce grabbed his shirt. "You don't walk off until we're done talking, Buck! I want to know—"

"I'm getting pretty tired of you grabbing me, Pearce." With strength born of disgust, he jerked his arm free. His face looked chiseled in granite. "I don't care what you want to know. As soon as the funeral's over, I'm heading for Chief Breedlove and whatever I say to him depends on you." He paused, looking his brother in the eye. "Your call, bro."

"I'll call it."

Pearce's head whipped about as Claire came out of the bathroom. "Before you start a heavy discussion like that, you should check to see that you're alone," she said dryly, then spread her hands. "Surprise."

"How long have you been in there?" Pearce demanded.

"Long enough." She moved to her husband and straightened his tie. "There's only one way in and out. And it's just about the only place in the house where a person is guaranteed privacy. You might want to make a note of that."

"This doesn't concern you, Claire," Pearce said in a repressive voice. "You've already filed for a divorce, so take off. We'll be down in a minute."

Fury flared in her eyes. "It doesn't concern me that Buck has just revealed I've been married to a murderer? It doesn't concern me that I've lived a lie for sixteen years?" Her face showed absolute disgust. "I've put up with a lot since the day I married you, Pearce. I'd planned to simply walk away— with Paige—and start a new life. But now I think that's a spineless thing to do. I've been weak and passive too long. Buck might be willing, but I'm not going to let you get away scot-free this time. The choice is not up to you."

She moved to the doors. "As soon as we're done with your mother's funeral, I'll be talking to Jack Breedlove."

"Yeah, I bet you will," Pearce sneered.

"As the chief of police," she added firmly. "In spite of your accusations, I'm not having an affair with Jack." She paused, looking at him thoughtfully. "I've been tempted to leave you many times, Pearce. Since I decided to do it, you'd be amazed how happy I've been." She wrenched the door open. "Take your time coming down. As I said, you have until after the funeral. It's not likely, but I guess you could do the right thing on your own, but we won't count on it, will we, Buck?"

"Hey…" Buck caught up with her. "Wait for me."

Anne stared at Buck in amazement. She wasn't the only one. Franklin gaped, too. And Beatrice covered her mouth to hide a smile. "You're telling me Claire was in the bathroom listening to you and Pearce and nobody knew it?"

Buck's smile was somewhat off-center. "Well, maybe I had an idea the bathroom wasn't empty." When everybody seemed to expect more, he explained, "Claire wears a pretty recognizable perfume."

"So she came out fighting mad? Claire?" This from Beatrice. "It's hard for me to imagine Claire on a tear."

"Like an avenging angel, she was," Buck said wryly. "She's having a taste of independence and she's liking it."

"And right then and there, she gave him an ultimatum?" Franklin, who was nursing a brandy that Buck would dearly like to share, smiled faintly. "One might call that poetic justice."

"Which may be the only justice possible, as unfair as it sounds." Buck finished his Earl Gray and stood up. "Don't think I'm entirely happy with the way it's all come down. I had a talk with Jack and we agreed it beats us how we could prosecute him on the words written in a journal over twenty years ago. Like me, Dad only suspected what happened. Neither of us had any proof and Pearce will go to his grave denying it."

"And you wouldn't want to reveal his motive," Anne said thoughtfully, moving to stand beside him. "That would cast a shadow on your mother's reputation and that seems somehow...dishonorable now she's gone." She rubbed his arm, thinking he needed a little affectionate stroking. "I can see how you chose to let all those old secrets stay buried."

Buck linked his arms around his wife, his arms crossed at her waist. "Yeah, the secrets stay, but Pearce loses almost everything. The way I see it, he's lost his chance in politics, he's lost his wife, he's forced to rebuild his career from scratch in D.C. without the prestige of Belle Pointe and all the doors that would have opened for him and finally, he knows that I know for certain that he killed a man in cold blood."

"The person I worry about is Paige," Beatrice said.

"Yes, me too," Anne said. "How was she today when you told her? I know Victoria was never very affectionate toward her, but still, she's a child. Losing her grandmother so suddenly must have been a shock."

"How could I have forgotten?" Beatrice opened an old-fashioned pie safe and brought out a chocolate cake. "I thought we needed a distraction today, so Paige and I baked a cake." She set the cake in the center of the round table.

"Franklin, will you hand me that knife over there, please? Anne, dessert plates are in that cupboard."

"Now you tell me." With a pat to Anne's bottom, Buck nudged her aside and sat back down at the table. "I'll take some of that, please, ma'am."

"Me, too," Franklin said.

Anne waved away an offer of cake. "About Paige..." she prompted.

"Yes." Beatrice cut two generous wedges. "When I told her, she was quiet, thinking it over. And of course, I didn't mention suicide. I simply said Victoria had been diagnosed with cancer and had decided against a long and difficult treatment." She placed the cake on dessert plates, then sat down as Buck and Franklin tucked into it. "Paige understood her grandmother well. She said Victoria would have hated walking around with no hair and looking sick."

"No tears?" Anne wanted to know.

"Sadly, no." Beatrice paused, thinking back. "I've yet to tell you the worst. Paige said Victoria's death was just one more change going on. She said she thought it wouldn't be long before her parents got a divorce. I knew you'd said Claire hadn't told her yet, Anne, so I was a little...distressed."

"That child," Anne breathed in wonder. "Claire hasn't a clue that she knows. So how did she find out?"

"She read the journal, didn't she?" Buck guessed.

"Yes." Beatrice nodded. "I don't know exactly when she read her father's awful secret. I just know that for a long time she's been distancing herself from Pearce. That's why Claire's drinking was so worrisome. The child was surrounded with dysfunction, her mother, her grandmother, her father."

"I guess that explains why she assumed that Goth look," Buck said. "Her whole life was pretty dark."

Anne touched Beatrice's hand. "Except for you. Thank goodness, she had you."

"If Claire is successful with AA," Beatrice said, "and she stays on an even keel while she divorces Pearce, I think Paige will be okay."

"Especially once Claire marries Jack," Buck said, earning three surprised looks. He shrugged. "She told me out of her own mouth that was her plan."

"She has certainly looked happy lately." Beatrice's eyes were soft meeting Franklin's across the table. "Love will do that."

For a long minute there was silence all round. Anne, watching the men enjoy their cake, took in a long breath. There was something she needed to do and it made her nervous, just thinking about it.

"Is something else bothering you, Anne?" Beatrice, rinsing teacups at the sink, paused in the task.

Beatrice had an uncanny radar where she was concerned, Anne thought, not for the first time. It was so strong that it amazed her she hadn't guessed their real connection before she was told. "Ah, there's something I'd like to show you," she told Beatrice. Flustered, she looked around for her bag.

"This what you're looking for?" Buck reached out and plucked the bag from the seat of an empty chair. She caught his eye and realized that he knew what she intended to do. Had urged her to do it.

"Could we go to the living room?" she said to Beatrice. "Dad, Buck, we'll be back in a minute."

Puzzled, Beatrice dried her hands on a tea towel and

dropped it on the countertop without taking her eyes off Anne. Gripped by a nervousness that drove her heart up in her throat, Anne walked quickly to the front room of the old Victorian. The house where Beatrice had been born. The house of Anne's own ancestors.

She sat down and patted the cushion of the love seat, inviting Beatrice. When she was seated beside her, Anne pulled a letter out of her bag.

"Oh." Beatrice knew instantly. A hand went straight to her heart.

"This letter was in the box you gave me. It was sealed with my name written on it. It's from Laura, my mother."

"I know." Beatrice's voice was barely a whisper.

"In spite of everything that has happened in the last few days, there's no way I was able to resist reading everything in that box." She touched Beatrice's hand. "Thank you for giving me that glimpse of your friendship with Laura."

Beatrice, beyond speaking, nodded.

"I'd like to read this to you…if that's okay."

"Yes, of course. Yes."

Anne took the letter from its envelope and smiled up at Beatrice. "You're gonna love this." She was beginning to feel more at ease. Actually, she was feeling just fine, she decided.

"It starts, 'Dear and Precious Anne.'" Suddenly she was choked up, reading the words of someone whose memory she treasured. She cleared her throat. "If you're reading this, you will have met your birth mother and now know the story of your father's love affair with Beatrice Jones and its wonderful consequences: you, my darling. When Franklin came to me, broken and riddled with guilt, and confessed he'd been unfaithful, my first thought was, 'Well, now he's done what

I knew he would do eventually. It's behind us and we'll just pick up where we left off and never speak of this again.' Oh, I was going to be noble and forgiving. So ridiculous, so impossible. My next thought was 'How dare he!' Of course, I was angry. Bitterly angry. I'm only human. I felt so sorry for myself that I just wanted to curl up and die right then and there. It wasn't fair. He was healthy and strong and virile, just as I used to be before MS struck. And now I was sick and weak and pathetic. Of course he'd had an affair. The mystery was why he hadn't done so before. And then, worst of all, I was struck with a terrifying fear that he was going to ask for a divorce.

But no, not Franklin. Perhaps I should have offered him one, but I was far more selfish—and am today—than your father, Anne. Instead, Franklin then said the words that explained why he'd been compelled to confess his infidelity. Yes, no prettying it up. Infidelity. A betrayal of our vows. But it was much worse than an affair. His lover was pregnant!

I wanted to scream. I hated him. I hated her. I had longed for a child with all my heart, but to no avail. It wasn't fair that he'd fallen in love with a beautiful and healthy woman, but adding insult to injury, she had conceived his child. Easily and naturally, in one short summer affair! While I sat stunned and heartsick, thinking up ways to punish him, he went on to say that this woman's father considered a baby born out of wedlock to be a disgrace to the family. She had been sent to a relative in another state and the baby would be put up for adoption.

Giving a baby away to strangers when I longed for a child? Knowing Franklin was responsible for a child and doing nothing about it? It would have haunted me forever. How can make you understand the emotion that consumed me from that moment? No stranger would have that baby. That baby was meant for me.

Selfish, you think? All about me, me, me? Maybe. But I thought of it as consolation for being stricken with a nasty disease that rendered me infertile. So God had simply made it up to me by giving me you."

Anne stopped, swallowed hard and brushed at a tear. "Sorry," she whispered and to finish, leaned against Beatrice whose arm had encircled her waist. Again, she cleared her throat. "And so, as the years have passed, I have shared your growing-up years with Beatrice Jones. She was there in spirit when you took your first step, when you graduated from kindergarten, high school and college. She was there when you married Buck. And when the day comes that you read these words, I hope you are sitting next to Beatrice Jones. If so, I hope you will be able to do this one thing for me. Tell her, thank you."

For a long minute, neither was able to get past the lumps in their throats. Tears from both blurred the image of the letter now lying in Anne's lap while each felt awe at the amazing generosity of Laura Marsh.

"I am so glad she thought to do this," Anne said finally, resting her head comfortably, naturally against her mother.

"She was…" Beatrice paused with her arm still around Anne, gently rubbing the soft sleeve of her T-shirt. "She was an angel, a very human one, but an angel just the same. My God, I owe her."

Anne reached up and covered Beatrice's hand on her arm, gave it a little squeeze, then leaned up and kissed her cheek. "No, Mom, I'm the lucky one."

Epilogue

Three months later...

Anne lay flat in bed and took in several long, deep, slow breaths. Eyes closed, she waited...waited. Beside her, Buck shifted, coming awake within a few minutes of the alarm going off. Oddly, he had his own internal alarm clock. Must be a farmer thing, she thought. As naturally as breathing, he turned over and reached out to pull her close.

"Don't touch me," she ordered. "Don't move."

He went still, but opened one eye. "I can't move?"

"No." She breathed in again, slowly. "Not yet."

Smiling, he straightened out and stacked his hands behind his head. "Okay, tell me when."

Suddenly, she threw back the covers and dashed to the bathroom. With a more or less empty stomach, there was little to upchuck, but she suffered through a series of dry heaves anyway. Same thing, every morning, like clockwork. Nothing she did, no remedy she tried worked to stave it off or prevent it.

Buck, now beside her, knew the drill. Wordlessly, he handed over a cold wet face cloth. Weakly, she wiped her face, then went to the sink and brushed her teeth. Buck, following routine, was back in bed, again flat on his back, his hands stacked behind his head. "Morning, sunshine."

She laughed, fully recovered now, and crawled back in bed. Plumping her pillow, she lay back, snuggled up against him. "I know it's crazy,"

He shifted to take her into his arms. His kiss was sweet, soft with sympathy and a little worry. "How much longer do you have to go through this?"

"Who knows? Who cares? What's a little morning sickness when you think of the reason?" She looked up at him, kissed his jaw. "Six more months and we'll have a baby!"

He angled back to be able to see her face. "And everything's okay? No complications?"

"Like last time? No, nothing." Because he looked worried, she reached up and swept hair from his brow. "The funny thing is that I'm not worried this time. I know this pregnancy is right. I know this baby is fine."

He searched her face gravely. "You've forgiven me?"

She touched his lips with a forefinger. "Long ago."

After a long minute, he leaned back, gathering her close again. Anne lay thinking about second chances. They wouldn't make the same mistakes again. She'd fled to Tallulah with her world in pieces. And from such a disastrous beginning, they were both renewed. Buck had found his place at Belle Pointe and she had found so much more.

She glanced at the alarm clock, then reached up to turn his face to hers. "We have ten minutes. Let's not waste it."

GENGU/MIRA6

MILLS & BOON ®

The best romantic fiction direct to your door

OUR GUARANTEE TO YOU...

The Reader Service involves you in no obligation to purchase and is truly a service to you!

Your books are sent direct to your door on 14 days no-obligation home approval.

Plus, we have a dedicated Customer Relations team on hand to answer all your queries

(UK) 020 8288 2888
(ROI) 01 278 2062

There is also a 24-hour message facility on these numbers.

MIRA

MILLS & BOON®

Pure reading pleasure

HOME	SEARCH	🛒 MY BASKET
MY ACCOUNT		0 books	Total £0.00
FAQs	find >	view basket / checkout

Visit millsandboon.co.uk and discover your one-stop shop for romance!

★ Choose and buy books from an extensive selection of Mills & Boon®, M&B™ and MIRA® titles.

★ Receive 25% off the cover price of all special releases and MIRA® books.

★ Sign up to our monthly newsletter to keep you up-to-date with all news and offers.

★ Take advantage of our amazing FREE book offers.

★ In our Authors area find titles currently available from all your favourite authors.

★ Get hooked on one of our fabulous online reads, with new chapters updated regularly.

Visit us online at www.millsandboon.co.uk

...you'll want to come back again and again!!

WEB/RS2